These Dreams

barbara chepaitis

POCKET BOOKS

new york london toronto sydney singapore

POCKET BOOKS, a division of Simon & Schuster, Inc.
1230 Avenue of the Americas, New York, NY 10020

ISBN: 0-7434-3750-0

First Pocket Books hardcover printing March 2002

10   9   8   7   6   5   4   3   2   1

For information regarding special discounts for bulk purchases, please contact Simon & Schuster Special Sales at 1-800-456-6798 or business@simonandschuster.com

Designed by Jaime Putorti

Printed in the U.S.A.

*to my sister, Norma Shook, for her lifelong support,
friend Debbie Colarusso for her kitchen table
—and of course Fran—
with thanks, for spinning those Wildwood dreams*

acknowledgments

Although the people and places in this book are part
of the imaginary world that distracts me from cooking supper
and paying bills, that imaginary world often has reality as a
source of inspiration. Therefore, I owe an inspired thank-you to
the most amazing Peter Dubacher, who started and continues to
nurture the Berkshire Bird Paradise, located in Grafton, New York.
I've spent many happy hours there face-to-face with emu and
hawk, or listening to the stories Peter has to tell about rescuing and
caring for injured birds. I encourage you to visit the place, or the
Web site at www.birdparadise.com.

Thank you, Peter. Thank you, birds.

I send lavish thanks to the generous women of the Amsterdam
Book Club, especially Nancy B., who invited me to meet with the
club to ask the women what they'd do if they were going to live as
if they had only a year to live. I am consistently delighted by the
extraordinary intelligence and wisdom expressed by seemingly
ordinary women.

Laurie Liss must always be thanked, in the diminishing hope

Acknowledgments

that someday I'll actually be able to thank her enough, and Emily Bestler must be newly thanked, for her insight in editing, which polished this gem smooth.

A humble thank-you goes to the mysterious crow that flew into my house as I was writing about the relationship between birds and healing. I'm hoping I heard her right.

Finally, a limitless thank-you to my sister, Norma, and my friend Veronica Cruz, two women who have done me the deep honor of seeing my life honestly, and believing in me anyway. Such belief is truly the stuff of which dreams are made.

In our deepest sleep, we enter synchronicity with
the trembling of the Earth. Dreaming, we become
the Earth's dream.

> —Diane Ackerman,
> *A Natural History of the Senses*

these dreams

Cricket Thompson *was on her way* to the supermarket after work when she felt the motion of change inside her.

It was soft and warm, like the almost-April wind, sweet but tinged with sorrow and the breath of fear change always brings.

She could pinpoint no external cause for this feeling and had no reason to suspect herself of making any changes in the near future. Her marriage and her children, her house and work, were all in order, for the most part. While she waited at a red light, she examined the feeling further for more information, but it was still just a feeling, ephemeral, tugging mutely at the center of her chest. She thought perhaps it was due to the lengthening spring days, or the fact that she'd put her first lettuce seeds and peas in the ground the day before.

She pulled into the supermarket lot, narrowly avoiding a maverick cart that bumped toward her, pushed by the light wind. She returned it to the stand, then entered the supermarket and groped for her list, which was somewhere in the bottom of her purse

1

among a pile of useless ATM receipts, half-eaten Life Saver packs, and loose change.

She wheeled her cart up and down the aisles, tossing items into it. Her husband didn't like grocery shopping, so it was her chore. He thought this only fair, since he mowed the lawn, though she didn't think mowing compared with grocery shopping at all. Shopping happened every week all year, for one thing, and required thought as well as physical energy. All he had to do was push a machine and whistle. She had to remember which deodorant he was using, which toothpaste her youngest daughter preferred, which foods her older daughter wouldn't eat this week, and deal with the coupons, the lines, and the clerks.

She rolled past a young mother, whose toddler sat in the cart seat banging his legs against the metal bars and periodically letting out a shriek. The mother looked tired, slumped into her own body as if that was the only place she could escape the noise.

Cricket remembered when her daughters were young, banging their heels against the metal of the cart, screeching, wanting everything. Teenagers were easier physically, but much more difficult emotionally. They didn't ride in the cart, but they still wanted everything, and everything was more dangerous when it included cars and boyfriends their fathers didn't like.

Cricket headed for the cosmetics aisle to get pine tar shampoo for her husband and herbal shampoo for her daughters. She picked up the mint conditioner she liked, checked to see if anyone was watching, then opened the cap and took a deep whiff. It was expensive and she could make do with the generic. But she wanted it. Just for herself. Her family didn't have to eat her whole paycheck, after all. She tossed the bottle in the cart.

Then, she felt guilty.

She had no right to such thoughts. She was a lucky woman. Her family was healthy. She was healthy. They weren't rich, but they weren't poor by any standard. She lived in a town full of good, reliable people she'd known all her life. She had a yard and a garden. If her life sometimes looked a little dull from the outside, or felt a little dull from the inside, that was normal. Sometimes life was dull. And what else could she possibly want? Excitement and adventure? Trips to Europe, or fame and fortune? All of that, she thought, was fine in fantasy, but a lot of trouble in reality, and dangerous, too. No. She needed nothing, and if she wanted more, it was just because she sometimes forgot how much she already had.

She put the shampoo back and pushed the cart down the aisle quickly, without looking back. She was probably just premenstrual, she thought, or she wouldn't even be having such disturbing thoughts in the middle of the grocery store.

Usually she'd think disturbing things in the mornings, when she rolled over and saw her husband on his back, his mouth open, his belly a soft hillock, rising and falling under the blankets. He turned forty last year, and seemed to enjoy settling into middle age. It was a time when he could relax, not push himself to be rich or handsome or sexy or powerful. He knew where he'd gotten, and the suspense of pretending he could get any farther was over. Clearly, he wouldn't. At least, that was her analysis. He only said that forty wasn't much different than thirty-nine.

She was glad for his attitude, though. It relieved her of the pressure to have a perfect body, or be a perfect wife. They'd been together long enough that neither had expectations beyond the norm, and this comforted her. Once in a while, she'd imagine herself being seen in the doctor's office or the bank or the grocery store by a man who was wealthy, eccentric, and suddenly in love with her. He'd take her away on his private cruise boat—not a jet, since she was afraid of flying—and buy her diamonds, and show her the world.

But, then, she'd have to make sure she shaved her legs regularly, and probably would have to learn to shine in public for people she didn't know. She'd have to be beautiful and sexy and smart in a consistent way, and she thought living up to that would be an awful burden. No. She preferred Jim, who rubbed her stomach when she got her period and knew everybody she knew and didn't complain about his job or need to chase after younger women. He was as safe and comforting as her favorite shoes, in spite of his insistence that lawn mowing was the equivalent of shopping.

Cricket made her way around the store, filling her cart. When all the items on her list were crossed off, she moved to the checkouts and stared at the lines. They were all long, but checkout three seemed to have people with lighter carts. She went and stood in it.

Four people ahead of her, the clerk got on the intercom and asked for assistance. Somebody needed a price check. Cricket sighed.

This was the part of grocery shopping she hated most—standing in line. After a long day at the high school where she worked as a secretary, typing and Xeroxing and answering phones that always seemed to have irate parents on the other end, and making sure kids signed in and out and saw the principal or the nurse or a parole officer when they were supposed to, she just wanted to get home. But even at home she had a pile of laundry or bills or dishes or all three waiting and her husband or children or the PTA would expect cookies for lunch or a Special Event the next day, and she couldn't remember if she was supposed to pick up fish food. Or if she had.

She stood in line looking over the ALIEN BIRTH headlines and the *Cosmo* breasts and the 100 WAYS TO COOK EGGS, wondering if she should change lines because this one was now stalled and obviously the wrong one, and the people in front of her were surely all idiots or psychotic killers who needed price checks or refunds or deodorant. She began to despair of world peace and an end to pollution, because how could those big cans of worms be managed when grocery shopping remained a hideous mass of confusion and aggravation?

She picked up a magazine and flipped it open to an article titled "Sex Every Day? No Way!" It was about how to put more spark in your marriage. It listed a variety of suggestions ranging from position changes to the use of dairy products.

She closed the magazine and put it back on the rack. Jim had never been the type to experiment. She didn't think any amount of whipped cream would change that. She wasn't sure she wanted it to.

She sighed again, and the man in front of her turned around and chuckled.

"Long line," he noted cheerfully.

"Yes," she agreed, trying to sound bright. He was a large and lumbering old man, wearing denim coveralls and worn sneakers. He didn't smell, and Cricket was grateful for this. At the other end of the cart was a woman—his wife, Cricket assumed—who was small and slightly shriveled with carefully curled white hair that was getting scrunched by a plastic rain hat, which Cricket wondered about since it wasn't raining.

"But we're moving. Yes, we're moving now," the old man said.

He pushed his cart forward and began pulling items from it. Cricket watched.

Celery and lettuce. Peanut butter and jelly. Bread. Eggs. Milk. Cheese. Orange juice. Birdseed, two bags. Then, one . . . two . . . three . . . four . . . five . . . six commercial-size bags of unshelled peanuts. Each bag was ten pounds' worth of nuts.

To keep from staring at them, Cricket picked up a *Cosmo* and turned to the horoscope, which said this month would bring Romance in the form of a New, Exciting Lover, something she doubted her husband would like. The bags of peanuts seemed more interesting than her imaginary love life, so she looked at them again, trying to figure it out. She creased her forehead and chewed on her lower lip. The old woman saw her and laughed gently.

"She wants to know what we're buying all this for, dear," she said to her husband.

"Of course," he said. "Of course she does." The deep wrinkles around his mouth pushed up as he smiled broadly. "Squirrels," he said. "We feed squirrels and other yard creatures."

She smiled back. "How nice," she said. "How lovely."

And she meant it. Standing in line, worrying about pollution and world peace, feeding squirrels seemed the most benign activity in the world. She imagined the old couple setting out the food in containers made of used coffee cans, then sitting in plastic fold-up lawn chairs, holding hands and watching squirrels chase each other up and down trees.

Cricket had two bird feeders in her yard, and often watched out the window while she washed dishes. She imagined she and her husband would retire someday and watch the birds together, though right now jobs and raising children made it impossible to find the time.

The peanuts moved slowly up the belt toward the cashier and Cricket began unloading her cart. "I have raccoons in my yard," she told the old man. "And woodchucks—a family."

She was inordinately fond of the woodchucks and loved to listen to them whistle or watch them burrow their noses into the clover patches she'd planted just for them. She'd named the woodchucks Abraham and Sarah. Recently, they'd had a little Isaac.

"Oh, yes." The old man chuckled. "I have raccoons, too. And birds. Hummingbirds."

"Really?" Just this year she'd planted honeysuckle and put out feeders, but so far they'd only attracted ants. They reminded her of loneliness, hanging unused from their black posts. "I put out feeders, but I haven't seen any. They come to your yard?"

"Ah," he said, and turned to his wife. "Do we have hummingbirds, Mary? Do we?"

"Oh, dear." His wife tittered. "You know we do. You tell her."

"Ruby-throated hummingbirds. We plant bee balm and honeysuckle and we get lots of them." He leaned over and spoke confidentially to her. "You have to be patient, though. Sometimes it takes 'em a while to spot the goods."

Cricket almost clapped her hands like a delighted child. "I have honeysuckle," she said. "And bee balm. They should show up, then, right?"

He nodded. "Of course. As long as your yard has a trans-dimensional portal, that is."

Everything in Cricket paused for a moment. She had that feeling you get as a child when you grab a hand and then realize it isn't your mother's hand at all, but some stranger's. "Oh," she said softly. "The . . . transportals. Of course."

"Don't worry. Most yards have 'em."

"That's . . . good."

"I can see you haven't had much experience with extradimensional beings," he noted.

"Not much," she admitted.

He turned to his wife and they exchanged nods. "Should I tell her, dear?" he asked.

"Of course," she said brightly. "After all, she's here."

He turned back to Cricket while his wife got out a calculator and added along with the cashier. "They're different from extraterrestrials. They move between dimensions as well as planets. I've seen both."

"Have you?" She settled into herself, quiet and comfortable. Why not? she thought. It had been a long time since anyone told her stories. She loved stories.

"Yes. I'm frequently visited by the Blue Starships. The Nordic ones, that is," he said, as he helped the cashier bag his items. "They're as blue as the morning sky, and they bring the Many-Colored Women of Light with them. They came to rest on my lawn one night, after a wild wind had blown away the energy field that blocked their entrance. They harness the power of blue quasars to travel. They're very blue."

"Blue," she said, and she imagined them. They were pervasively blue, a quiet blue that soothed and cajoled into calmness. They had nothing to do with pollution or loneliness or bounced checks or standing in lines or worrying about the mortgage or her daughter's boyfriends. In their world, she wouldn't have to feed anyone, get to work on time, create happiness in her home, get a good night's sleep or eat right. The Nordic Starship men and the Many-Colored Women of Light were all-calm and all-knowing and all-happy with themselves. Everyone, including herself, walked slowly and spent a great deal of time feeding yard animals and birds.

The cashier snapped her gum at the old man. "That'll be thirty-five sixty-five."

The old man turned to his wife.

"She's right, dear," the woman said, putting her calculator in her purse and holding out her hand. The old man handed her a wad of crumpled bills, which she began carefully smoothing and counting.

"At first, I was afraid," he said to Cricket, wiping his hands on his pants as if to remove the smell of the money. "It seemed as if I was in the tracking presence of angels of death, who had come to take me from my earthly existence. But that wasn't their purpose. They came to bring me dreams."

"Good dreams?" she asked, as he began helping his wife put their items back in their cart and the cashier started rolling Cricket's goods down the line.

"True dreams. I stood in my yard and received a message from one of the seven."

"Seven?"

"Yard dwarves. You know—the ceramic ones."

"Oh. Um . . . Sneezy?" she asked.

"No. Doc. It was Doc. He told me what to do."

He reached over and touched her on the arm. She looked at him fully, and saw that his eyes were as blue as the story he told. They gazed into her with an intimacy and intensity she thought inappropriate to the setting. "I can tell you what he said," he whispered.

She wanted to pull away, but didn't want to be rude. She nodded.

"What would you do?" he asked.

She waited for him to say more. He didn't.

"Do?" she asked.

"What would you do," he repeated, "if you were going to live as if you only had a year to live?"

She heard the words, but she wasn't sure if they made sense. "I don't understand," she whispered, frightened for reasons she couldn't explain.

His hand on her arm grew heavier, and his fingers clutched her wrist. "Live," the old man said, his voice fervent with some meaning he seemed to want to press into her. "Live as if you only had a year to live."

Cricket looked over his shoulder at the old woman, who was smiling and nodding at her. It was okay, her face said. It was all okay.

"Okay," Cricket said. "Okay."

He breathed in and out, then released her. "Here," he said, rummaging in the chest pocket of his coveralls, "I have something for you." He pulled out a cassette tape, white and carefully labeled in blue marker: "Nordic Journals—Blue Spacepeople." He held it out and she took it from his hand.

"I had it with me, expecting I'd meet someone who needed it," he said, smiling kindly at her and patting her arm. "I was right."

"It's been so nice talking with you," she replied, as he and his wife waved their old hands at her and began pushing their cart out of the store.

The cashier shook her head and rolled her eyes as she watched them leave. "You got a lot of patience," she said. "Guys like that, they put me to sleep."

Cricket shrugged, and began packing. She always helped to pack.

On the ride home, she put the tape in her cassette player and listened. The old man had a deep, soothing voice, but after only five minutes of describing the nature of blue quasars, the tape slowed, then stopped. She heard something like a click and hit the eject button.

She pulled the cassette out, and a long string of tape remained stuck in the player. She tugged gently, as gently as she could, but it snapped. Brown tape hung like hair out of the end of her tape player, and out of the end of the cassette.

She tossed the cassette on the floor of her car and drove home.

t w o

When Cricket got home, her older daughter, Janis, was sitting at the kitchen table looking morose. Her younger daughter, Grace, was in the living room watching TV and reading a book, something Cricket continually told her would ruin her eyes, though she had done the same thing and it hadn't ruined hers. She knew her husband was home, but he wasn't visible. Probably watching a basketball game in the den, she thought.

Balancing bags, she looked at Janis. "There's more in the car if you want to help."

Janis rose with a deep sigh, and went out to get more bags.

Cricket followed, and when they returned, Grace had bounced into the kitchen and was peering into a bag.

"You get more Oreos?" she asked.

Cricket nodded, put down her bags and went back out, while Janis put her bags on the table and began rummaging. Two more bags and she was done, except for the unpacking and putting away. Then, of course, there was dinner to produce, and dishes and homework and showers and bed and perhaps sex, but probably not because it'd be late and Jim would be sleepy from beer, and she'd just be sleepy.

Grace found the Oreos and retreated to the living room with them. "Don't spoil your appetite," Cricket called to her.

"Won't," she said. Then, as an afterthought, "What're we having?"

"Um—chicken something."

"Didn't we have that last night?"

"Last night," Janis chimed in, flopping back into her seat, "we had fish something. Can't you tell the difference?"

Cricket kept unpacking. Janis watched her with dull eyes, then sighed deep and long.

"Everything okay?" Cricket asked.

"Maria got her license today," she said.

"Well, that's nice," Cricket said cheerfully. "Tell her I said congratulations."

Janis sighed again. "She got a car, too."

"That's even nicer."

"Be nicer if it was me," Janis concluded glumly, and put her head down on her arm.

Cricket nodded. Janis wanted her license, but didn't really want to spend a lot of time learning how to drive. Both Cricket and her husband had explained the importance of learning to drive to getting a license, but Janis only pulled at one of the half-dozen earrings weighting her left lobe and said something disparaging about parents who name their children after dead rock stars. Cricket thought she needed to go to a driving school, have someone who was not her parents teach her. Jim thought she was just being contrary.

"You need an attitude shift." Jim had glowered at her. "If you think—"

"Jim," Cricket had reprimanded him softly, stopping him before they got into one of their regular arguments. Janis, who had an attachment to the truth, wouldn't soften her words to prevent a battle. And Jim wasn't one to leave a battlefield unless he was the winner.

The problem was that they were both definite people. They were definite in what they wanted, and in what they thought they knew. Cricket admired this about both of them. Her mother had been that way, and had scolded her father for his lack of clarity. He could always see too many sides of a question. It was more admirable, she thought, to be like Jim and Janis, even though it created a lot of difficulty for her, since she was always somehow in the middle, seeing what they both saw, trying to get them to meet on that common ground. She supposed she was too much like her father after all, as her mother always told her.

"Honey," Cricket started to say now, but Janis made a noise between a groan and a growl and stomped out of the room. As she passed through the living room on her way to her own attic room, Cricket heard Grace squeal, "Ouch—*quit* it."

Cricket didn't intervene. She'd gotten a book on adolescent girls and it said that they should fight their own fights or stop fighting altogether, and either way she should stay out of it. Instead, she opened the refrigerator and stared into it, looking for inspiration.

"Hey," her husband's voice said behind her. She turned and smiled as he put a hand on her shoulder. "Don't you yell at the girls for that?" he asked.

"What kind of chicken sounds good to you?" she asked.

"Cooked," he said. "Did you get the salsa?"

She pulled out a jar, handed it to him. He held it up and frowned. "This isn't Ortega."

"It's organic," Cricket said, pointing to the label. "See?"

He snorted, an unpretty sound, Cricket thought. "And what's nonorganic salsa made from? Old crayons?"

"You know what it means," she said patiently. "It's better."

"It costs more." He opened the jar and sniffed suspiciously. "Oh—your sister called. Said she might stop by." As he spoke, there was a quick knock on the front door. It opened and Cricket's sister, Peggy, stuck her head inside.

"He-ey there," she said, swooped down on Grace and kissed her on top of the head, then stepped over her recumbent form on the way to the kitchen.

Peggy's house was only about two miles from Cricket's, and they were as used to stepping into each other's kitchens as stepping into their own. They were born less than a year apart, married less than a year apart, and had their children less than a year apart, with Peggy producing two boys, and Cricket producing two girls, which they both somehow felt was appropriate. Their husbands joked that they would die less than a year apart, and they joked back, "Yeah. Just watch out if one of us gets a divorce."

"Hey, Jim," Peggy said cheerfully. She flung her purse up on the table and ruffled her smooth pageboy hair with her fingers. To Cricket, it resembled a bowl of dark silk placed perfectly on top of her head. They were both small women and their features were similar enough to mark them as related, but Peggy had inherited her mother's dark brown hair and eyes, while Cricket got the honey hair and fair skin of her father. Peggy was also more conscious of her looks and the reaction they got from men. Their mother always said that Peggy liked to flirt the way her mother did, and Cricket liked to dream the way her father did. Cricket thought daydreaming was easier than flirting, and probably safer.

"Hey, Peggy," Jim said. "How's it going?"

"Not too bad. You?"

"Good. Only, I got this game I'm watching."

"Don't let me stop you," Peggy said, and he didn't.

Cricket gathered up the empty bags and stuffed them into one bag. She saved them and reused them until the packers at the store started eyeing them as if they might be infectious, at which point she brought them to the recycle bin and got another bunch. Peggy looked at the little pieces of carrot top and other produce bits on the floor, and made a clucking sound with her tongue on the roof of her mouth.

"I was shopping," Cricket said. "I just got home. I'm cleaning it."

She felt irritation rise and fall, then disappear. Peggy was neat, and thought Cricket was messy. Cricket was casual, and thought Peggy was anal. But what really bothered Cricket was that Peggy seemed to be naturally anal, whereas she tried to keep her house neat and just couldn't. She had many books on how to live simply, how to avoid clutter, how to let your living room be a reflection of your soul. She read them, she tried them, and when they didn't work, she guiltily stuffed them into the bookshelves among the novels, books of affirmations, and healthy-eating cookbooks. Then Peggy would come over and cluck her tongue at the mess.

In spite of this occasional irritation, they never really fought. Long ago, they'd made an unspoken pact that no matter what one of them did, the other would continue to accept her pretty much as she was. They never argued over boys or clothes, instinctively protecting their bond over any consideration of romance or fashion.

"Don't get mad at me, Peggy," Cricket would say, "but I spilled soda on your sweater. I borrowed it yesterday." And Peggy's face would go tight, but then she'd laugh it off. "You're such a slob" would be all she'd say about it.

"If you're not going out with Billy anymore," Peggy would say, "I was thinking of trying him out," and Cricket would say sure. Why not? Billy didn't matter all that much after all.

Now Peggy sat at the kitchen table, and put her chin in her hand, looking very much like Janis but less morose. "You have such a nice husband," she said.

"Nice?"

"Yeah. Nice. He talks to people." She waved a hand in the air. "You know. He's not antisocial."

Cricket laughed. "Pete's not antisocial. He's just quiet. I think it's sweet."

"Sweet. Ha. And where's Jim taking you on vacation this year?"

"We're just going to the beach," Cricket said. "You know he doesn't like big vacations."

"Virginia Beach," Peggy reminded her.

Cricket smiled tightly. It was true that Jim always planned a nice vacation for them, some time between the girls' camp and school, while Peggy argued every summer with her husband to get him to go for a weekend at the lake. Cricket felt a vague guilt about it, as if there was something she should do to atone to Peggy for this, though there wasn't a resolution she could think of. Pete was just like that. On the other hand, he did the grocery shopping, so Cricket thought maybe it was a trade-off. Some husbands were difficult one way, and some were difficult another.

"Coffee? I can make a pot."

Peggy shook her head. "Tea, maybe." She sighed.

Cricket put the kettle on the stove and got cups down from the cupboard. "You okay?"

"How do you know," Peggy asked, "if your husband's having an affair?"

Cricket put the cups down on the table, then sat down. "What?" she asked.

"If he's not home much and he has no interest in sex, is that a sign of an affair?"

Cricket cast about for an answer to this. "Peter wouldn't have an affair," she said.

"Why not?" Peggy asked.

"Well, look at him," Cricket said, and then put her hand over her mouth. Peggy giggled.

"Yeah. You'd think the absence of hair and the extra gut might make him less than Mr. Superstud, huh?"

"Peggy, I didn't mean . . ."

Peggy waved a hand in the air. "I know. But, really, what do you think?"

"I don't know. How long . . . I mean, when did you start thinking this?"

"A few months now, I guess. Just a weird feeling, you know?"

Cricket knew. She and her sister both believed in feelings. There were bad feelings—sure signs of upcoming trouble. There were weird feelings—signs of unexpected events either good or bad. And there were the rare good feelings—signs of happiness or imminent good fortune. They'd both had good feelings throughout their pregnancies. They both had bad feelings right before their father died.

"But not a bad feeling?" Cricket asked. Peggy shook her head.

Cricket breathed in relief. "Then just sort of watch him for a while. Maybe it's prostate trouble or something."

"I suppose," Peggy agreed. "But what if he is? Having an affair, I mean."

"Then I guess you'll leave him," Cricket said.

Peggy closed her eyes and considered. "Maybe. Maybe not."

Cricket raised her eyebrows. "Maybe not?"

She would if it was Jim. At least, she assumed she would, though all the movies she saw on the Lifetime channel taught her otherwise. People had affairs, and sometimes split for a while, then got back together. But first you had to leave them to show that fidelity was good. Affairs were bad. People who had them should be left. The clarity of that was reassuring. It would be very different than just saying, as Sheila at work did, that the marriage was dead. Cricket didn't know how Sheila had the nerve to leave a nineteen-year partnership based on something as ephemeral as that. The marriage was dead. But wasn't there always a way to revive it, or learn to live with the corpse? Cricket thought there must be, and if you didn't try, then you were the bad one.

"Well, there's the kids. Of course, Andy's so into his video games he might not notice. Little Pete'd take it hard, though." Peggy shook her head. "And if I leave him, I have to deal with all the boxes," she said.

"Boxes?"

"Packing. Sorting. This is yours, this is mine, and what about these pictures from our honeymoon." Peggy shivered. "I don't know if I could. And what if it's just one of those things. A fling. Meaningless sex. Do you wreck a marriage for that?"

Cricket shook her head. "Sex isn't meaningless."

"Yeah? And you've been married how many years?"

Cricket blushed, and Peggy laughed just as if she could see the times when Cricket, tired or uninterested, had faked orgasm while thinking of the next day's to-do list. "That's different, Peggy. We're married. You know—"

"Yeah, I do know. That's why I wouldn't really blame him if he had a fling. I mean, didn't you ever think about it? Really?"

The kettle whistled and Cricket went to it, brought it to the table. She didn't want to think about it. Fantasizing about, for instance, Harrison Ford wasn't the same as someone really having an affair. Fantasies should stay where they belonged—inside your head.

"You want chamomile?" Cricket asked. Peggy nodded, and Cricket poured, for Peggy and then for herself, and the two women sat and considered their tea.

"Well?" Peggy asked again. "Haven't you?"

"Not for real. Maybe if I was dying or something. Like if I knew I had a year to live." She scrunched up her face. "If you were going to live as if you only had a year to live, what would you do?" she asked.

"What?" Peggy said.

"If you were going to live as if you only had a year to live, what would you do?"

Behind her, she heard her husband laugh. "Whoa," he said. "Now there's a line to come in on. Is there something I should know here?"

She twisted around to him. He went to the refrigerator and opened it, took out a beer.

"It's just a question someone asked me," Cricket said.

"Helluva question," Peggy said. "What would I do if I only had a year to live?"

"That's not it," Cricket said. "It's if you were going to live *as if* you only had a year."

"So, you're not dying? You're just . . . pretending you only have a year to live?"

"I think so," Cricket said uncertainly.

"Oh," her husband said. "That's different."

"Is it?" Cricket asked.

"If you know you'll die in a year, you can be as stupid as you want," he explained. "If you're just pretending, you have to keep a lid on it."

"You do?" Cricket asked.

"Sure," Peggy agreed. "I mean, if you max out all your credit cards—which I would do—you don't have to worry about paying them if you're dead."

"But who asked you that question?" Jim insisted.

"I told you, just somebody."

"What somebody? Just somebody in the streets?"

"At the store," she said.

"Somebody at the store," her husband said. "Somebody you know?"

She shook her head. "No. But . . . he gave me a tape," she said, as if that legitimized the conversation. Jim didn't like the way she talked with total strangers—in stores, in the streets, on the beach, at the mall. He kept telling her it wasn't safe. "He was a nice old man. His wife was there. He said I should. Live that way, I mean."

Jim snorted. "C'mon, Cricket."

"No, really," she said, and sighed, then told them the rest of the story. When she got to the part about the Nordic Spacepeople, and struggled to explain how it was soothing and good, Peggy giggled, and Jim snorted more.

"But it was *beautiful*," she insisted.

"Cricket, he was nuts," Peggy said.

"It was beautiful," she repeated, as if that explained everything, and to her, it did. Beauty didn't need a reason to exist except for itself, she thought.

"You are so much like Daddy," Peggy said.

"Jesus," her husband said, "I hope you didn't give him our address."

Cricket stifled a rising impatience. "Anyway," she said to Peggy, "what *would* you do? Besides max out the credit cards."

Peggy sipped her tea, smiling as if at something she saw just outside the window. "I'd go to a beach," she said, "where the water is so clear blue I could see my feet at the bottom."

"See your feet," Cricket mused. She knew what Peggy meant, what the pleasure of that would be.

"Yeah. See your feet. What about you, Jim? What'd you do?"

"That's easy," Jim said. "I'd have an orgy."

"Jim!" Cricket exclaimed.

"Well, I would. Then I'd watch football and eat pizza and ice cream as much as I want."

"Ha," Peggy said. "Do enough of that, you won't be welcome at any orgies."

Cricket felt her face grow warm.

"You've got a point," Jim said. "I guess I better have the orgies first, huh?"

"Orgies?" Peggy said. "Plural? Now it's plural?"

"Might as well. Burn up a few calories. Like push-ups?"

"Yeah. Pec flexes, too."

Jim lifted his arm and made a muscle for her, which she waved a dismissive hand at. Jim laughed and left the room. "Break's over. Back to the game," he said as he exited.

"Save your strength," Peggy called after him. "You'll need it."

When he left, she put her hands on the table and pushed herself up. "I gotta go. Andy has early Babe Ruth practice, and I'm supposed to be at the store by ten for inventory. No rest for the weary."

"Me, too. Up early."

"You? You don't work Saturday."

"There's a lot to do at the sanctuary."

Peggy rolled her eyes. The sanctuary was the short name for the Birds of Paradise Sanctuary, where Cricket volunteered. Peggy didn't approve. She thought it was strange.

"Pass built a butterfly house," Cricket said. "I told you. We're planting for it now."

"Pass," Peggy groaned. "Pass Christian. What kind of name is that, anyway?"

"I told you. The name of the town where he was born. In Mississippi. I saw it on a map," she added, as if that lent it more respectability.

"Southerner," Peggy said. "Southerner with a strange name who still takes care of baby birds. I mean, that's something you do when you're a kid, right? They fall out of the nest and you try to feed them with an eyedropper and they die, then you have a funeral. We did that, remember?"

Cricket remembered, but this was different. "Injured birds," Cricket corrected her sister. "Injured, and endangered. He breeds them. And Grace likes it there."

Peggy leaned back in her chair and called into the living room, "Grace, honey?"

"Yeah?" her voice answered.

"C'mere a minute, would you?"

There was the rustle of movement, and then Grace came into the kitchen and stood by Peggy's chair. Her hair was tousled and her eyes looked dreamy and far away, as if she still occupied the story she'd been reading.

Peggy put an arm around her, and Grace leaned into her. "You're such a sweetie," Peggy said. "You know that?"

Grace squeezed closer to Peggy. She still looked like a child, though at thirteen, that was something that could change any day. She was Cricket's affectionate daughter, the one who liked to hug and be hugged, the one who would sit and talk nonsense and laugh for long periods of time while Cricket combed and braided her hair. She was a Cancer, one of the signs of the zodiac that was about feeling and connection, while Janis was a Leo, with a Scorpio ascendant, which made her both regal and honest, but not necessarily affectionate. But it was Janis she called on when she needed to move furniture or clean closets or do anything that took extra energy. Grace didn't focus for long on those kinds of tasks.

"Listen," Peggy continued. "I wanted to ask you about that bird place. You like it there?"

Grace smiled and nodded. "The emus are cool," she said.

"And the man who runs the place?"

"He's nice. He didn't yell when I scared the ducks off their eggs."

Cricket tilted her head at Peggy, and allowed herself a moment of smugness. She didn't know why she bothered to defend Pass to Peggy, except that doing so defended her own involvement, which seemed to need explanation.

Cricket had first gone when she chaperoned Grace's fifth-grade field trip there, three years ago. Pass told the children that he'd moved here to work as an assistant to a veterinarian. People would bring in injured wild birds, and he would take them home, care for them, and set them free if they recovered, keep them if they didn't. He learned more and more about the wild birds, and before he knew it, he was running a sanctuary instead of working for a veterinarian. He said that was the way you made a life, by doing what you liked most and seeing what happened next.

As he spoke to the children, she stared at his eyes, which were strange. They were hazel, but one was more gold, and the other more green, so that when the light was on them, he looked as if he was one person viewing the world out of two different eyes. At one point, he stopped talking and turned his gaze fully toward her. She ducked her head down, sure she was blushing, and he turned his attention back to the children.

Then, as they walked among the birdhouses, she had been

enchanted by the pretty feathers left like soft messages all along the paths, the emus that ran with the fallow deer in the fenced, wooded acres behind the cages, the scent of pine forest and the rich loamy earth with its ferns and wildflowers. It was a magic kingdom, an enchanted forest.

While the children ate lunch, she excused herself and went back to that area, at first just listening to the odd drumming sound the emus made, then going to investigate a small stand of trillium nestled under a pine tree. She crouched over it like a brooding mother goose over a nest of eggs, stroking the leaves.

"Hey," a voice had said, and she jumped to her feet to see Pass standing over her. She almost fell down again, apologizing to him, but he just grinned at her.

"There's no fine for leaving the path. What caught your eye?" he asked, his voice a slow and gentle drawl.

She showed him the trillium, named some other plants she saw. He listened carefully, regarding her with his strange eyes. "How do you know all that?" he asked, and she told him she'd worked for a landscaper during the summers when she was in college, and might have continued except that she was allergic to the pesticides and had to quit. Then he asked if she'd advise him on landscaping.

She said yes because she didn't know how to refuse, and came back the following week, thinking she'd do this once, and that would be it. But Pass had other ideas, and so she came back again and again. Sometimes Grace would go with her and play with the ducks. More often she'd go by herself. In the last three years, she'd planted an herb garden, landscaped the paths, and started a wild-flower field. Soon they'd have a butterfly house.

Maybe it was the idea of having such a large garden to play with for free, or maybe it was the pretty feathers she collected from the path, or maybe it was the sound of eagles and hawks calling, but the truth was the place still enchanted her, though she felt constantly apologetic about that.

"You want to go with me tomorrow?" Cricket asked Grace now. Grace shrugged. "Maybe."

"I'll wake you up when I'm leaving," Cricket said.

Grace nodded, and extricated herself from Peggy's arms. "Buffy's on," she said.

"Buffy?" Peggy asked.

"The Vampire Slayer. *You* know."

Peggy grinned. "Not really, but that's okay. You go ahead."

Grace skipped back to the living room, and the two women listened for a moment. They heard the TV, and then Janis's voice talking to Grace as she entered the room, Grace giggling at something Janis said.

"How's your wild child?" Peggy asked, referring to Janis.

Cricket listened a moment. "Seems okay right now."

"Hey, Janis," Peggy called out.

"Yeah?" Janis called back.

"Your mother get you a car yet?"

Janis appeared in the door of the kitchen, grinning. "She insists that I have to learn to drive it first. Can you believe it?"

"Terrible," Peggy laughed.

"Awful," Janis agreed, but from the tone of her voice and her grin Cricket could tell that Janis's mood had shifted. If you gave her time and some space, Janis was very good at coming to terms with reality. In fact, Grace would brood and weep for much longer over a perceived wrong. For Grace, a hurt was more totally encompassing and needed more assuaging than it did for Janis, whose instinctive sense of fair play led her into and out of a bad mood with dramatic suddenness.

"Mothers," Janis said, rolling her eyes dramatically.

"Kids," Peggy replied.

Janis shrugged and turned to leave. Then, in a darting motion, she went to her mother, hugged her briefly, and shot back out of the room. Cricket felt warmth spread through her at the unexpected gift of connection. Janis's sudden gestures of affection reminded Cricket of the way swallows seek food, skittering through the air, their course unpredictable, and swiftly changed.

Peggy turned back to Cricket. "What does Janis think of the bird place?"

"She doesn't go. She met Pass once, though. When he came here to drop off some seed catalogs. She said he had weird eyes, but he was cute anyway."

"He is. Like a mix of Sam Shepherd and Joseph Fiennes in dirty jeans. Y'know, you oughta at least have him kiss you."

"What?" Cricket said, shocked.

"He's screwing you, he oughta kiss you."

"Peggy!"

"Well, he is. Getting all that free work. And if he's *not* kissing you, what's wrong with him?" Peggy and Jim once had a conversation about whether Pass was gay. Jim said he figured Pass for swishy, which was why he didn't mind Cricket spending time with him.

"What's he doing out there alone with that weird brother of his, anyway?" Peggy continued.

"Law's not weird. Just . . . well, disabled."

"Law. Another great name," Peggy said. "I'd be afraid to be alone out there."

"They're very respectful toward me."

"They say gay men are," Peggy commented.

Cricket started to say something, then changed her mind when she realized her thoughts were far too complicated for the sentence or two Peggy expected in response. First, what did it matter if he was gay? There was nothing wrong with that. Then, part of her wanted to encourage the notion because then she wouldn't have to answer questions about what she did there. But once, as she knelt next to a bed of miniature irises, admiring their color and shape, she'd turned suddenly to find him staring at her, not in the way a man who cares nothing about women would stare. He'd walked away before she could say a word.

She didn't want to tell Peggy that, though. It seemed too private, somehow. And it wasn't as if he ever flirted or joked the way Jim and Peggy would, or even hinted at anything sexual. It was just a look he gave her. Cricket sighed and said nothing.

"Yeah," Peggy said, then laughed. "Listen, who cares anyway, right? As long as you're enjoying yourself." She stood and started toward the door. Cricket followed, and they stopped in the living room to gaze down at Grace and Janis, who lay on the floor peering at the television. "Don't you two ever have homework?"

"I did it at school," Grace said.

"I paid someone to do mine," Janis said. Grace giggled and Janis leaned over and whispered something to her. She giggled harder, and rolled over.

"Ha," Peggy said. Then, to Cricket, "You bringing the kids to church on Sunday?"

"Not me," Janis said. "Religion is the opiate of the people."

Peggy raised her eyebrows at Cricket, who sighed. "She's reading Marx in her advanced placement history class," Cricket said. "Aren't you going?"

"I guess. I was just thinking it'd be nice to sleep in."

"I'm going," Grace declared. "This is the week they give out that grass."

"Palms, honey," Peggy corrected. "It's Palm Sunday."

"I'm going. I can take the boys," Cricket offered, out of some need to make amends for Pass and the sanctuary. It was one of those gestures she often made out of hopelessly irrational motives. Peggy didn't approve of the sanctuary, so Cricket reestablished her legitimacy by doing something Peggy approved of. Usually, at her own expense. Peggy didn't ask for it. Cricket just did it.

"That'd be great," Peggy said. She walked to the door and stepped outside to the cool night. Cricket followed, walking her to her car. "I'll make a big breakfast for Pete and we'll relax, alone for a change. Maybe I'll be able to figure out what's happening with him."

"He's not," Cricket said, keeping her voice low. "He's not having an affair."

"Well, if this keeps up, I'll have to find somebody else to sleep with," Peggy said, getting into her car. "Honest to God, I can't stand it."

When she went back inside, Cricket decided that cooking a frozen pizza would be a much better idea than chicken something, and if she made a salad with it, she could call it a complete meal.

DREAM #1

flight

That night, when Cricket crawled into bed next to Jim, she tried to imagine him at orgies. At first, the only image that came to her mind was of her husband completely naked except for his socks. He had cold feet and often didn't take his socks off when they made love. Sometimes she would reach down and feel the wooliness while he was inside her. It was oddly comforting. And it seemed at odds with the idea of group sex. Then again, so did he.

The familiarity of his skin when she curled next to him, his warmth and particular scent, gave her a sense of all being well with the world. Peggy was right. She had a nice husband. Feeling that, and seeing him sleeping on his back with his mouth open, made it difficult to think of him in intricate sexual positions with many people. Perhaps if he was sleeping on his side, one hand tossed casually across the pillow, he would look sexy and daring. On his back he looked vulnerable and slightly foolish. He was not a man who went to orgies. He was her husband.

His value was in his capacity to be solidly there, solidly real.

She'd met him at her father's funeral, which he attended because he'd just started a job at the state office where her father worked. He was respectful when he took her hand and patted it firmly, telling her how sorry he was, how much he'd liked her father, though they hadn't known each other that long. "You have his smile," he told her, and she burst into tears. He brought her a glass of water. A week later, he called to see if she needed anything. Two years later, after she graduated from the community college she had decided to go to so she wouldn't have to leave home, they were married.

They'd been married seventeen years. He was with her at the birth of both girls. She had stayed in the bathroom and held a sieve for him to pee through when he had kidney stones. She relied on him for his good sense, counted on him to be the Jim she expected. And all that she knew about him, all the books she'd read about relationships, had not prepared her to know that he would want orgies, even in fantasy.

This frightened her. What else was she missing of his interior life? They'd talked about his sexual fantasies when they first slept together, but that was a long time ago. She was still in college then, and she would go to his apartment after class. They'd make love, then he'd cook spaghetti with sauce from a jar, and they'd lie in bed eating it and talking and giggling about nothing. When they were done, Cricket would strip the bed and wash the sheets.

That all seemed to change when they were married, as if they had to get serious then. As if becoming his wife meant she was no longer his playmate. When she thought about it, she couldn't remember the last time they'd had a conversation about anything more intimate than what kind of car to buy next time around. Maybe she should get the magazine with the article about Sex Every Day. Maybe she was failing him, not creating the spark a marriage needed to thrive. Of course, when the girls were little, they didn't have time for much else besides child-rearing and work, but now that could change. They would have time.

She closed her eyes and tried to sleep. She'd have to be up early, and ready to work. In the greenhouse, she had many sets of plants that were attractive to butterflies, or provided a place for them to lay their eggs. Some were ready to go into the ground. All needed to be fed and checked. They also had to order plants for inside the butterfly house to feed the larvae and provide nectar for the butterflies.

Pass asking her to work on the butterfly house made her feel special, though she knew that most of the sanctuary was run on volunteer efforts. School groups came to clean and build cages. Computer experts who stopped by to visit ended up building him a website, PR people came for a quiet Sunday afternoon and returned to help with fund-raising.

It was odd, she thought, that he should be able to attract so much help when he was himself a reticent man. Aloof and, she sometimes thought, arrogant. Or maybe just withdrawn, as if he looked out onto the world from deep inside himself. Maybe it was his unusual eyes, but sometimes she wasn't sure if he saw her there at all. She would show him a new flowering crocus, admire the light passing through its petals, so delicate and detailed, and he'd nod and say, "The old apple tree behind the goose pond needs pruning."

But, in some way, it was his aloofness that put people at ease. It made them think that since he wasn't paying too much attention, they could just be themselves.

What Peggy said about him disturbed her. Of course, she'd fantasized about Pass now and then, wondering how he would kiss, what he would look like naked. She'd seen him working with his shirt off, and admired the muscles of his shoulders, defined from years of physical labor. But that was just fantasy. It meant nothing. And fantasy, she knew from reading Nancy Friday, was healthy as long as it was kept separate from reality.

Jim teased her about Pass a little, but he wasn't the jealous type, and didn't complain about her time at the sanctuary. He played golf, he said. Why shouldn't she play with birds and butterflies? He did want her to think about doing some real work, as he put it, now that the girls were getting older. Office work at the high school was fine for when the girls were little and needed her, but her talents were just wasted there now. She should look for a better job, especially since they'd need money for college expenses. Maybe, he suggested, Pass could start paying her. But she didn't want to see the sanctuary as a commercial endeavor. It was, to her, a dream that came true, not a place to foster her personal ambitions.

She pushed herself down under the covers and let go of that thought, focusing instead on what she might want to dream that night.

Cricket always dreamt, and often about what she wanted to dream. Sometimes, her dreams were bits and pieces of images that never quite held together in a narrative. Other times, they were startling in their clarity. Some, she believed, were a sort of spirit visit from dead people, or even living people who were thinking about you. And, on some nights, they were just sensations, frightening or pleasurable. Sometimes, she would pose herself a question or a problem before she fell asleep, and begin to find the answer in a dream. Other times, she would just imagine what she wanted to feel as she slept. Her father taught her to do this when she was little and had nightmares. Her mother scoffed at the idea, but it worked for Cricket, though not for Peggy, who rarely remembered her dreams. She said she was too afraid of having one that might come true.

"But you're dreaming anyway," Cricket would point out to her. "So if it's going to come true, it'll come true if you remember it or not."

"It will?" Peggy would ask. "Will it? Then I *really* don't want to know. That's way too much responsibility."

If you knew, then you had to do something about it. If you didn't, then it didn't matter.

Cricket thought dreams were the one place where you didn't have to be responsible. If she dreamt she was unfaithful, she didn't have to feel guilty. If she dreamt she was happy, then she was, at least for the time that she dreamt.

Waking, she thought, was where the responsibility came in.

Pass told her once that he'd dreamt about injured birds all the time he was growing up, and during the years before he started the bird sanctuary. The first time he set a wing, he said, he made no errors because he'd already been doing it in his sleep for so long.

But Pass was unusual, and maybe that was what frightened Peggy, and the other people in town who talked about him. The bird man, they called him at the Agway where she bought seed. And they'd chuckle, and roll their eyes.

Pass took his dreams and made them real. There was something vaguely threatening about someone who did that so nonchalantly, and to no self-serving end. He wasn't getting rich. He didn't have a lot of stuff or women, or even a nice car. He just did what made him happy, and managed to make a living at it. Maybe, Cricket thought, it made people wonder what they were missing.

Behind her closed eyes, Cricket had a flash image of his face as he held a recently healed crow in his hands, then lifted it high and opened his hands to let it fly away. They had watched it spread its wings and soar to the top of a nearby tree, where it landed and cawed at them before taking further flight. Pass's smile had been one of pure satisfaction. She supposed that if crows had feelings, that was how the bird felt, too.

Tonight, as she drifted into sleep, she thought she'd dream about flying.

When she was a child, her father caught her trying to jump off the top of the back stairs with an umbrella, like Mary Poppins. He'd stopped her and explained that flying was good, and she could do it if she tried hard enough. But there was a rule about flying, he said.

She must always fly from the ground up, he said. Never from someplace high down.

She was five and believed him without question. He was her father, after all, and he knew so very much. When she looked into the clear blue of his eyes, she was reminded of the pictures of God she saw in Sunday school, though her father didn't have the white hair and beard, or the look of frightful power that God had. But there was something in his eyes that was about knowing everything.

She didn't jump off the stairs again, but the next windy day he found her leaping around the yard with her umbrella, pointing herself up, running to try and catch the wind.

"That's my Cricket," he said to her. "Keep at it. You can do it."

She huffed and puffed and kept jumping.

"You shouldn't tell her that," her mother said, but he shook his head.

"Don't ever discourage a dream," he told her. "You never know when someone'll make it come true, right, Cricket?"

"I wish you wouldn't call her that," her mother had said.

"It suits her," her father had said, smiling. "Suits her just fine."

He'd given her the nickname Cricket after Jiminy Cricket, when he found her outside in the middle of the night trying to find the right star to wish on. She was going to wish for an elephant, she said, as soon as she found the elephant star. Years later, she read in a book by Mary Gordon that in Italian, the word *cricket* is another word for the clitoris. It made her feel better about never having gotten to Europe.

When she and Peggy went to college, their father broke the rules about flying, and fulfilled a lifelong dream by taking skydiving classes. On his first solo jump, his parachute failed, and he plummeted to the ground. She overheard the doctors saying that his head exploded like a melon on impact. Her mother, through her tears, had said, "I *told* him not to."

Later there was an investigation to determine what went wrong. It turned out that his parachute didn't open because he never pulled the cord. It happened sometimes, the skydiving people said. People passed out, or panicked. It happened.

Now, when she dreamt of flight, she always started on the ground and ascended, either with wings or by simply floating with her arms out in front of her.

As she lay in bed, thinking about flight, she waited for wings to carry her up. But in the drifting manner of presleep thoughts, the images behind her eyes became mixed with other portions of her day and she saw her sister standing in water, looking down at her feet, which were bathed in clear blue and had wings at the heels. These feet became her husband's feet, with socks. And then a sort of orgy began, and she sat in the middle of it with pen and paper, listing the various types of flight.

There was the hovering, controlled flight of hummingbirds. The soaring of eagles and hawks on warm air. The majestic flight of birds with large wings, like herons. The absurd flight of turkeys and bumblebees.

There was the flight of angels, and the flight of Blue Nordic Spacepeople in sleek silver crafts. There was the flight of old men from death, and the flight of teenagers who knew no fear, and took chances. There was the flight of an affair. The flight into fantasy. The flight of a dive into water so clear you could see your feet at the bottom.

As she sat making her list, people around her rose from the ground into whatever kind of flight she named. Her husband became a turkey, seeking a mate. Her sister became an angel. The old man in the store was a tired blue heron, his wings soiled and tattered. Her daughters appeared, holding hands. Grace became a hummingbird, and Janis a heron.

She waved and yelled to them, "Do you have everything you need? Do you?"

"Don't worry," they shouted. "We don't need you half as much as you think we do."

Then, in a deep heron's voice, Janis added, "But you better check your flight plans, Mom. It's getting late."

Suddenly, Cricket found herself struggling with a hand full of tickets. One of them was hers, and would take her somewhere beautiful, perhaps in the sleek silver ship of the Nordic Spacepeople. But her hands were stiff and clumsy. The tickets spilled from them onto the floor and she couldn't find the right one. She bent to search, and felt a hand on her shoulder.

When she turned, Pass stood in back of her. "Here," he said. "You'll need these."

And he attached two butterflies to her back.

"Don't worry," he told her, "you'll live long enough to mate."

She rose up and up, her flight smooth and easy. She wasn't at all afraid.

Below her, she saw many people, but not one of them seemed to see her.

t h r e e

Cricket woke to the sound of the Doobie Brothers singing "Black Water." The radio was set to the classic rock station. Funny, that rock music used to be about revolution and now it was classic. She lay still and listened for a while, then rolled over and out of bed. Her husband didn't wake while she showered and dressed in jeans and a sweatshirt. The daffodils were in bloom, but it was still cool out.

Before she left, she sat on the bed and touched her husband lightly on the arm.

"Jim," she said softly. "Jim, I'm going now."

He rolled toward her, flung an arm around her waist. "Can't you stay a little?" he asked. She moved away from his grasp. He woke amorously, regardless of her schedule.

"I've got to go," she said. "Don't forget you're taking Janis to the mall today."

At this, he groaned. "You know I'm playing golf with John and Bert before the stag party. You know I had it planned."

"I know," she said. Bert, who worked with Jim, was getting

married for the second time, and Jim had helped plan his party, though he assured her he wasn't the one to get the stripper. "You can drop her off first. Terry's mother is bringing her home."

"Who?" he asked. He didn't keep the names of his daughter's friends at the tip of his tongue the way she did.

"Terry," she repeated. "You know. The one with the braces."

"Oh," he said. "That boy won't be there, will he? I told her—"

"He won't," she said quickly.

She didn't want him lecturing Janis about Gary. Jim hated the boy, though Cricket was neutral. Jim said he was only out for one thing. Peggy, who heard some of this discussion, said sharply, "How do you know she isn't out for the same thing?"

Cricket thought Jim was going to have a heart attack, his face turned so red. She'd turned the conversation with laughter and cajoled him back into a good mood, but from then on, her job had been to placate Jim, and make sure Janis didn't go into complete revolt at being denied her right to choose a boyfriend. Mostly she did this by turning a blind eye to Janis's meetings with Gary, and making sure that Jim never asked her about him. It was a task that required delicate attentiveness. She sometimes found it exhausting.

"She's going with her friends," Cricket said. "Don't give her a hard time. She's trying to grow up."

"That's the trouble," Jim grumbled, and rolled away from her, back into sleep.

She rose from the bed. Her next stop was Grace's room, to see if she wanted to come along. If Cricket forgot to ask her, she'd feel left out, and when she felt left out, she tended to brood. Cricket thought that was natural for the younger daughter, though in most other ways, she was so truly good-natured that accommodating her wasn't a problem.

Of course, her good nature might be simply a reaction against Janis, who was what Cricket's mother called of High Temperament. "She'll be an artist if you don't watch out," she said, as if that was a life-threatening illness. Cricket sometimes blamed herself for this.

She had named her daughters after her two favorite female singers—Janis Joplin and Grace Slick. Janis was only trying to live up to her name.

But even if Cricket sometimes found her eldest daughter's outspokenness baffling and even frightening, she nurtured a quiet pride in her dramatic talent. For the last two summers, Janis had gone to drama camp, and now, at the end of her junior year, was looking into theater programs in New York City and California. Cricket, who was frightened when she had to speak up at a PTA meeting, was both amazed and excited that she'd produced a daughter so unlike herself.

Cricket opened the door to Grace's room, which was cool and clean and filled with space and light. It was painted white, with peach trim around the two windows and the chair rail. Her clothes were always in her closet or her drawers. Her bureau had two pictures on it—one of Grace with her sister, and one of the ocean, which Grace loved more than any place else in the world. The only other ornament was a goldfish named Country Joe, which swam in a pretty glass vase that sat on top of her bureau. It was the opposite of Janis's attic room, which was spilling over with scarves and beads strewn about, every inch of wall covered by movie posters.

Cricket stood for a moment, admiring the clean space and the face on the pillow. She felt a sense of peace. Grace had that effect on her, especially when she was sleeping and still had something of her childhood in her face. She was fair-skinned, with her mother's honey hair and hazel eyes. Janis was her mirror image, with deeper skin tones, dark hair, and vivid blue eyes that were certainly from Cricket's father. When Janis tanned in the summer, her light eyes were startling in the rich brown face surrounded by her long and wild dark hair.

Even in sleep, Janis looked as if she wrestled with something larger than herself. A dream, perhaps, because she was an active dreamer like her mother. Or maybe some dramatic tension she was trying to drum up out of her unconscious for a play. She might look young in sleep, but she still looked wild, while Grace looked innocent.

Cricket wondered if Grace really was that way, or if she'd adopted this demeanor to separate herself from Janis. She'd read in one of her child-rearing books that sisters feared losing their identity to each other. Especially younger sisters. She could remember making a decision as a teenager not to behave like Peggy, not because Peggy was bad, but because she knew she couldn't ever keep up with her. She wasn't as outgoing, flirtatious, or assertive. She couldn't compete with Peggy's skills, so she'd have to find her own.

She wasn't sure if this was her self, or just a self she'd adopted to be different from Peggy. Or maybe that was the only self you had—the one you created under pressure, like coal into diamonds. But, even so, she wasn't displeased with the results in herself or her daughters.

Cricket went over to the bed and leaned down, touching Grace lightly on the shoulder. "Grace, honey," she whispered. "I'm leaving soon. Did you want to come?"

Grace mumbled something, opened her eyes and stared unseeing at her mother. "Is the coach here?" she asked.

Her mother smiled and smoothed Grace's hair back from her face. "No, honey. It's me. I'm going to the bird sanctuary. Did you want to come?"

Grace shook her head, and closed her eyes. She mumbled something into her pillow as she turned away. Cricket let her sleep. She'd read that adolescents actually need more sleep than infants to negotiate their physical changes.

She left her daughter's room quietly, then left the house and only needed to return once for the car keys, which were on top of the TV instead of in her purse as they should have been.

It was still early, not yet nine, and so the roads were quiet. Not that they were ever very busy in this small town, but later on in the evening, the appearance of boys, sober and drunk, showing off in Camaros and GTs, would make driving unpredictable. Every year, a few teenagers were hurt or killed in car accidents. Every year, the PTA sponsored a campaign against drunk driving. Driving recklessly, drinking too much, and painting graffiti on the overpass out of town had been the favorite activities of teenagers in Dansville, New York, until the mall opened up three years ago.

Now that's where teenagers went to drink a lot of soda, maybe shoplift a little, find partners and then go to the empty field behind the mall and make out. Parents complained that the field was littered with used condoms. Peggy said she'd think parents would be happy to know they were there.

There was very little traffic today, which meant she could drive without tension. She hated driving in heavy traffic, and thought that was probably what kept her in the town where she was born. The traffic patterns were predictable. Just about everything else was, too, and that meant she could pursue her thoughts without the distraction of the unfamiliar. And Cricket liked her own thoughts better than anyplace in the world.

Cricket drove under the overpass that had JENNY LOVES GREG graffitied in blue paint, next to the bold red words EXIT HELL HERE. She took the highway that led from town toward the next largest city, which was about forty-five minutes away. When the girls were little and Cricket and Jim took them there to shop for fall clothes, Grace had asked Janis, "Is this where the big people live?"

"Yup," Janis replied. "In the big houses."

Cricket looked out the car window and saw the high-rise apartment buildings they went past. Jim, driving, chuckled softly while Grace and Janis continued a solemn discussion.

"When I'm big, I'll live in the big houses," Janis said.

"Not me," Grace said. "I want to live in the small house, just like ours. With a bunny."

And that hadn't changed. When Grace talked about her future, it always had something to do with being in the country, and having animals. Sometimes, it was a goat farm. Sometimes, it was a place for boarding cats. It was always outside the city limits. Janis, on the other hand, couldn't wait to get to a city, preferably New

York, and live in the big buildings, with the big people they imagined so long ago.

In between their town and the city, in a desolate spot, was the bird sanctuary, four miles from the mall, but tucked down a side road you could easily miss. Pass had put up a sign last year and, with the opening of the mall, was getting more visitors, and more donations.

The sign led you down a small road that became a gravel road that turned into a narrow, steeply inclined dirt path. After a snowfall, it was terrifying to drive. During a heavy rain, you could get in, but if the creek ran high, you couldn't get back out up the hill. Cricket told Pass he ought to get the town to pave and plow the road. Pass said he'd rather not. First of all, he was between city and town, and couldn't get either one to do it without a lot of fuss. Second, he liked letting the elements dictate his schedule. It gave him time to be alone and catch up on his reading. He read more than anyone Cricket knew, including herself.

Today the road was wet from runoff, melted snow coming down the mountains and leaking up from the bottom of the earth to saturate the surface. It wasn't deep enough to cause trouble, and she turned into the driveway without skidding.

She stopped her car and sat in it, adjusting to stillness. There were no traffic sounds here. The cool air was filled with early morning moisture, and the bright sun seemed to soak into it and linger as a sheen of transparent hung gold. The peacocks were making their mournfully frantic cries. Take me, the males said. Take me. The geese answered in honks, and a hawk's cry pierced the air with an arrow of sound. The clack and rattle of the sand hill cranes lifting their heads and the thrumming of the emus made a percussive backdrop.

When she first came here, she was intimidated by the birds, preferring to focus on the flowers. The birds were beautiful—the cranes lifting their long necks, turning their heads toward the sky and clacking out their call, the eagles with their following eyes, the different kinds of pheasants dressed in shades she'd like for a dress. But birds might bite. Flowers didn't. And some of the birds were big. Pass told her you just had to remind them that you were a predator, and they wouldn't hurt you. She wasn't sure if she was, though. Or if she wanted to think of herself that way. She reached a tentative peace with her own fears through time and association, though, and no longer jumped if a goose honked at her or an emu stuck its curious face into hers.

She got out of the car and walked toward the house, stopping briefly at the monitor, which Pass had set up at the front of the house. It was trained on the two eggs of nesting golden eagles, due to hatch any day. Pass was hoping to get good footage of the hatching, which *National Geographic* said they'd like to buy.

It was a big deal, she knew, to have brought these two golden eagles to a point where they'd breed, and hatch eggs. The female was missing a wing, and the male missing a leg. Both were permanent residents of the sanctuary. Pass wasn't sure if they'd mate, if eggs would result, or if they'd care for the eggs or hatchlings properly.

She went to the front door and knocked. After a short while, it opened, and Pass stood on the other side, as he always did, looking her over as if he expected her to be someone different this time. Not unfriendly, just not sure, as he often looked. She thought that he was actually a shy man, more at home with birds than with people.

"Just me," she said.

He nodded, convinced. "Come on in."

He stood to one side and let her by. She walked through the kitchen, which was, as usual, marvelously neat—just as neat as Peggy's ever was. In fact, when Peggy gave her a hard time about working here, she'd say, "You should see his kitchen, Peggy. It's so clean."

Beyond the kitchen was his study, also neat and spare, with a donated IBM computer on the desk next to a blue vase that held feathers, books filling the shelves on three walls, and on the fourth wall an old-fashioned black-and-white photo of his mother, who was a pretty and sad-looking woman. She held a five-year-old Pass on her lap, who looked up at her with open worship, while she gazed at him as if she saw all the world and the harm it might do. The picture always made something move in her chest.

"I was just ordering plants," he said. "After that, we can go check the seedlings."

"Okay. That's good," she said, as she stood and looked at his captured childhood.

"The way you look at that," he noted, "you'd think it was a Rembrandt."

She turned her head to him and smiled. "It's sweet," she said. "You were a sweet little boy, I'll bet."

"When I wasn't raising hell," he admitted.

"I'm surprised some little girl didn't grab you up and marry you," she said, feeling a little nervous and hoping she didn't sound it. She never asked about his personal life.

He was quiet a moment. "I was married," he said flatly, matter-of-factly. "We were real young. It didn't work out."

She felt triumphant, the way she would when she was a little girl and Peggy would ask her a riddle that she would guess correctly. She'd found him out.

"Let's get some work done," he said a little brusquely, and went to his desk and sat down. She pulled up a chair beside his, and peered at the Web site of an organic nursery.

"Go to butterfly bush," she said, and he moved the mouse, clicked on to the picture that opened into a palette of pinks, purples, and blues. She sighed with deep satisfaction.

"Get the Ruby Slippers," she said. "You can plant some outside the house, too."

"How many?"

She calculated quickly in her head. "Ten. Eight in, and two out. And six of the Black Knight, six of the White Cloud. It'll be a good mix."

He placed the order, nodding. "What else?"

"Munstead lavender, a dozen. And liatris, the same. Then we'll need some plants for the eggs and larvae. Milkweed for monarchs, nettle for the question mark and comma—why do butterflies have punctuation names?"

"Orderly creatures," he said. "Admirable of them."

They actually were orderly, she'd learned. Their lives proceeded with brevity and grace. Some had such short life spans that they were born without the necessary apparatus for eating. They spent their two weeks of life mating and then, having sucked themselves dry of nutrients, they died.

"Admirable," she agreed. "Queen Anne's lace grows here already. You'll want parsley, fennel, and dill, though. I'll set up a new herb garden for that. I know just where it can go. Order rosemary, too. Yours isn't doing very well."

They went through the rest of the plant ordering, which delighted Cricket as nothing else did because she could buy as much as she wanted and not worry about the cost. They had a planting budget from a grant, and it would cover her yard ten times over. She could be as profligate as she wished, and so she chose with wild abandon and a sense of unlimited abundance.

They talked of flowers and birds as they waited for orders to go through, and she had a sense of summer starting, which always excited her, as if every summer was the first one, full of wonder and growth.

Pass told her it looked as if the eagle's egg would hatch any day, and he would call her when it did. She told him about her daffodils, which were in bloom, her lettuce and peas, which she'd planted two days ago, and that she thought she'd put her hummingbird feeders up early this year, on the recommendation of a friend. This made her remember the old man she'd met in the grocery store, and she laughed.

"What's funny?" he asked.

"Just this man I met," she said. "Talking about hummingbirds reminded me."

"He was funny?"

"Sort of." She smiled at him. His gaze was focused on the screen, and his face turned down in a sort of a scowl that she knew wasn't angry, but a way he had of thinking hard.

"He said I should live as if I only had a year to live," she explained.

"Oh," he said. Then, after a pause, he looked at her instead of the screen. "Will you?"

She was taken aback. She hadn't expected to be asked that. Peggy and Jim hadn't asked her. "I don't think so. I don't know what I'd do, really."

"It's easy," he said. "Find what makes you feel most alive. Do that."

"Oh. Easy." She laughed, and he grinned back at her. "Would you?"

His scowl deepened. Then, his entire face smoothed over. "I already do," he said, then paused. "With one or two notable exceptions. Things I can't have just by wanting."

"Like what?" she asked, and he moved his face half an inch, looking at her with his gold eye. She found her heart beginning to beat a little harder than was natural, and the moment lengthened itself in silence.

He opened his mouth to say something, closed it, and turned away. "Things," he said.

"Oh," she said, not sure where to go from there.

Something had happened, hadn't it? Or maybe not. Probably not. Jim always told her she overanalyzed, reading into the smallest gesture a larger meaning that just didn't exist. In this case, she hoped it didn't exist. She didn't want to have to worry about him feeling things for her that she couldn't feel back. Not that he wasn't attractive. He was. Very attractive. Though of course she wasn't attracted to him. She wouldn't be. Or couldn't. She was happily married, and loved Jim and her family. Of course.

"Let's check the seedlings," he said.

He rose, and she followed. They went outside where the air was warming as the day progressed. She took a deep breath. "Spring," she said.

"Nice," he agreed.

They walked around the duck pond and behind the baby emu house, stopping to watch the chicks run in their flocking patterns, trying out new legs. Cricket was fascinated by them and would stand for as long as Pass let her, watching them circle and recircle and spiral in toward some invisible center, only to break open and circle again at signals she couldn't discern. It was like watching the motion of water or fire, mesmerizing and pointless and soothing.

Pass stayed with her. He was rarely impatient, and certainly not while watching the birds. He became treelike in his stillness, only his eyes moving like leaves in the light. He stood next to her silently, but she could see that he was smiling at her pleasure, pleased by it.

The sun warmed her back and the scent of green growth and rich loam filled the air. She breathed it in, and breathed out. She was deeply happy. Watching the emus, standing in the warm air, knowing her children were well and her home was secure and her life followed discernible patterns, she knew there was nothing she lacked.

"Everything is so good," she said softly. "Isn't it?"

He laughed. He had a nice laugh. Relaxed, and real. "Sometimes it is," he said.

They moved into the butterfly house, where shelves of seedling packs lined the plastic interior. They were little, but sturdy. Not one was leggy, and none, as she examined them, showed signs of mildew or rot or mites. They were doing well.

"Beautiful," she murmured, as she examined them. The butterflies would love them. They would feast on them. They would lay eggs like tiny jewels, and by next year they'd have butterflies of all kinds to stock their house with.

"We'll transplant next weekend," he said. "I've got a Boy Scout troop coming in to help."

He reached down and stroked one of the small false leaves of the zinnias with the tip of his finger. He had fine hands, with long fingers. Without thinking, she reached down and touched the plant he touched, her finger brushing his. He startled. She pulled back immediately, embarrassed. So intimate a gesture. She didn't mean to do that.

"You were in my dream last night," she said quickly to create a distraction, and realized that only sounded more odd and intimate than her gesture.

"I was?" he asked, but he didn't look at her.

"You were giving me butterflies. To use as wings." She felt strange to herself, as if she were saying words beyond her own understanding, the way she did in dreams sometimes.

He seemed to shake himself lightly, then took a few steps away, moving to the next tray of plants. "And did you use them?" he asked over his shoulder. His distance shifted the feeling, relieved her of her own strangeness, and the tension dissipated.

"Yes. I did," she said, then added, "Flying dreams usually mean new power, but I think this one meant something else."

"What makes you think it means anything?"

"Well," she said, "it's a dream."

"Right," he said. "It's a dream."

"But you dream. All the time. You told me."

"That's right," he said. "I dream every night. In color. Last night, I dreamt I was giving you butterfly wings."

She gasped, and her eyes opened wide. "Really?" she asked, and saw he was grinning broadly. "Oh, you're teasing me. But don't you like to know what your dreams mean?"

"I think," he said, "they mean exactly what they say."

"Well, how do you know what they say until you figure them out?"

"You know what they say by living it, not figuring it out."

She chewed on this. She thought of the possibilities, and decided she didn't want to discuss any of them, especially the bit involving orgies. "I think there's more to it than that," she said definitively. Pass was one of the few people she'd argue with this way. With everyone else, she'd say something neutral if they disagreed. Something like, That's an interesting opinion, or I see what you mean.

"Maybe," he said, "you think too much."

She was wondering whether to be hurt by this, and how to respond, when the door opened. She looked toward it, and saw Law standing just inside, his broad form blocking the sun. Cricket tried not to stare. She didn't know the right amount of eye contact to maintain with him, since he seemed to look somewhere over her head with his soft gray eyes. He worked his hands in and out of fists, his face, with its perfect skin and heavy brow, indicative of no emotion.

"Hey," Pass said.

Law shuffled his feet, looked at Cricket, and then at his brother. "Going out," he said, his voice thick and slow with effort. Cricket rarely heard him speak, and when he did, it always seemed to be pulled from a place that was unfamiliar, unvisited.

"Okay," Pass said. "Do you need money?"

Law scratched at his arm and thought, then pulled a ten-dollar bill out of his pocket.

Pass dug into the pocket of his jeans and pulled out a wallet, removed another ten-dollar bill and gave it to Law. "Just in case."

Law backed into the door, opening it with his rear, bobbed his head up and down a few times, and left.

Pass went back to examining leaves. Cricket frowned. "Where's he going?"

Pass shrugged. "Out."

"Just out?"

"Sometimes he goes out walking," Pass said. "Sometimes he goes to the end of the road and catches a bus to the mall."

"Is that safe?" she asked hesitantly.

"What?"

"That he goes out. Alone. Is it safe?"

"Safe?" Pass said a little sharply. "Safe?"

"Don't you worry about him?" she asked gently.

"I showed him how to take the bus, and how to use the phone booths at the mall. He knows when he's hungry and he knows the way back here."

He moved away from her, toward another tray of seedlings. She stayed where she was, shielding her face by examining more leaves. She'd been rebuffed by his answer, given in colder tones than he ever used. His coldness made her feel lonely. She let this thought roam through her for a moment. She was lonely. His coldness only emphasized the feeling. She was lonely, and only noticed it now.

She walked down the aisle of the greenhouse to where he stood.

"These look good," he said pointing to the tiny leaves.

"I'm sorry," she said.

He lifted his head and tilted it, his eyebrows coming down over his eyes. "What?"

"I'm sorry if I said something wrong. About your brother. I hope I didn't offend you."

"No," he said, sounding genuinely surprised. "Of course not."

"I guess you don't like to talk about him."

"There's nothing to talk about," he said. "Is there?"

"Well," she said, "maybe how you feel, taking care of him. If it's hard to do that. If you ever worry about him. That sort of thing."

He lifted his chin an inch and looked up at the top of the greenhouse. His lips moved, as if he were repeating her words. Then he shook his head. "Law's my half brother," he said. "We had different fathers. You knew that?"

She shook her head.

"Oh. Well, we did. And he's . . . disabled, I guess they call it. He gets around okay, so long as he's in familiar territory, but, well, part of his brain doesn't work right. That's all."

She nodded.

"So it doesn't matter how I feel. It's still like that."

"It does matter," she said, her voice sounding a little too high and breathless to her own ears. "Everybody knows that. I mean, it matters. To me."

His face smoothed into stillness. His mouth became almost a smile, then decided against it. He looked at her hard, as he had in his office. This time, she knew she was blushing.

"Thank you," he said, very softly, and then was silent. She waited for more, but nothing came. He just stood there, looking at her.

"We better look at the planting plans," she said.

He nodded and they moved on.

The rest of the morning was spent in details of landscape planning. She kept far enough away from him that her hand couldn't make gestures without permission. She wondered if she was flirting with him, maybe because she was upset about her husband wanting orgies. She had discovered she was lonely, and that was a dangerous sign. Why was she lonely, anyway? Did she want Sex Every Day? Whipped cream? She wasn't sure, but she decided she'd stop and get that magazine after all. She couldn't go around lonely, unconsciously flirting and starting trouble she couldn't deal with. No. If her marriage was feeling a little dull and lonely, she would do something about it. Quickly.

They were done by one o'clock, and though Pass asked her to stay for lunch, as he always did, she declined. She had to get to the bank, stop at Wal-Mart and pick up a video for her daughter. "Errands," she said. "You know."

He raised an eyebrow at her. "If you were going to live as if you only had a year, would you spend it doing errands?"

She grinned at him. "Probably," she said. "I'm just that stupid."

"No," he said. "You just like to make people think you are, so they'll leave you alone. Not interrupt your thoughts. See you next week?"

"Sure," she said, not certain if he was teasing her again, or if he'd said something true. But if he had, he wasn't pursuing it, which she thought was all for the best.

"I'll call if the eagle hatches," he said.

"Oh, yes. That's good."

When she was in her car, she opened the window to the warmer afternoon air. She let it stay open, let the wind blow in as she drove, maybe a little faster than usual, back down the highway toward town.

When she got to the bank, it was closed, and she had to use the drive-up ATM, which she didn't like because her arm was too short and she always dropped things out the car window. She also felt funny about depositing her check to a machine, though she knew it wasn't money, but just numbers, traded back and forth. Her school sent her numbers, she sent them to the bank, the bank sent them to the mortgage company. Just numbers that somehow allowed her to live in a house and buy food and clothes.

She headed toward Wal-Mart, another place she didn't like to go, but one where she often ended up. It seemed to suck her toward it relentlessly, always needing her to buy something for the house, her husband, her children. Grace asked her to pick up a video she'd ordered—a copy of *Fly Away Home*, which they both loved and which made them both cry. Even Janis would sit and watch with them when they rented it and sniff back tears now and then.

She steeled herself and entered, making a beeline for the video section, ignoring screaming children and older couples who stood directly in front of her staring at things like cheap aluminum foil and plastic bags. She finally got the attention of a salesperson, got the tape, and made another beeline for the checkout. The store made her dizzy if she looked around. It had too much stuff, and all of it wanted to be bought.

As she stood in line, conversation reached her from the

woman ahead of her, who talked loudly, with a downstate accent.

"Closed," she said. "Can you believe that? And on a Saturday. I mean, how can they close? Don't they know people *need* things?"

The woman in front of her replied in a softer voice that Cricket couldn't really hear except as a series of murmurs.

"I don't *know*. All I know is they got the road blocked off, or else I'd a gone to Sears, y'know? I wanted to go to Sears because I have a *card* for there, and I get *points* when I use it. Here I got *nothing*. But the *road* was blocked off."

Cricket began to get interested, though she wasn't sure why. Just something tapping at her insides like an importunate finger. She heard more murmurs from the other woman, and then the city woman replied.

"Well, I *guess* so. I turned on the news on the way over, but they didn't have nothing *about* it. Just that there'd been an *incident* and the mall was *closed* for further notice."

Now Cricket felt something cold and unfriendly creeping down her spine. Janis was going to the mall at what time? At noon? And coming home at seven, after seeing a matinee. Something about the mall?

She cleared her throat and leaned forward. "Excuse me," she said to the city woman. "Is there something going on at the mall?"

The woman turned, and Cricket saw her lavishly red lips open, about to speak, when the voice of a child interrupted them. "Hey, Ma," it yelled across the store to a woman who stood in line one over.

"Hush, Sam," the woman said. "Don't yell."

"Ma, listen—there's a shooting at the mall. Some crazy guy is killing people with a gun."

Cricket's hand began to tremble. She watched it move. A shooting at the mall? That didn't make sense, so why was her hand shaking? She dropped the video, and the next thing she knew she was walking rapidly toward the exit.

four

Much of what happened that day would remain forever unclear to Cricket, while strange, small details would never leave her mind. She got in her car, started it, and listened to the engine hum to life. The radio came on, and played a song Grace liked—Green Day, singing, "It's something unpredictable that in the end is right."

The phrase repeated itself over and over in her mind as the song ended and a commercial for the Great Escape amusement park came on. There was no news of a mall shooting. It could be just a vicious rumor, started by people who had so little to enlarge their own lives they had to steal the tragedies of Arkansas, of Colorado, of anywhere but here, where they did not really want to be but were afraid to leave.

She saw a dead raccoon on the side of the road. It was on its back, and bloated like a balloon. When she got to the access road for the mall, a police roadblock stopped her, and the officer who came and spoke to her had a spot of mustard on the shoulder of her uniform.

"My daughter's in there," she said reasonably. "I have to go in."

"Nobody's going in," the officer said. "Everybody's being taken out."

"Then what do I do?" she asked. "Where do I go?"

"Go to the high school. We got a real mess to clean up here, but we'll be bringing the underage survivors to the high school, and reporting on the victims."

"Survivors?" Cricket asked. The officer said nothing. "Survivors?" she repeated as the officer walked away.

Then, she shouted, "Survivors?"

The officer stopped and turned around. Nodded.

Cricket drove to the school and was stopped by a roadblock about a quarter mile away from the building. A different officer took her name and number and told her to go home. It would take time to get the kids here. She would be called.

She thought briefly of her husband. He should be here, she thought. He would tell this officer that they couldn't leave. They would believe him, too. For some reason, she was sure they wouldn't believe her.

"Survivors?" she asked.

"Ma'am?" The officer had very white flesh. She would remember very white, thick flesh.

A white van pulled up next to her car and a woman in a pretty blue suit got out. She had a microphone that said CNN. She stuck the microphone in the officer's face and asked, "Officer, any official word on how many?"

"Survivors?" Cricket whispered to herself.

"Not yet," he said. "Nothing official."

"Unofficially?" the reporter asked.

"More than ten," the officer said. "Some killed in a crush on the escalator, too."

"Survivors?" Cricket asked.

The reporter turned to her like a hawk spotting prey. The microphone moved toward her. "Are you a parent?" the reporter asked. "Is it your child?"

"I want to know about the survivors," Cricket said.

The reporter waited. Maybe she asked something else. Cricket wasn't sure.

"My daughter," Cricket said.

"Your daughter?" the reporter asked with sympathy and a barely disguised eagerness. "How old is she? Was she with friends? What does she look like?"

Cricket shook her head. No more words wanted to come out. She drove away and headed toward home. In her rearview mirror, she saw the CNN reporter, turning back to the officer.

She would remember nothing of the drive home, but she recalled sitting in her driveway and looking at little pieces of grass that broke through the tar. It would have to be resealed, she thought. She got out of the car and went inside, turned on the TV to CNN and sat down on the couch. There was a deodorant commercial on. She closed her eyes, willing it away, and when she opened them, magically, it was gone and the news was on. She saw the school she'd just been at, and the reporter in the pretty blue suit.

Ann Taylor suit, Cricket thought. It looked very Ann Taylor, but these reporters probably had their suits custom-made.

Then Cricket saw herself, her face looking strange and blank as she said, "My daughter," and nothing more. She looked the way Law sometimes looked. Her face said nothing. Her eyes were looking at something nobody else could see.

Cricket pushed herself up from the couch. She still had her car keys in her hand. She moved toward the door, to her car, got in it and drove back to the school. Halfway there, she remembered she'd left the TV on.

When she was stopped at the roadblock, she parked her car, got out and walked. Nobody stopped her. Other people were there. Parents, she supposed. People like her, whose sons and daughters went to the mall for fun on a Saturday afternoon. People who were all saying the same word, with a question in it. Survivors? Survivors?

She supposed they all had been told to go home. She wondered how many of them had gone and come back, as she had,
and how many had simply refused to leave. After all, what could
the police do? Shoot them? Arrest them? For the first time, it
occurred to her that the police only had the authority that she gave
them, or the authority of their guns.

The others all stood against the fence that surrounded the
school grounds, their faces pressed to it, their hands grasping the
mesh. As she approached, many of them turned to her. Their faces
all asked the same question.

Survivors? Survivors?

"My daughter," she said as she took her place at the fence. The
man next to her nodded, and turned back to watching the school.

"It'll be a while before they get the kids here. They didn't catch
the shooter," the man said. "They're still trying to clear the mall."

They stood and stared. The police came around and had the
parents give the names of the children they were waiting for,
then left again. She supposed a long time passed. The sun
seemed to shift, the angle of light changing from afternoon to
late afternoon, to early evening. The air grew cooler. At one
point, she lifted her head and sniffed the air as if she could smell
the night coming on.

"It'll be dark soon," she said.

The man next to her, who had not moved, nodded.

A woman came over to them. Cricket looked at her. The
woman was named Annie. Cricket knew that because the woman
had told her at some point earlier, though Cricket couldn't remember when or why. But she remembered that Annie had gone to get
information. She said it was a sin the way they were making the
parents wait. She said something had to be done. Cricket figured
she'd see Annie's face on CNN.

"They're letting the first group out," Annie said. "The cops'll
be coming with lists of names, see if they're ours."

"Survivors?" Cricket asked.

"Survivors," Annie said. "If your kid's hurt or . . . anything, they'll find you, talk to you."

"How many?" the man to Cricket's left asked.

"Eleven dead," Annie said. "A lot more wounded. Some pretty bad. There was a panic, and a bunch of people got hurt trying to get out."

The man kept looking forward. "My son is very alert," he said to nobody in particular. "He runs the five hundred meters on the track team. Last year he won a medal."

Cricket remembered that race. She'd gone to the track meet because Grace was running, and she'd seen the little boy who won the five hundred meters. He didn't look old enough to be in high school. He was a thin, shy boy who wore prescription glasses with elastic holders to keep them on his head as he ran.

"Darren," she said. "Darren Holabee."

The man turned to her. "That's right," he said. "You know him?"

"I work at the high school," she said. "I know all of them."

"He's alert," the man said. "Very alert."

Cricket nodded. She saw, in her peripheral vision, a policeman and a policewoman approaching them. She had a sudden urge to run. Instead, she stood very still. The two officers handed out pieces of paper, which were passed down the line. Then, they began working their way down the line of parents, stopping to talk to them. Cricket saw couples clutching each other's arms, their faces turning white. She heard sobs, and groans. She heard someone praying loudly. When Annie handed her the list, she read it three times. Each time she did not see her daughter's name on it. The police kept moving down the line.

She closed her eyes, not wanting to gauge their progress, wishing she could avoid this moment somehow, knowing it couldn't be avoided. Even if she left, whatever had happened wouldn't unhappen. She tried very hard to think of nothing at all. Not "let her be alive," or "take his son instead," or "I'll do anything." To think anything might tempt the fates, might be the wrong wish to make, might backfire as wishes so often did.

Cricket heard the officer speaking to Annie in a low voice. She opened her eyes.

"Seward," Annie said. "Mrs. Seward. My daughter's Jeannie."

The officer said something, very softly. Cricket, trying not to watch, saw anyway that Annie's legs were buckling and the officer was grabbing her elbow, holding her up. Then Annie began to moan, a low sound, a horrible noise like a machine that's broken and keeps grinding away anyway, unstoppable.

It's her heart, Cricket thought. That's what it sounds like when it breaks.

Cricket saw that the man on her left had his eyes closed, and his lips moved as if in prayer. He held the paper close to his chest. Then he opened his eyes and smiled at Cricket.

"I told you," he said. "My son is very alert."

He walked away briskly and the officer moved on. Cricket watched, and then shouted after him, "Hey. Hey!"

The officer stopped and turned to her.

"My daughter," she said, and it was all she could say. "My daughter. Please."

The officer came up to her. "Name?" he asked.

"Thompson," she said. "Janis Thompson. She's tall, and pretty. Dark hair."

The officer thumbed through his list. "We've got a Jack, last name T-O-M-S-I-N."

"No. Janis. A girl. Janis T-H-O-M-P-S-O-N."

The officer shook his head. "Not on the list of victims."

"Oh my God," Cricket said. "Oh my God."

"Does she carry ID?"

"God," Cricket repeated. "God."

The officer put a hand on her shoulder. "Look," he said, "if she was in the school, we'd have her name. We got them all. But some of the kids got out, got their own way home. And some—well, not everybody's been identified yet. Best thing you can do is go home. She might be home, waiting for you."

"What if she's not?"

"Someone will call," he said.

Cricket turned and walked away.

She had the feeling of settling into a nightmare. It must be a nightmare, she thought. Her legs wouldn't move as fast as she wanted them to. She couldn't say a lot of words she wanted to. Soon, she'd probably see that all her teeth were falling out, or her car had become a giant white sea slug.

When she got to it and put her hand to the door, she saw that it hadn't. She got in and drove home, only to once again sit in her driveway considering the grass, listening to the TV, which she could hear from outside. After a while, she got out of the car and went into the house. She walked to the TV and turned it off, then stood in the living room listening for any sound of human presence. There was none.

She went to the phone to pick it up and call someone. Peggy. Jim. Maybe she could find him, though she wasn't sure where to call at this point. Some bar they were going to, she thought. When she put her hand on it, she saw that it hadn't been cradled properly. She was always telling Janis to make sure it was cradled properly, but Janis was always in a hurry, darting out of the room practically before it left her hand. She picked it up. The line was dead. She clicked the receiver and brought back the dial tone. She put it down and looked at the answering machine. There were no messages. It had probably been off all day.

She stood in the silence, waiting. Maybe if she just stood here quietly, something good would happen. Jim would come home. Peggy would show up to criticize her housecleaning. The night would turn back into day and none of this would have happened.

In the silence, Cricket asked for that miracle, or one just as good. A miracle was what she needed. It wasn't just for her, she explained, but for all the parents who stood with their hands clenching the wire fence or waited in their silent houses for the phone to ring.

Please, she asked, let there be a miracle. She folded her hands and put her forehead down to lean on them, something she hadn't done since she was a little girl at church. Then, she did it because she thought it looked important. Now, she did it because she wanted to rest inside something more reassuring than reality. Please, she prayed. Let there be a miracle. She heard a car go by, slow down and stop. Then, her front door opened.

"Mom?" a small and frightened voice said.

She lifted her head from her hands and turned toward it. It was Janis.

Cricket took one step forward, then reached out and grabbed for her as if she was a balloon in danger of flying out of her hands and up into the sky. She grabbed Janis's arms and pulled her into the house, put her hands on her shoulders, touched them, touched her face, pressed her hands into her forearms. "Oh," she said. "Oh. Oh."

Then, her phone rang. She jumped, and went quickly into the kitchen, still hanging on to Janis, dragging her along to the phone. It must be Jim or Peggy, frantic, trying to get her all day and just getting a busy signal.

She picked up the receiver and asked, "Hello?"

"Is this Mrs. Thompson?" a male voice asked.

Of course, she thought. Telemarketing time. "I don't want any—"

"Do you have a daughter, Mrs. Thompson?" the voice asked.

"Yes, but I'm not buying—"

"Ma'am," the voice continued, "this is Officer Halloran. Do you have a daughter who was at the mall today?"

Cricket's grasp on Janis tightened. "Yes. She's here. She's right here."

There was a long hesitation. "Is your daughter named Grace?"

"No," Cricket said automatically. "Janis. My daughter is Janis."

A white heat moved through her. Grace wasn't at the mall. Janis was. "Wait," she gasped. "Wait." She looked at Janis, who seemed dazed and a little pale. "Did your sister go with you today?"

Janis nodded.

"Grace?" she asked the person on the other end. "My daughter Grace?"

"We tried to call earlier and couldn't get through. She's at Sacred Heart Medical Center, ma'am, and they had to—"

"Grace?" she asked again.

"Grace Thompson. Thirteen years old, lives at—"

"I'm on my way," Cricket interrupted, and hung up. She stood for a moment with one hand on the receiver and the other on Janis.

"Mom?" Janis asked, sounding young and fragile.

"There's chicken in the refrigerator," Cricket said. "You can eat while I'm out."

"I don't want chicken," Janis said. "I'm going with you."

Cricket shook her head. Something wasn't making sense. Grace? She had forgotten she even had a daughter named Grace. She hadn't noticed Grace's absence, hadn't thought to call her, look for her, worry about her. But Grace was in the hospital. Cricket hadn't asked how badly she was hurt. No. She didn't want to know anything bad. Didn't want to hear any bad words said. Only wanted to hear that it was a mistake, wasn't true, was a different Grace Thompson after all. T-O-M-S-I-N.

She stared at the phone. Maybe they would call back and say that. T-O-M-S-I-N.

Please, she prayed. Let there be another miracle. *Now.*

The phone rang. She blinked at it, then picked it up.

"Hello?" she whispered.

"Cricket?" the voice on the other end said. It was male. A male voice. "Is that you?"

"Yes," she said.

"Oh. You sound strange. I thought you should know—"

Male voice. Not the hospital, though. They didn't call her Cricket. It must be Jim, though she couldn't tell if it sounded like him.

"It's okay," she said quickly, to avert more news. "I know. I already know."

There was silence on the other end. She waited for it to be filled.

"How did you find out?"

"The hospital called and told me. Is this . . . this is Jim, isn't it?"

"It's Pass. What's the hospital got to do with it?"

"I . . . I thought you were Jim. My daughter, Grace, was at the mall."

There was a long pause. "I don't understand."

"Don't you know about the shooting?"

"What shooting?"

"At the mall. My daughter . . ." She couldn't go on. Couldn't make herself say it.

"I'll be right there," he said.

"No," she said quickly. "I have to go. I have to go to the hospital."

"Okay," he said. "Okay."

"Why did you call?" she asked.

He breathed in and then out.

"The eagle hatched," he said. "I thought you'd want to know."

children's dreams

The mall was the gathering place for teenagers and almost-teenagers, and on any given Saturday, if you went there, you'd see them milling about the food court in groups of threes and sixes and more, eating junk food, playing games in the video arcade, boys looking at girls and girls looking at boys and all of them looking at each other to see some image of who they might be reflected in the eyes of their friends. Mall rats, running the interior space, looking for food and fun and themselves.

This Saturday was no exception. The mall was busy. A clown made balloon animals in the food court. A man demonstrated remote-control helicopters. A woman walked giant mechanical tigers and pandas in a circle around the food stands, offering rides and pictures to children. The air was full of sound—people talking, music from stores and the central loudspeakers, crying children, laughing children, scolding parents. Sound was a living force, like a giant insect whose wings vibrated at many pitches at once, each one harmonic with the others. There was barely any room for anything but sound.

Grace and her friends, Karen, Deborah, and Julie, stood in

front of Arby's, Grace drinking a Coke, Karen and Deborah sharing fries. Karen had a bag of body glitter and tiny butterfly hair clips that moved their wings if you moved your head. She was a big girl, already five feet eight inches and towering over the boys in her class, but when she closed her eyes, she saw herself diminutive, sweet, with butterflies in her hair.

Deborah, who really was diminutive and blond, with large blue eyes, had bought herself a fake leather vest from Limbo Lounge. She wanted a pair of leather pants to match, but her mother said no. She hoped to get a tattoo in a place her mother wouldn't see, as soon as she was sixteen, when the tattoo parlor said she wouldn't need parental permission.

Grace hadn't bought anything. She didn't know what she wanted, except that she sometimes saw herself in long red silk dresses. When she saw herself this way, she was usually lounging on a satin couch, with a man who looked remarkably like Pierce Brosnan bringing her flowers.

Grace and her friends knew many of the other kids hanging around the food court. Janis's friends were at Arby's. Grace didn't talk to them, because she thought most of them were weird. They all wanted to be on the stage, and spent a lot of time putting on makeup.

A group of boys stood just outside the arcade, milling and buzzing around each other like horseflies in constant erratic motion. Frank and Joshua and Dave and Jonathan were there, all boys on the football team. They were in the next class up from Grace, and all considered hot. Grace and her friends tried to pretend they weren't looking at them, but they were.

"Wanna go play a game?" Deborah asked casually.

"I don't know," Grace said, not wanting to seem too eager.

"Might as well," Karen said. "Nothing else to do."

They made their way over nonchalantly, talking easily to each other about what style of jeans from the Gap would best suit Karen's hips, Grace's legs. The boys stopped talking as they approached, and when they were just even with them, one of them whistled softly. Grace lifted her chin in the air. Deborah giggled.

"C'mon," Karen said, "let's get some tokens. I feel like shooting something."

They went into the arcade, traded their dollars for little metal coins that would be useless anywhere but here, and looked around.

"Here," Karen said. "Zone of the Dead. I'm good at that."

"I suck," Deborah said.

"You can watch," Grace said.

Karen put four tokens in the slot and picked up a pink pistol that was attached to the game. When the enemy—an alien with pointed teeth and one green eye—appeared on the screen, she turned the pistol sideways, the way she saw it done on TV, and started to fire. Grace, with her own pink pistol, started her game and fired at the alien. Deborah kept an unobtrusive eye on the boys, who were still milling and circling at the entrance. She saw them punch each other in the arm, look their way, punch each other more. Then, Frank grabbed Dave by the arm. His face expressed shock. Deborah saw him fall to the floor.

"Grace," she said, "something's wrong. Stop it—*stop* shooting."

Grace put her pistol down. The noise of the arcade was all they could hear, but Deborah pointed outside, where Joshua and Jonathan had become a pile of boys on the floor with Dave and Frank, and somebody was screaming, screaming, screaming.

Deborah pulled at Grace, and Grace pulled at Karen, who lifted her pink pistol and began firing at nothing, at everything.

"Stop," Deborah screeched, girl voice high and thin. "*Stop.*"

Stop what, Grace wanted to ask, but she felt a sting near her jaw. She lowered her gun and turned to her friends.

"Debbie?" she tried to ask, but her mouth wouldn't work. Something hurt and she was afraid. "Mommy?" she tried to ask, and couldn't. Something was wrong, terribly wrong, she could tell because Debbie was staring at her and screaming, screaming and for some reason getting smaller, swallowed into darkness as if she were being sucked into a hungry throat.

"No," Grace tried to say, but she couldn't.

"*Grace,*" Debbie shrieked, and grabbed at her, but Karen tugged her back.

"You can't help. You can't help," she yelled over Debbie's screams and dragged her still screaming to the back of the arcade, pushed her into the tight space between a surfing game and the wall.

"Shut up," Karen commanded. "Close your eyes and shut up," and Debbie did. They were still.

They knew how to dream about jeans, and their hips, and boys. They knew how to dream themselves into adulthood as they saw it in the lives of their parents or in the magazines or on TV. They knew happiness was one of their constitutional rights. They were raised to expect good things, to be safe, to have a lot, to be happy. They did not know how to live a nightmare. They were not raised to live a nightmare. They did not know how.

As they huddled behind the surfing game, they heard screams, people running, people crying. They didn't see a large man with unfocused eyes and a Glock in his hand walking through the crowd, firing, the sounds of the gun hidden under the sounds of canned music, of high young voices echoing in the high-ceilinged interior, the shots and pings and bells and screeches of arcade games. They didn't see his eyes as he fired into the crowd, as he watched the children fall or run screaming away. They didn't see the people stumbling over each other, knocking each other down to get away.

They didn't see the man with the gun turn the weapon to his own head. They didn't see another man fling himself at the shooter and knock him down, or the gun skittering from his hand. They didn't see the shooter scrambling out from under and running, running away in the mass hysteria of people pushing toward the escalator, out, anywhere safe.

And they didn't see their friends left on the floor of the food court, or all the dreams that would not be dreamt that night.

five

The sliding automatic doors opened and Cricket walked through to the lobby, which was hushed and smelled of lingering blood and body fluids mixed with the odor of Pine-Sol. Looking back, she could see the WTXT van, and reporters using microphones, talking to people they didn't see. They'd tried to stop her on the way in, but she just kept walking, and they moved on to someone else.

Cricket looked around the lobby. Two older women sat on the cranberry plush couch, speaking quietly. Church voices, Cricket thought, or funeral voices. The kind of voice you use when you're talking about something normal, in the middle of something sacred or tragic. One of the old women giggled softly, then covered her hand with her mouth and looked around guiltily. On the wall, a portrait of Jesus with children clustered around his knees smiled benignly in their direction. His heart was exposed and bleeding, an image Cricket thought was inappropriate for a hospital lobby.

She approached the front desk.

"My daughter," she said to the woman who sat on the other side, a phone to her ear. "My daughter is here."

The woman held up a finger and mouthed the words, "Just a minute."

Cricket made a strangled noise of impatience. The woman continued her conversation, which had something to do with accounts receivable. As she spoke, Cricket watched the second hand on the clock behind her sweep a circle, then another, then another. She imagined herself reaching over the desk and ripping the phone out of the woman's hand and screaming at her, though she knew she wouldn't do any such thing. She could feel a stiff smile pasted carefully on her face. She could feel herself trying not to think about what came next.

When the woman hung up, she turned her own frozen smile at Cricket and said, in bright but sympathetic tones, "Can I help you?"

"My daughter," Cricket said, "Grace Thompson. She was brought here with . . . the kids from the mall. The shooting—there at the mall. She's here. Somewhere."

The woman made a clucking noise as she started working her computer.

"Horrible, isn't it? So many dead. Mostly kids. You have to ask yourself what the world is coming to, don't you? Now let's see—we didn't get too many. Just the overflow from Mercy Hospital. They have the larger facility. And they all checked in at Emergency, so . . ." She turned her sympathetic yet professional smile at Cricket.

"How do you spell Thompson?" she asked.

Cricket spelled it out and the woman clicked more keys. Then she shook her head. "She wasn't admitted here," she said.

"But . . . somebody called. They said here. Sacred Heart Medical Center. Here." She stabbed at the portrait of Jesus with her finger to emphasize the point.

"She's not here," the woman repeated. Then her phone rang, and she picked it up, turning one last shrug at Cricket.

Cricket looked around for any sense of direction. She stared at the Jesus portrait, the bleeding heart, and in her peripheral vision saw a sign that said EMERGENCY ROOM.

She turned away from the desk and walked toward it, then down the long white hall, past nurses and doctors and orderlies who didn't ask her if she needed help either because they didn't care, or it was obvious that she was beyond help.

The hall opened up into a room where people sat in chairs, looking sick or hurt or dirty or afraid. There was an old man who looked remarkably like the old man in the supermarket. There was a nun, holding a little girl. There was a toothless young man talking to himself.

She saw a man in a white coat, studying papers on a clipboard. Cricket went to him, and grabbed his arm.

"My daughter," she said.

He jerked his arm back. "What the hell?" he asked.

Cricket took a step back, embarrassed. "I . . . I'm Mrs. Thompson," she explained. "My daughter, Grace. Thompson. T-H-O . . ."

"Oh, God, I'm sorry," he said. "I didn't know. There's been reporters getting in all night, driving us nuts."

"My daughter," Cricket repeated.

"Yes. I worked on her when they brought her in. She's been in the OR a few hours. We called, but couldn't get through, so we had to go ahead. I'll bring you now."

Cricket held a hand out, to ward something off or plead for something. "Wait," she said. "Wait."

The doctor stood still. "Do you need to sit down?"

"No. Just . . . tell me. Where?"

The doctor blinked, frowned, then looked her over. His eyes were a very sharp blue, she thought. He lifted his hand and touched her jaw at the joint. "The bullet entered there, from behind," he said. He moved his hand up and touched her temple. "It exited there." He touched her upper back. "A second bullet entered there, pierced the lung and lodged in the upper ribs." He dropped his hand. Cricket closed her eyes.

I will not, she told herself. I will not. She didn't know what the words meant, but she kept saying them to herself as if they were a prayer. I will not. I will not.

"She's alive," she said, when her prayer was done.

"Yes," the doctor said. "She's alive."

"Take me to the OR," she said.

They rode the elevator to the fourth floor and he led her to the waiting room, which was spacious, painted in soft colors, occupied by plush chairs and couches upholstered in subdued mauve and sage green. Windows looked out onto the night sky, where a thin young moon was washed in wisps of moving clouds like veils drawn across a woman's face. There was a TV in the room, tuned to CNN. Only one old man was there, reading a magazine. He stood up when they entered, then sat down again, shaking his head.

"I'll let the surgeon know you're here. She'll talk to you when surgery's done," the doctor said. "Who's her regular doctor?"

"Dr. Davis," she said. "Greg Davis."

"Okay. I know him. I'll see he's notified."

He turned to leave the room, and it occurred to Cricket that he had saved Grace's life. "Doctor," she called after him.

He turned back to her, his hand on the door.

Cricket realized there were no words adequate to the task she wanted them to do, which was fill him with some kind of blessing for what he'd done, and perhaps ask him to continue, somehow, to keep her alive. As if he were a god who could do that. "Thank you," she said at last. "Thank you very much."

His face expressed confusion, then concern. "You're welcome," he said, and left.

Cricket stared at the door. There were things she should do. Find Jim. Call Janis. Call Peggy. But if she made the calls, she'd have to say the words. She couldn't do that. They should be here, she thought, but she couldn't say the words, couldn't talk to them, couldn't listen to them.

The sound of human voices on TV compelled her attention, asking her to listen. But listening hurt, as if someone was rubbing sand against sunburned skin. She couldn't listen. Couldn't not listen. She went to the TV and turned it off. The man who sat there looked up at her, then got up and left the room.

The silence was no better, because it asked her to wait, and she couldn't wait. She picked up a magazine, but couldn't look. To feel any awareness was to court disaster. She went to a couch and curled herself into a corner, closed her eyes. I will not, she repeated to herself, will not. Will not. Will not.

She wasn't sure how long she sat there, how many times she repeated the phrase, before she felt a hand on her shoulder, massaging it lightly. A soft male voice said her name. Jim, she thought. She sat with her eyes closed, feeling the touch. It doesn't hurt, she thought. Touch doesn't hurt. Maybe it was just the words that hurt. How wise of Jim to know that, she thought. Eyes closed, she turned toward the warmth, and arms were around her, rocking her gently, a hand stroking her hair.

She mumbled into the soft cloth of his shirt, "How did you find out?"

"You told me," he said.

The rocking stopped. She pulled back, and looked up. It was Pass.

Her hand flew to her mouth. "I'm sorry," she said. "I thought you were Jim."

"I figured," he said, running a hand through his hair. "A doctor downstairs said Grace is in the OR. Did they tell you how long?"

She shook her head.

"Do you want anything? Coffee? Or I could get you some brandy or something?"

She shook her head again.

He breathed in and out deeply. "Then we wait," he said.

"Pass, you don't have to."

"I know. I know that."

"No, really," Cricket insisted. "You've got things to do. And there's the baby eagle."

"The eagles take care of their own," he said. "Anything I do would be interfering."

"But you can't want to be here."

He paused a minute and put a hand on the back of the couch. "Do you?" he asked.

She closed her eyes and opened them again. If it was anyone else, she'd think it a cruel question. Knowing Pass, she recognized it as an honest one. "I have to be here," she said. "You don't. And if you're here, then I'll have to . . ." She struggled with this. If he was here to help her, she had to make sure he felt good about it. Be a hostess, somehow.

"What? Take care of me? Entertain me? Forget it."

"Pass," she said, "you can't do anything."

"No," he said. "I can't."

"Then, why be here?"

He took his hand off the back of the couch. The silence that followed was long and rich. His answer, when it came, was simple.

"Because you are," he said.

She lifted her eyes and looked at him. She had always shown him, and the rest of the world, she supposed, a bright face. Now it was as if that brightness had blinded her true vision, and as it cracked and fell away, she saw truths that had been hidden.

She saw that Pass loved her. She saw that she didn't have to do anything about it. She didn't have to earn it or be grateful or ward it off or explain it. It was out of her control.

And she was glad. Glad to be loved in just that way. Glad to have him here. She wanted him here more than she wanted Jim right now, because he wasn't here as a father or a husband. He was just here, because she was.

Some time earlier in this same unending day, she'd touched his hand, and now she wanted to touch it again. She wanted to go back to where they were in the morning and take her clothes off, take his clothes off, and kiss his mouth and his neck and his shoulders. She was appalled with herself for thinking this now. She was a horrible mother and horrible wife, but she wanted to be in his bed, while the hawks gave their piercing cries and the emus ran in circles and the sand cranes clacked. Horrible. Horrible. She was horrible.

She put her hands over her face and moaned into them. He would think nothing of it. He would think she was moaning for her daughter when she was really moaning for herself and what she couldn't do, what she wanted to do. She rocked back and forth, moaning softly.

"Cricket," Pass said. He put a hand on her shoulder. She stopped rocking, stopped moaning, dropped her hands into her lap and stared ahead at nothing. There was nothing to see. Nothing she wanted to see. She felt his hand leave her. She was suddenly cold, and alone. She couldn't kiss, couldn't think, couldn't talk, couldn't do anything anymore. She had to do nothing but make sure her daughter stayed alive.

She'd read in all her books that belief was essential, positive thoughts had real influence, and will was crucial in matters of health. She wouldn't think about kissing or touching. She would just think about Grace. All her thoughts would be positive, and they would keep her daughter alive. There would be room for nothing else.

"Do we have to talk?" she asked.

"No," he said. "Of course not."

He walked to the window and stared out of it. Cricket observed how his shoulders were broad for such a slim man. Something that looked like a bleach stain discolored a patch on the right side of his T-shirt, which was a faded forest green. Cricket stared at it, and thought of Grace, needing to stay alive. Grace needed her. He did not need her. He did not need her. Cricket felt immense relief. He doesn't need me, she thought. Thank God. Thank God. She could turn her attention where it should be, which was toward Grace.

The waiting room door opened and her heart pounded as she pushed herself to stand, but it was only Peggy, walking toward her hard, Jim and Janis right behind. Cricket sat down.

Peggy came to the couch and sat next to her, hugging her hard. "Oh my God, Cricket. Oh my God. Why didn't you call? I kept trying your house and it was busy and then nobody answered. I went to the mall and couldn't get in, went to your house and you weren't there."

Peggy released her, and pulled back to look at her. Cricket looked up. Janis and Jim stood in front of her, staring down.

"You could've let me know," Jim said a little truculently. "Janis was frantic when I got home. Jesus, what the hell happened?"

Cricket blinked around at them, then stared at Jim. He wasn't really angry. She knew that. She could tell by his eyes that he was terrified, finding refuge from his fear in anger. Normally, she'd comfort him, but now she couldn't. She didn't want to talk. Talking only distracted her from willing her daughter to stay alive.

She got up and walked over to the TV, and turned it on to CNN.

six

They sat on the plush mauve couch and waited, watching CNN. Peggy said "Oh my God," at regular intervals, and put her arm around Janis, who sat stony-faced and silent. Jim put a hand on Cricket's shoulder and squeezed hard. She patted it, to let him know she understood his distress. Pass stood staring out the window, unremarked by anyone. Cricket wondered if he was praying, and if so, to whom. She kept an image of her daughter, surrounded by light, sitting in her room brushing her hair, held firmly in her mind.

When CNN broke for a Visa card commercial that showed people vacationing on a sunny island, Peggy shook herself and turned to Cricket. "I talked to Reverend Braxton," she said. "He'll come over as soon as he can."

Reverend Braxton, who was tall and thick as a tree trunk and smelled of Old Spice, taught Sunday school to the girls when they were little, just as he had taught it to Cricket and Peggy. She remembered that when her grandmother died, she'd asked him if children ever died, and he said Jesus waited eagerly to gather children to him.

"No," Cricket said.

"What?"

"No. He can't come here. Call him right now. He is not to come here."

"Cricket, I can't do that. He'll . . . it's his job."

"No," Cricket said again. "Call him. Tell him no. We don't need him."

Peggy gaped at her, then at Jim.

"Call him," Cricket said. "Tell him not to come."

"Okay. I'll take care of it," Peggy said. "Don't worry. I'll just call now." She pushed herself up and walked toward the phone that was kept on a table next to the coffeepot.

Cricket was vaguely aware of Peggy talking, sounding apologetic, then hanging up and coming back to the couch. She was vaguely aware of the TV making sounds. Of Jim and Peggy talking to her, of Janis sitting silent and pale next to her, of Pass standing silently by the window, but none of it seemed to matter. She was in a cocoon, she thought. She was not who she used to be, and not yet what she would become. And none of that mattered. All that mattered was Grace. She would be fine. Fine. Fine. Cricket kept thinking of that.

"Where're you going?" Jim asked her, when she stood to go to the bathroom.

She gave him a slightly surprised smile. "To the rest room."

"I was talking to you," he said.

She stood there, still surprised. His face was dark and glowering, the way Janis would look sometimes. She knew what that meant. He felt guilty for not being home, frightened and helpless and angry at himself for being helpless, and not sure how to deal with any of it. He wasn't good at talking about his emotions, and certainly not emotions regarding his children. She'd always helped him with that. She knew how. Only, she'd never expected to have to do it under these circumstances.

But here he was, obviously in as much pain as she was and

unable to express it. They should comfort each other. She put a hand on his arm. "I'm sorry, Jim," she said. "I'm just— Well, you know."

"I know," he said, a little gruffly, but he put his hand over hers. "I'm sorry, too."

She put her arms out and he walked into them, held her, squeezed her briefly. "It'll be okay," he said reassuringly. "It will."

"Yes," she said firmly. "Yes. Of course."

He released her, and tossed a nod toward the rest room. "Go on. I'll come and get you if the doctor comes."

Cricket went, noticing on her way that the TV had a commercial on for a movie. It showed two men struggling to pull a woman out of a raging river. As Cricket watched, the waters took her away. She turned her face from it and went into the bathroom, which had only one stall and that occupied. Cricket waited, staring at the white and beige floor tiles.

The door to the stall opened, and Janis came out. When she saw her mother, her face darkened with anger. Like her father, Cricket thought. She looked like her father. But that was to be expected, Cricket thought. She was angry, out of fear.

"You okay?" Cricket asked.

"Why didn't you call me?" Janis demanded.

Cricket lifted a hand to her heart as waves of pain flowed through her. She hadn't called. First she forgets one daughter, then the other. What was wrong with her?

"I'm sorry," Cricket said. She put a hand out, then let it drop. What good did her hand do now?

"You should've," Janis said.

"I know. You're right."

Janis chewed on the end of her thumb, and her eyes reddened and filled with tears. "Mom?" she asked, sounding young now, the anger stripped from her fear. "Mom, is she gonna be okay?"

"Yes," Cricket said firmly. "Yes. She is."

Janis shuddered, and closed her eyes. Cricket put a hand on

Janis's shoulder, aware that she had to reach up to do that. It didn't seem possible. Her daughter was taller than she was. She realized that she didn't know what happened to Janis, if she'd seen the horror, heard the shots. She knew nothing at all.

"Are you okay? Did you see the . . . shooting?"

Janis ducked her head down. "I . . . wasn't there."

"Weren't there? At the food court?"

"At the mall."

Something clicked into place for Cricket. Of course she wasn't there. That's why nobody could find her. "But you were supposed to be there."

"I went, but I left."

"Then Grace was there alone?"

"She met her friends. I saw them before I left."

"But . . . where were you?"

Janis mumbled something, talking into her chest.

"What?" Cricket asked.

"I was getting tested," Janis mumbled louder.

"Tested?" Words weren't making sense. "Tested? There's no school. It's Saturday."

"Not that kind of test," Janis said. "You know," she said.

"No, I don't," Cricket said. "I don't know."

"At the health clinic," Janis said. "I took a bus to the clinic. To get tested for stuff."

"Janis, what stuff?"

"Diseases and . . . things."

"What kind of diseases?"

"Like STDs. AIDS and stuff."

"Oh God," Cricket said. "Oh God. Oh God."

"And pregnancy," Janis said.

Cricket found herself leaning on the sink, holding herself up against its cold edge. The day was one long nightmare that started at Wal-Mart and wouldn't end. She must have done something horribly wrong, she thought.

This sort of thing didn't happen if you were a good mother, an attentive mother, a mother who set the right boundaries and loved your children enough. No. This sort of thing only happened to mothers who were not disciplined and had aberrant thoughts about flying and sex and men and listened to crazy stories in grocery stores. This only happened to mothers who forgot their daughters, abandoned them at malls, and went off to play with butterflies and birds while people shot at their children and killed them.

"You have a disease?" she asked quietly.

Janis shook her head. "I don't think so. Some tests won't come back right away."

"Then," Cricket started, then stopped. She stopped looking inside at her own fear and lifted her face to view her daughter who was so young and so tough, so angry and so afraid.

"You're pregnant?" Cricket asked.

Her daughter's face was tight and angry, but her voice was small and frightened. "I thought I was. But I'm not. The test came back negative."

Cricket leaned against the wall, her shoulder pressed into cold tile. She waited for the right words to emerge, but all she could think of was Thank God. Thank any god. Thank any god that she didn't stay at the mall. Thank God she thought she was pregnant, and went to the clinic and didn't stay at the mall. Thank any god. Thank the devil, too. She put a hand out to touch Janis, but Janis stepped back away. Her face collapsed and she took her two hands and made fists, beat them against her own face.

Cricket reached over and grabbed her hands at the wrist and held them. "No," she said. "No, no, no."

"I should've been there," Janis growled, struggling against her mother's grasp. "I should've been there. I'm so stupid, stupid, bad and stupid."

"No." Cricket held on fiercely, shook her daughter. "No. No. No. You're not bad. You're good. You're *good.*"

She pulled her close, thinking this is the closest Janis has let me since she was ten years old. Thinking, Why does it take horror to make us admit we need love? Thinking, She's alive. She's alive. It's good she wasn't there. Good she did the wrong thing. She's alive.

For a brief moment, they were still, then Janis wrenched herself away, put her head against the wall and grabbed at her hair with her hands. Cricket stood still, waiting for her to give some signal of what she needed next. Half the job of parenting teenagers, she thought, was just standing still while they ran in circles around you and you watched to see what they needed next. And God help you if you took your eyes off them, pulled your thoughts away while the rest of the world lay in wait.

"I don't want Daddy to know," Janis said at last, keeping her face to the wall.

"I won't tell him," Cricket said. "He doesn't have to know."

Some part of her knew that was wrong, but it didn't matter. Janis was alive. She didn't have a disease and she hadn't been shot in the mall. She was alive. Who cared if her father knew? Who cared if she did the wrong thing?

"But you should get some contraceptives. Some condoms. Maybe a diaphragm."

Janis was silent.

"I'll take you," Cricket said. "I'll make an appointment for you. I don't know how long Grace might . . . might need to stay in the hospital, but when she's better, I'll take you."

Janis whispered something Cricket couldn't hear.

"What?"

Janis turned to look at her mother, her face mottled from crying. "We were in the car, and Grace said she wanted to get a CD but she didn't have any money. I got it for her, but I left it home. I meant to bring it, but I forgot."

Janis sounded so mournful at her small oversight, Cricket had to will herself not to cry out "oh, how sweet." But Janis did that sort of thing, her generosity as swift and unexpected as all her other emotional gestures.

"That's okay," Cricket said quietly. "She can listen to it when she gets home."

"What if she doesn't?" Janis whispered.

"Doesn't what?"

"Get home."

Cricket felt the words sink through her skin, crawl up and down her spine. She did not want to hear them. Did not want the words that expressed what everyone was afraid to think. No, she said to them. I will not. I will not.

The door to the bathroom opened and Cricket turned around. It was Peggy. She tilted her head back toward the waiting room. "The surgeon's here."

Cricket pushed past Peggy and back to the waiting room.

A doctor, wearing green scrubs, pulling off something that looked like a shower cap, spoke to Jim. Cricket went over to where they stood. The doctor stopped talking, one hand lifted in a gesture she was waiting to complete.

"This is my wife," Jim said.

She tilted her head at Cricket as if they were being introduced at a dinner party. Her graying hair was thick and wavy. Cricket expected her to say something like "Charming to meet you."

"Mrs. Thompson," she said, holding out her hand. "I'm Dr. Harrison. I was just telling your husband that Grace came through the surgery. She's on her way to recovery."

Cricket took two steps away.

"Whoa," Jim said, and grabbed at her arm. "Where're you going?"

Cricket stopped and turned back. "To see her. If she wakes up alone, she'll be afraid."

"She won't be conscious for some time," the doctor said. "We should talk about her prognosis."

Cricket shook her head. "Prognosis?"

Dr. Harrison cleared her throat. "You know that she had a head injury?"

"Yes. I know."

"Her recovery is . . . ah . . . unpredictable. The brain is a mysterious organ. We can't tell yet how much function she'll recover, or how long that will take."

Cricket looked at Jim. She became aware that Peggy was standing behind her, Janis next to Peggy. She wondered briefly where Pass was, if he was still in the room. She turned to look for him and saw him still standing at the window, staring out. As her eyes found him, he turned toward her. Nobody else seemed to see him. Maybe he wasn't there, she thought. Or maybe he was a ghost. She nodded at him as if answering a question. Okay, she said. Okay. He closed his eyes and opened them again, nodded at her once and, still ghostlike, walked across the room and out the door. Nobody looked to see who had left or entered when the door opened and closed.

"She's alive," Cricket said firmly. That was all that mattered, really. The rest would be okay. It would have to be.

"And breathing on her own, which is a good sign. We just don't know the extent of the damage or if she'll—"

"Where is she?" Cricket asked.

"Cricket," Jim said, "let the doctor finish."

"Where is she?" Cricket asked again.

Dr. Harrison glanced at her, at her husband. "Recovery," she said. "She'll be in ICU within the hour. You'll have to wait until she gets there to see her."

"Why?" Cricket asked.

"Hospital regulations."

"Where's Recovery?"

"Down the hall and to the left, but you can't go in."

"When they bring her out, I can walk with her to ICU, can't I?"

"Cricket," Peggy said, "maybe they don't want you to."

Cricket looked at Peggy and laughed, a sound that was strange even to her own ears. But did they seriously think she cared what anyone else wanted? Or were they just so used to her caring that they didn't know what to make of this? "Can't I?" she asked the doctor.

"Yes," Dr. Harrison said. "You can."

When Cricket left, she was still talking to Jim, completing the gesture she'd started earlier, as if nothing had intervened.

She walked down the hall, the smell of antiseptic and body excretions stinging her nostrils. Grace won't like this, she thought. Grace liked the smell of lavender. She reached a small lounge near the door that said RECOVERY—STAFF ONLY BEYOND THIS POINT, and she stood, waiting. After some time passed, Jim and Peggy and Janis joined her. Peggy put a hand on her shoulder.

"Don't you want to sit down?" Peggy asked.

"No."

"Oh. Well. I guess I will."

"Okay."

She did not know how much time passed. She didn't count it. She didn't have to. She only had to think of Grace, healing, getting well, coming home. Jim and Peggy talked softly, Janis stayed silent. Cricket leaned against the wall between the lounge and the hall, thinking of light and strong bodies.

The door to Recovery opened, and a gurney came through, pulled at the foot end by a young man with dark skin and hair, who spoke with an accent.

"You hang on, dolly," he said. "We're just taking you for a little ride."

Cricket stepped forward, blocking the stretcher's progress.

On the stretcher was a small figure, head wrapped in bandages, body connected to clear tubing in many places, her mouth and nose blurry under the oxygen mask. Her arm had bruises coming up around the tubing. Her eyes were both black and blue, as if she'd been hit hard. Her mouth was open, and a little drool came out one side.

It was Grace.

Her chest was moving up and down. Up and down. She was alive.

Cricket stood, stunned into immobility, fearing that if she moved, this image would dissolve, a trick of her vision or her desire. She looked at her, examining her face, the little mole on the left side, the way her mouth was slightly crooked.

"Grace?" Cricket asked. "Grace?"

Her legs were weak and she felt them start to buckle, but she got hold of the side of the gurney and held on, her hand touching flesh. Grace's flesh. Grace's arm. "Grace," she whispered into her ear. "Grace."

Her flesh was transparent, as if all the wounds she'd received in her life were visible behind this thin veil, so easily torn. Her flesh hadn't looked this way since she was an infant, when Cricket would cradle her and talk to her to keep her awake long enough to get a good feeding. Janis had been a loud and active baby, but Grace was so placid Cricket was sometimes frightened that she would simply fall into the deepest sleep and not return. As if she resented coming out of the dark quiet of the womb. As if she wanted to remain asleep, to dream and dream inside the watery dark.

"Grace," Cricket said. She touched the bandage and felt a shiver of horror at what her daughter had seen and felt in that moment when the shooting began. She must have been afraid. Must have wanted help. Must have felt pain and shock and fear, abandoned by all the rules of the world as she knew them.

Inside her chest, Cricket felt a sensation that was unfamiliar, as if her ribs were made of thin new ice, and a beast raked claws against them. Everything in her shattered, shooting shards of ice and bone into her heart, and she was glad of the pain because she had no right to peace in a world that shot her daughter. Nobody did. Nobody. Least of all herself.

She thought she heard someone—a man—speaking. She

thought she heard the quiet voice of a medical person talking. At some moment, she became aware of something pressing on her shoulder. She shrugged, trying to get rid of it, but it persisted. She turned and saw through a haze, as if she looked through water, that a tall woman in white leaned over her.

"What?" she asked impatiently. "What is it now?"

"Mrs. Thompson, we have to get her to ICU. You can come along."

Cricket straightened herself, letting the water float away from her eyes. "Of course. Then, let's go."

The stretcher moved down the hall, and Cricket followed.

DREAM #3

girl dreams

As Cricket sat next to Grace in ICU, listening to the beep and hum of various machines, she wondered if Grace dreamt, and if so, of what. Jim was still outside talking to doctors. Peggy brought Janis in to see Grace and then took her home. She'd stay with her at Cricket's house, she said. The room was quiet, except for the occasional sound of someone moaning. Cricket watched Grace's eyes twitch under her eyelids and thought maybe that was REM movement, and she was dreaming. She knew that the brain needed no external stimuli to dream. In sleep, the brain talked to itself, re-creating the world in its own image. Knowing Grace, she imagined her dream world was full of light peach-colored curtains, small fish, white clean walls, and windows full of light.

Cricket knew a lot about dreaming, and the motion of the brain in that activity, an interest that had started when she was little and her father had encouraged her to talk about her dreams, and to find out what they meant. He believed they meant something. She did not question his belief until her science teacher said her father was wrong.

The teacher said dreaming was simply a temporary psychosis of the brain as it washed itself clean and resynthesized proteins. The process was purely biochemical, isolated from emotional or psychological function. That people tended to see it as meaningful was our mistake.

Cricket didn't tell her father what the teacher said, but she started researching on her own. In the process, she discovered something fundamental about the nature of reality. People disagreed about it. A lot. Some said dreaming was a dip into the unconscious mind of all humanity. Some said it was our deepest wishes, greatest fears, and nastiest fantasies. Some said it was the ancestors speaking. Nobody believed what anyone else said.

This knowledge was both frightening and empowering. It meant she might never know what was real, but it also meant if nobody knew, she might as well come up with her own answers. Recently, she'd read that the brain in dreaming vibrates at the same rate as the earth. Somehow, this seemed important now. If Grace dreamt, she was still connected to the earth. Still of the world. Still alive.

Cricket could see Grace's eyes twitch under her eyelids. She looked at the nurse, who was making notes about the machines. "Is she dreaming?" she asked.

The nurse raised an eyebrow. "Dreaming?"

"Her eyes are moving. See?" Cricket pointed it out. "I thought maybe she was dreaming."

"Oh. Well, probably not. That sort of movement—it generally doesn't mean anything."

But she's wrong, Cricket thought. It means she's alive.

Maybe later she would remember her dreams, and tell Cricket about them.

As her father had, Cricket encouraged her daughters to tell her what they dreamt, and when they were little, they would do so. Janis had dreams that were cryptic and brief. Once she told her mother she'd dreamt she saw a whale break the surface of the water, then resubmerge. That was all. Cricket thought it was a dream of approaching adolescence. Janis thought it had to do with the show she saw about whales on the Discovery channel.

The night before Janis got her first period, she dreamt she was having a sword fight with an old woman who was dirty and ugly, and so frail you could see her bones through her skin. Her face was almost a skull, with thin gray hairs growing on her chin. Janis thought she could easily beat her, but the woman lunged forward, and her sword went right through Janis's belly. She stared down at it, amazed that it didn't hurt, but terrified that she would die. She woke to find that she was wet between her legs, and blood stained her sheets.

Grace tended to dream intricately curved and moving dreams full of color and motion. She dreamt shape-shifters and riding magic carpets and walking on water and leaving the planet on the back of a dragonfly.

"Mom," she said one morning, "I dreamt about a woman who grew three eyes. They were green, and one was in the middle of her forehead. A third eye."

When they looked these symbols up in Cricket's dream book, they found that dreaming about a beautiful woman meant success in business. Eyes meant things secret. The color green meant growth and abundance. Altogether a very good dream.

Of course, they'd laugh at themselves, looking up dreams in a book that listed symbols in alphabetical order. Still, it always gave them a thrill to have a dream with good signs, and always made them edgy when the signs were bad.

As the girls grew older, they had dreams they would never tell their mother. They dreamt of being beautiful and pursued, which was their definition of love. They dreamt of changing body parts, of sexual encounters with strangers, with women, with anything. They woke, not sure of who they were, or where they were, or why. They woke anxious and angry about it, then went back to sleep to dream some more.

Cricket sat next to Grace and watched her eyes twitch under the lids. "Sweet dreams," she whispered, in spite of what the nurse said. She kept a hand lightly on her arm, wanting her life to expand as if it were a tent Grace could rest under until she was well. Her will must make up for any medical deficiencies, she thought. That must be so.

"Hey," a voice said behind her, and she turned to it. It was Jim. She motioned to a folding chair. He pulled it next to her and sat. He cleared his throat, but when he spoke, he sounded as if he was about to cry. Cricket didn't look at him. Tears were about defeat, surrender, grief. There were no acceptable tears.

"She looks younger," he said. She heard him blow his nose. "I think the guy in the bed next to us is dead," he said. "This place is creepy."

"I don't think they'll give us cots," Cricket said, "but I could get you a chair."

"I can do that," Jim said. "I can see about it." He looked around, then seemed to sink into himself.

Cricket looked at him. After so many years of anticipating and responding to his unspoken moods, she could clearly read what he was feeling now. He didn't want to stay. Of course, he would stay because that was the right thing to do, but he didn't want to. To stay here was to be helpless, to merely watch his daughter without the ability to fix her, make her all better. It was too much for him.

She stifled a feeling of resentment, then a feeling of sorrow. She wanted him to stay and be with her, even if he couldn't fix Grace. But she didn't want to have him there if he couldn't do that. She wanted him to be able to do that. But she didn't want to teach him how. Not tonight. Not here.

"Maybe you should go home," Cricket said softly. "Janis is home."

"Peggy's there," he said tentatively. Then, with conviction, "You need me here."

"She might need you there. You're her father," she said. "She'll need you." And of course that was true. They should work as a team, each one doing what they were best at. That made the most sense.

"Yeah. You're probably right." He put a hand on the top of her head. "Will you be okay?" he asked.

She leaned toward him, stifling her disappointment that he should take the exit she offered. "I'll be okay when she is," she said.

"Sure," he said, his voice rough with emotion withheld. "I know. I'll come back in the morning. She'll be okay. I love you, Cricket." He pressed a kiss against the back of her head and left.

When he was gone, she felt an unexpected relief. She didn't have to worry about his emotions, or the ones he inspired in her. All conflict gone, she could focus, her will directed toward one end—keeping her daughter alive. She kept the tip of her finger against Grace's arm, rested her chin on the iron railing of the bed. It was cold, and put the taste of metal in her nose and mouth.

A doctor came by and pulled up Grace's eyelids, shone a pencil-sized flashlight into her eyes, and made a note on the chart. Cricket wanted to ask if he could see her dreams. If his light showed that.

"Is it okay?" she asked instead.

The doctor stopped, as if he was surprised to hear a human voice. "Okay?" he asked.

"What you saw in her eyes. Is it okay?"

"Oh," he said. "Oh. That. Well, yes. Her pupils dilate normally. That's good."

He left, but Cricket hung on to his words. Good, she thought. Good. Grace had survived the shooting, survived surgery. A doctor looked in her eyes and saw something good.

She leaned on the bed rail with her hand on Grace's arm and closed her eyes. She thought of sleep, but every time she did, she would hear the sound of something sharp and close, like bullets being fired nearby, and she would wake with a start.

That happened three times, and on the third time, she woke to find she was staring into the eyes of a man she didn't know. Half asleep, she rose clumsily from the chair and moved to put her body across Grace.

"Hey," the man said, pulling her back. "It's okay. I'm Detective Dennaro."

Cricket let the words sink in, then pulled herself upright. "I'm sorry," she said. "I was dreaming. I thought you were . . ." She let the sentence trail to silence.

"That's okay," he said. "It's a tough night all around. Are you Mrs. Thompson?"

She nodded.

"I just need to talk a little with everyone involved in the incident," he said, and he pulled a notebook out of his pocket.

"I wasn't there."

"I know. But your daughter was."

Cricket looked at Grace's still form. "She can't talk yet. She's . . . asleep."

Detective Dennaro licked the end of a pencil. When he spoke, it was with deliberate neutrality, like detectives on TV. "Do you know of anyone who might want to hurt your daughter, Mrs. Thompson? Boys who wanted her attention, or boys she'd made angry?"

That was so ridiculous, Cricket laughed. Detective Dennaro lifted his eyes from his notebook and regarded her without emotion. "No," Cricket said. "I don't think so."

"Can you give me the names of any of her friends who might know?"

"There's Karen Whitehall. And Debbie. Debbie Larson. And Veronica Lopez. They're all friends. Why are you asking this?"

"It's routine, Mrs. Thompson. Do you have their phone numbers?"

"Not here. At the house. Are you saying someone was after Grace?"

"No, Mrs. Thompson. We're just checking into all possibilities at this point."

"Then, you didn't catch anyone?"

"Not yet."

"Were a lot of people hurt?"

"Eleven dead," he said, still neutral. "A lot of wounded. There was a rush for the escalator when the shooting started." He was big and had a paunch. His arms and his neck were thick, like a football player, but his hand clasping the pencil was white and smooth, like the surgeon's.

"Oh," Cricket said. "Oh."

"Is your husband at home?" he asked.

"Yes. With our other daughter, Janis. She wasn't there," she added hastily, then, fearing that the detective would tell Jim that, she amended her words. "I mean, she didn't see anything. Can't tell you anything. Officer—"

"Detective."

"Detective, whoever did this isn't going to come back and look for her or something?"

"We don't believe so," he said. "It should be perfectly safe."

"Safe," Cricket repeated, as if it was a word she had to learn all over again, or a word that didn't belong to her anymore.

Officer Dennaro held up a finger. "One thing," he said. "There might be newspeople out there. When you leave."

"I'm not leaving," Cricket said.

"Pardon?"

"I'm staying here. I'm not leaving."

"I see. Well, they might still be there in the morning. We'd prefer if you didn't talk to them just yet. You probably don't want them to know why you're here, anyway."

Cricket blinked at him. "What?"

"If you don't want them bothering you for a story," he said.

Cricket absorbed what he said, and realized she'd been part of an event that might be the biggest she'd ever see. How odd, she thought, that she was newsworthy because she'd participated in horror. She didn't do anything good or bad. She just happened to be there. Somehow, that increased her public worth.

"I don't understand," she said softly.

"Well," the detective said, "they want the stories. Human interest. You know. So it might be best to just say your daughter's here for tonsillitis or something."

"You mean, I should lie?" Cricket asked. Wasn't the news based on people telling the truth? But here was an officer of the law, telling her to lie. She wished someone would tell her something that fit in with the world as she knew it, as she wanted it to be.

"Yeah," he said. "You can lie."

"Oh," Cricket said. "Well, thank you very much." She put out her hand and he took it, shook it firmly, and let it drop.

When he left, Cricket returned to her post, dozing fitfully as nurses came and went like soft angels in tennis shoes. She was aware of sounds around her—creaking carts, low voices, someone snoring. She had no idea of day or night in this windowless place, but at some point, she had a sense of increased motion, the way she would when the birds announced morning in her yard. A nurse came in and touched her arm.

"Mrs. Thompson?" she said softly.

"I'm awake," Cricket said.

"Mrs. Thompson, there's some forms I need you to look over and think about."

Forms. There were always forms. "All right."

The nurse handed her a clipboard with papers on it, then put a hand on her arm. "You don't have to sign them right away, but we recommend that if you want this, you should, in case something happens."

Cricket stared at the papers. Words danced and blurred under her eyes. She pressed the palm of her hands to her eyelids and looked again. "What's it for?" she asked.

"DNR orders," the nurse said.

Cricket shook her head. "I don't know what that means."

"Do not resuscitate orders. They're if you don't want extreme measures taken in case your daughter . . . in case," the nurse concluded.

Cricket stared up at her. She was blond, and her hair was tied back in a high ponytail. She looked like a high school cheerleader. She offered Cricket a perky smile, and patted her shoulder. "It's just in case," she said.

"But what does it mean?" Cricket said.

The nurse dropped her arm at her side. She kept her voice simultaneously perky and sympathetic, a combination Cricket found irritating. "I can have the doctor talk to you about it," the nurse suggested.

"Just tell me what it means," Cricket said. "If it's important enough to wake me up . . ."

"Well," the nurse said, her voice getting a little higher, "if your daughter should . . . if there's cardiac arrest, do you want her revived? If her kidneys fail, do you want her on dialysis? If her brain . . . if she can't breathe on her own, do you want her on a respirator?"

Cricket stared at the nurse, then at the papers in her lap. Grace lay on her back, eyes closed, chest moving up and down. Cricket could remember the first time she saw that motion, when Grace emerged bloody and silent into the world, her mother's blood still beating into her through the cord. Then the cord was cut and her chest seemed to sink in from suction, then press out. She didn't cry. She just started to breathe and was alive.

Cricket touched Grace's arm, and was aware of the blood flowing in the veins beneath her skin. In her own hand, she could feel years of that small motion, years of holding her daughter's body close and watching her breathe and helping that breath to produce words and laughter. She had years of holding that small body when she wept from hunger or fear of monsters or from grief when her gerbil died and she didn't understand. It still looked like her gerbil. What did it mean that it was dead?

"Maybe Daddy was wrong," Grace had said. "Daddy makes mistakes sometimes, you know," she had confided as if this was a secret just for them, never to be told to Daddy.

And Grace wanted to have a goat farm, or cats, or maybe both, and she wanted to live in the small houses, with a bunny. All of this Cricket felt in her hand touching Grace's arm.

She'd read somewhere that scientists could find cells of a fetus in a mother's body up to thirty years after the baby was born. Cricket looked at the skin of her arms, at the blood pumping through arteries that still carried those cells into her skin, into her hands. She looked at the DNR forms.

"I can't," she whispered. "She's in my hands."

The nurse swallowed. "Excuse me?"

Cricket lifted her hand off the form and held it out toward the nurse as if to show her where Grace resided, under the skin of her palm.

It was a futile gesture that explained nothing. The nurse couldn't see. Couldn't know. She dropped her hand into her lap.

"I have to talk to my husband about it," she said. "I can't sign anything like this without him. I'm sorry."

"Oh, no," the nurse said, sounding relieved. "That's fine." She took the clipboard back. "You talk to him. If you want, you can talk to your doctor, too. It's fine."

She hurried from the room. Cricket wondered how long she'd been a nurse, or how long she would remain one.

She pulled her chair closer to the bed and curled into it, one hand on her daughter. She went back to dozing fitfully, dreaming of the sound of gunfire and of rooms made of ice, where everything was quiet and cold.

seven

Cricket stayed at the hospital through the night, and the next day and the next. Jim and Janis brought her clothes and a toothbrush and told her about the news and how reporters kept trying to call.

"Tell them she has tonsillitis," Cricket said.

Jim offered to stay, but the nurse told them that they could only stay overnight one at a time. If he stayed, she had to leave, and she couldn't. She just couldn't bring herself to walk out the door. He could stay when they moved her into her own room. Then they could stay together. Or they could take turns staying, when Grace was just a little bit better. For now, Janis needed him. He seemed relieved.

Janis used one-word sentences in response to her mother's questions. Are you okay? I'm fine. Do you need anything? No. Do you want to talk about it? No. Then, unexpectedly, Janis put a hand on her shoulder. "Do you need anything, Mom?" she asked, her chin held high and her wide mouth held tight.

Janis was the elder daughter. She was trying to be the grown-up of the family. Trying to be strong. Cricket wanted to stop her, but didn't know how.

By that Monday, she felt as if she'd established a new life that revolved around changes in shifts and the language of machines that wrote Grace's story on their screens with a series of lines and squiggles and beeps. The hospital was her turf, and she was learning its rules and language. She wasn't sure if the nurses or doctors liked her being there. She thought they were sometimes irritated by her persistent questions.

"What's that?" Cricket would ask when they moved a bag of fluids.

"Just IV," the nurse would say.

"What's in it?"

"Liquids. Antibiotics. I'm checking the level to see if I need to get another for her." She patted Cricket on the shoulder. "We don't want her to get thirsty, do we?"

"You should go home," the night nurse said to her. "She'll be fine here with us."

"I'm fine here with you, too," Cricket said, and settled into her chair.

On Tuesday, they moved Grace out of ICU and into a room. There were two other beds curtained off, both empty. Cricket was given a cot to sleep on, and the nurses were friendlier, more responsive to her questions. She thought she'd get some flowers to decorate, maybe a poster or two from Grace's room for her to see when she woke up. The room had windows that looked out onto the Mohawk Valley. Cricket could watch the sun set.

"She should be up soon, right?" she asked the doctor when he came in.

"Be patient," he said. "It could take time. You should go home, Mrs. Thompson. Get some real food. See your family."

"They come here," she said.

She watched the nurses carefully to see what they did when

they turned her, flexed her legs and arms, washed her. "Should I do that?" she asked. "Would it help?"

"Well, yes," a plump young nurse named Marianne said. "It would help."

"Is there anything else I can do?"

"There's no scientific evidence," Marianne said, "but I think that if you talk to her, play music, touch her a lot, that helps. Keeps the neural connections going. And we don't know what a person in a coma can hear." She took Cricket's hand, wrapped it around Grace's. "Do like this." She leaned over and spoke close to Grace's face. "Grace, honey. If you can hear us, squeeze your mother's hand."

They waited. Nothing happened. "Grace, if you can hear us, squeeze on your mother's hand. C'mon, honey. One little squeeze. Give it a try."

They waited. Grace's hand remained still in Cricket's.

"Well," Marianne said, "keep trying."

"Wait," Cricket said when she started to leave. "Is she . . . I mean, does it hurt her?"

Marianne had clear, fair skin and a round face that seemed like a container for kindness. Cricket didn't want her to be too kind, though. Her kindness was dangerous because it made Cricket remember that she couldn't stand the thought of Grace in pain, or afraid. That was what would kill her, make her unable to see this through. If she thought of her daughter frightened, seeing bullets, seeing death, afraid and wanting her mommy. If she thought of Grace in pain now, while her mother stood by helplessly, she couldn't stand anything. She would have to lie down and never get back up.

"She's not in pain," Marianne said gently.

"Are you sure?"

"I'm sure. They don't feel pain in a coma, you know."

"But . . . how do you *know* that?" Cricket almost whispered the question. She preferred to believe her daughter was just dreaming, sleeping comfortably, but if that wasn't true, she had to know. Then she would know how much she had to suffer, too.

Marianne came closer to Cricket and looked at her closely. "I've been working ICU for thirteen years," she said. "When somebody's in pain, I can smell it."

Cricket breathed in, and let her breath out slowly. "Thank you," she said. "Thank you very much."

"No problem," she said. "Just keep at it. You're both doing fine."

Cricket called home and told Jim to bring Grace's Walkman, with some tapes. And the teddy bear that sat on her bed. And the bottle of lavender perfume from her bureau. If she needed stimulation, Cricket would make sure she had it.

On Wednesday, when Janis visited, she told Cricket that Jim had gone to work that day.

"He did?" Cricket was surprised. She couldn't imagine how he could get any work done. Then, it occurred to her that Janis should be in school.

"Still closed," Janis said. "Until Monday. There's all these memorial services."

Cricket shuddered. She knew from Jim that none of them were close friends of Janis, but all were known to her. Cricket knew them, too, had seen them in the hall, or let them use the phone in the principal's office, or taken their late passes. It was a small school.

But she couldn't bring herself to go to the services. No. I will not, she thought. I will not. She reached toward the bed and patted Grace's leg. It twitched under the covers.

Janis clutched her mother's arm. "Mom? Did she . . ." The question trailed off into silence and both Cricket and Janis held their breath, waiting to see what would happen next. Some minutes passed, and nothing did.

Janis let out breath loudly and her shoulders sagged down.

Cricket shrugged. "That happens sometimes. I think it's a good sign."

"Yeah," Janis said. "A good sign."

Cricket saw Janis's face was tight and pale. It reminded Cricket that she had another dilemma to deal with. And she would. When Grace woke up, she could go back to normal. Everything would be okay. "Honey," she asked, "do you want me to call the doctor and make an appointment for you? For the . . . for contraceptives."

Janis frowned. "Dr. Lowry?"

"Well, yes. They do that in his office—Pap smears and so on, too."

"I can't go to him," she whispered, glancing at Grace as if she might hear. Her face expressed horror.

"Why not?"

"Well, I *know* him. And he's . . . he's a man. He's . . . like an old man."

Cricket bit back on a smile. Good to have something to smile about, she thought. "Then I can call Planned Parenthood, okay?"

Janis mumbled something into her chest.

"What?" Cricket asked.

"I said, you don't have to," Janis said. "I mean, you're here and Grace . . ." She didn't complete the sentence. Grace needs you more than I do. I'm the older one, so I can wait. Cricket wondered which of those sentences would finish the thought. Or maybe there was the sentence that said, you don't love me as much as you love Grace, so you don't have to do anything for me. Or I don't need you to do anything for me because I can take care of myself. It could be any of that, or all of it mixed together.

"I will," Cricket said. "Tomorrow. I'll call and make an appointment. I can bring you. We'll go to the one in Schenectady."

"She'll be okay?" Janis asked, nodding toward the bed, her hand moving toward Grace, then retreating.

"She'll be fine. It just takes time. The doctor said it takes time." And time moved on.

On Thursday, Pass stopped by with a bouquet of flowers from his garden and a silver helium balloon that said "Feel Better Soon" on it. When he walked into the room, Cricket's heart beat off-rhythm for a moment, then settled into a thrum of happiness.

"Hi," she said, as if she were welcoming him into her new home, "Sit down."

He put the balloon and flowers on the windowsill, fussing with them, his back to her. When he turned around he didn't touch her, or even look at her too hard. His face pushed itself into a smile, then relaxed.

"I brought you this," he said, and dug into his denim jacket pocket, pulling out a can of ginger ale and a chocolate bar. He always had these two items at his house for her when she came to work. He said it was the least he could do. He handed them to her, but before she could thank him, he said, "Eagle chick's doing good. Mama and Papa are feeding it just fine, and I'm getting tape of the whole thing." To Cricket, he sounded as if he was being deliberately hearty and cheerful.

"That's great, Pass."

"Some magazines called to do stories. That'll be good. Get some more funding."

"I'm so glad. I'm sorry I can't be there. To help."

"That's silly. You have your own chick to take care of. Don't worry about a thing."

The conversation melted into silence. There were emotions being felt that were too complicated to express, and it held them still. If they could touch each other, it would be okay, Cricket thought, but they couldn't. Too much of her attention was focused on Grace for her to be able to control touch once it started. She didn't dare risk it. Some words would have to be found instead.

Cricket ran a hand through her hair and realized it had been some time since she thought about how she looked, what her face or hair was doing. "I'm not ever worried," she said. "But I'm not ever not worried." She wrinkled her brow. "Does that make sense?"

Pass nodded, and when he spoke, he sounded more like himself. "You only worry about things outside of you," he said. "This is inside you and around you. It *is* you, right now."

Yes, she thought. He understood. And if he kept a distance it was because he understood. Right now, she belonged to another realm.

He stayed and watched her exercise Grace's legs and arms. He talked to Grace as if she could hear, and then he went home. When he left, Cricket realized that she was lonely. Everybody came and talked to her—Peggy, Jim, Sheila from school, the nurses, friends of hers and mothers of Grace's friends—but her emotional life was solitary. Nobody occupied the realm she was in, and somehow only Pass or Janis seemed to know how to get inside and visit. Jim seemed stuck in his own room of terror that she couldn't get into either. She talked with him about the DNR orders, and he told her she should sign them, if she thought it was best.

"Why don't you?" she suggested.

He licked his lips and said nothing for some time.

"Well?" Cricket asked.

"Okay," he said. "I will. You get them, and I'll sign. Before I leave."

But neither of them remembered.

And somehow they'd both forgotten about him staying in the hospital once Grace was out of ICU. Every time he came, Cricket meant to ask, then didn't. Maybe, she thought, she didn't want him to stay. Maybe she was being selfish, keeping the care of her daughter all to herself. Or maybe she knew he didn't want to, and was reluctant to press him beyond his own limits. Everyone had limits, and had to be forgiven for that. He was a good father, a good husband, doing everything she asked him to do, bringing her what she needed, taking care of the house and Janis while she had to be with Grace.

If he could not rescue her from this, she had to forgive him. Or at least not think about it.

On Saturday, Peggy was there, with her husband and her children. "She looks like she's sleeping," Andy said, touching her and withdrawing quickly.

"It's okay," Cricket said. "You can touch her." But Andy didn't try again. Instead, he hovered in the corner with his brother, who looked out the window and stayed silent. After a while, Peggy had Pete take them to the cafeteria.

"They don't know what to do here," she said apologetically.

"I know," Cricket said. "I understand." She smiled, to prove that she did. "They're getting big," she noted. "Pete's hair is getting dark."

"Voice is changing, too." Peggy sighed. "Boys. I don't know quite what to make of them. Especially with this. All the memorial services, all the stuff that can't be explained."

She shrugged, and told Cricket about the services, which she'd gone to, the shell-shocked community that seemed so far away to Cricket right now, and how the school was hiring a team of counselors to talk to the kids. They'd have an assembly at the school on Monday, when classes resumed.

"You look awful," Peggy said. "You should go."

"What's looking awful got to do with going to school?"

"I mean, you should get out of here. This place'll make you crazy."

As if, Cricket thought, the rest of the world wouldn't do that, too. She shook her head. "What if Grace wakes up when I'm not here?"

"The nurses are here," Peggy said. "Honestly, Cricket. It could be weeks yet, and when she does come to, you'll have your hands full. Physical therapy, maybe speech therapy. You need to pace yourself. Besides, it's not fair to Jim, is it?"

"What?"

"Well, he's got to go to work, go home to that house which must seem awful lonely to him. I mean, he's a man, but he's gotta have *some* feeling."

Peggy was grinning and Cricket stared at her a moment before she recognized what was happening. Peggy was teasing her. Talking like everything was normal. Trying to pull her back into the world. Cricket felt herself resisting, but with guilt. Jim needed her in the world. Janis needed her. Peggy was right. "Okay," she said. "I will. I'll go home. Soon."

"When?"

"Soon. Tomorrow. She's got another MRI and EEG today and I want to be here for that. Tomorrow I'll go home for a night. Okay?"

"And go to the assembly on Monday?"

"Peggy, whatever for?"

"The counselors. They might be helpful. You always say counseling is a good idea."

"Okay," Cricket said. "Okay. I'll go to the assembly."

"That's a good idea," Peggy said. "A great idea."

The MRI and EEG showed nothing new. Swelling had gone down, healing was going on, but nothing was waking her up yet. Patience, the doctor said. It took time.

And, yes, the doctor said when she asked, he did recommend that she sign the DNR orders. She wouldn't want to see her daughter suffer needlessly.

Inside a rough and heavy blanket of unreality, Cricket signed.

She went home on Sunday, and felt herself a stranger, as if she were using somebody else's bathroom and sink and utensils and plates. The phone was more silent than she remembered, without the constant stream of callers for Grace, then Janis, then Janis, then Grace. The silence was oppressive. Cricket couldn't relax in it. She made a meal for her family—meat loaf and mashed potatoes, which were favorites of Jim—and she talked cheerfully about the weather, asked cheerfully about Janis's classes, Jim's work, but he was politely withdrawn, and Janis ate in nervous silence, finishing quickly.

"Stay and talk," Cricket said, when she got up to go to her room. "I want to talk to you."

"I have homework," she said. "I have to do my homework."

"I never saw you rush out of the room to do homework before," Cricket said, smiling.

Janis closed her eyes, her face growing tight. "I can't *sit* here," she said. "Everything is wrong." She opened her eyes and gestured toward the empty seat across from her, where Grace always sat. "I can't sit here," she said, and turned and left the room.

Cricket looked to Jim, her face asking him questions. He shrugged. "It's hard on her, Cricket. What do you expect?"

She nodded. "Maybe I should stay home a few nights and you can go stay with Grace?" she suggested.

"Sure," he said. "If you want."

"Don't you want to?" she asked cautiously, not sure she wanted to hear his answer.

He hesitated, ran a hand through his hair.

"I mean," she said, "I know you don't want to. I don't want to be there either, but would it make you feel better to be with her? Spend time with her?"

He stood up, looked around the kitchen as if he'd lost something, then shook his head as if he knew it wasn't there after all. "I'll stay if you want," he said. "You know I will."

She felt a stabbing in her chest, a motion of pain she hadn't expected. Pain was a new animal alive inside her. She wasn't sure what it wanted from her. Whether she should feed it and care for it until it grew more friendly, or starve it and make it go away.

"I know," she said. "I know that. I just thought maybe . . ." She let the sentence go away. She didn't know how to finish it.

"You just let me know," he said. "I'll be in the den."

She sat at the table for a while, letting the pain quiet down. Janis was upset. Jim was upset. He would stay if she asked him to. Her heart beat out the phrase that she shouldn't have to ask. Shouldn't have to ask. Shouldn't have to.

She asked herself if she wanted to talk to him about it. There were things she could say to start a conversation. I know this is hard on you, she could say. I'm sorry if I'm neglecting you. You must be terrified and hurt. Usually, she said those kinds of words when she noticed that his emotions were unnameable, unmanageable without her assistance. That was one of her jobs in the marriage, just as his job was to be solid and real. He was the reality janitor, and she was the emotional janitor. It was what they did.

But, now, she couldn't do it. They were in a version of hell, and she couldn't do her regular job in hell. She wasn't asking him to do his.

She went into the den, where he sat drinking beer and watching the Mets, and she sat next to him, but she didn't say anything. Maybe if she sat there long enough, he would talk first.

The game broke for a preview of the evening's news, and a reporter said something about the latest theory that the shooter's body was among the eleven dead in the mall. That turned out to be a rumor started by a high school student interviewed after he'd gotten the bullet taken out of his arm.

"I seen him," the boy said. "He was big. A big guy. And old. I saw him shoot himself."

Autopsies indicated that none of the dead had shot themselves. The killer was still walking the streets, or more likely sitting home and watching CNN, seeing the stricken faces of parents and sisters and brothers and friends.

"I better go take care of the dishes," Cricket said, standing up and heading for the door.

"I'll stay with her," he said as she walked out. "You know that. I will."

Cricket stopped. "I know," she said. "I know that. You just do what you think is best."

He sighed deeply, and she knew that was her cue to offer more reassurance, but she couldn't. She felt something niggling at her, and if she stopped to name it, it would probably be resentment. She didn't want to feel that. She washed dishes instead.

Apparently, what she'd said was enough. When they got into

bed, he pulled her to him, whispered that he was glad she was home. They made love silently, and it wasn't until he rolled over to go to sleep that she realized he hadn't looked at her once. They were separated, living on different islands of fear and grief, not able to feel each other even when they touched. She was chilled, as if the act had taken heat from her body. If their marriage had been dull before, now it was soiled. It had been marred. Something bad was happening between them, and there was nothing she could do to change it.

On Monday morning, Cricket awoke to Aerosmith on the radio and wondered who brought the radio to the hospital, and when Aerosmith had become a classic. Then she remembered she wasn't in the hospital. She was home. She lifted her head to look out the window, and saw that the sky was overcast, dull and gray.

Cricket got up and showered, dressed, and went to the kitchen to put the coffee on, as if there had been no break in the routine of their lives. She heard the shower running. Jim, she thought. He always got up a little later than she did, and she often envied him the extra minutes of sleep he could squeeze out of morning.

Janis wasn't out of her room yet. Cricket ascended the stairs to her attic room, knocked softly on her door and waited a moment, then opened the door and went in.

Janis was sitting up in bed, groggy and tousled. "I'm up," she said.

"Okay. Get ready. I'm taking you today."

She went back down to the kitchen, got orange juice and milk on the table, English muffins in the toaster, and cracked three eggs into a blue bowl.

"Cricket," Jim called across the house, "where's my *socks?*"

"In your drawer, honey," Cricket called back, trying to sound gentle.

"My *dark green* socks," he called back. "The ones that go with my dark green suit."

Cricket stopped beating the eggs. She put the bowl down and went to the laundry room just off the kitchen, opened the dryer and saw that it was full.

"Look in the dryer," Cricket suggested. "There's clothes here."

"Honey, do me a favor and you look."

Cricket sighed and knelt down in front of the dryer as if worshiping. She had to finish the eggs. She had to talk to Janis. She had to get their cat to the vet because he came home with a swollen foot and was now huddled miserably on the couch, looking at her as if she'd personally bitten him. She had all kinds of things to do that she wasn't doing because she couldn't. Grace was in the hospital and needed her to be there. Being away this long made panic rise at the back of her throat as if something awful was about to happen.

Cricket pulled all the laundry out of the dryer and let it fall onto the floor. She picked among the underwear, her husband's plain white, which were wearing thin, her daughter's silk and cotton and flowered and multicolored bikinis, her own assortment of high-cut and bikini and lacy and plain. She was the only person in the house who saw everybody's underwear, because she was the only person who did everybody's laundry. Sometimes, Jim or the girls would do a load of their own if they needed it in a hurry, but nobody ever did hers, and only occasionally would Janis or Grace do each other's, and that either to get a fee, or pay off a debt.

Cricket was the only one who saw it all. She didn't know if that had any kind of significance. When she thought about it, she figured it probably didn't.

She found the socks and went to her room. "These?" she asked Jim, holding them out.

He nodded, and held out one hand, his other one busy working a tie.

"Thanks," he said, "and close the door on the way out, okay?"

Cricket did so. She leaned against it for a moment and breathed deeply, searching for some good thoughts to put into the day. She'd asked Jim to stay home from work and go to the hospital, but he said he couldn't. He had meetings up the wazoo.

She couldn't find any thought that was good. Just some that were less grim than others.

Janis was not a morning person, and the ride to school was short and silent. When they got to the door, Janis put a hand on Cricket's arm. "Don't say anything embarrassing," she said. "Okay?"

Cricket frowned. "Embarrassing?"

"Like, don't say anything about me, okay? Don't ask questions about me, or . . . say anything about me. Okay?"

"Honey, everybody knows your sister's in the hospital, don't they?" Cricket asked, not sure what Janis was getting at.

"That's not about me. Just . . . I don't want to have to talk about it all the time. Every time I talk about it . . ." She paused, and ducked her head down to her chest.

Lately, Janis was the master of the unfinished sentence. And Cricket didn't understand. Didn't know what her daughter needed from her. How could she give it, if she didn't know what it was?

"What?" Cricket asked. "What happens when you talk about it?"

"It hurts," Janis said, speaking into her chest, her voice a whisper. "Every time someone talks about it. Every time I get reminded. It hurts. I can't—it hurts."

Cricket heard herself gasp. She didn't mean to, but it was pulled out of her. Janis lifted her face to her mother's and stared at her hard, then shook her head and walked away

Cricket stood in the hallway and watched her go, marveling at the phenomena of distance and age—that the farther away your child got from you physically, the younger they became. It was a law of some kind, she thought. A law of physics that nobody had bothered to identify or name because it only happened to women.

"Hey," a voice said behind her, and Cricket turned.

It was Sheila, who had left her dead marriage. Cricket spent a moment admiring her suit. Sheila always had great suits. This one was maroon, some soft material that wasn't wool. The jacket was long and straight, the skirt straight and short. She wore nothing under the jacket, which was cut low.

"Good to see you here," Sheila said. "How's Grace doing?"

"Better," Cricket said. "Much better. All her reflexes are working."

"That's good, right? It sounds good."

"It's good," Cricket said.

"And you? You okay? You must be exhausted."

"Fine. I'm fine."

Sheila smoothed down her beautifully cut auburn hair, making a *tsk-tsk* sound with her tongue as she did so. "Don't go into delayed shock on me, okay?"

"No," Cricket said dully. "I won't."

"So are you coming back now? Back to work?"

Cricket tilted her head to one side and rubbed the back of her neck. She'd forgotten about work. It was no longer a part of her mental landscape. She'd have to make some kind of schedule, she supposed. She couldn't quite wrap her mind around it, though. "Maybe," she said. "We'll see."

Sheila let a minute of silence pass. "You're not saying much," she noted.

"What?" Cricket asked.

"I said, you're quiet. How're you doing, really? This must be terrible for you, and for Jim. Something like this puts an awful strain on a marriage. Are you two holding up okay?"

Cricket frowned. Were they? How do you hold up when the bad thing happens? He was doing the best he could. So was she. That had to be good enough. It always had been.

"It's difficult," she said carefully, weighing her words. "Jim has a . . . a hard time seeing Grace this way. He feels helpless, I guess. He likes to fix things when they're broken."

"That must piss you off," Sheila said.

Cricket stifled nervous laughter. Of course she wasn't pissed at him. He had feelings about it. Deep feelings. She needed to respect them, that was all. He wasn't doing anything wrong.

"He's doing the best he can," she said.

"The problem," Sheila said, "is that most of the guys I know grew up in houses where the father was the center of the world, and some part of them expects they'll get the same thing. That the house revolves around their needs. I mean, they've got all these words they say about their children, and child-centered houses and the new fathering, but it hasn't sunk in. Not really. Of course, most of the time they can fake it, but when something like this happens, they can't deal. They just can't deal."

She turned her sharp eyes toward Cricket. Bore down on her with them. "Right?" she asked.

Cricket wanted to say no. Wrong. Jim wasn't like that. Jim worked for her, for the children. His family was his life. But she couldn't say that. Didn't know if it was true. Didn't know what was true anymore. Didn't want to think about it. Did Sheila expect her to answer, to agree? Or could she not say anything, and that would be taken as agreement? She chewed on her lip, and shrugged. Then, surprising herself, she asked, "Sheila, if you were going to live as if you only had a year to live, what would you do?"

Sheila frowned. "What?"

"You heard me."

"If I had a year to live?"

"No," Cricket said. "If you were living *as if* you had a year."

"Oh," Sheila said. "Oh. Well, that's . . . that's a really strange question, Cricket."

"Is it?"

"Well, yes. I mean, what with—"

"But what would you do?" Cricket cut in quickly, before Sheila could say anything more about her or Jim or Grace.

Sheila tilted her head to one side and lifted her eyes as if peering into her own mind. A slow, soft smile formed on her face.

"Travel. Go places I've never been. Ditch the job and the kids and go. I already ditched the man, so I'd be clear of that, at least."

"Where?" Cricket asked. "Travel where?"

Sheila closed her eyes and the smile grew. "India," she said. "I've always wanted to go to India. I've heard the cities are filthy and they smell and they're packed with beggars."

Cricket ran her gaze up and down Sheila's suit, her lovely hair, her expensive shoes.

"India?" she asked.

"India." Sheila sighed. She opened her eyes, and tilted her head up to view the clock. "Hell. Gotta run. Gotta get the counselors set up. Listen, if you need anything, you call me, okay? And don't worry about Jim. He's a good man. He'll come through for you."

Yes, Cricket thought. Of course he would. Of course.

After Sheila left, Cricket went into the office and observed that a stack of Xeroxing she was supposed to do before the shooting still sat there, accusing her of inattentiveness and irresponsibility. That was nothing new. She accused herself of it often enough. She shuffled items on her desk as the announcements came on and the Pledge of Allegiance was said. The principal came out of his office and patted her shoulder absentmindedly, as if he knew that he should for some reason but couldn't quite remember why.

Everyone in the office except for Maria, who would stay on the phones, was attending the assembly. They walked silently through the halls, and Cricket noticed how quietly the students walked as well, whispering here and there, but not laughing or pushing out of line as they usually did on their way to assemblies. For the most part, they kept their heads down and their mouths shut. Some of the girls walked with their arms around each other. Most of the boys were hunched into their own chests, hands in pockets, faces blank.

Cricket wondered if they were afraid, or just shell-shocked, unsure how to behave in a world that had changed so radically in such a short time. Many of them had lost friends. Some had seen them killed. Maybe some of them waited for the killer to appear among them again because out here, in the world, Cricket remembered that the gun that shot her daughter had another human being at the end of it, and that human being was still free in the world. He could even be here, now. Panic rose at the back of her throat. As she took her seat up front with the rest of the school staff, she twisted to see where Janis sat, trying to establish some invisible shield around her just in case. Just in case.

She spotted her toward the back, with a group of girls dressed in black. Janis and her friends wore neutral tones. Blacks, grays, tans.

When everyone was seated, the principal briefly addressed them, saying all the right things. There were too many dead, he said, and read the names of the students who were killed—from the high school, six shot to death, one crushed trying to escape. He talked about grief and the great loss to the parents, the siblings, the community.

He said more right things about the nature of violence and the need to develop the mind so that irrational events didn't occur. He talked about the need to apprehend the criminal and see to it that he never walked the streets again. Murmurs of agreement rose and fell.

The principal ended his speech and introduced the counselors. There were four. Two young women, a young man, and an older man who had flecks of gray in his beard and hair, which was long and pulled back into a ponytail. They were all dressed casually but neatly. Cricket recognized an Abercrombie & Fitch shirt on one of the women because Janis had the same one at home in her closet.

The principal said things about their credentials, and then stepped back as the older one, a man who called himself Michael Winston, walked forward to speak.

"Hi," he said, less formal than the principal. "How is everybody?"

He waited, as if he expected an answer to this, and the students began to mumble and shift in their seats. Cricket directed a smile at him so he wouldn't be embarrassed, which she thought he must be, so exposed up there actually asking such a stupid question on a day like today. How were they. How should they be?

"It's okay. Don't tell me. I know," he said, and Cricket realized the question had been rhetorical. This made her angry at him. He was using their discomfort to make a point. That didn't seem fair. She decided not to smile at him anymore. Let him fend for himself.

"How you are is frightened, angry, and confused," he said. "You can't even be sad about the people who were killed yet, because you're still too scared. The bottom's dropped out of your world. You look around, and everything you see is a little out of focus. You walk down the hall expecting violence at any moment. You walk down the streets and see someone with a hand in their pocket, and you feel panic. Everybody looks like a stranger, and none of them are friendly."

Now Cricket heard murmurs of assent around her, saw people nodding. Michael nodded back. "I'm here to tell you, it's all normal."

Cricket heard the word, and repeated it to herself softly. Normal. It's all normal.

He continued to speak, but Cricket ceased listening. Normal, he said. It was all normal.

In her mind, she saw the old man at the supermarket, heard Jim calling him nuts. The old man was nuts. This, what they were going through now, was all normal.

Then, she heard Peggy's voice calling Pass crazy. Pass was crazy. The fear they felt was normal. She thought of all the times her own daughters referred to a classmate as weird because they wrote poetry, or a geek because they did well in math class. She thought of the women she worked with gossiping about someone who had gone nuts and was taking courses in astrology. Crazy. That was crazy.

She whispered to herself, "Normal."

Around her, the audience was listening attentively as this stranger named Michael Winston fielded questions. Somebody asked how they could feel less afraid. He said it would take time.

She thought it would take more than time. It would take willful ignorance, too. She felt something move inside her with the same soft power she'd felt when her daughters had first shifted in her uterus, first fluttered their hands or kicked their feet against the inside of her skin. But that was a joyful moment, and this was not. It was not normal, she thought.

Somebody asked him what they could do for the families of the victims. He recommended letters and flowers, staying in touch, talking to them, not ignoring their pain and rage. Their feelings were normal, he said again. She thought, What do their feelings have to do with it? Something happened. Something horrible happened. Nobody can make that unhappen, or make what it means go away. And it wasn't normal.

It especially wasn't normal for them to be sitting here making little jokes and whispering and smiling when out there somewhere someone who gunned down children was walking around, maybe buying a newspaper, maybe getting gas or having a cup of coffee at the diner. Maybe working out at the gym. Maybe walking his dog. Or maybe even in this room, listening, asking questions, getting ready to shoot again.

She stood up and tried to get the person next to her to move her legs so she could pass.

She saw Michael looking at her out of the corner of his eye. Then he pointed at her. "Yes?" he asked. "You have a question."

She looked left and right. People were staring at her. She just wanted to leave.

"It's not normal," she said quietly.

"I'm sorry. I didn't hear that," he said. "Maybe—could you speak up?"

"It's not normal," she said, this time too loudly. "None of it is normal." She realized she sounded belligerent, angry, a little hysterical.

"Of course," he said reassuringly. "Of course it's not the norm. That would be horrible, wouldn't it? What I meant is that what you feel is normal, and okay."

"No," she said vehemently. "It is *not* normal to feel this way. It is not, not okay." She punctuated the words with her finger, jabbing it in the air with every negation of what he said. "None of it is okay, not any of it, not *any* of it."

She waved an arm to the people gathered in the room. "Can't you tell them the truth?" she insisted. "It's not okay. It will never be okay again. Nothing," she said, "nothing will ever be the same."

There was a gasp from the audience. She whirled around and saw that Janis was staring at her, red with fury or shame or both.

Cricket's face grew hot. What was she doing, torturing people with the truth? The truth was a form of torture, she knew. She'd learned that long ago from her mother, her father, from everybody who told her it was better to think positively, make people feel good about themselves and they'll return the favor. All her self-help books espoused the value of positive thinking. All the talk show hosts agreed.

She raised her hand to her mouth as if to keep more words from coming out. She pushed her way around the people in the aisle and left at a fast clip. As she retreated up the long aisle toward the door, she heard Michael speaking.

"You've all felt that, haven't you?" he asked. "And the truth is, things won't be the same. But maybe we can make them better."

A collective sigh went up around the room. Cricket left the auditorium.

She stopped briefly by the office to write a note to the principal saying that she wouldn't be coming back to work. Her daughter needed her.

Dream #4

tulips

In the weeks that followed, Cricket dreamt of flowers. She knew what Freud said about dreams. They didn't mean what they said. They meant what they hid. She knew about Carl Jung and dream archetypes—images all people shared, across the globe and across time. She knew what the scientists said about REM sleep and neural firing. None of it explained why she dreamt persistently of flowers.

Her life shifted to include in it the fact of her daughter's wounds, and after a month, nothing changed except the kinds of flowers she dreamt about.

She moved her daughter's legs up and down, flexing them, bending them. She talked to her and played music for her, and while she slept in the cot next to her, she dreamt of roses. Though scientists said dreaming didn't include scents, in her sleep she would smell their thick scent as she stood in a garden with dazzling white fountains engulfed in brilliant orange roses climbing like mad children all around.

They were alive, these roses. They had spirit and voice. They laughed continuously. They wanted to embrace her and she let them. But their thorns drove into her flesh and she began to bleed in a thousand places. Her life seeped away, the roses drinking it from her, growing darker and darker as her blood became theirs.

When Jim came, he stood at the foot of the bed and looked uncomfortable, reached out toward Grace and then pulled back.

"You can touch her," Cricket said. "It's okay. It's good."

"She looks so strange," Jim said. "Like she did when she had measles, and her fever went so high we had to put ice around her. Remember that?"

Cricket did. Jim cracked the ice out of holders and she stuffed it into plastic bags while Janis ran with it into Grace's room, putting it all around her, talking to her, telling her, "Don't lick it. You tongue will stick."

Grace was limp as a rag doll, her skin translucent and hot. They all slept in her room that night, and the fever broke by morning. Janis was triumphant, as if she'd saved the world all by herself. Over the years, she told the story to Grace again and again, each time her fever getting a little higher, the work a little harder, the moment of change more dramatic. Grace would laugh and say, "Tell about the thing you said again. About not licking the ice."

Jim sighed, and tapped a newspaper against his leg. He always brought the newspaper to the hospital.

"Read it out loud to her," Cricket suggested.

"I feel silly," he said.

"Read it," she insisted. "The doctors say it's good for her." Even if Jim couldn't stay the night, he could do some things. Cricket knew he'd feel better about himself if he did, so she always gave him tasks, like making tapes for Grace, finding things in her room to bring to the hospital, reading to her, talking to her. That way he'd stay connected to the process, and would perhaps adjust better to what had happened.

Reluctantly, he started reading an article about post-traumatic shock in witnesses of violence. It included an interview with a mother who saw her son shot at the mall. She was getting him a Big Mac, she said. "I turned, and there was blood coming out of his throat," the mother said. "It was just coming out and he was looking at me, and I was standing there holding his Big Mac."

"Stop now," Cricket said. "That's enough."

Shortly after that, another child was moved into the room, but only stayed one night. Cricket heard the mother crying quietly, but with a grief that seemed to rise up from her belly and emerge as a living thing into the night. Cricket fell asleep to the sound and dreamt about an early blooming tulip. It was white, with soft pink markings at its center. It seemed to absorb and then give off light, phosphorescing in the sun. It was beautiful. Too beautiful. She was afraid of the power it had to draw her into the world, which was not safe. She was afraid its power was too much She was afraid its power wasn't enough, and she felt that if she continued to stare at it, death would come into her yard and take her.

In her dream, day seemed to turn into night and the tulip closed. She wanted to open it, and knew she couldn't. When it opened, she knew she could not make it shut. When she woke, the bed next to Grace's was empty.

The school sent home sheets of paper with titles like "Family Facts: Understanding Violence," and "You Can Heal," and "Learning to Live: Community Violence and Recovery." They drove Cricket mad, made her scratch at her head and twitch

The list of risk factors to watch for—previous aggressive behavior, a history of abuse, firearms in the home—seemed useless, a pointless restating of the obvious. If someone had guns, they didn't recognize the risk. And how many abusive families would look at their children and say, Gee, we abused them. Better watch out now.

She stopped reading the handouts Jim brought to the hospital.

After the fifth week of Grace's hospital stay, Cricket dreamt of a certain purple weed that grew in her yard. It was the only weed she felt truly unfriendly toward because it was so voracious, taking all space and letting nothing else in. In her dream, she was pulling them out, pulling them out, but as fast as she pulled one, two more grew in its place.

She had made a deal with Jim that she'd stay home at least three nights a week, but when she was home, she couldn't relax. She went out into her vegetable garden and saw that all the beans had been chewed down to nubby stems that stuck out of the ground like an army of dead sticks. A quick rage filled her, then dissipated into guilt. The woodchucks had eaten her garden, which they didn't do when she was here. Maybe they felt abandoned, too.

By the seventh week of this schedule, Jim said she was always turning toward the hospital, even in her sleep. He began to hint that she wasn't being responsible to Janis, who was withdrawn and silent. She ate dinner with them silently, then went to her room and locked her door. Cricket followed her one time, and when Janis let her in, she asked, "What is it, honey? What's wrong?"

"I'm tired," she said. "And I've got homework. I'm in the school play, you know. I have lines to memorize." She tried to sound truculent, but only sounded edgy and tense.

Cricket felt shame flood her. She hadn't known. She should have. She would have to make it up to her. She called Planned Parenthood and made an appointment for Janis. She would take her. Maybe they could have lunch together. Maybe they could talk.

She dreamt of a lotus, such a simple plant, really not beautiful except in its simplicity. In her dream, she was sitting in front of a bowl of them, and each one reflected her face in some aspect— smiling, concerned, calm, amused. When she lifted her face from them, she saw a great mirror with a golden frame. It reflected nothing.

When Grace had been in the hospital two months, the TV news announced that the police had run out of leads on the shooter. Survivors were interviewed again, but their reports were contradictory. One woman described a very large man with a pale face leaning over her when she was on the floor bleeding. He was crying, and he had a gun. But when the police probed, she lost her surety.

"I *guess* it was a gun," she said. "He looked like the type. You know—not all there."

Another witness remembered seeing an angry woman waving something that looked like a gun. Reporters fell on this like vultures and ripped off every piece of flesh. A woman shooting children—now that was a different angle. Women whose ex-husbands worked at the mall were checked, and nothing was found except two men who were arrested for not paying child support. Then, men who had ex-wives at the mall were interviewed. Even a local family court judge was questioned, but he had an alibi. He was with his mother.

In the absence of a real killer to talk about, the news gave special reports on theoretical killers. Some said they had a faulty genetic code that made them too aggressive. This could only be cured with medication. Others said this kind of crime was the inevitable result of a generally violent culture. Some said it was the millennium, or godlessness, or working mothers. Some said it was a child with a too rich fantasy life and too many video games.

Such children weren't evil, the news said. They were innocent. Innocent of the knowledge of consequences, or the pain of others. And innocence could kill. How could that be, Cricket wanted to know. How could anyone be innocent of the pain of others?

But then she realized there wasn't one person on earth who understood the pain they might cause. Nobody was innocent. She had two cars, blow-dryers and a TV—all of them sucking the earth's energy dry. Americans used up the vast majority of the earth's resources, and she was an American. There was no way to live and be innocent. She began to be afraid of herself, of her own existence. She stopped watching the news. If Jim or Janis turned it on while she was home, she left the room.

She dreamt that she went out into her yard and saw that the trees had been burned to the ground in a terrible war, leaving only smoking stumps and seared brown grass. She went into the vegetable garden to search for food, but the plants were just blackened twigs, and the earth stank of smoke and death. She had no food to give anybody. They would all starve.

The only time Cricket felt a relief of tension was at the sanctuary, where she would go once or twice a week for an hour or two between the hospital and home. She went guiltily, hungry for a quiet that felt like peace rather than suspense, but not sure she should allow herself this luxury. She told herself she needed it as a time to shift from the hospital to home and back again. The sanctuary was a cocoon, where the rules of neither world applied. But she had an almost physical hunger to be near Pass, who drew the injured and the wild to him without effort, by nature of his being. He was a pool of peace she could wash herself in, if only she could stand next to him now and then.

This made her feel as if she was being unfaithful, though Pass had not been seductive by word or deed. Still, she couldn't shake the feeling that they had made an unspoken agreement not to act on something they both felt. Not yet.

Now? She seemed to ask when he came over to her car to greet her. Now? his eyes seemed to ask in return. Every time the answer was no, but that had nothing to do with Jim. Being unfaithful to him wasn't the issue. What mattered was being unfaithful to Grace, and the realm Cricket occupied with her.

But this, Cricket told herself, was only in her mind. It was just a fantasy she used to distract herself. In reality, Pass was no different than usual—self-contained, considerate in an aloof way, intensely present to the moment without imposing himself on her. He was, perhaps, more gentle with her, and he always asked about Grace.

Sometimes, he'd come to the hospital and visit. He asked questions, helped with her exercises, and showed the same interest he would in the repair of any broken creature, the same quiet hope she felt in him when he changed a splint on a hawk's leg. To Pass, Grace might as well have been a small eagle, with broken wings.

Cricket dreamt of crocuses, which bloomed and disappeared so quickly they seemed to be formed from the snow they emerged out of. She picked one, held it in her hand, and watched it dissolve into water, running through her fingers and back to the dark earth.

Cricket bought pretty silk scarves in peach and lavender and sky blue, with flowers of all kinds, to put on Grace while her hair grew back. She bought scarves with irises on them, and lilies of the valley. She wanted to think about pretty scarves for her daughter rather than the man who made her need them. She wanted the scarves to make his existence moot.

But the people who came to visit her and Grace wouldn't let her forget. The town was on the map because of this. There was a sickening sense of excitement about it all.

"Did you hear that Jane's going on *Sixty Minutes*?" Grace's teacher said when she came to visit. "That's something, isn't it?"

It was something, in a place where nothing much happened that anyone could tell. But she did not want to think that about the people she lived with, her neighbors and friends. She did not want to think that they would greedily devour disaster because it was bigger than the lives they'd consented to.

"What would you do if you were going to live as if you only had a year to live?" Cricket asked the teacher, to change the subject. The teacher was startled, but then looked dreamily out the window as if the answer were there.

"I'd eat anything I wanted to eat. I'd just eat chocolate for a week. I wouldn't worry about my weight anymore."

When the guidance counselor, who had a patronizing manner and bad breath, came by and started talking about the shooting, Cricket asked him the same thing. It seemed to be the only question that distracted anyone.

"What would I do?" he asked.

"Yes," she confirmed.

"Well, I guess I'd have a lot of sex," he said, nodding. She bit her lip to keep from asking whom he thought he'd have it with.

"What would you do," Cricket asked the woman who came in and washed the floors at night when she commented about the killer still being free, "if you were going to live as if you only had a year to live?"

The woman stopped pushing the mop, and looked out the window for a minute. "I'd quit my job and do nothing but read and eat mashed potatoes all day."

"What would you read?" Cricket asked.

"Dostoyevsky," the woman said. "He's a Russian writer. Ever hear of him?"

"Do you think," Cricket asked Peggy when she told her about all this, "people want to do what they can't?"

"I think people like novelty," Peggy said. "And that it wears off, and then they want something else. And I think you're obsessing."

But Cricket kept asking. She felt as if she were harvesting the unused dreams, the unlived lives of her visitors, and presenting them to her daughter as a kind of medicine to help her heal.

Here, she wanted to tell Grace. Take these dreams. This is what you have to come back for. Don't pay attention to their terror, their unwillingness to look at you too closely, their talk about *Good Morning America*. Take the dreams they'll never have the courage to use, and live.

If it was an obsession, it was the best one she could come up with, given her choices. The doctors were beginning to shake their heads when they examined Grace. They looked at her as if they were sad, and Cricket would turn away to avoid seeing.

"What would you do," she asked the neurologist, "if you were going to live as if you only had a year to live?"

"I'd raise horses," he said, running his finger up the bottom of Grace's foot. "On a farm way out in the country. I wouldn't see anybody for weeks at a time, except the horses. If your daughter doesn't wake up soon, she'll have to be transferred to a long-term facility. You know that, don't you?"

"What kind of horses?" Cricket asked.

After two months, Cricket dreamt of flowers made of ice that broke if you touched them, their slivers sounding like glass when they hit the ground.

Cricket bent Grace's legs and played music for her and talked into her closed face, where she could hardly see her daughter, her little girl, her Grace, anymore. Her face was bloated from fluids, but her skin was thin and seemed fragile. Jim would dutifully help her when he came, but each visit seemed more difficult for him. He paced the room restlessly, looking out the window, fiddling with the remote for the TV, channel surfing.

When Cricket went home, he would ask, "How's everything? How is she?" Cricket noticed he rarely said her name anymore. It was always "she."

"Fine," Cricket would say. "She's fine."

"Any change?" he would ask hopefully. Cricket would shake her head, and he would look deflated. No. No change. Not today.

"It's been three months," he said one night while she was brushing her teeth, getting ready for bed.

She stopped brushing, rinsed out her toothbrush, rinsed out her mouth and spit. She had no idea it had been that long.

"Huh," she said. "Really?" She calculated and realized he was right. The shooting was the end of March. Now it was the end of June. She hadn't even noticed spring turning to summer.

"Don't you ever wish it was over?" he asked.

She shook her head. "Over?"

He put his hand on her shoulder and rubbed it lightly. She looked at him. His touch was soft, but his face was full of darkness.

"Cricket," he said, "how long can we go on like this?"

"I don't know what you mean."

"Yes, you do," he insisted. "Yes, you do know. You're not here anymore. Janis is a mess. We're a mess. We have to . . . to do something."

"What?" Cricket asked.

He cleared his throat, rubbed at her shoulder, his voice getting more gentle. "She needs to go to a place where they can care for her. A . . . a long-term facility. She won't just get well any day now, the way we thought. We . . . we have to let go of it. Find a way to . . . to live our lives. Let go of her, a little bit."

Cricket shook his hand off and took a step back from him. He'd become someone she didn't know, saying words she couldn't comprehend. Yes, the doctors said something about long-term care. But not yet, Cricket thought. It wasn't time yet. And they never said let go of her. Let go of her? Let go of Grace? Grace, who was in her hands, still in her bloodstream, her flesh and bones.

"Let go of her?" she whispered. "How?"

"We have to stop pretending," Jim said. "Stop pretending she'll get better."

"I'm not pretending," Cricket said. "Are you?"

"No. Of course not. But you can't act like she'll just wake up and go back to the way she was. Like you believe—"

"I do believe," she cut in. "I believe she'll get well. Don't you? *Don't* you?"

He lowered his head, rubbed a hand over his face, looked away from her.

"You don't, do you?" Cricket said, amazed. So that was his problem. He didn't believe Grace would get well. When he saw her, he didn't see her getting well, didn't envision her with her beautiful hair grown long again, and her body lithe and strong. He saw her as she was now, simultaneously shrunken and swollen. Or maybe he saw worse.

A horrible thought flooded through her. When Jim saw her, he saw her as already dead.

Fury rose up in her. How dare he do that? How dare he, when Grace was alive and needed all their faith, all their positive thoughts and feelings and imaginings. How dare he?

"She's not dead," Cricket said. "We can't pretend she's dead."

He mumbled something Cricket couldn't hear.

"What? What did you say?"

"Nothing," he said. "I just— We have to live our lives. We can't let this run everything. Grace wouldn't want that. Especially since . . ." He paused.

"Since what?" she asked.

"Cricket, the doctors all say the same thing. After one month, maybe. After two months, there's still a chance. But when someone's been out this long. . . . I don't think it's a good idea to believe in something that can't be."

She made a fist, and punched him in the shoulder. He stepped back, shocked.

"What do you believe in?" she asked angrily. "Basketball games? Beer? Orgies?"

"Jesus, Cricket. It's not like that. You know—"

"I know you won't be with her," she said, yelling now. Words kept coming out of her, and she couldn't stop them. "I know you won't even *try*. You're supposed to try, at least. You're supposed to be my husband, not some guy who leaves me alone in the hospital or . . . or yells at me when I come home or . . . or abandons our daughter. *Our* daughter, Jim."

"And what about our other daughter?" he yelled back. "What about Janis? While you're at the hospital in some fantasy world, the real thing is falling apart right here. You're throwing it away, Cricket. I'm warning you, you're throwing it away."

Warning her? What did that mean? Was he threatening? It seemed ridiculous. He had nothing to threaten her with. The worst had already happened.

As suddenly as it had erupted, her anger dissolved. He wasn't someone she knew anymore, and why fight with someone you don't know? They'd done nothing together for years, beyond eating and sleeping together, having sex, talking about things that didn't matter to either of them, because somewhere along the way, they'd ceased mattering to each other.

Was that true? They didn't matter to each other anymore? If it was true, would her heart break about it, or did it matter so little that she wouldn't even feel it?

"Maybe this is real," she said, "but it's not real deep."

She went to bed.

That night, he slept as far away from her as possible. She dreamt of nettles, sharp in her hand as she tried to grasp them and pull them up. When she woke in the morning, he was already gone.

Another child was moved into Grace's room, a one-year-old boy with a brain tumor. He had no visitors, and was comatose. Marianne would come in and sit next to him and rub his arms. " 'Would you like to swing on a star,' " she would sing in a sweet, rich voice, " 'carry moonbeams home in a jar.' " Cricket tried not to listen.

That week, Cricket was moving Grace's legs and talking to her when she felt a shiver run down her spine. She held her breath. Something had changed. She felt the motion of it inside her, change that must occur and she did not know how to keep it from her.

She turned her head very slowly to look at Grace, trying not to think of anything at all.

Her eyes were open.

"Grace," Cricket whispered. "Grace."

She lowered her leg carefully, her hand shaking. "Grace, honey, it's me. It's Mom."

Grace didn't move. Cricket leaned close to her, grabbed her hand. She didn't react.

"Grace," she said again. "Grace, I love you."

Still, no response.

But Grace's eyes were open, staring at her. Cricket stared back, trying to see what they saw, why they were open, but looking into them was like looking down into an endless hole that erased boundaries and perspective as you fell farther and farther into them. Her eyes were bottomless, a container for forever.

Grace stared at her, showing her forever.

Cricket reached for the button at the side of the bed and pressed it hard once, twice, three times. She needed a doctor to tell her what it meant. She needed someone to pull Grace out of her bottomless eyes and bring her back here, away from forever to now.

She heard footsteps padding down the hall and entering the room. She turned and saw Ron, who was the day nurse on this floor. "Look," she said. "Look at her eyes."

But Grace's eyes were closed, as if they'd never been open at all.

The next day, the neurosurgeon told her it was just a reflex. It meant nothing regarding consciousness, one way or the other.

At night, at her daughter's side with a finger resting on the flesh of her arm, Cricket dreamt of a garden where all the flowers were birds tied to green stems, their wings leafy and wild and in constant motion, in a desperate and futile attempt to be free.

eight

Cricket knocked on Janis's door softly. "Honey," she said, "time to get up."

"I'm up." She heard the muffled reply from the other side. "Just a minute."

Janis emerged from her room, wearing jeans and a T-shirt that said "Free Leonard Peltier."

"You okay?" Cricket asked.

She bobbed her head up and down, but said nothing. Her face was tight and there were dark circles under her eyes. "Let's just go, okay?"

They left the house and got in the car. Jim was at work. Cricket had stayed home the night before, and had tried talking to Janis, but had found her withdrawn, edgy. "I don't want to talk about it all the time, Mother," she said. "It's too embarrassing."

Cricket didn't blame her. She felt the same way.

They were both quiet on the ride to Planned Parenthood, Janis staring out her window, Cricket concentrating on driving and trying to keep from talking when she knew it would only make Janis angry. She envied Peggy for having boys. All she'd had to do was tell Pete to get some condoms and explain it to them. And when he did, they told him they already knew all about it from health class.

When they stopped at a light a block from their destination, Janis exclaimed, "Jesus Christ. What's that?"

Cricket looked where Janis pointed. She squinted. The bishop? The pope? Standing in front of Planned Parenthood?

The light changed and she drove forward. They had to pass the building and pull around the corner to the right for parking and as they drove by Cricket realized it wasn't a real bishop or pope, but men dressed up as a bishop and pope, kneeling in prayer.

Behind them a few women and little girls stood holding signs. The little girl's sign said, "WOULD YOU MURDER ME?" The women's signs said, "Lord forgive them for they know not what they do," and had images of fetuses superimposed on the cross.

"What is it?" Janis said, her voice edgy and high. "What're they doing?"

"Nothing, honey," Cricket said. "They won't bother you."

Janis turned an angry face to her mother. "Yes, they will," she said. "That's why they're here, isn't it? To bother people?"

Cricket shook her head. "I won't let them," she said, but she was frightened because she knew these people sometimes carried guns and shot people. She cared about her daughter's life. About Janis, this daughter she had right here in the car with her. She loved her with a fierceness that wouldn't allow them to even breathe the same air she breathed.

"They won't bother you," Cricket said firmly.

As they got out of the car, a woman wearing an orange vest that said Planned Parenthood approached them. "Hi," she said. "I'm your escort. Best thing to do is just keep walking. Don't talk to them. They can't touch you."

She stood on Janis's other side and they walked quickly to the door and opened it. Janis and the woman in orange went in ahead of Cricket, and as she stood just behind them a woman from the group got in front of her and raised a closed hand.

Cricket gasped and backed up, as her skin grew cold with fear. Was the woman going to hit her? Shoot her?

"We'll pray for the baby's soul," the woman said, and held out a white rosary.

Cricket didn't move because she was shaking, and didn't know if she was going to faint. The woman shoved the rosary into Cricket's hand and Cricket stared down at it. The plastic was cheap and shoddy, as if they bought them wholesale from a trinket vendor.

The door behind Cricket opened and the woman with the orange vest tapped her on the shoulder.

"Better come in," she said.

Cricket turned around and saw that Janis stood just behind the woman, looking horrified. She let the rosary drop from her hand and went inside.

"Did you have to?" Janis said through her teeth.

"I didn't do anything," Cricket said, stung. "They did. I was just there."

Janis took a step back and ducked her head down. "Let's just go in," she said.

They were admitted into the locked door and directed to a waiting room, where they sat among a group of women of various ages, some looking depressed, some bored. Across from them a young woman sat with a young man who kept patting her hand. Her eyes were rimmed with red as if she'd been crying for a long time. Two seats down, a very fat woman smiled at the TV on the wall, where Ricki Lake was asking a woman if she knew her sister was having an affair with her husband. "Hell, no," the woman said. "And now I know, I'm gonna clean her clock."

The camera cut to Ricki's surprised face, then back to the girls, who were being held apart by a man who was apparently husband to one of them, lover to the other.

"Guess the day didn't turn out like you planned," Ricki said.

"That's horrible," Cricket muttered.

"What?"

She pointed to the TV. "To do that to your own sister—on national television."

Janis opened her mouth to reply, then shut it hard and picked up a magazine. Cricket let her be, and quietly watched the clock move its hands around. Their appointment was for eleven, and it was already eleven-thirty. Janis kept reading her magazine. Just before noon, a door at the end of the room opened and a woman in a lab coat came out and asked, "Janis?"

Janis put her magazine down and looked up. The woman tilted her head in the direction of the door and Janis rose, went toward it. Cricket stood with her and went to the door.

"You can wait right out here," the woman said. Janis cast a look at her and then nodded. Cricket walked back to her seat.

The noontime news came on and a reporter said that police were investigating recent threats against a Planned Parenthood in Hudson, New York. Other threats were going on around the state, during Right to Life Week. Cricket found her heart beating harder. A policeman was interviewed. Local Planned Parenthoods were on full security and full alert. Patients had no reason to be afraid.

Cricket stood up and walked toward the door her daughter had gone through. She put her hand on the handle and jiggled it. It didn't open. On the other side, she saw two youngish women chatting. One of them looked toward her and frowned. Cricket waved, indicated the closed door. One of the women came to it and opened it.

"I just . . . um . . . is my daughter okay?" Cricket asked.

"Your daughter?"

"Janis. Janis Thompson."

"She's fine," the woman said.

"I want to see her," Cricket said. "Now."

"She's with the counselor," the woman said.

"I want to," Cricket said, her voice rising. "The news—did you know about the threats?" The woman patted Cricket's arm. She looked over Cricket's shoulder at the people in the waiting room. "Why don't you just come in here and we'll find you someone who can tell you about your daughter."

Cricket was led into a room with a desk and a chair that said COUNSELING on the door. The woman closed the door and Cricket sat there, staring at a model of the vagina, ovaries, and uterus. After a while, the door opened and a woman with hard blond hair and a red suit came in and sat down behind the desk.

"Mrs. Thompson?" she asked. Cricket nodded.

"I'm Betty Lark," she said, putting out her hand. Cricket took it.

"I just . . . I want to know if she's okay. I saw this news report about threats to Planned Parenthood and— I wanted to make sure she's okay."

"She's just here for contraceptive counseling, isn't she?" Betty said uncertainly. She was looking at Cricket suspiciously, as if she expected her to leap up with a gun at any minute.

Cricket shook her head, wanting to tell her it's not me. I'm not the enemy. "Yes. But the news. My daughter was in the mall shooting and— I heard the news. About threats."

"Mrs. Thompson, are you okay?"

"I— yes. I'm fine. It's just the threats . . ." She was beginning to realize how crazy she must sound, and she attempted to pull herself back together. She laughed lightly. "I guess I panicked. Wanted to make sure she was okay. I heard this news story . . ."

"I understand," Betty said, nodding sagely. But Cricket could see that she didn't.

"All those people outside," Cricket said. "Are we safe?"

"Safe?"

"Yes. I mean, they're so strange."

"They believe in what they're doing," Betty said, professionally neutral.

"Yes, but they won't hurt my daughter, will they?"

Betty frowned, then her face relaxed as if she understood at last. Cricket wasn't harmful. Just another neurotic mother. They were manageable.

"We have police protection for days like today," Betty said. "Your daughter's safe."

Cricket felt some of the tension in her dissolve. "Oh. Of course. Thank you," she said. "Thank you so much."

"Not at all," Betty said. "Would you like to stay here and wait for . . ."

"Janis. My daughter is Janis."

"Janis."

"Yes. I think so."

"You said she was in the mall shooting?"

Cricket shook her head. "My other daughter. She's not dead. She's getting better."

"It was a horrible thing," Betty said. "And they never caught the killer, did they? Makes you so aware of how fragile life is, doesn't it?"

Cricket smiled uncomfortably. She didn't want to talk about this. Then, she thought of something. "What would you do if you were going to live as if you only had a year to live?"

Betty blinked. "What?"

Cricket wondered why she always had to ask this question more than once. People didn't seem capable of hearing it the first time around. "If you were going to live as if you only had a year to live, what would you do?" she asked again.

"You mean, anything I wanted?"

"Yes. Anything."

Betty chewed at her lower lip, rubbing away some of the pinkish lipstick with her teeth. Then, her neutral eyes brightened and she leaned across the desk, closer to Cricket.

"I'd get a gun and shoot all those people outside," she said. "Then I'd know I'd done something good with my life. I could die at peace."

No, Cricket almost said. She had it wrong. Not that you only have a year to live. That's not it. But the pleasure in Betty's eyes stopped her. She nodded. She stood up.

"I'll go and wait outside," she said.

It wasn't much longer before Janis emerged with a bag full of condoms and a diaphragm, and a handful of brochures about AIDS and pregnancy prevention. Cricket didn't stop to talk to anyone on the way to the car. She just got in and drove away, and breathed with relief as the building receded behind them.

"Sure you're okay?" she asked Janis.

"I'm fine, Mother," Janis said. "They didn't *do* anything to me."

They rode in silence. Cricket tried to think of a good way to phrase the question she wanted to ask, then decided to just ask it. "Janis, why didn't you use birth control before?"

Janis shrugged.

"Don't they tell you about it at school? About using condoms?"

Janis turned toward the window and mumbled something.

"What?"

"He said he doesn't like them. Taking a shower with a raincoat or something."

"But what about . . ." Cricket started to ask, then stopped. What about you, she was going to say. Why did you let him place his convenience above your safety?

"Honey," Cricket said, "you don't have to please him all the time for him to love you. Really, the more he sees you take care of yourself, the more he'll take care of you."

Janis snorted, sounding like her father. "Yeah," she said, "right."

Hot shame filled Cricket's blood. Of course Janis wouldn't believe her. Why should she when everything Cricket did taught her otherwise. No matter that she was a working woman who paid her own bills and drove her own car and had her own checking account, she taught Janis that the needs of others came first. How could she possibly undo that learning? What words would shift the behavior Janis had observed in her mother all her life?

"You don't have to do what he wants. You know that, don't you?"

"Jesus, Mother," Janis said angrily. "I mean, can't you just leave it alone?"

"It's important, Janis."

"I don't want to talk about it anymore," she said, her voice rising in volume and pitch. "Don't you *get* it?"

Cricket took a deep breath and silently counted to ten. She had to talk to Janis. She had to be her mother, remember that she was the adult, and Janis still a child, really. Still her child, at any rate. "I know you're angry at me," she said calmly. "I get that. I just don't know why."

"Yes, you do know," Janis said, slapping her hand against the dashboard to emphasize her words. "I told you. I told you. You just didn't listen."

"Honey, don't," Cricket said, reaching toward her, then pulling back as Janis waved her away.

"You talk to me," Janis said. "You just keep talking to me like it's all gonna get better. And it's not. It's too late for that. It's just a fantasy, and I can't stand it. Any of it."

"Any of what?" Cricket asked. She wanted to pull over and talk quietly, not have to worry about driving, but she couldn't see a parking place.

"You know what," Janis insisted.

"I don't," Cricket said, wanting to cry, but not wanting to let Janis see her cry. She had to keep it together. This was important.

Janis brought her hands up to her face and pressed them into her eyes, groaning loudly.

"What?" Cricket asked. "What is it?"

Janis let her hands drop into her lap. "You *remind* me," she said. Cricket let the words sink in. "I remind you?" she asked.

"About Grace. You remind me about Grace. All the time. Whenever I see you. When we sit down to eat and she's not there. When you ask me about *Buffy the Vampire Slayer.* When you talk about getting music for her, like she can hear it. When you go to the hospital. When you come home. You *remind* me."

"That she's sick? But . . . I can't do anything about that," Cricket said. "And . . . and she'll get well. You know it just takes time. You know—"

"I know you're the only one who believes that anymore," Janis cut in. "Aunt Peggy doesn't. Daddy doesn't. You don't know what he's doing, but I do. I know. I'm not stupid or blind. And I hear them talking. They *talk* about you, and it all *reminds* me."

Something like fire burned the inside of Cricket's veins. What did Janis mean? What was Jim doing? What was he saying that Janis heard and couldn't say? Cricket felt as if she was going to faint. She wanted to pull the car over and sit with her head on the steering wheel and make all this go away. Just make it go away.

But she was the adult. She had to be the mother. Had to help, somehow.

"I know you don't want to think about it," she temporized. "I don't want to, either. You just want everything to be like it was. So do I. It's horrible, what happened to her. Everything reminds me, too, and I just want her back. I know that."

"That's not it," Janis said, shouting now, the way she used to when she was little and would wake from a bad dream, calling out her distress to everyone in the house, waking them all. "It's not Grace. It's me. It's *me.*"

Cricket heard the words, but couldn't get them to make sense. "You?" she asked. "You?"

"*I'm* supposed to be in the hospital. Not Grace. Me. I was supposed to be there. It's me. It's *me.* Every time I see you, it reminds me that it's supposed to be me."

Janis drew in a ragged, sobbing breath.

Cricket felt a sense of keen understanding, piercing as knives. She remembered once when the girls were in grade school, Janis had gone ice-skating with Grace, and Grace had fallen, cut her chin on the ice and needed five stitches. In the rush to get to the emergency room, Janis was largely ignored, but when they returned from the hospital, Cricket had found her in her room, sobbing hysterically.

"I pushed her," Janis said. "I pushed her."

"Why?" Cricket asked. "Were you mad at her for something?"

"No," Janis said, angry in her tears. "She wanted me to push her across the ice. So I pushed her, and she fell."

No matter how many times Cricket reassured her that it was an accident, Janis was inconsolable about her part in it. Cricket was shocked. Until then, she hadn't realized how seriously Janis took things, under her dramatic bravado. She demanded as much of herself as she did of the world, and that was a lot.

Only Grace coming in to the room to laugh and show off her bandage dried Janis's tears. But Grace couldn't do that now. And all Cricket had were words, which seemed totally inadequate to the task.

"Janis," she said softly, "it's not you. You're not supposed to be there. I don't want you to be there."

"You'd rather it was me than Grace," Janis shot back.

"No," Cricket said. "No. That's not true."

"Yeah? And if you had a choice? Which one would you pick?"

"I'd shoot myself," Cricket said quickly, wanting to knock on wood or cross herself to ward off the hex of words like that. Janis said nothing.

"Do you believe me?" Cricket asked, and Janis didn't answer. "Do you?"

Janis mumbled something.

"What?" Cricket asked.

"It should've been me," Janis said distinctly, and then was still, her face turned back to the window.

They were almost home, Cricket thought. Almost home and then she could stop the car, talk to Janis reasonably. If Cricket could talk to her quietly, and in stillness, she'd understand. It would just take time. That was all. She drove slowly, carefully, not looking at Janis, not letting herself cry.

When they got to the house, Janis went up to her room and shut the door hard.

Cricket started to follow, then stopped and stood in the middle of the living room, waiting for something to happen. Waiting for something to tell her what to do. Nothing happened. She was told nothing.

She climbed the stairs to Janis's room and knocked softly on the door. A muffled voice on the other side told her to go away.

"Janis, I just want you to know that I love you. That's all. I love you."

The muffled voice said something Cricket couldn't hear, and was still.

Cricket sighed. She wanted her words to change Janis's feelings. To make her feel better, or at least feel bad in a different way. Cricket went to her room and lay down on the bed. She stared up at the ceiling, waiting for what might happen next. She thought about cooking supper, but couldn't make herself get up. She dozed on and off, the way she did in the hospital. When she opened her eyes around midnight, she looked at the pillow next to her and saw that Jim wasn't there.

She got up and walked through the house, but he wasn't there. It was midnight, and he wasn't home. She was tempted to call Peggy. To talk to her? To see if she was home? She didn't know. She no longer wanted to know her own mind. Clearly, she didn't know her husband's, or her sister's. The sense that she understood other people, their motives and probable actions, was an illusion. She knew nothing about anyone, including herself.

Cricket went back to bed.

She did not care, she told herself. She did not care. It was all too complicated. She could not care anymore.

Jim came home some time between midnight and morning. Cricket heard him grunt as he took off his shoes, the way he always did. She thought about asking him where he'd been, but instead she pretended she was asleep. When she woke the next morning, he was already gone, and so was Janis. Cricket got dressed and made coffee and left the house alone.

On her way to the hospital, she stopped at the bookstore to pick some books on grief and healing for Janis. She could just leave them on the table for her, and the books would explain that it wasn't her fault. And Janis might listen to the books better than she'd listen to her mother right now.

Near the self-help section was a table with flyers of various kinds. She picked up one for "An Adventure in Consciousness" workshop. The workshop leaders, it said, were recently requested to ramp up the energies on Mother Earth, and release new information on how to live in that State of Being called Unconditional Love by activating DNA strands. They had worked with various Angelic Beings, who came here to help the Ascension process on earth.

She knew it was ridiculous, but part of her yearned to be in the presence of people who believed in something strongly enough to make a flyer about it. Or to meet someone who still believed in angels, and spoke to them.

As she was reading, she became aware of a shallow, stertorous breathing over her left shoulder. She waited to see if it would go away. It didn't, and she couldn't walk forward because a table was directly in front of her. She turned around.

"Oh," she said. "Oh, hello."

It was the old man from the grocery store, wearing what appeared to be the same overalls. She was incredibly happy to see him, as if his presence boded well, though she didn't know why.

Maybe because he came from a day before the horror began, and reminded her that such a time still existed.

"Good to see you," he said, smiling. "That's an interesting bit of reading there."

She held up the paper. "This? Well, I guess it is."

"Myself, I've never dealt with the Angelic Beings or the Ascended Masters. Nor have I ever had a Walk-In. Seems damn uncomfortable if you ask me."

"A walk-in?" she asked.

He pointed to a paragraph explaining the difference between a Walk-In, which sounded like possession, and Occupation, which required your consent. It sounded like the difference between sex and rape, but she didn't think it would be polite to say so.

"I see," she said. "How have you been?"

He blinked his sharp blue eyes at her, and she noticed they looked distant and rheumy.

"Fine," he said. "Just fine. And you?"

"Oh," she said, "you know. It's been very difficult with the . . . the incident at the mall. My daughter is, well, she's in the hospital still. It's very difficult." She felt for some reason that explaining it to him would help. As if he really could intercede for her on some celestial plane. "And it's funny, but I keep thinking about what you said."

"Yes?" he asked. "You do?"

"I do. I keep thinking maybe I should do it. I mean, live as if I only had a year."

"Yes," he said. "What a good idea for you."

He was silent, ruminating into his beard, eyes blank and hollow.

"How's your wife?" Cricket asked. "Is she with you tonight?"

"My wife," he repeated, and he shook his head from side to side slowly. "No. I don't feel her presence tonight. Not tonight. Not here."

Her presence. Cricket tried to interpret, but before she could, he explained.

"She's gone on ahead," he said. "Yes. She couldn't wait. I hear from her occasionally. But mostly, she's gone."

"I'm sorry," Cricket said. "I'm so sorry to hear that."

"Yes," he said, then his face brightened. He looked at her directly, and put a hand on her shoulder. "I have something for you."

He dug into the chest pocket of his overalls. "I brought it with me, thinking I would run into someone who needed it, and I was right."

He pulled out a tape and handed it to her. It was labeled, "Nordic Spacepeople Journals."

"But you already . . ." Cricket started to say, and then realized he had no idea who she was, had no memory of having met her before. He patted her shoulder.

"Thank you," she said, putting the tape in her purse. "I think . . . I guess I better go now."

She backed away from him as he stood, nodding at nothing, eyes hollow and blank. When she couldn't stand it anymore, she turned around and bolted from the store.

DREAM #5

jim's dream

Jim didn't dream very often, but when he did, his dreams were pleasurable. He dreamt of floating in quiet places while soft hands stroked him, and everything was fine without him having to do a thing about it. Or sometimes he dreamt of Cricket holding him, rocking him as if he were a baby. These dreams would fade into dreams of his mother, and he a child suckling at her breast.

He never told Cricket about them, though she asked about his dreams all the time. They weren't the kind of dreams you wanted to tell your wife, whom you were supposed to protect and support and seduce into sex. Instead, he would laugh and say, "I dreamt about you. The way you looked the first time I took you out to dinner, with that pretty pink dress you used to have."

She would smile, and ask no more questions, though clearly she knew he wasn't telling the truth. But he said to her once that he'd decided to marry her on that first dinner date because she looked like a dream come true, standing in the front hall of her mother's house, wearing something pink and frothy, her smile radiant. He had fallen in love with her smile, he said, and wanted to be able to see it every day.

And if the dream was a lie, she knew that was true. He'd married her because he wanted that smile near him every day. It felt like his reward for working at jobs he didn't necessarily like, and worrying about bills he didn't generate, and raising up two daughters whom he loved, but who somehow didn't feel like a part of him the way he thought children were supposed to. It would have been different, he supposed, if he had sons, which was another dream he had sometimes, that he was holding a baby in his arms who was a son. In these dreams, he felt a pure elation, as if he'd won a great victory and the baby he held was his ally in the winning. But then in the dream something always went wrong. He'd look down and see that the baby was horribly disfigured—a great purple birthmark across his face, or his entire body covered with wiry black hair. Or the baby would scream with hunger, but when he tried to feed it, he remembered he had no breasts. Or sometimes Cricket would appear to take it away, and it would become a baby girl.

He didn't tell Cricket about these dreams, either. If he told her, she'd try to figure it out, and God only knew what she might come up with. Wish fulfillment, alternate lives, archetypal fears—it could go anywhere. Women were like that, he thought. They made things complicated, when really things were very, very simple.

Not that he had anything against her analyzing dreams. She enjoyed it and so did their daughters, though Janis seemed to like it less than Grace. Janis was always more like him, though. At least, that's what Cricket said. He couldn't really tell. He thought it was probably easier for a mother to tell these things.

Not that he didn't love his daughters. He would die for them. He would kill for them. Every day he went to work so they could have a nice house, go to a good school, someday go to the right colleges. Sometimes, when they were very young and they all sat at the table together, Cricket feeding Grace with a funny little spoon and Janis patting her hands in a bowl of cut-up vegetables, his heart filled with a feeling for his family that made him have to leave the room in order to steady himself. Sometimes, he thought it would make him cry for no reason.

No, he obviously loved his daughters, even if they sometimes seemed like creatures from another planet, just visiting, disconnected from him in a way that they weren't disconnected from their mother. Still, he loved them. He just didn't always understand them. But he didn't think he had to. That was more Cricket's job.

Since Grace was hurt, he'd realized the truth of that even more. He sometimes lay awake at night, revisiting the shooting in his head, how it would have been different if he was there. He would have thrown himself in front of Grace, taken the bullet for her. She would have lived, and known that her father had died to save her.

He could imagine his funeral after that. He would have been a hero. Cricket would have grieved for him, the hero who saved her little girl. It would have been something to see, even if he wouldn't be there to see it.

But it hadn't happened that way. He was playing golf when she was shot. And while Cricket was desperately searching for her, he was drinking and watching a young woman who was not much older than Janis take her clothes off and caress her breasts in front of howling men.

Of course there was nothing shameful in that. A stag party was a stag party, after all. It was just tough for him to think about it in those terms. If his daughter hadn't been hurt, he wouldn't have a qualm about it. He would have drunk his fill, given the girl some money, gone home and danced Cricket off to bed for some good sex. But now he had to remember that while his daughter was in the hospital, he was stuffing a twenty down a girl's lace panties. For the rest of his life, he'd remember it that way.

A few nights ago, he'd dreamt that a stripper was lap dancing with him, but when he looked up, he saw Grace, her face shattered and bloody. He woke fighting her off, yelling, "Get off me." When he realized it was just a dream he turned to Cricket to see if he'd woken her, but she wasn't there.

He was angry at Cricket then. Suddenly and completely angry. Angry at her absence, at the way she silently faulted him for not taking better care of his daughter. She never said that, of course, but she felt it. He could tell by the way she looked at him and by the soft tone of voice she used when she asked him to come to the hospital and stay. He was angry at her that he couldn't do that. Angry at her for expecting him to fix what he couldn't, angry at her for making him fall in love with her so long ago, promising him a life they didn't have now. He resented that they'd had kids before he got his M.B.A., resented that he never got to start his own business because it was more important to take care of her and the children. She could have gotten a better job. She could have supported him while he started something good.

And sometimes, just sometimes, he wished Grace had either woken up right away, or died on the operating table. This in between was a kind of living hell, holding them all in suspended animation with her, unable to live, unable to grieve. And he couldn't tell anyone that, because what would they think if he wished his daughter dead? Good fathers didn't do that. Not under any circumstances.

All of this swept over him in an instant when he woke up from a bloody dream about his daughter and found that his wife wasn't there. Then, just as quickly, he closed it down. Those were strange and unreasonable feelings. He didn't have to feel them.

But he knew his life was falling apart, going places he never imagined it would, and he had no map to guide himself with. He was lost. So much so that when Bert, a computer programmer at work, asked him how he was holding up, he actually talked about it.

Things were bad, he admitted. He wasn't feeling good about things.

Bert didn't press. He didn't ask for particulars. He just said,

"It's tough. Bad enough to have this happen to your kid, but then something happens with a kid, the mother just goes and stays with them, right? No way we can compete. Not that we want it any other way, but it's tough. Leaves you out in the cold."

Jim nodded. Bert was speaking some basic truths.

"Maybe you ought to find a little interim relief," Bert suggested.

Jim didn't know what he meant at first, then he caught on. "You mean, another woman?"

"That's it," Bert said. "Take the pressure off, right? Just make sure it's not someone who wants a permanent thing. You don't want to mess anything up for when things go back to normal. But if you find some relief, just for now, you'll feel better, and that'd make it easier on your wife, in the long run."

Jim thanked him. It seemed like good advice. Not that he was sure he'd take it. He'd never had an affair. Wasn't sure he knew how to go about it. Go to a bar? A whorehouse? He didn't really want to sleep with a strange woman and risk diseases, but he didn't know anyone offhand who would suit the circumstances.

When he tried to imagine it, the only thing that came to mind was a moment in the hospital, when Cricket had left to go find Grace and he had turned to put his face in his hands, uncertain that he was ready to face seeing her so badly hurt. Then, unexpectedly, Peggy was there holding him, her arms around him, her breasts soft and full against him. In spite of himself, he'd felt a stirring at her touch. He'd wrapped his arms around her, even kissed her neck. She hadn't pulled away.

Then he remembered that Janis was there, and he let go.

A few days later, he came home and found Peggy there making supper. She thought it'd be nice for Janis, she said. He thanked her, grabbing her hand, pulling her to him and quickly kissing her. It was a real kiss, too, with his mouth on hers and his hands rubbing her behind. She hadn't said anything about it one way or the other, not objecting and not offering to go further, but she hadn't stopped it either.

He shook his head. Peggy was Cricket's sister. She wouldn't. He couldn't. Could he? But in these extreme circumstances, who would blame him for considering it? Who would blame her? In a weird way, they were both taking care of Cricket, making sure everyone got what they needed while she did what she had to do. He could see it that way, especially since just thinking about it made him less angry at her, and at the whole damn mess. He didn't have to lie in bed alone and boil about the things he couldn't control. There were things he could do to feel better. Things that didn't have to hurt anybody, if it was all managed well, and he was a good manager.

With that, he rolled over and fell asleep, to dream of nothing, dark and soft.

nine

$\mathcal{J}$ *Saturday morning,* Cricket looked out of the hospital window to see that it was raining steadily and insistently. Saturday was one of her at-home nights. That was the deal she'd made with her family.

What family? she wondered, as she put together a bag of things to take home, which would be changed on Sunday for a bag of things to go back to the hospital.

She pressed a hand against Grace's arm, brushed it lightly against her face. "I love you, honey," she whispered. "See you tomorrow."

She left the hospital, and stood outside in the parking lot, feeling the cool rain on her face. She didn't want to go home. If she did, what seemed to be happening there might take shape and become real.

I am lost, she thought. I live between worlds. I am lost.

She would go to the sanctuary first, she decided. She could stay an hour and watch the eagle chick on the monitor, maybe check the seedlings. Then she would go home. By then Jim would have a game and Janis would have rehearsal or friends and everyone could pretend to be their usual selves.

But the rain was worse than she thought, and her ride down the road to Pass's house was treacherous, white-knuckle driving through mud and water. To brake was to risk sliding off the road into a ditch. Not to brake around the curves and down the slope was impossible. She wasn't thinking properly. She had forgotten what the rain could do here. Or maybe she didn't want to remember, because if she did, then she'd have nowhere to go.

Pass was standing at the door looking out when she arrived. "I saw you coming down the hill," he said. "Didn't know who'd be crazy enough to try it today."

She looked back at her car, covered with mud, at the road, running with rivulets of water.

"I didn't think," she said.

"Supposed to rain like hell all day," he said. "There's flood warnings along the Schoharie. Better come in before you drown."

She followed him into the house and took off her raincoat and her shoes, and shook the rain out of her hair.

"I was just making some soup," he said.

She padded after him into the kitchen, and sniffed the air. The aroma of herbs in oil, garlic, and tomatoes made her hungry. The sanctuary was the only place where she felt hungry anymore. "Soup?" she asked.

"With all those herbs you planted for me. Sit down. I'll be done in a minute and then it can just simmer."

She took a seat at the kitchen table and watched him work. He moved around the kitchen, deep in his task. She thought it was lovely to watch him, so normal and good to see someone cooking. The rain pattered against the roof, and there was nothing she could do but sit and listen to it. Being lost, she thought, wasn't awful when somebody was cooking and nobody was angry at you. In these circumstances, being lost felt light, and easy, and free.

For the first time in a month, or maybe in her whole life, she felt all those things.

"There's some brochures on the table," Pass said as he worked. "You might find them interesting."

She saw them and picked up the top one. "What is it?" she asked.

"Some stuff I got from the Internet. Brochures for butterfly farms."

She opened one, which offered butterflies for sale to be released at weddings. "Each butterfly is hand fed and exercised prior to being placed in an origami envelope and thermally insulated shipping container, and mailed to your event," she read to him. "How do you exercise a butterfly?"

Pass grinned, and made a motion of someone pushing and pulling small wings with his fingers. "One two three, one two three," he said.

She giggled, then stopped. It was an unfamiliar sound, one that raised immediate guilt. She thought of herself moving Grace's legs up and down. One two three. One two three. She was horrified at herself for laughing. She pressed her hand against her mouth and looked down at the floor. Pass, watching her, stopped smiling. He took two steps to her, and put a hand on her shoulder.

"Jim doesn't believe," she said softly. "He doesn't think she'll get well."

She didn't look at him, and he didn't speak. "Do you?" she asked him.

She felt his hand move on her shoulder. "I can't answer that, Cricket," he said. "I just don't know the answer."

"But you don't think she *won't* get well. I mean, you don't think that's inevitable."

"No," he said tentatively. "I just don't know."

She lifted her face and looked up at him. "Don't you think it's important to believe?"

He closed his eyes, opened them again. "I think there's some things that won't happen unless you believe in them, no matter what anyone says. And there's other things that won't happen no matter how hard you believe in them. I just don't know which one this is."

She stared at him a moment, and saw he was telling her all the truth he knew. She lowered her head. Jim would not rescue her. Pass would not rescue her either. Nobody would. Nobody could.

"I'm sorry," he said softly. He moved a strand of her hair back from her face. She sat very still. He smoothed her hair down. "I'm really sorry," he said. Then he moved away from her and back to the stove.

"The soup can cook itself now," he said, "Let's go check the greenhouses."

The rain pelted at Cricket's plastic raincoat and ran off the hood into her eyes. She had to keep shaking her head like a dog to see the raised-bed plantings they'd put out in the last few weeks. Looking at them, Cricket saw they could have a disaster on their hands. The ground was thick with too much water, and the roots could drown, the young plants be washed away. All her hours of tender nurture would disappear in an abundance of rain.

"Hell," Pass said, needing to raise his voice above the pounding rain. "What'll we do?"

"We need plastic," Cricket shouted back. "A lot of it."

They hunted through the sheds and found as much as they could, then collected stakes to create little plastic houses over the seedlings. It wouldn't help the groundwater, but it would keep them from getting further saturated and pounded into the earth. If it was sunny tomorrow, or at least dry, Cricket thought, they'd be okay.

They worked in silence, the rain making talk an effort. It got in their eyes and made them slip as they walked. Once Cricket almost came down right on her face, but Pass put an arm out in time and grabbed her, lifted her back to her feet.

"Okay?" he asked.

"Fine. Thanks."

He didn't let go of her arm immediately, and she stood trying to see him, with water running into her eyes. "What're you doing?" she asked. "What's happening?" She felt him release her, and they went back to work.

They had all but one plot covered when Pass dropped his end of the plastic and said, "Shit," very loudly.

Cricket looked up and saw, through the rain, that one of the young hawks was out.

"How the hell did that happen?"

The hawk had a broken wing that Pass had splinted, hoping to give it a full recovery. It couldn't fly away, but it could hobble into the woods and be lost, attacked and eaten. They had to get it back.

"Here"—he motioned to Cricket—"go around back. If he comes to you, move him to me."

"But," she started to protest, and then stopped when she saw he hadn't heard her, was already moving. She was afraid of the big birds, she wanted to say. She didn't work with them. Their wing-spread was so big, and their beaks and talons too strong. She couldn't handle them. But he was motioning her to go. She made her way around the bird. Pass stood in front of it, waiting for her to scare it toward him, but it turned and started hopping toward her.

"Shoo," she said, making grand flailing motions with her arms. "Shoo. Go away."

The hawk lifted its head and gave its piercing cry, which seemed to strike somewhere deep inside her. It was the sound of sky, and wind. Of open places, and of being alone. It terrified her. She put her hands to her throat and stood there. It hopped toward her.

She stood very still, not listening to Pass yell to her to do something. The hawk stopped at her feet. It stared up at her, and she stared back, looking at its golden eyes, and the way the pupils dilated as it shifted focus to her. She found herself lifting her hand, reaching down, slowly, very slowly, touching it on the head. "Oh," she whispered. "Oh."

Then Pass was in front of her, too. He made a successful grab for the bird and wrapped his arms around it. "Can you finish the plants?" he yelled to Cricket over the sound of wind and rain. "I gotta get her in, see what happened."

She nodded. He took the bird, still struggling, back around to where the cages were. She returned to the pea patch and finished putting up the plastic.

When Cricket got back inside, Pass was already there to take her coat and shake it out. "You're soaked through. I'll have to get you some other clothes," he said, shaking his head like a mother hen. "Anyway, I got the hawk's cage taken care of for now. Looks like a raccoon tried to get it. Bit through the wire. I'll have to put some glass around the bottom."

Cricket said, "I better call home. Jim will be waiting for me. I'm late."

Pass shook his head. "You're not late," he said.

"What?"

"You aren't going anywhere." He pointed out the window toward the road, which ran with water, a small river.

Cricket felt panic rise in her. She was trapped. She couldn't go home.

"If I could make it up your road, I could get out," she said.

"You can't make it up my road," Pass said, and she was angry at him, as if he were the enemy, trapping her here.

"It's okay," he said. "You'll be okay here. You can have my room and I'll sleep on the couch. Or if you'd rather, you can have the couch. Tomorrow'll be better, probably."

"I can't," she said. "I can't."

She walked to where her coat was and put it on, pulled on her boots. Pass came up behind her, put his hand on her shoulder, said things she didn't hear. She had to go. Had to go. "Grace," she said to him. "Grace."

"It's okay," he said. "It's Saturday. You don't go to the hospital on Saturday. Right?"

She was surprised he knew. She didn't remember telling him. But that wasn't the point. If she was home and Grace needed her, she could get there. If she was trapped here, she couldn't.

"I have to go," she said.

"Cricket," he said, "you can't. You can't beat nature. You'll be killed trying."

"I *have* to," she insisted, and pulled away, but he held on to her arm.

"No," he said. "You will not. You won't go out there and get killed, you hear?" he said, his hand wrapped around her arm, his eyes holding her gaze.

She whirled on him, then drew in breath, short and hard. His face was smooth and quiet, but intently focused on hers. It was a look she recognized immediately. She'd seen it in the eyes of the hawk when it regarded her. And she'd seen it on her own face, catching sight of it in the mirror when she worked on Grace's legs, all her will focused on the singular purpose of making Grace well. He willed her to safety. Willed her to stay.

"I can't go?" she asked.

"Too risky," he noted, his face relaxing as he released her arm. "Really, Cricket."

Her shoulders relaxed. She relinquished the fight, a little relieved at having the decision removed from her hands. "I'll call Jim," she said. "I have to let him know."

"Okay," he said as she left the room. "Tell him you're safe."

The phone at her house rang, and she heard Jim's voice saying a muffled "Hullo?" In the background, the television blared. A Bud Light commercial. He must be watching baseball.

"Jim, hi. It's me."

"Hey. What's up?"

"I stopped at the sanctuary on the way home," she said. "And it's raining hard."

"Yeah. Coming down like crazy here, too."

"Yes. Jim, the road's washed out. I can't get home."

There was a silence. "Hell," he said. "He should've caught that. It was right in his glove."

"Jim," she said again. "Did you hear me?"

"Yeah. You can't get home. So I'll see you later?"

"No, Jim," she said. "I can't get home until the rain stops and some of this dries up. Probably tomorrow, if it lets up."

"Tomorrow? One of the few nights you're supposed to be home and you're staying there? That's just great."

She paused. He sounded almost smug, as if he enjoyed her doing something wrong. She thought about asking him where he was the last time she was home. What or who kept him away until after midnight?

"I'd come home if I could. *I* don't have a choice," she said, emphasizing the pronoun. Jim was silent.

"I want you to go to the hospital tonight," she said.

"Why? Nobody's supposed to be there tonight."

"I know. I just— I'm stuck here, Jim. It makes me nervous. I'd feel better if you just stopped in. Or get Peggy to go. She'll go."

"Cricket," he said, and then was quiet.

"Play her some of the tapes. Tell her where I am. Tell her I'm not that far away."

"When will you get home?" Jim asked.

"If the rain stops, tomorrow later in the morning, or early in the afternoon."

"I guess I'll see you then."

"Kiss Grace for me," she said. "Tell Janis what happened, and she can call me here if she wants anything."

She went back into the living room, where Pass was standing at the door, helping his brother take off his raincoat. Law stood like a tree, his eyes distant, face soft and almost smiling, hair matted and wet, while Pass struggled with the zipper, which had gotten stuck.

Cricket remembered similar moments with her daughters when they were small and got stuck in jackets or snowsuits. Law was much more patient than her daughters had been. They would scream to be released as if they were trapped inside a collapsed coal mine. Law just stood, smiling at whatever it was he saw, waiting. Pass talked to him as he worked, asking where he'd been, didn't he know enough to come in from the rain, wasn't he starving? His voice was a soft drawl, more of the South in it than when he talked to Cricket.

"I think I got it, buddy," Pass said at last, and eased the zipper down. "There it is," he said. "We got it now. Oh— wait. You got a leaf on you."

Pass licked his thumb and wiped it under Law's eye, removing a piece of leaf and the dirt that adhered to it. Law smiled, and nodded, then laughed, an odd, guttural sound.

Cricket had never seen a man tend to someone in that way. She felt warmth move through her, spiraling from her belly to the surface of her skin, twining like the small dance of fire into her arms and legs and hands and face.

"You go on ahead, now," Pass said. "You can watch TV. And there's soup and a sandwich for you in the kitchen."

Law left the room. Pass watched him go, then turned to Cricket. He looked as if he was going to say something. Something like Are you hungry? or Everything okay at home? But the words stopped before they left his mouth.

He said nothing, but his eyes asked questions. Now?

Cricket walked toward him, her body a wave of warmth in motion. Now, her eyes answered. Now.

She stood in front of him, looking up. He lifted his hand to her face.

"I want to kiss you," he said.

Cricket had a brief moment of fear. It had been so long since she kissed a man who wasn't Jim. She might not remember how. She nodded anyway. He pulled her to him, and his mouth was on hers, tender and searching. He was tasting her, she thought, the way someone who loves wine tastes it. It felt very good. Tender and searching, like the tide licking at her toes. Like standing in clear blue water that was warm. Like kissing. She reached her hand around the back of his neck and kissed him back until he broke away and held her face in his hands.

"Your green eye is gold," she said, reaching a hand up to touch his cheek.

"I want you naked," he said. "I want you," and he took her hand, led her up the stairs to his room.

When he opened the door, she noticed that it was warm and dark, cavelike, with russet covers on the bed and his bureau strewn with feathers and bones. She was looking around when she felt him behind her, tugging at her shirt, pulling it up over her head. Then he struggled briefly with her bra, until she reached back and got it undone, undressing herself while he took off his own clothes. She stood in front of him with nothing on, trying not to cover herself with her hands, feeling self-conscious about whether her behind was sagging or her belly not firm enough, if her breasts were shaped wrong or her legs too thin.

He stared at her for what seemed a long time, and she was about to cover herself with her hands when he pulled her close and smoothed her skin with his hands. His skin was silky and smooth to her touch. She never imagined he'd have such smooth skin, skin that would feel so good under her fingers. She stroked his back, his belly, his legs, her hand finding its way to his erect penis and stroking that, feeling how hard and long it was as he moaned under her touch.

"I want to fuck you," he whispered into her hair, and the word, which Jim never used except in anger, and which usually repulsed her, now sent a thrill through her. That's what she wanted. Something that simple. To fuck.

She turned toward the bed and he was behind her immediately, close against her back. She gasped and leaned over, her hand grabbing for the side of the bed. His hand smoothed the wetness between her legs.

"So nice," he whispered. "So nice."

He pressed himself into her, and she lost all words, all thought, becoming pure sensation that started in her groin and radiated out to the rest of her in all directions. He huddled over her back, one arm wrapped around her holding her close, the other arm at her hip, guiding the rhythm of her movements with his.

"Pass," she whispered, "I'm coming. Pass, hold me."

His grip on her tightened and she came, the pulse of contraction and expansion rocking her, making it impossible to stand. She collapsed onto the bed with him still inside her. He pulled out and turned her onto her back, stroked her face, his eyes open and holding her to him. "That's good, baby. That's so good," he crooned, and he entered her this way, now moving in and out of her slowly, his eyes open and his hand on her face, watching her as she felt her body convulse again, as if it held years of orgasms just waiting to emerge from her, just waiting to shake her body in this way.

"Pass," she cried, "don't let me go."

"Never," he whispered back. "Never let you go."

And in spite of all she knew about the temporary nature of life, in spite of all she knew about men in malls with guns and marriages that didn't last and dreams that died slowly or were smashed on the ground, she believed him.

When they next looked at the clock, more than three hours had passed. It was dark, and still raining, though not as hard as before.

"Better go check on Law," Pass said. "Want some soup?"

She was hungry, she realized. Very hungry. "My clothes," she said.

"I know. Wear this." He gave her a blue terry cloth robe that was too big, and they went downstairs and found Law in front of the TV, asleep. Pass woke him and told him to go on to bed now and he went, silent and seemingly unaware of her presence. They put their wet clothes in the dryer, heated the soup and ate it with thick chunks of bread and cheese. It tasted better than anything she'd ever eaten.

Pass kept his eyes trained on her as they ate, as if he was afraid to stop looking. When she was done, she put her bowl in the sink and he was standing behind her, pressing into her, then turning her around so that she felt her back pushed into the lip of the counter.

"Again," he said. "Again."

He opened her robe and his hands ran over her belly, her groin, then pressed between her legs where she was already wet, wanting him again. Again. Again.

"Not here," she whispered. "Your brother."

"He won't wake," Pass said. "He never does. He likes his dreams too much."

Cricket held that thought in the quiet dark, then tilted her head as if listening for something—for music or for dreams, or something that could be heard only here, in this night.

"What does he dream?" she asked.

There was a long pause. "He dreams he can fly," Pass said. "That's what he tells me."

By the time they returned to the bed and slept, her breasts against his back, his skin soft and silky against hers, it was very late. The darkness seemed absolute as she closed her eyes, and for the first time in weeks, her sleep wasn't disturbed by her thoughts or the sounds of the hospital, which had no real night at all. She slept, fully and deeply.

The next she knew, her eyes were open to a darkness that was softer, and she was on her back and he had taken her hand and moved it down between his legs where he was hard and ready for her. She stroked his penis, enjoying the feel of it in her hand. He rolled over and on top of her, kissed her mouth, her neck. Put his mouth over her breast and took the nipple between his lips, sucking on it, his hand moving between her legs and stroking her.

It was still dark, but as he climbed on top of her and in her, the darkness began to give. She could see his eyes, golden in the dim light, watching her, seeing her, wanting to know her pleasure. "Come, baby," he said. "Come for me."

She did, waves of pleasure washing through her, clinging to him as he murmured, "Nice. So nice. So nice."

She felt full of water, like the sky, and all of it pouring out of her, the way it had when she went into labor and her water broke.

We are birthing each other, she thought. Birthing each other into water and morning, emerging from the darkness into each other, into the flood, into the day.

The morning came up sunny and warm. At some point in the night, the rain had stopped and enough water had run off the road to let her through.

"Will you be okay?" Pass asked her as she dressed. "I mean, with your . . . with Jim and everything?"

She smoothed her shirt over her skin and paused. "I don't know," she said. "I don't know what any of it means."

He sat on the bed, his hands on his knees, looking thoughtful. "Maybe it's like dreams," he said. "Maybe you shouldn't try to figure out what it means. You should just let it happen, and see where it wants to go."

"Maybe," she said uncertainly, and continued dressing.

He offered her breakfast but she declined, anxious to get home and then to the hospital. They walked to her car and stood next to it, awkward because saying good-bye was different now.

"Do you want me to call you?" he asked.

She thought about it. "No. I think . . . you better not."

He brushed the skin of her face with his hand. "I love you," he said.

She shook her head. "You can't. You shouldn't."

"I do," he said.

She shifted uncomfortably, pulled her car keys from her jacket pocket and fiddled with them, then was still. "I'm scared," she said.

"Of what?"

"I don't know. Everything. Like everything's falling. Or maybe I'm the one who's falling. Like nightmares where you're falling faster and faster, and you can't stop."

He nodded, and stroked her face. "It's not falling until you hit the ground, Cricket. Up until then, you're flying."

She lifted her eyes and stared up at him. She was falling. Flying. Falling. His eyes were green and gold, and she fell into them, or flew through them. She could no longer tell.

"I'll be right here," he said, "between you and the ground."

He kissed her, his sweet hands on her face and his eyes watching her.

She thought they continued to watch her when she got into her car and drove away. She thought that if they could, they would continue to watch her all the way home.

Cricket expected Jim to be sullen and angry when she got home, but when she walked in the front door, she was surprised to see him sitting in the living room chair, his face darker than any she'd ever seen. Apparently, he was angrier than she thought he'd be.

She stood still and waited for him to speak. He didn't.

"I'm home," she said.

"The hospital just called," he told her. "Grace is dead."

t e n

Cricket felt the words like an explosion in her body that separated all her molecules from each other, dispersing them around the room. She watched the explosion occur, viewing it as if she were very far away. This is good, she thought. Soon, I'll be unconscious and I won't feel what just happened.

She wondered if that's what Grace felt like when she was shot. She wondered if that's what it felt like to die. Soon, she knew, it wouldn't matter. One could not sustain a wound like this and survive.

She stood in the living room and watched herself disperse.

"Are you listening?" Jim hissed through his teeth. "Do you hear me?"

Cricket blinked. "Where is she?" she asked.

Jim's mouth dropped open. "Where is she? Where *is* she?" He stood up and grabbed Cricket's shoulders, shook her. "She's at the *morgue*. What the hell is wrong with you? She's dead, and she's at the *morgue.*"

He shook her again and it didn't matter, and then Janis came

164

into the room and he turned and looked at her, looked at his own hands, and he collapsed onto Cricket's shoulder, sobbing.

Cricket stroked his head, put an arm around him. Looking over his shoulder, she said to Janis, "Did he tell you?"

Janis, pale and tense, nodded.

"Did he call Peggy?"

Janis nodded again. "A few minutes ago. The hospital just called. I answered the phone."

Cricket couldn't tell what Janis felt. Horror, or maybe pride at being the one to answer the phone. It was something she'd done, taken responsibility for. Something that made her part of the act.

"You should've told me last night," Cricket murmured into Jim's ear. "If something was wrong, you should've called me."

"Nothing was wrong last night," Jim said, words caught between sobs. "The doctor said nothing was wrong last night."

Cricket's hand paused. "The doctor said?" she asked.

Jim clung to her the way the girls used to do when they knew they'd done something wrong. She recognized this gesture. Submissiveness. One-downing himself for safety.

"Did she open her eyes yesterday or . . . anything like that?" she asked.

Jim muttered something into her shoulder.

"What?" she asked softly.

"I didn't go," he said.

She stroked his head. He didn't go. No. Of course he didn't go. He was angry with her, and this was how he showed it. He wouldn't do what she said. He was angry at her like a child whose mother asks him to start doing chores after years of telling him he didn't have to do a thing. He was angry at her, so he didn't go. Cricket stroked his head. She didn't blame him. Nothing had prepared him for this. He didn't have a clue how to deal with it.

The door opened, and she twisted around to see Peggy standing there, eyes wide with grief and horror.

She wasn't looking at Cricket. She was looking at Jim.

Cricket turned back to Janis, and saw how stiffly Janis stood, her face tight, lips pressed into a thin line of anger, though she couldn't tell who the anger was meant for. It occurred in the briefest of moments, without words, and then the world tilted back in a different direction. Peggy came inside and went directly to Cricket, pushing Jim aside and enveloping her in a hug.

"Oh my God," she said. "Oh my God, oh my God."

None of it matters, Cricket thought. She stroked Peggy's hair, was aware of the difference between the way it felt and the way Jim's hair felt. None of it mattered at all. She was dispersed. She did not exist. This did not matter at all.

When Peggy let her go, Cricket turned back to see that Janis had left the room.

nightmares

When Cricket was a little girl, she had a recurring nightmare of being dead, in a coffin, but conscious of her deadness. In the dream, people would come up to the coffin and touch her, say things about her. "Look how pale she is," someone would say. A hand would lift her arm and let it fall. "Her skin is so smooth," a voice would say. Her body felt cold and rubbery when it was touched.

All the while, she would be aware that they were going to bury her soon. She couldn't talk, couldn't move, couldn't see anything, but she knew she was about to be buried and inside she was screaming, screaming for someone to notice that she was still alive. When she woke, she would be unable to move for some time.

She usually told her father about her dreams, but she never told him this one. It was too scary. She was afraid of what it meant. Eventually, she just stopped having it, not even remembering it until Jim told her about Grace. Then, for a moment, the horror of it, the feel of cold and rubbery flesh, swept over her. She didn't want to feel that, so as soon as she could, she walked out of the living room and went into Grace's bedroom. She sat on her bed and stared at her peach-and-white curtains, at the stuff still on top of her bureau—barrettes and a comb and a box of hair bands. Her fish, which Janis had continued to feed.

Her old nightmare was coming true, she thought, but reversed. Now she wasn't alive, but people thought she was. She no longer existed, and everyone treated her as if she did.

Somebody knocked softly on Grace's door, and Cricket said, "Come in."

It was Peggy. "Cricket, you want to stay in here?"

Cricket nodded, not looking at her. How could she look at her, when she wasn't alive? If she did, she probably wouldn't see her.

"Okay. Listen, honey, we'll take care of all the arrangements. Okay?"

That's the way she said it, all the arrangements, making it sound like a wedding or a vacation. Jim called the morgue and had Grace's body sent to the funeral home. Peggy called the cemetery and secured a plot. He called Reverend Braxton to perform the services, and they stayed on the phone for a long time.

All Cricket did was sit on the bed thinking nothing because people who don't exist don't have to think. Periodically, Jim or Peggy would come in to tell her what they'd just done. Periodically, Cricket would think that she should be angry with them, and then decide that dead people didn't feel anger. If she wasn't dead, she'd probably be angry at Jim, though not really at Peggy. Peggy always knew when Cricket was done with a boy.

When Peggy came in the last time, she went to Grace's closet. "I need to get some clothes," she said. "To take to . . . you know. For Grace to wear."

Grace needed clothes. That wasn't Peggy's job. Peggy didn't know what Grace liked to wear. And wasn't Cricket the best person to go to the funeral home, since she wasn't alive? She wondered when people would start to notice. Or maybe people were really quite stupid about knowing who was alive and who wasn't. For instance, she finally realized that the person who shot her daughter was probably dead, and that's why they couldn't find him. He'd probably been dead for a long time, and certainly was dead when he walked into the mall and started shooting. Maybe if everyone had noticed sooner, they could have buried him before he killed anyone.

But nobody noticed. People were stupid about it. Maybe they didn't even know it about themselves, if they were dead or alive.

The edge of a new thought sliced its way into Cricket's mind. If people didn't know who was alive and who was dead, how could they be sure about Grace? Cricket might be the only one who would notice. After all, Grace was her daughter.

"I'll do it," she said.

Peggy hesitated. "Do you think that's a good idea? I mean, you're not . . ."

She didn't finish the sentence. Not alive, she was probably going to say, Cricket thought. "I'll do it," Cricket said definitely.

She picked Grace's favorite shirt—a purple T-shirt with hummingbirds flying in a cluster that looked like a flower about to open, and the jeans she liked best. In spite of Jim's protest, she took them to the funeral home. When she walked inside and was let into the office to meet with the director, she told him, "I'll dress her." Grace wouldn't like it if strange men dressed her. She'd never forgive her mother for letting that happen.

"That's our job, Mrs. Thompson," he said, patting her shoulder.

"No," Cricket said. "It's mine. I'll do it."

He cleared his throat. "It will only upset you," he said, "needlessly."

She gaped at him. She wanted to laugh, and did. His face turned red.

"I'll dress her," Cricket said. "Bring me to her."

He relented with obvious reluctance, bringing Cricket to a room where Grace's body lay under a sheet on a metal table. Before he removed the sheet, he asked, "Are you sure?"

She nodded. She had no fear. Dead people have no fear. They have no need of it. But then she felt her heart pounding in her chest, and thought maybe she wasn't as dead as she thought, or as dead as she'd like to be.

When he pulled the sheet back, her heart settled into normal rhythms. She saw only her daughter, naked and very still. She seemed more naked than she had at the hospital, where she always had a gown or a towel covering part of her. Now she was as naked as the first time she was put into Cricket's hands.

Cricket stroked her arm. It felt cold and rubbery, just the way her arm felt in the nightmares. Yes, she thought. Just like her dreams. And, clearly, Cricket thought, this beautiful almost-woman, almost-child, with her face smooth and calm and pretty as always was not a dead person. She was too beautiful to be dead.

"People make mistakes," she said to nobody. "It happens."

She'd read stories about people being buried alive, and doctors thinking someone was dead when they weren't. There was such a tiny difference between alive and dead. There was breath, and no breath. Heartbeat, and then none. Such a small difference. Such a little thing.

"Excuse me?" the funeral director said.

She turned a smile to him. "She's cold," she said.

The funeral director cleared his throat. "It's necessary, Mrs. Thompson."

"I'm going to dress her," she said, "and then I want her brought home."

The funeral director nodded courteously, but his head stopped midway. "Home?"

"She can't stay here," Cricket said. "She's cold. She'll have to come home."

"We can't . . . Mrs. Thompson, she can't . . ."

She patted his arm. "She needs to be home, where I can watch her."

The funeral director looked over her head, around her, around the room, his face a study in conflict. She was a paying customer, but what was she saying? How could he respond courteously, and sensibly?

"We do provide services for home funerals, Mrs. Thompson, if that's what you'd like," he said after some thought.

"That's it," she said. "That's right. I'll dress her, and you take care of everything else."

He bowed slightly at the hip, and left her alone.

As soon as he was gone, Cricket dressed her daughter, talking to her as she worked. "Don't worry, honey," she said. "People make mistakes. Mom'll take you home."

When Cricket got home and told Jim, he was at first confused, then appalled.

"Home? A funeral in our home? A . . . a casket in our house?"

"It's not a bad thing," Peggy said uncertainly. "Less impersonal."

"Yes," Cricket said. "Exactly."

The last funeral she'd been to was her mother's, five years ago, which was at Craig's Funeral Home. Grace thought the men who opened the doors for them and spoke in deliberately hushed voices were butlers. "Tell the butler I want a drink of water," she whispered to her mother. She was afraid of them, Cricket remembered, though she wasn't afraid to go up to the casket and talk to her grandmother. Grace had hushed Janis at one point, telling her not to wake Grandma up. Janis had rolled her eyes and said, "She's dead. She's not asleep. She died *in* her sleep."

It was a very different funeral than her father's, because everyone felt his life had been tragically cut short, while Cricket's mother had lived her full time. And she died peacefully in her sleep, with the TV still on.

"We'll have it here," Cricket repeated. "Grace would prefer it."

Jim opened his mouth, but Peggy shushed him with a look. "We better move the couch."

"They'll bring the chairs," Cricket said. "They said they would."
"I'll let Reverend Braxton know."

As furniture was being rearranged, Janis came into the room and looked around. "What's going on?" she asked.

Peggy and Jim exchanged glances. Cricket went over to Janis and patted her arm. "It's okay," she said. "We're bringing her home. That's all."

Janis's eyes got big. She made a sound that Cricket couldn't interpret. Then she left the room, and Peggy quickly followed her.

Cricket continued to talk to Grace in her mind, telling her that Janis didn't understand yet, but she would. It would be okay. Sometimes people made mistakes, but it would be okay. Mom would be there.

The next day, neighbors peered out of their houses when they saw the hearse pull up to the house, and bring a coffin into the house. Burly men with arms like slabs of meat brought it and put it where the couch usually went. Cricket looked at them and said, "Open it."

They did as she said. Cricket leaned over the coffin. "Mom's here, honey," she said. "It's okay."

The men left quickly.

Chairs were put into place. Cricket sat between Janis and Jim, Peggy and Pete and their two boys sat next to Jim. Andy and little Pete were still and wide-eyed, made quiet by the specter of death that occurred outside the world of TV. When little Pete put a hand out and she took it, all he said was, "I'm sorry, Aunt Cricket. I mean . . ." He shrugged, and after she patted his hand, took it back from her and sat down next to his brother. She noticed that his voice was cracking when he spoke, but she didn't know if it was from grief, or puberty, or fear.

People came and greeted her and sat down and talked in hushed tones, and drank coffee or soda while they waited for Reverend Braxton to arrive. They said it was horrible. They said they were so sorry. They cried. Cricket kept her eyes on the casket, on Grace, who looked like herself in her pretty shirt, with a lavender scarf around her head and her teddy bear tucked in her arms.

Janis sat stone-faced, looking ahead as hard as Cricket did, which made Cricket wonder if she had figured out what was happening. She wanted to test her on this, so at one point, she took her hand and said, "Honey, people make mistakes. It happens."

Janis stared at her in horror, then her face crumpled into sorrow and tears. Cricket put an arm around her, drew her close. Janis let herself be drawn, pressing her face into Cricket's shoulder. Cricket wanted to tell her it would be okay, but she could see that Janis didn't understand. Didn't know after all. But Janis would soon see that everything was fine.

Grace's classmates came all in a group. They approached Cricket slowly and uncertainly, like birds who had lost their flocking pattern. Debbie and Karen were there. Debbie handed her a red rose.

"Hi, sweetie," Cricket said. She put a hand on her face and patted it. It was a nice face. She'd fed it enough times to know that.

Karen burst into tears. Cricket put her arms out and drew her close, rocked her, even let herself cry a little. Not because anything was sad, but because Karen was sad, and sad children always made Cricket cry. "I'm sorry, sweetie," she said. "I'm sorry."

Then, a group of Janis's friends showed up, clumsy in grief and in sympathy for the grievers. They shook hands with Jim. Leaned over and kissed Cricket, then huddled around Janis, whispering. There were too many of them to sit up front, so Cricket said to Janis, "Maybe you want to sit with your friends, where you can all be together?"

Janis shook her head stoically. "I'll stay with you and Dad."

"Go on," Cricket said. "It's okay. Really."

They retired to the back of the room, occupying two rows of chairs.

More people came. Sheila and the principal and the guidance

counselor and teachers. People who worked with Jim. Friends, she supposed. There seemed like too many, though. She didn't remember having this many friends. They distracted her from talking to Grace, from watching her. She didn't know when Grace would wake up, though she was such a polite girl, Cricket thought she'd probably wait until they were alone so as not to make a fuss. She had a hard time splitting her focus, though. It was so difficult, she almost missed Pass, almost treated him like one of these other people who were supposed to be friends.

She had his hand, but she was looking around him, at the coffin.

He saw where her gaze went and how it was focused. He squatted down in front of her, ignoring the angry look her husband shot their way. He didn't ask her if she was okay. He didn't offer his condolences. He just looked at her, then back at Grace, then at her.

"Cricket?" he asked.

She started. "Pass?"

"That's right. It's me."

She leaned forward. She could tell Pass. He would understand. He would know. "People make mistakes," she said softly. "You know they do."

His face, old with the knowledge of pain and dreams, moved in thought, then settled down. He lifted a hand and turned Cricket's face to look directly at his. "Is that what you think?" he asked.

She flushed, then her lips became a tight line. She nodded hard.

"Okay," he said. "Okay."

Peggy stood up and came over, knelt next to Pass. "Is something wrong?" she asked, nervous, looking around.

"No," he said, releasing Cricket and standing up.

Cricket relaxed. He understood. He would watch with her. Peggy took his arm and led him to a seat at the back of the room.

Reverend Braxton came and said some prayers, announced the

time for the morning funeral service, and then left. Other people began to leave, saying the same things on the way out as they'd said on the way in. Cricket shook their hands, kissed them. Janis asked if she could go with her friends for a while. Cricket said yes. Pass lingered after the others, and when he leaned over to briefly hug her, he whispered to her, "I'll stay just outside. You'll see me out there, okay?"

She nodded, squeezed him, then let him go. That was for the best. If he stayed inside, he might get the wrong idea because certainly after Grace woke up, Cricket couldn't sleep with him again. But she wanted to be his friend. It was just the sex she'd have to stop. She'd love him as a friend.

At last, the only people left besides Jim were Peggy and Peter, and their boys.

"Do you want me to stay?" Peggy asked.

Cricket shook her head. "No. I'm okay. I'll use the air mattress."

"What?" Jim asked.

"The air mattress," she said. "It's in the den. Don't worry. I'll take care of it."

Peggy exchanged a significant glance with him. "Honey, what're you talking about?"

"I'm not sleeping on the floor," she said.

Jim groaned, and left the room. Peter jingled his car keys, touched Peggy's arm and said, "I'll take the boys out."

When they were gone, Peggy sat down next to Cricket and took her hand. "Cricket," she asked, "what're you doing?"

Cricket told Grace she'd be right back, and turned to Peggy. "I'm staying with Grace."

Peggy paused. Cricket turned back to Grace and told her it was okay.

"You want to sleep here tonight?" Peggy asked. "That's what you mean?"

Cricket nodded.

"Why?" Peggy said.

Cricket wasn't sure if she should say something. Peggy was probably sleeping with Jim, which made her untrustworthy by association. Jim hadn't gone to see his daughter. Jim didn't know how to keep watch. Still, Grace always liked Peggy.

Cricket leaned close and said, "People make mistakes. They do it all the time."

Peggy flushed a deep red. "They . . . do," she agreed.

Cricket nodded and patted her hand. "It doesn't matter. You go ahead. I'll just stay in case she wakes up."

Peggy didn't say anything for a moment. Then she made her face deliberately smooth.

"Honey," she said, "Grace won't wake up."

Cricket heard the words. She's not going to wake up. Of course, Peggy was right. Grace would probably sleep well now that she was back home. She needed her rest. She'd been badly hurt.

"I know," she said. "I just want to stay."

Peggy breathed out with relief. "Okay. I better go, though. I'll be here early to help out."

Cricket was glad when she left. She didn't want to talk. People said the strangest things, frightening things. After Grace woke up, they wouldn't do that, and everything would go back to normal. Jim and Janis wouldn't hate her anymore. Peggy would find some-body else to sleep with. Cricket wouldn't sleep with Pass again. Everything would be as it was, only they'd all love each other bet-ter because that's what it was all about, wasn't it? Everyone loving each other better. Cricket looked out the window and saw that Pass's car was parked down the street. That was good. He would stay to make sure nobody fell and hit the ground in the meantime.

She told Grace she was going to get the air mattress from the den, inflated it, and laid it next to the coffin. She hoped Grace could see her, but just in case she kept talking to her as she dozed on and off, a way of sleeping she'd become so accustomed to she wondered if she'd ever remember how to sleep through the night again.

Jim came into the living room early, but she was already awake, leaning over the coffin, stroking Grace's hand.

"You better get dressed," was all he said. He still seemed angry at her, and he was spending a lot of time letting Peggy pat his arm, but that was okay, Cricket knew. It would all change after Grace woke up. Peggy was only doing this to keep him busy while Cricket kept an eye on Grace. Cricket was grateful for the help. Glad to know he wasn't alone or without comfort. And Pete didn't seem to mind, either. At least, he didn't look angry or upset when Peggy talked to Jim, or put her arm around him. That was good, too. Everybody should understand at times like this.

She told Grace where she was going and left to get dressed. When she returned, Peggy and Janis were there, talking in whispers. They stopped talking when she entered the room. Janis looked upset, and turned away.

"What?" Cricket asked. She was wearing a dark brown dress. She didn't own any black. It washed her out. "Isn't this okay?" she asked, pointing to it.

"It's fine," Peggy said, and went up to her and squeezed her hand.

The funeral service was not too long. Most of the people who had been at the wake were there again. Pass came in and took her hand and patted it, then went to the back of the room. He looked tired, disheveled, but his eyes were clear and focused on her.

Reverend Braxton spoke about Jesus' love for children, and how he welcomed them, which almost made Cricket laugh out loud. Jim got up and said some very nice things about Grace, and even about Cricket and what a good mother she was. Peggy got up and said some things about how much Grace loved being alive, what a peaceful child she was, how much she loved her sister. Cricket kept touching Janis's hand, and she would look at her with her mouth open, as if she was afraid of her. People walked up to the coffin and put flowers in, which Cricket thought Grace would really like.

Then they all piled into the cars to go to the cemetery. The hearse came and took the coffin, closing it before they put it in the back, but Cricket had the chance to reassure Grace that it would be okay. Soon it would be okay. When she left the church to get into the limo, she noticed that the air was warm, and the sun strong on her arms and face. It seemed like a long time since she felt sun. She'd spent so much time inside, at the hospital.

The limo with her and Janis and Jim rode behind the hearse, with the pallbearers, mostly friends of Jim, and one of Grace's favorite teachers whom Cricket had asked. She thought he'd want to be there when Grace woke up. It would make him happy. When they arrived at the cemetery, the coffin was just being put on top of the plot it would occupy. She saw the pallbearers step back and other people crowd around. She pressed her way through them to the coffin, and stared at it, horrified.

She went up to the coffin and put her hand on it. Then she turned to the crowd.

"Why is it still closed?" she asked, trying to keep her voice even, smiling at them.

They didn't know. They didn't mean any harm. Maybe they just wanted to keep the sun off Grace's skin, she burned so easily. But she couldn't let it go on.

"Why is it still closed?" she asked again. Some people moved uncomfortably. "I'm not angry," she said. "But you have to open it. Somebody has to open it."

Nobody said anything. A few people looked down at their feet.

"She can't breathe," Cricket said, her voice getting higher and louder. It was important that they open the coffin now. It was *important*, they must realize that.

"She can't breathe," she said louder, almost shouting.

Nobody moved. They didn't understand. They were stupid people. Idiots. Assholes who couldn't tell the difference between alive and dead.

"Do you *want* her to die?" She was screaming at them now, but she didn't care. "You want your children to die locked in boxes? You shoot them and lock them in boxes? Lock them in boxes where they can't breathe, or . . . or see anything or *be?*"

They stared at her, then stared at the ground. They were jealous, she thought. They were jealous because they were dead, and Grace was alive, and they didn't want anyone to be alive when they were dead. They wouldn't help her.

She turned to the coffin and found the place where the lid met the bottom, started pushing at it with her hands, but she couldn't pry it up. Jim went to her and put a hand on her shoulder. "Cricket," he said. "Stop. You've got to stop."

She turned around and slapped him hard. Once. Twice. Three times.

"Fuck you," she screeched. "*You* didn't go to the hospital. You're *dead* like they are, and you want her dead, too."

He put a hand to his face and backed away. Everyone was staring at her except Janis, who had her face buried in Peggy's chest. Everyone was staring but nobody would help, just like in her nightmares, nobody doing anything to help her help her help her.

"She can't *breathe,*" she screamed at them. "Don't you understand? If you don't open this lid, she'll die. She'll *die.*"

She turned and pounded the top of the coffin, dug her nails into the place where it opened, pushed her shoulder against it. Hands grabbed her and turned her around. It was Pass. He would understand. It wasn't falling until you hit the ground. He would help.

She stopped struggling and looked in his eyes.

"Cricket," he said, his voice a slow and gentle drawl, "you have to stop now. She's dead."

She looked closely at his eyes and saw he wasn't lying. His eyes were telling the truth. But he had to be wrong. He had to be. Not her child her baby her daughter. Not Grace with her laugh and her fish and her pretty scarves and her soft peach-colored curtains and friends and life. Not Grace who was in her hands, in her blood, still in her body, in her hands.

Cricket held up a hand. "She's here," she said. "Here."

He took her hand, held it for a minute, then pressed it against her chest, where she could feel her own heart still beating. She was alive. Grace was dead.

She felt herself begin to shake, then somebody was screaming. My baby, someone screamed over and over again. *My baby my baby my baby.* It was in her ears, this screaming, so loud and so horrible, it hurt her ears. Somebody should make it stop, but it kept going and going. The screaming was everything, filling her and surrounding her, and becoming her, until darkness came and, under its cover, she fled.

eleven

When Cricket opened her eyes again, she had the feeling some time had passed without her being a part of it. Maybe days. Maybe years. She couldn't tell. She saw that she was wearing her white cotton nightgown. She had no idea who had put her in it. She looked around and saw that she was in her bedroom, in her bed, the bed she'd bought with Jim when they got married.

She had vague disjointed memories of faces—Jim's, Peggy's, Reverend Braxton's. She remembered feeling an intensity of pain she'd never felt before. She remembered asking for Janis and hearing Jim shout something at her. She remembered Pass's voice talking in his soft drawl, Jim yelling at him. Pass kept talking. She'd called to him, she remembered that, and he was there, and so was somebody with a needle. Then there was a merciful oblivion.

Now, as consciousness returned, so did the pain. There was nothing that didn't feel horrible. She lifted a hand to her chest to press against where it was worst. Then she turned to her left, and saw Pass sitting in a chair next to the bed, his eyes closed, one hand on her arm, just the way she'd slept with Grace.

"Pass?" she asked.

He opened his eyes, his pupils dilating. Was he afraid, she wondered?

"Hi," he said, his face watchful and quiet.

"Where's Janis?" she asked.

"She's with Jim."

"Oh. Are they in the kitchen?"

"No. They went away."

"Away?"

He sighed, and rubbed at his face. "He thought it'd be better if Janis didn't see you so upset, and if you had some time . . . to be upset without worrying about her. He took her to see his cousins in Buffalo. He said you'd know where they were."

She nodded. He had cousins in Buffalo. They went fishing together every summer. They had been at the funeral, she thought. It made sense, though she didn't think Jim had expressed it as kindly as Pass did. The pain increased, and she pressed harder at her chest.

"Peggy?" Cricket asked. "Is she here?"

He shook his head.

"Did she go home?"

Pass shrugged. Cricket understood. Peggy went with Jim and Janis. She wondered how Pete and the boys felt about that. But, of course, it was fine, because it was an emergency and Janis needed her. And, truthfully, Cricket was glad Peggy would be with her, though she supposed she should feel angry and betrayed.

"Did Jim say how long they'd be gone?" A day, a week, forever?

"He said maybe a week. Maybe more. Nothing definite." Pass cleared his throat, uncomfortable with being the messenger. "He said Janis'd go to camp after that. He wanted to make sure you knew that."

She nodded. He didn't want her near Janis. That's what that meant. Janis needed to be protected from her own mother.

"Why did you stay?" she asked.

"You asked me not to leave," he said. "Jim came and told you what he was doing, and you asked me to stay."

She closed her eyes. Her husband was gone. Her daughters were gone. Her sister was gone. Everything was over. There was nothing left to hope for, or think about, or try to do. And there was nothing that would fix it.

"I think I should die," she said. "I think that's all I can do."

Pass considered. "That'd be selfish," he said.

"No, it wouldn't," Cricket said. "Then Peggy could marry Jim and take care of Janis."

"And how do you think Janis would feel about it?"

"Relieved."

"You're wrong. That's not how I felt when my mother died. I was just about Janis's age, too."

"You didn't hate your mother."

"That just makes it worse. If you died, Janis would never have the chance to forgive herself, or you."

Cricket sighed. That was cruel of him, she thought, making her responsible for Janis's well-being when she obviously couldn't take care of her children. "It hurts too much," she said quietly.

"It's supposed to hurt," he said, speaking gently, stroking her hair. He could state the most difficult truths in that gentle way, so that it got into you, and you felt it. "Your daughter died. That's one of the worst hurts there is."

She was flooded with pain not so much at his words, but at the kindness in him. She'd never seen a face so kind. He seemed to know so much about pain, but he accepted what he knew without stopping his life or growing mean with knowledge. Her throat felt full of water, but she didn't want to cry because tears did no good. They wouldn't solve her grief. They would just express it, and what was the point in that?

She clutched at Pass, and he got onto the bed and held her. She pushed her face into his chest and breathed in and out slowly. Not crying was heavy as stones, but crying would hurt like knives.

"It's all gone," she whispered. "There's nothing left."

Pass stroked her hair and rocked her. "When I was a kid, I went to this school where the Franciscans taught. They said when you lost everything, that was perfect joy."

"What?"

"When you lose everything, it's perfect joy because that's when God can find you. That's what the Franciscans said."

"That's horrible," she said. "Horrible."

"I always thought so. I just don't know if it's also true."

She shook her head. "I don't believe in God," she said. "Not a God who'd take everything away just to find you."

Pass shrugged. "Me neither. And I don't believe in chasing what hurts you so you can find God. But maybe it's not about God. Maybe we blame God when it's just the way things work, because I know that when you're hurt worst, you find things you never thought you would. It happens like that, Cricket. Only it takes a long time."

"I can't believe in that," she said. "I just can't."

"I know. You don't have to. Right now, you just have to believe in staying alive."

She leaned against him, listening to his heart beating smooth and easy inside his chest. She was sure hers didn't sound like that. It must be making noises like an angry animal, howling or snarling. His was so quiet, so regular.

"What do you believe in?" she asked.

"You," he said.

"No," she said. "Not who. What. What do you believe in?"

"I'm not sure," he said, speaking slowly, with great care. "I know there's things at work I don't understand. Could be just energy. Spirits. Beauty. Or maybe love. Sometimes, I think that's where it all starts and ends. Just that."

Cricket shifted uncomfortably. She had loved Grace without knowing what a fierce and unbending force love was, or that it continued beyond reason or hope. She thought love was a winged dove, not a beast with claws slashing the inside of your chest, making you bleed. Not a terrifying specter waiting to slay her.

"But I loved Grace. Why did she die?"

"Because somebody shot her. It's a tragedy. Just a tragedy."

Sorrow swelled in Cricket's throat. She swallowed hard and felt sick with the taste of it. "Pass, don't the birds die sometimes? They're so hurt, they just can't live?" She'd seen them sometimes when they were brought in, one that was wrapped in barbed wire. Another with a fishhook protruding from its throat where it had swallowed the wrong thing.

"Sometimes," he said.

"And sometimes, isn't that a mercy?"

"Sometimes," he admitted. "But not this time."

"How do you know?"

"I know about pain," he said, and she knew from the kindness in his face that this must be true. Only someone who understood pain could be this kind. "It doesn't go away, but if you don't run away from it, it changes you, and you get bigger. After that, it teaches you instead of chewing you up. Only, you have to stay alive long enough for that to happen."

She rested her head against his chest again, listening to his heart tap out his life. It's a code, she thought. If I could decipher it, I'd know the secret to being alive. But I can't.

He stroked her face, cupped it in his hand, and she had a vivid memory of watching him hold a chickadee that he found stumbling about under a nest, one wing hanging loose and broken. "There, there," he whispered to it. "It's okay. Okay."

He sat and held it in his lap while it stared up at him, panting, and then just stopped breathing. It just stopped. She had gasped, but he had held a hand out for her to be quiet. He sat for some time more, then took the body and put it under the tree where he'd found it.

He had looked at his hands, then went inside the house and washed them. She hadn't said anything to him. He didn't seem to want her to. And he didn't stay morose, nor did he try to joke it off. It was sad. He let it be sad, but he didn't let it be bigger than that.

Cricket lifted her head and looked up at him. "What if I can't?" she asked.

"Stay alive?"

She nodded. She wasn't sure she knew how anymore. Things like working and eating and talking to people all seemed pointless, awkward tasks, performed in the maximum of pain.

"Try it," he said. "Give it a year. If I'm wrong, you can check out then."

"What'll I do in the meantime?"

"Cry," he said. "Maybe laugh sometimes. Sleep and eat. Live."

She thought of the old man in the grocery store. Live, she thought, as if she only had a year to live. That's what he said. But he was just a senile old man who hallucinated and made tapes about it. Besides, what she wanted was Grace. All that she would choose had been stolen from her. So what would she do now? Just live, anyway?

"Listen," he said. "I was thinking about going on a trip this summer. I have some business to take care of in New Orleans, and I wanted to see some butterfly houses. You can come with me. You shouldn't be in the house for a while."

It might help to leave, she thought. Here, every moment would be a reminder of how she'd failed, or a moment of reliving the nightmare, or waiting for it to end. And it would not. But to leave the place where she'd rocked her daughter, saw her first steps, nursed her through chicken pox—that seemed too hard, as if there wasn't a lever in the world big enough to pry her away.

"I don't know if I can go. I don't know if I'm up to it."

"You don't have to do anything except sit in the car if that's what you want."

"Pass, you don't have to baby-sit me."

"I'm not. I want you to come with me."

"Why?"

"Because I love you," he said.

She breathed in and out, trying to make her breath match the rhythm of his heart. She had nothing in her for love. It all hurt too much. Could she even make love with him? She didn't know, because she wasn't sure what parts of her were still alive. And what did his love matter? It did nothing to change her pain, or the events that brought her that pain. She opened her mouth to tell him all this, but when she looked at his face, his eyes were full of kindness and truth. She breathed in, and breathed out.

"Okay," she said. "I'll go with you. Okay."

twelve

She called Jim at his cousins', to tell him she was going away for a little while.

"A little while?" he asked. "How long is a little while?"

"A couple of weeks," she said.

"That's all?" He sounded disappointed.

"Maybe more. I'm not sure yet."

She waited for him to ask where she was going, but he didn't. "I'll let you know where I am, in case Janis needs me."

He didn't say anything.

"Let me talk to her," Cricket said.

"She's out," Jim said. "At a movie with her cousins."

"Oh. Well, then let me talk to Peggy."

There was a pause. "She's not available."

"I see."

"Yeah? I don't know what you think you see, but you're wrong," Jim said. "And you can't sit there and think you got it all figured out, either. I warned you that you were throwing it all away."

"I know. I remember."

"And is that bird guy there with you?"

"No," she said. "Not right now."

"Right."

She didn't argue with him. She didn't have anything she wanted to prove. "Where's Peggy's kids? Are they there, too?"

"They're with Peter."

"Does he . . . know?"

"Know what? That she's here taking care of her niece? Of course he knows."

Cricket felt a small pinch of pain in her forehead between her eyebrows. Her third eye was hurting, Grace would say. It saw things Jim didn't want her to see. Things he didn't want to talk about. Of course, he could be telling the truth. There was that possibility. She'd know if she talked to Peggy.

"Look," Cricket said, "just let me talk to her."

"I won't have you insinuating—"

"I'm not going to. I just want to talk to her. She's my sister, Jim."

In the background, Cricket heard muffled voices. She supposed Jim had covered the receiver with his hand and was talking to Peggy. Then she was on the line.

"Cricket?"

"Peggy?"

"I'm here."

"With Jim," Cricket commented.

There was a pause. "Sort of," Peggy agreed. "But not . . . not really. Y'know?"

They were silent. They didn't need a lot of words to understand each other. In the brief sentences between them, Cricket knew that Jim was lying. She also knew that what was happening was probably not the affair he thought it was.

Cricket's first feeling wasn't anger, though she thought it probably should be. She ought to be screaming at Peggy, like the women on the Ricki Lake show, but she didn't feel angry. She slept with Pass, and Jim slept with Peggy as the world fell apart. She'd read somewhere that when Pompeii was drowned by volcanic ash, people began having sex in the streets, their skeletons discovered hundreds of years later clutched in amorous embraces.

When the world fell apart, that's what people did. Cricket could hardly blame Peggy or Jim for being human. And while she could see herself getting angry at Jim, if her feelings ever returned, the unspoken pact of acceptance between her and Peggy was deeper than jealousy, older than any marriage, and so much a part of their genetic code that it wasn't possible for either of them to abandon it entirely.

What Cricket felt most was surprise that Peggy wanted to sleep with Jim. He didn't seem like much of a catch. Of course, maybe she didn't want a catch. Maybe she just wanted a distraction.

"You mad at me?" Peggy asked.

Cricket sighed. "I can't really tell. Would you be mad if you were me?"

"Maybe. Or maybe not."

"Yeah. You sure you know what you're doing?" she asked.

"Probably not," Peggy said. "You?"

"Not really. What about Peter?"

"He's okay for now. There's nothing . . . been decided. I just . . . Cricket, I don't know how to explain."

"Don't try. It doesn't really matter, Peggy. I guess it's more your problem than mine right now. I'm just worried about Janis."

"I know. But you're the last person who can help her. She needs somebody to blame, and you're too easy a target."

"She blames herself most of all."

"Yeah," Peggy said. "And she can't believe you when you try to talk her out of it."

"I think she's upset about you, too," Cricket said.

"I know. But I'm not her mother, so I'm allowed to be stupid."

Cricket leaned her forehead against the wall. It was cool, but did nothing to soothe the pain between her eyes.

"I'm going away for a while," she said.

"I think that's a good idea," Peggy said positively. "I think it'll help."

"How?"

"I don't know. I guess . . . I don't know. I just think it will."

"Maybe," Cricket said. "Anyway, I'm going, whether it helps or not." She had to go. Had to stay alive long enough to know if it mattered to Janis, or herself.

"Put Jim back on, okay?"

"Okay. Let me know where you are, huh? Be okay."

She didn't respond.

A brief silence, and then Jim's voice. "Yeah?" he asked.

"What're your plans, after Buffalo?" she asked.

"Janis wants to go to camp, so I'll take her. Then, it'll just be business as usual."

Cricket couldn't help it. She laughed.

"Jesus Christ, what's that for? Just because I have a life and I want to get back to it. Because I have a daughter, and a job and—"

"Jim, somebody came here and *shot* people. Shot our daughter. Killed her. Whoever it was didn't even know her."

"It'd be better if he did?" Jim shot back.

"No. But this way—it wipes out everything about her. Her existence, her life, ours—it's all erased. And you can go to Wal-Mart and play golf and work as if that never happened? As if it didn't change anything? It changed everything."

"It didn't change me," Jim said. "I didn't change."

Cricket sighed. "That's the problem."

"Christ," Jim said with disgust. "You need a shrink."

"No, I don't," Cricket said. "I need a new world."

"Well, you're not gonna get it."

Cricket was silent. He was right. Even when he was being an idiot, he had to be right.

"Look, I gotta run," he said wearily.

Of course he did, she thought. He was never comfortable with this kind of talk anyway.

"Sure," she said. "I'll let you know where I am."

"Fine."

When she hung up, she imagined him turning to Peggy for comfort. That's what men did with their mistresses, didn't they? She wondered if that was different when the mistress was your wife's sister. She could imagine Peggy sleeping with him, maybe out of some subliminal need to hurt her own husband, or maybe because she wanted sex, or maybe because in some backwards way she thought she was doing Cricket a favor. But she couldn't imagine Peggy listening to any malicious whining from Jim about his wife.

Somehow, that was consoling to her.

She went up to her room and packed her bags.

It felt strange to leave this way, with nobody to say good-bye to, but the next day, she drove to the sanctuary, glad of the warmth of the sun that filled the car. It was the only thing that didn't hurt.

As she pulled in, she saw Law standing just outside the house, rocking back and forth, smiling at nothing. He had a Walkman in his hand, and headphones in his ears. She suddenly wondered what he'd do without Pass. A couple of interns were coming from a local college to take care of the birds. Would they look after Law as well?

She stood for a moment, hoping Pass would come out and she wouldn't have to walk past Law alone. She was not afraid of him, but she felt shy in his presence. She didn't know how to communicate with him, didn't know if what she said might hurt him, and so was reluctant to say anything at all. His eyes, which always saw things beyond her or behind her or above her, made her nervous. She had no clue what his thoughts might be.

The door behind Law opened, and Pass appeared, carrying a backpack and a suitcase.

"Hey," he said as he brought them to the car. She opened the trunk and he threw them inside, then he put a hand on her shoulder and kissed her forehead, his lips lingering for a moment against her skin. "Two more bags," he murmured. "Then we're ready."

He went inside, came out again with two duffel bags. He tossed them in the trunk, then looked around, shrugged. "Well, what I'm forgetting is forgotten. C'mon, Law," he said. "Time to go."

Law didn't move. Pass walked over to him and pulled an earphone out of his ear. "Time to go, buddy," he said again. Law looked at him slowly, and then walked toward the car.

Cricket stood outside the driver's side of the car, staring.

Law got in the backseat, next to the cooler of snacks and drinks she'd packed. He was humming softly and tunelessly to himself.

"Um," she said, as Pass went around to the other side of the car. He didn't hear her. He opened the door on his side and then smiled up at her over the roof of the car. When he saw her face, he tilted his head at her inquisitively. "You forget something?" he asked.

She shook her head, and pointed to the backseat. "He's coming?" she asked.

"Sure," he said. Then he laughed. "You didn't think I'd just leave him, did you?"

She frowned. "I . . . didn't think."

He leaned on the roof of the car. "I guess it's a little late to ask if it's okay, then."

She said nothing.

He sighed and closed his door, opened the backseat door. "Okay, buddy," he said. "Sudden change of plans."

"No," she said. "What . . . what're you doing?"

"You don't seem too keen to have us both here," he said. "And I'd rather not make it worse for you."

"No," Cricket said again. "It's not . . . I just didn't know. I have to get used to it."

Pass tapped a finger on the roof of the car. "You really didn't know?"

"No. I didn't."

"I should've said," he said. "I'm sorry. I made an assumption. That was stupid."

"It's fine. I mean, you know if it'll be okay. It'll be okay?" she asked, hoping to get a reassurance from him that didn't exist. Because of course it would be okay, but of course it wouldn't. Law was outside her pain, not a part of her grief. To have him along was a constant reminder that something did exist other than that, and asked for her attention. She didn't think she could give it. She didn't know that she wanted to.

"Fine," he said. "He'll be fine. He likes to travel. If you're sure?"

She wasn't, but she nodded, and got in the car.

When she started it, he said, "Wait. There's something."

He dug into his pocket and brought out a box. It was a box that said "Drill Bits" on the cover. He handed it to her.

"What is it?" she asked stupidly.

"Open it," he said. "You'll see."

She took off the lid, and was engulfed in fragrance. Sweet and overwhelming, it filled the car. In the backseat, Law breathed in deeply and said, "Aaah."

It was a rose, dusty pink, small with many petals. Cricket recognized it as rugosa, an old-fashioned type.

"It's the first of the season," Pass said. "I thought you should have it."

Cricket felt his kindness as soft wings brushing the inside of her chest clean of sorrow, but just as they did, she remembered the smell of roses at the funeral, so thick from the flowers people brought to put in Grace's coffin. She saw herself watching them, a madwoman whose reality was different than anyone else's in the room. Water filled her eyes and she pressed them shut to keep it in.

From the backseat, Law made a sound—something like groaning, and something like laughing. Cricket opened her eyes and saw that he was gesturing toward the rose. She handed it to him reluctantly. It was her present, after all. As he took it, she didn't quite let go, and a thorn pierced her thumb. Blood welled up and then trickled out. Law, holding the rose, made a panicked sound.

"It's okay," she said, looking at Pass to make sure she was doing this right. "It's not your fault."

But the sounds he made increased in volume, and changed rhythms to a panicked crying. His eyes filled with water that streamed down his face, and he waved his hands in the air around his face, then hit himself over and over again, as Janis had done, she thought.

"Hey," Pass said. "Hey. Don't do that." He reached back over the seat and grabbed Law's hands, held them in one of his and with his other hand grasped Law's face so that it looked directly at his. "Hear me? Don't do that," he said sternly.

Cricket was shocked at the tone of voice he used. So rough. She would've thought gentleness was called for. Law was crying, upset.

"Blood," Law said mournfully. "Blood."

Pass considered this, then looked at Cricket's hand. He took it in his and brought her thumb to his mouth, moved his lips over it, then showed it to Law. "Gone," he said. "It's gone. Look."

Law shivered, and grew still. As quickly as the panic had started, it was gone. He leaned back in his seat, looked out the window and hummed softly to himself.

Pass turned back in his seat and said, "Let's go."

"Is he okay?" Cricket asked.

Pass nodded. "Just the excitement. He'll settle down fine. You'll see. I'll drive first?"

She nodded. He started the car, and they went.

The first few hours on the road she was sustained by speed and music, motion without intent substituting for the need to think or do.

Pass had a tape of oldies—Santana, *Abbey Road*, Steppenwolf, *Pearl.* He played them one after another—born to be wild, black magic woman, once there was a way to get back home. She opened the window and put her head out, letting the wind suck her breath away while Janis Joplin sang that freedom was just another word for nothing left to lose. The Franciscans called it Perfect Joy. Janis called it freedom. She hadn't wanted either, but they were hers anyway.

A guilty excitement rumbled beneath her pain. She was going somewhere. She'd never really done that, just gone somewhere, setting out on a road she didn't know, for unfamiliar destinations. Santana sang, and Janis, and Steppenwolf, and they drove down the thruway, down the turnpike, and onto the roads of Delaware. She was going.

He drove for four hours, and then she drove for two. She tired easily, and when she tired, everything became very dark and sleep was the only place of refuge. She would curl up in her seat and not hear the music, or feel anything except the need to escape her own skin. She apologized for this, but Pass said it was fine. They were polite with each other, realizing that the rules were different now, and neither of them knew what they were.

Pass was right that Law was not a bother. She forgot he was in the backseat until she heard a keening sound, and Pass turned around and asked what he needed. "Drink," he said mournfully, and Pass got a soda for him from the cooler they'd brought along.

They were just into Virginia as it was getting dark, and Pass said they should stop and get a place to stay. They'd already decided that they'd alternate between camping and hotels, to save money, and it was a fine, soft night, so they found a campsite with pine trees to pitch their tent under and hardly anyone else there. Cricket was beginning to wonder how Law would fit in the tent with them when she saw Pass pitching another, smaller tent.

"Is that . . ." she started.

"For Law," he said, then smiled at her over the tent pegs. "You didn't think he was gonna sleep with us, did you?"

"No," she said. "Of course not."

"Yeah," he said. "You did."

"Well," she said, "maybe."

He stopped his tapping on the tent stakes and looked up at her. "Look," he said, "I'm not making you responsible for him. He's my brother. He's my responsibility."

"How come?" she asked.

"How come what?" he asked.

"How come he's your responsibility. I mean, you don't have any other family?"

He was silent for a moment, then he nodded. "There was just me and Law and my mother."

"What happened to her?"

Pass tapped at the stake again, and for a minute she thought he was going to simply ignore her. But he didn't.

"She had a brain tumor," he said. "I was fifteen. Law was about six. She had surgery, and she lived about a year after that, but she just got worse and worse. Didn't know her own name, didn't know who I was. Then, she died."

Cricket mused for a moment on the way tragedy made some people kind, and some people mean. "What about your father?" Cricket asked.

"My father, or his?"

"Both," she said. She'd forgotten they had different fathers.

"My father didn't stick around. I never really knew him. Law— he's from her stepdaddy."

Cricket didn't say anything. Nothing at all. Pass tapped the stake the rest of the way in, and went around to the others. She stood watching, silent. When he was done, he stood, pressed a hand against his back and stretched.

"So," he said, "you maybe don't care to sleep with white trash like me?"

Cricket lifted her head and looked at him. His eyes on her seemed to listen to the inside of her for an answer, seemed to listen to the cells of her body. He could make her reach orgasm by kissing her and she did not understand her body's response to him. Even now, when she knew that pain was her closest friend, she could still feel herself grow warm, wanting him.

She could not say she loved him, because she couldn't allow herself that feeling. But he was a shelter in her pain, a pair of arms that would hold her without question and see to her physical pleasure as if that were important. So she turned to him, and asked herself if that's what love was, a turning toward something.

Once, looking up a word for a Scrabble game, she'd stumbled across the definition of the word *desire*. In its original French definition, it meant to turn away from the stars. Desire was to turn away from the stars. Love was to turn toward something, inexplicably, inexorably, motion without premeditation or volition. She turned toward Pass. Perhaps she did love him. Or perhaps she would have to love him, for being there when she turned.

"I want you," she said softly. "That's what I want."

He ran his hand up and down her arm. "Supper first, okay?"

They made a fire and cooked hot dogs. Pass opened a beer and had one, and so did Cricket. The day brought itself down into darkness, and the moon rose. Pass settled Law into his tent, and Cricket deliberately withheld from helping. Instead, she went and settled herself in her own tent, and when Pass entered it, he found her naked.

He took his own clothes off quickly, knelt down next to her, and brought his mouth to hers, then to her breast, then between her legs. She had never felt anything as soft and light as his tongue, like butterflies kissing her, only thousands of them. She came quickly and hard, and he entered her, watching her come again and again and again, his eyes always open and on her face.

He was present to his pleasure in a way she'd never seen any man be either during sex or outside of it. In fact, most people she knew seemed to live mostly in the past or the future, as she had until her life fell apart. It frightened her, and it held her, this capacity for attention to the moment.

They made love until he gasped and she knew he was coming. She held his face with her hands and watched him, saw how he fell softly into this pleasure, letting himself go entirely. He was open, free of himself, free of her. He trembled, and let himself fall onto her, and then she held him in her arms, stroking his hair, his back.

She felt immense gratitude, as if he'd given her a gift, showing himself trembling, showing her his orgasm, letting her see how fragile and powerful that moment was.

"Thank you," she whispered. "Thank you."

In the night, the wind picked up and beat against the outside of the tent like the hands of importunate children trying to get in. It woke them up, and Pass groped for a flashlight while Cricket said, incoherently, "Who is it? Who is it?"

"I don't know," Pass said, and shone the light outside, then opened the tent.

"No," Cricket said. "Don't go out there."

"I just want to check on Law."

"No," she said. "There's something out there."

"Something? Like a bear or something?" Pass peered outside the tent, moved the light around. "I don't see anything."

"It's . . . things we can't see. Spirits. Ghosts."

Pass frowned. "Ghosts."

"Maybe. Maybe angry ghosts. Maybe . . . maybe it's the children. Grace."

He blinked at her, then shook his head. "Grace wasn't angry. She didn't have time to be angry."

Cricket brought her hand to her mouth and pressed it there, pushing words out on the edge of sobs. "What if she did? What if she saw the man who shot her and he— What if she knew, if it hurt? Maybe she's angry that I wasn't there or didn't make him stop."

"No, baby," he said, pulling her close. "Cricket, no. It's not like that. Really, it's not."

"How do you know? How can you know? Maybe all the children are there, all of them, angry and . . . and hating us. We failed them so badly."

"No, Cricket. They're not. They got better things to do now. What do they care for our crazy world?"

She felt the frantic words subside, the rumblings of pain retreating to their den in her chest. Maybe he was right. Why would they want this? What for? She wasn't even sure she did.

"Listen, I need to go check on Law. You okay for a few minutes?"

She nodded, and pulled back. "Aren't you afraid?"

He thought a minute, then shook his head. "If anything's out there, I can't see it, so what does it matter?"

"What if it sees you?" she asked.

He blinked at her in the strange light. The wind slapped at the tent. "I'll be right back," he said, and slipped out the opening, leaving her in the dark.

She could hear him moving around, and the mournful whistling that circled their space. Come home, it cried. Please come home. Don't leave us. Come home.

She thought of Janis, and was panicked that she was so far away. It made her want to get up and run to the car, drive home as fast as she could. But of course Janis wouldn't be there. She was in Buffalo, or maybe at camp already, getting sympathy from her friends for having a dead sister, a crazy mother.

The wind screamed, asking for something she couldn't give. She pressed her hand along the inside of the tent and felt it drumming against her skin. She closed her eyes and tried to hear beyond it. She had a memory of Grace running in the park, holding a helium balloon and laughing as she watched it trail behind her. "Look, Mommy. Look at me," she yelled. She was five and at the look-at-me stage, when nothing was as important as her mother's eyes observing her capacity to do this, and that, and everything.

"I see you," Cricket had yelled back, and Grace stopped running, lifted her arm, and opened her hand.

The balloon rose in erratic spirals, whipped by the wind. Cricket gasped, sure Grace would scream to get it back, but Grace only laughed and twirled in circles on the ground to match the circles of the balloon above her, until it disappeared from view.

"Look, Mommy," Grace had squealed happily. "I made it fly."

Cricket dropped her hand into her lap, conscious of the feeling of emptiness and absence of motion.

The tent flap unzipped, and Pass came back in.

"It's okay," Pass said. "He's asleep. It's just the wind. Come here and warm me up, woman."

He drew her to him, and she curled into him and lay there, feeling his skin and listening to the pleadings of the wind.

dolphin dreams

They traveled for another day and night, taking their time, stopping to camp along the way. The road became a refuge where there were no sights or sounds to remind her of what she'd lost, or how it felt to lose it. Inside herself, she felt no better, and no worse, but she was alive and aware of being alive, which she supposed was something. Her skin had feeling again, prickling against the sticky hot seat at her back. Her eyes saw what passed along the road, though her mind had no comment to make about it. The smell of the trees, the sound of them whispering in the night, was not comforting, but she was aware of it as not painful, either. When Pass reached over to squeeze her hand, she noticed his fingers were smooth, and there were calluses on the palm of his hand.

When they got into Alabama and he said something about finding a campground, Cricket said, "I think we should stop and maybe go to a hotel." She wanted a shower, and a bed. She was, somehow, alive.

Pass got out a map and consulted it. "We're just outside

Mobile. Let's find someplace, and we can go on to New Orleans tomorrow." He studied the map for a moment more. "Oh, hey," he said. "We're right near Dauphin Island."

"Dolphin Island?"

"Dauphin. It's in the Gulf. I used to go there sometimes when I was a kid, when we lived in New Orleans."

She considered him, surprised. "You didn't tell me you lived in New Orleans."

"You didn't ask. But I told you about the Franciscans, right? That's where they were. We can go swimming tomorrow," he said, "if you like. Been years since I swam in warm water."

They found a microtel, got two rooms and went to a diner. As she studied the menu, she realized she was hungry, and that she hadn't really been aware of hunger except as an inconvenience since the shooting. When Grace was in the hospital, she'd eaten hospital food with no appetite for it. When she was home, she felt too guilty to eat. Now she ordered steak and eggs, and was able to eat most of it before a sudden sinking told her she was tired, and with fatigue came the dark feelings.

As she curled next to Pass in the squeaky hotel bed, she thought of warm water and whispered to him, "Will it be nice?"

"Beautiful," he said. "You'll see."

Dauphin Island was silver and beige in the pervasive light and heat. The water was womb-warm, salty. Not clear enough to see her feet at the bottom, because the motion of the waves stirred up the thick sand and silt, but she thought even Peggy might be satisfied with this.

"Nice," Pass said, and dove under a swell, hung upside down, then reemerged next to her. They floated, drifted on their backs, supported by salt and warmth, looking up at the misty sky. Then Pass put an arm around her waist and pulled her to him, holding her at his hip. She rested there, buoyant, fully alive. She resisted the feeling, not sure she could sustain it when it lived so close to her grief, but the salt water held her up, and the sun was warm regardless of her pain, and her body, as reluctant to give up her soul as her soul was to give up her body, responded. She didn't know it would be like that. She didn't know her body would teach her how to live. She always thought it was her mind.

"Look," he said, pointing up, and she saw flocks of gulls circling overhead, then some small bird she didn't recognize, and then the pelican.

"Watch," he said. "This is great."

The pelican, which seemed so unlikely in flight, so not built for it, folded its wings up and down, slowly like a puppet of a bird whose strings were being pulled. It seemed to pause midair, then dropped like a stone into the water, coming up with a fish in its mouth, which it swallowed quickly.

"So beautiful," she said. "Beautiful."

"Look there," he said, and pointed beyond the pelican.

Just beyond the birds, she saw the dolphins, their backs curving in and out of the water as they fed, following the birds. They were about thirty yards out, she judged.

"Should we swim to them?" Pass asked.

"What about your brother?" she asked.

He looked back to shore. Law was sitting in the sand just where the breakers lapped at his legs, patting his hands in the water. "He's okay. He doesn't swim, so he'll just stay there." She shook her head and clung to him. "Too far," she said. "You go. I'll wait here."

"I could take you," he said.

She shook her head harder.

"I want to be with you," he said, and began to walk out, carrying her with her legs wrapped around his waist.

"No," she gasped. "Don't. I'm afraid."

He stopped and stroked her hair. "I won't. I'm just walking a little ways. Really, you trust me?"

She nodded hesitantly.

"Yeah. Well, not all the way, but you will. I don't hurt people."

He held her at the waist, walking her out no deeper than her chest. They stayed there and watched the pelicans dive, the small birds nip at the surface of the water, the gulls circle and call, the dolphins swim in and around the birds.

"When dolphins sleep," Pass said, "they only sleep with half their brains."

"What?" she asked.

"They don't stop swimming. They just put half their brains to sleep at a time, and keep going. That's how they sleep."

Cricket saw them leaping in and out of the water, half-moons, crescents, arcs of motion. "Do they dream?" she asked.

"Yes," Pass said. "They dream us."

At least, that's what she thought he said. They dream us. But she wasn't sure because the warmth of the ocean, the warmth of being held, created a cocoon of soft pleasure that made all words blur into something like poetry or song. He pulled her closer, and moaned with pleasure. She could feel him growing hard against her. She looked at him and saw his eyes piercing hers, asking a question. Yes, she nodded at him. Yes, of course. Here.

His hand moved between her legs, and though there were people at the shore, she and Pass were in a bubble of dreams, warm and wet, with nothing except what was here at the beginning of time and would be here at the end of time. Water, sun, sand, and pleasure deeper than any pleasure that had ever existed anywhere, in any form.

His voice crooned to her from far away as he pulled her closer, his hand moving her toward orgasm, someone—was it him? Must be him—encouraging her, saying, That's right, baby. Just like that. Just like that. Come, baby. Come for me. So nice.

Then his long sigh of wonder, his voice saying, "You're calling them, Cricket. They're here. They're here."

Her body contracted and expanded like the tide, her womb pulling in and out, pleasure and more pleasure in salty climax, and like the turning earth moving her, Pass circled her around and she saw the faces of the dolphins, no more than ten feet away, regarding her closely, as if she mattered.

As if they saw her, and considered what they had dreamt.

"Pass," she gasped. "Look. Oh my God, they're here."

"You called them," he whispered in her ear. "They're here for you."

This is a dream, she thought. A dream of pleasure the dolphins are dreaming. A dream of us.

When the dolphins grew tired of watching human sport and swam away, Pass wrapped an arm around her and kissed her, and she wished the dolphins would never wake again.

thirteen

They left Alabama in the morning, and drove toward New Orleans, going through Pass Christian in Mississippi.

"Do you want to stop?" Cricket asked.

"What for?"

"To see things," she said.

"Things?"

"Like your old house, your old neighborhood. Where you used to live."

"What for?" he asked again, and drove on.

His face was tight with tension. His eyes kept flicking to the rearview mirror, looking at Law, she supposed. He drove faster than the speed limit, and she put a hand on his arm.

"Are you okay?" she asked.

"What? Oh. I guess. Just . . . it's funny coming back. Like seeing a ghost of yourself, when you're still alive."

As they entered New Orleans, they began a series of difficult maneuvers down narrow one-way streets to find a hotel. Pass's tension increased as they saw sign after sign that said no vacancies.

"We could just drive on and camp. We don't have to go to New Orleans," she said.

"I do," he said, a little sharply. "Anyway, I just need to stop driving. Get out of this car."

"Okay," she said. "I have the guidebook. Let's go to a bar and call a few places."

They did so, and as Cricket made calls, Pass looked around him nervously. "This is a funny place," he said.

"How many nights?" Cricket said into the phone. "Um . . . two? And . . . um . . . two rooms."

"There's only men here," Pass whispered.

Cricket, waiting for the clerk to check her credit card, lifted a magazine off the shelf below the telephone. The cover showed two men caressing each other.

"Hell," Pass said. "Figures, it's a gay bar."

"So?"

"Well, what if someone tries to pick me up or something?"

"Then you say no. Women do it all the time."

He shifted uncomfortably, and Cricket frowned, irritated. Wasn't he the man who helped her call the dolphins yesterday? And, today, was he suddenly someone who was afraid of the advances of gay men, and anxious about hotel plans? She went back to the phone call, trying not to think about it. She liked him better yesterday.

They found a bed-and-breakfast in the French Quarter, and by the time they collapsed into it, he had retreated into himself, gruff and silent. Cricket felt his disapproval keenly. He didn't need to chastise her, she thought. She chastised herself enough when things didn't go smoothly, whether it was her fault or not. But, she realized, she did so silently. Nobody knew because she was so busy trying to make the other people involved feel better. Today, she decided, she would not do that.

"I feel like shit," she said. "And if you stay mad, I'll keep feeling like shit for upsetting you."

He rolled over on the bed and stroked her face. "It's okay, baby," he said softly. "It's just strange to be here. That's all. I'm not upset with you."

He pulled her closer, but she froze under his touch, suddenly overwhelmed with a complex feeling that was something like sorrow, and something like dread. What was she doing here with this man? Who was he to her, to call her away from her pain and make her forget her daughter? He was an unknown quantity, and she was far from home, far away from her own life. She had no orientation to whoever's life it was she was now living.

Pass paused, and without saying a word, he withdrew from her. They lay next to each other in silence. She felt cold, alone, and afraid.

Suddenly and inexplicably, she missed Jim. She missed his sameness, the way he let her float in the dreams she spun without interruption. It was so comfortable there, and so uncomfortable here, where she had to create a life instead of simply living out a familiar role. She missed her house, the beautiful patterns in the slate around the fireplace, the way the sun came into the kitchen, the snow that fell on her garden, her life that was shedding her like an old skin that had enough of her after all.

It had all been so predictable, and then, without warning, it was not. She wondered what would have happened to her life if Grace hadn't died. Would she ever have seen the illusions she was spinning? Or were they only illusions because something came along to change everything, irrevocably, without mercy. It frightened her, how quickly and completely things changed. Once she could not imagine living without her mother and father. Now she couldn't imagine living with them. Once she couldn't imagine feeling joy without her marriage, her home, her garden. Then Pass had caught her with joy unaware. She resisted the motion of it inside her. If everything else could go, this could go just as easily.

Pass gathered her to him. "You okay?"

"Sure."

"No. You're not. What is it?"

She curled her legs up against him. "I don't know. I don't know what I'm doing here."

"Here in New Orleans? Here with me?"

"Here," she said. "Here."

He ran a hand up and down her back. "Listen," he said to her, "maybe it's not my place to say this, but you know you don't have to stay, right? I mean, you should go back if you need to."

"Back?"

"To Jim. Back home."

He was offering her exactly what she wished for, giving her an out. But she didn't want him to. He had no right. She had a moment of anger, then realized she wasn't angry at him. She was angry because the offer wasn't possible any longer. She couldn't go back to Jim. Not ever. What had happened had changed her, and she could not fit herself into her former skin. It was too late to pretend she could.

"I can't go back to Jim," she said. "I can't be there. I just don't know why I'm here."

His hand traced spirals on her back, soft and light. "I guess I can't tell you that," he said. "But I can tell you why I'm here."

"Why?" she asked.

He was still for so long, she was about to ask him again, but then he spoke. "I'm making the world a better place."

She moved away from him so that she could see his face. She didn't understand.

"There's something between us that's not about all the grief and evil in the world," he said. His face was as serious as she'd ever seen it, his words chosen carefully, as if he'd thought about this for some time. "All that happened to you, to me, all the ugly stuff can't touch what we have. It's . . . it's good, and sweet. It's about beauty. And it's alive, between us. You know that?"

She nodded. She knew. Even when she couldn't feel it, she knew what he meant. It was what brought her to his bed.

"And we need to . . . to take care of it. To grow it. That's all we can do. Take the good stuff and grow it. The birds, the gardens. Loving you. Loving anything. That's beauty, and it's the only thing that wipes out the rest of it. That's why I'm here."

"But it gets stolen. Murdered."

"Sometimes," Pass agreed. "But that doesn't mean we shouldn't grow it anyway. If you don't, you leave more holes for the ugly stuff to come and live in."

She leaned into him, tucked her arms around him and felt the smooth skin of his back. They fit together perfectly, like two parts of a puzzle that could interlock no matter which way you turned them. That didn't mean anything, she knew, but it also seemed to mean everything, as if there was nothing else.

"You really think that matters? Beauty?"

"I guess I do," he said. "I guess I think that matters more than anything else does. You think so, too."

"I do?"

"You know you do," he said. "That's why you make gardens." He lifted her face from his chest and cupped it in his hands. "What happened with the dolphins—did you ever feel anything like that?"

His gold eye and his green eye looked at her as if there were no other time but this, no other place but here.

"That was beauty," he said. "As real as it gets. And it's what we make together. Seems to me it's a sin to let it go by, when the world's so hungry for it."

His words went into a place inside her where she knew the truth. They warmed her, softened something that had been holding tight. His words were true, but the truth seemed so light, as if it would fly away from her at a moment's notice and she couldn't possibly hold on to it. She wanted to ask him how he knew that, and what if he was wrong. She wanted to ask how to live that, how to grow it, how to keep it safe. She wanted to ask him to answer all her questions. Instead, her stomach rumbled.

"Time for supper?" he asked.

She shook her head. If she was hungry, she didn't know it.

"I could use some food," he said. "And I'll bet Law's hungry. Let's go walk around, get something to eat."

Their hotel was in the French Quarter, and they left it to go walking on Bourbon Street. They got fried fish for Law, oysters and beer for themselves, feeling the heat penetrate them and make their steps heavy. As the daylight began to fade, the air grew a little less hot, but no less heavy. It might cool down more if it rained, Pass said. Either way, it would stay sticky. There was no relief from that in this city in the summer.

They got ice-cream cones and went to Jackson Square to sit and eat them while watching the people. Street theater, Pass said. Cricket felt herself filled with new color and motion.

Two street people sang the blues and a large woman in a leopard pantsuit kissed her poodle repeatedly. There were women reading tarot decks, men reading tarot decks, a circle of children dressed in scruffy clothes playing hackysack. A heavily tattooed man sat on a bench eating an orange and mumbling to himself.

Law pointed at a juggler, made a sound of happiness, grabbed Pass by the arm and made him watch.

"Pretty cool, huh, buddy?" Pass grinned at him, then turned to Cricket. "I think he might remember this crazy old city."

"You lived here for a long time?" she asked, realizing that she knew his history as a patchwork quilt, with pieces that must connect together somehow beyond chance. He lived here. He lived in Mississippi. He told her once he'd lived for a while in Arizona. His life had so many more chapters than hers, which was all played out on the same stage. But she didn't know the chronology, the reason for each move or how he felt about them.

"About ten years, I guess. When Law was younger, mostly. We spent a lot of time on these steps, watching the world go by."

"Did you like it?"

He leaned his chin in his hand and stared at the crowd in the plaza. "I was alone here," he said. "It's a good city to be alone in."

She was going to ask him what he meant by that, but he shook himself and stood up. "I want a soda." He pointed to a shop on the other side of the plaza. "You want anything?"

Cricket shook her head. "Should we come with you?"

"Nah. Sit here and relax. Or sit and sweat, like everybody else." He tapped Law's shoulder and got his attention. "I'm going for soda," he said. "You want some?"

Law blinked, as if making an effort to think about it. He shook his head, and went back to smiling at the jugglers, waving a large hand at them.

She watched his back retreat across the square, and had a moment of anxiety when he passed out of the circle of brightness that the streetlight shed on him, and she couldn't see him anymore. She had never been alone with Law before.

Almost immediately, he reached across the gap between them and patted her arm, made sounds at her, then waved toward the crowd.

"Yes," she said, "I see. That's nice, isn't it?" When Pass said things like that, it sounded like natural conversation between them. When she said it, it felt strained and unreal. She had no idea what he was communicating to her, really. She hoped she was answering appropriately. He returned to waving his hands at the crowd, and she decided to relax. After all, she knew about children. This couldn't be that different. She shouldn't be afraid.

She let her attention wander from him, but turned back quickly when he made a strangled sound, different from his grunts and squeals of happiness.

He was rocking back and forth, hands over his ears, staring ahead at a little boy who walked slightly behind his parents and pointed a toy gun at imaginary enemies and fired. He fired all around, at the people, then pressed the gun into his mother's back and said, "Blam-blam. You're dead, Mom."

"Yeah," she said. "Right. Tell my insurance agent."

The boy kept firing. Law's strangled sound became a sob and he moved his hands helplessly in front of him, as if he were trying to part an ocean. The sound he made grew louder.

Cricket gasped, uncertain what to do or say. She put a hand on his arm and he shook it off, stood up. She stood, too, thinking she had to do something, but didn't know what. He was like the hawk at the sanctuary, a wild creature that was frightened and might do anything. Where was Pass? He should be here.

"Law," she said, "stop. Please, stop."

He took a step forward and as an instinctive response, she put herself in front of him, her arms out, the same way she once stood in front of Janis when she tried to run into the road after a ball.

"Stop," she said. "Don't look at him. Don't look."

Law wrenched his attention toward her, his face collapsed in tears. She hadn't seen a face so full of grief since her daughters were little, before they learned to hide what they felt, or complicate it with notions of what they should and shouldn't do. It was unmitigated grief, pure as gold, and it resonated inside her like a bell.

"I'm sorry," she whispered. "I'm so sorry."

Then, she felt a hand on her shoulder. She turned and saw that Pass stood behind her. "What is it?" he asked.

"I don't know. He got . . . he saw a boy with a toy gun."

Pass quickly got in front of her, put a hand on Law's shoulder, another on his face.

"Look at me," he said. "Law, look at me."

Law stopped moving his head. He looked intently at Pass, and the noise stopped, though he breathed heavily, as if he'd been running.

"It's okay," Pass said again. "It's okay."

They stood like that for a full minute, then Pass released him and he sat back down.

Pass turned to Cricket. "You okay?"

"Yes. Fine. I just . . . I didn't know what to do."

"You did fine. Just fine. I'm sorry I wasn't here."

"No. That's okay. It's just that he doesn't know me well, and I didn't know what to do."

"He trusts you well enough," Pass said. "He didn't run away. If he doesn't trust someone, he just leaves. It helps if you touch him, though. Put a hand on his face or his arm or something. That helps."

"What scared him?" Cricket asked.

Pass took her hand. "I'm not sure yet. It's a new thing. Maybe from . . ." Pass shook himself lightly, as if rejecting some thought. "Could be from something he saw on TV. He gets ideas stuck in his head, sometimes. For a while, he started crying every time the toaster popped. I never figured that one out."

"What happened?" Cricket asked.

"Nothing. It just stopped."

"Can't he tell you what's scared him? He understands words, doesn't he? He knows what you're saying when you talk to him?"

"He understands. Words just aren't as important to him. He doesn't use them if he doesn't have to." He grinned at her. "Sometimes in the winter, when nobody much comes around, me and him'll go days without saying a thing. Law'll turn the TV on without the sound, even. After a while, it gets so quiet inside my head I forget how to use words, too."

Cricket could see the two of them, silent figures stalking through the big old house, the quiet in the rooms matching the absence of sound inside their skulls. But she had a hard time imagining what it would be like to silence the ongoing conversation in her own head. She talked to her interior almost constantly, and thought that if she was left alone, she'd just talk out loud to herself.

"Is it hard, not having words?" she asked.

"Sometimes. Usually not. Way I look at it, if you don't use words, you can't tell lies."

She supposed that was true. And she knew that interior silence was supposed to be good for you. All the yoga tapes and meditation books said so. She wondered if that was what made Pass simultaneously so compassionate, and so aloof. He lived with silence. He knew the broad sweep and depth of it. It did not make him afraid. He could stay at ease without the words that explained how or why something happened, the words that held the world together in recognizable form. For Pass, some things were mysterious, and that was okay. He could let them be. She didn't know if she was capable of that kind of patience.

He looked over at her and saw her chewing her lip. "What?" he asked. "You got a face full of questions."

"I just wonder how you do it," she said. "Take care of him. It seems so . . . big."

His face grew distant, and he answered quietly. "Remember that wife I told you I had? She thought it was too big. Wanted to send Law to a home. I wouldn't, and she left. I always thought nobody could take care of him as good as me. Lately, I wonder if maybe I was being selfish, keeping him for my good more than his. If maybe he'd be better off somewhere with more people, where he could get some real care." He shrugged, and held a hand out, palm up. "Hard to know your own motives, much less anyone else's, isn't it?"

She nodded agreement. People were bundles of mysterious motion, no matter what the psychologists figured out.

His expression lightened, and he smiled at her. "Depends on the day, I suppose. For the most part, if he's on his own turf, he's no trouble at all. You tired?"

"A little," she said.

"Me, too. Let's head back, okay?" He reached over with his free hand and tapped his brother's arm. "C'mon, Law," he said. "Let's go."

They walked away from the square, back to the crowded streets of the French Quarter, into the cacophony of voices and music all around. As they walked, Law began making happy sounds again, and pointing at people in colorful dress or the glitter of cheap beads and voodoo dolls and trinkets in shop windows.

"Now there's some fine folks," Pass said, when Law pointed at a woman who carried a poodle in a baby carrier at her belly, walking with a man in a pink polyester suit. "You suppose they're retired, and going around the country in their RV, or are they CIA out looking for some New Orleans organized criminals to arrest?"

Cricket smiled. "CIA, definitely. What about that one?" She indicated a man in drag, who was scratching his behind, peering at a shop window.

"That," Pass said, "might look like a man in drag, but it's really a movie star, who's dressed up to look like a man in drag so nobody'll recognize her and bug her for autographs. Madonna, for sure."

"Of course," Cricket agreed. She hadn't played this game in a long time. She used to play it with the girls, making up stories about the people they passed in cars when they went on trips. Jim would sometimes join in, but he wasn't as good at it as the girls were. Janis, especially, could weave stories that would last for days afterward, becoming the jumping-off point for bedtime tales that the girls whispered to each other late at night, during the days when they still shared a room.

"There's a love story." Cricket noted a young man and woman who stood in the middle of the street, their foreheads pressed together. He was talking softly. She was frowning.

"Not a happy one," Pass said. "Her fish died."

"Her fish?"

"Yes. A very special fish that her mother gave her. A . . . Yugoslavian fish. The last of its kind that belonged to her family when they were still princes and princesses. She's sad about it, but he's telling her that now they're free to make a whole new life, together."

"New fish," she said.

"That's right. And what about— Hey." He stopped walking, and looked around. "Where's Law?"

She thought he was walking next to them. She shook her head. "He was right here."

"Hell," Pass said, and grabbed her arm. "C'mon."

They turned and walked back the way they'd come, Pass scooting out into the streets, looking into shop doors, as he went. Cricket spotted Law first. He was in front of a bar that had open doors, and music pouring out of it. He was swaying and moving his arms as if they were the slow wings of a very large bird. He made a sound that was almost singing. Clusters of people stood near him, watching suspiciously.

"Pass," she said. "There."

Pass stood still, and looked where she pointed. His face tensed into anger, then relaxed. " 'Mustang Sally,' " he said. "Of course."

"What?"

"It's one of his favorite songs. We used to walk down here in the evening just because we knew that, sooner or later, somebody'd play it."

He walked toward Law and Cricket followed. "Hey," Pass called. "You could've let me know, huh?"

Law turned toward Pass's voice, startled at first, then just grinning and moving his arms harder, his feet going up and down now. He laughed, his face as full of open delight as it had been of grief a short while ago. He put a hand out toward them as they approached, and when Pass was within reach, he grabbed him and moved his arm up and down.

"Okay, okay," Pass said. "Don't rush me, though. It's been a while."

The people who had been looking suspicious now began to smile, as Pass joined in with Law's birdlike dance, Pass laughing at himself, Law just laughing out of pleasure in the song.

Cricket clapped her hands in time, until Pass curled a finger toward her, drawing her to them. "C'mon," he said. "You, too."

"No. I can't. I couldn't."

Law waved his hands at her, singing something that was almost "Ride, Sally, ride." She shook her head, smiling. Law moved toward her and Pass took a step, too, looking a little concerned, then stopped and stood still, watching. Law reached down and took her hand, pulled her over, indicating that she should do what he did. Embarrassed, uncertain, she imitated him, and he nodded at her, making sounds of approval, as if she were a child who'd gotten a lesson right.

Pass came nearer to her, and the people gathered around began to join in, clapping and singing. Cricket had never done anything like this. It was like flying, she thought. Full of freedom and peace. She didn't have to worry about how she looked, or being a good dancer. All she had to do was follow Law. His infirmity was her permission to do what she wanted to, and her protection from ridicule.

When the song was over, the crowd that had gathered applauded wildly, then began to disperse, moving toward whatever adventure came next. Cricket saw patches of damp on Pass's T-shirt, and realized sweat was dripping down the back of her neck as well.

Pass stood next to her and took her hands in his. "Thank you," he said quietly. He ran a finger down her cheek. He looked over at Law. "You happy now, buddy?" Law grinned and nodded.

"That's good. I'm glad. And I think we better call it a night. Tomorrow's the butterfly house, and a few other places I want to check out."

"Other places?" Cricket asked. "Where?"

He shook his head. "Just a place. From when we lived here. It's . . . well, it's got to do with Law. He liked it here. Still does, it looks like. And I'm thinking he might need a change."

"A change?" She didn't understand.

"We'll see tomorrow," he said. "See how it goes. Right now, I'd rather get you somewhere where we can get these sticky clothes off."

Pass moved his hand along the back of her neck, then leaned over and kissed her there.

"Okay," she said. "Okay."

f o u r t e e n

"*I always feel a little funny* about zoos," Pass said as they stood in front of a monkey exhibit, watching them walk like humans across a log. "I know they breed animals, and preserve species, and it's nice to see animals I wouldn't get to see, but . . . they're in cages."

Cricket felt the same way. She nurtured a vague guilt for being here, and had the urge to apologize to the animals or set them free, though she knew that would kill many of them.

Law was the only one who had no moral reservations. He got as close as he could to each habitat, which was what they called them instead of cages, leaning over the fence that looked down on the gorillas and laughing, pressing his face against the glass enclosure where the capuchins ran up and down a jungle gym. At one point, one of the monkeys came over to him and pressed his face on the glass just on the other side of Law, and he laughed so hard Cricket was afraid he was going to make himself sick. Pass laughed with him, and Cricket realized how much he relaxed when Law was happy, how tense he got when Law was not.

The zoo was large, and they walked all of it, stopping for lunch just outside the seal habitat, where the seals hung upside down in the water and blinked their large liquid eyes at the people who stared at them.

"Just like you," Cricket said to Pass. "They hang upside down in the water, too."

"Hey," Law barked. "Hey, hey."

Pass laughed. They were like a family with a toddler in tow, albeit a large one.

"Butterfly house," Pass said, "and then let's get out of here."

The enclosure was larger than the one they planned, a dome of glass that seemed filled with mist. They had to go through a sort of alcove, then they went into the house itself, where at first they just stood in the quiet and the warmth.

Cricket felt the soft flutter of silent wings moving the air around her, the strange soft energy of flying flowers. There were other people walking through—quite a few of them. But they were all quiet, too. Made quiet by the softness of the space, trying to breathe in something as ephemeral as these colors, these shapes, these motions.

"Pretty," Pass muttered, and she saw him staring up, his eyes following a painted lady in flight to the top of the enclosure. He walked, following its flight. They all wandered, like the butterflies, in random ways, knowing they could find each other easily if they needed to.

Cricket stopped at a feeding station where a group of butterflies sat in a plate, drinking from sponges soaked in sugar water. As she watched their persistent feeding, she heard a sound behind her and turned to it. It was Law.

She stood to one side, to let him close. He bent down to the sponge and held his hand out. The butterflies turned to it, walked clumsily to his hand and began to each find a place to cling to his fingers, as if he were a lightbulb or a flower. He smiled, laughed his odd laugh. Something inside her turned warm and expansive.

Law moved his hands and the butterflies worked their wings, floating upward like flower petals defying gravity.

One clung to his index finger and he turned to Cricket, offering it to her.

"Let it go," she said to Law, but he only brought it closer to her. She took a step back.

"I can't," she said. "You can't touch them. If you do, you can hurt them. Kill them. I can't."

Law frowned at her, holding it out. She looked around for Pass, but he was at a different station, his face bent over a cluster of butterflies.

"I can't," she said again, and turned around and left the dome.

When she got outside, she found she was breathing hard, as if she was afraid. What happened? She'd behaved badly, turning away a gift like that. She could have just said thank you, and let it walk onto her finger and then encouraged it to fly away. That wouldn't have hurt it.

But she couldn't touch it. Butterflies attached themselves to your fingers, and it was hard to shake them loose. She would hurt it if she touched it. She couldn't touch it.

"Hey," Pass said, when he came out of the dome with Law and found her. "Where'd you go?"

She looked at him, and at Law, who was smiling vaguely. He probably hadn't noticed her distress, or didn't remember.

"Here," she said lightly. "Resting my feet. Ready to go?"

"Yeah. Let's get out of here. I'll drive. There's a stop I want to make."

They drove through the garden district, but didn't stop to admire, so Cricket would only remember passing views of trees and flowers that looked southern, rich and red and luxurious and sensual. Law made a sound, and she turned to look at him. His eyes were big and he had a finger pressed against the window, pointing at something she couldn't see. She felt warmly toward him, partly for not giving her away, but also because she was beginning to see something beautiful about him, too.

Maybe the beauty was in the caring his presence brought out

in other people. If he required love, in a sense he had created it. She could see that her life would be beautiful if she devoted it to loving him, this child who would never grow up. She could imagine herself and Pass somewhere, in a house—in her house, in fact—and Law in the backyard, swinging on the swing set they'd put up for the girls. She would be shelling peas in the kitchen, making supper for them, and maybe that decision, to care for someone like Law, would redeem her heart, her losses, and her life.

Pass took a couple of turns and swore softly to himself.

"What?" she asked.

"Nothing. I just— I can't remember."

"Remember what?"

"A place. A place I wanna see. Some people I wanna talk to."

"People?" she asked. "What people?"

"Some people I knew. Here it is," he said. "This is the street." He turned right, and drove slowly, counting numbers. "Should be right— Shit. Hell." He pulled into a parking space that had a hydrant, and got out of the car. He opened the back door and tugged at Law's arm. Law had his earphones in, but he looked up at Pass, who made a gesture to him. "Come on," he said. "A walk."

Law got out, and Pass walked quickly down the street, Law by his side. She watched him walk down the street, then got out and followed.

"Pass, what're you doing?"

"I'm . . . looking," he said, without stopping. He entered a building that said "Southern Indemnity" on the front of it. An insurance office. Why was he going there? She followed him inside, casting a glance at Law, who sat down on the curb and rocked back and forth to his music.

Inside, she saw Pass standing at a receptionist's desk, talking. "No," he was saying. "I don't have a claim. I'm looking for the Brothers. Franciscan Brothers. They lived here."

"Funny. You don't look the type," the girl drawled softly, looking up at him from her heavily made-up eyes.

Pass's face clouded with anger. "They lived here," he said, and pressed a finger on her desk. "Right here. And they had an orphanage, and a garden, and a school. Did they move?"

"Sugar," the receptionist said, "I wouldn't have a clue. I been working here about two months, and for all I know that's all the building's been here."

As she spoke, a security guard came over to listen. "Bettina, you don't know much," he said to her, then put a hand out to Pass. "Hi, there," he said. "Y'all from out of town?"

Pass nodded. "But I used to live here. Long time ago. This was a Franciscan friary."

"That's right," the guard said. "Used to be. Tore it down a few years ago. Put this up instead. Don't know where the Brothers went. Lot of 'em died."

Pass frowned, stood looking around at the office art—splashes of color without form. Then, he walked to the door and left.

Cricket stood gaping for a brief second, then went after him. She had to clip fast to catch up. He was standing on the street, looking around helplessly. Law sat on the curb, listening to his music, humming tunelessly.

"Pass," she said. "What is it? What's wrong?"

"I didn't know," he mumbled. "I didn't know they were gone."

"Does it matter that much?"

He stopped walking and covered his face with his hands. Cricket grew afraid. Something was going on here that was beyond absent priests, or childhood nostalgia. He brought his hands down and turned a stricken face to Cricket.

"I wanted to bring Law back," he said. "When he was a kid, they took care of him. After our mother died. I lived with them, and so did Law. They told me . . . they said bring him back anytime. When I told them I was moving North. They said that. Bring him back anytime. He'll always have a home here. He . . . helped them do things. In the yard. In the house. They liked him."

"You were . . . going to bring him back? To live here?"

Pass nodded.

"Didn't you call?" Cricket asked.

"I thought—they're Brothers. Where would they go?"

Cricket felt as if she was still not understanding. "But why were you bringing him back?"

"He needs more than I can give him," Pass said. "I can't . . . I don't know how to take care of him anymore."

"No," she protested. "You do fine."

"I don't," he insisted. "I can't."

"Well, there are programs you can get him into," she suggested. "Something closer to home so you could see him."

"I . . . can't," he said. "He needs to be away. To go away."

Pass made fists with his hands, then unclenched them. He turned his face up to the sky, then down. Something cold walked up the back of Cricket's spine. It was the bad feeling she or her sister would get before an unpleasant event. A bad feeling.

"Go away? From what?" she asked hesitantly.

Pass drew in a ragged breath and let it out. "The day of the shooting. Law was . . . he went out. Remember, he left? You were there. Remember?"

"Yes," she said. "Yes."

"He didn't come back until late. I thought he was out in the woods. He goes out in the woods sometimes. There's nothing can hurt him there. But when he came in, he had blood on his jacket."

"Blood? What're you saying, Pass?"

"I think he was at the mall. The day of the shooting. I think he was there. He was all messed up when he came back. He couldn't stop crying. And now he cries sometimes and can't stop. I can't . . . I can't keep him safe."

The mall. Yes. She remembered Pass saying he knew how to go. That he went sometimes. But she didn't think to ask about it after. There was so much else to think about. And now Law was afraid of guns, afraid of blood. But that was horrible. Horrible.

"And . . . later on that week, I found a gun," Pass said.

Cricket paused to let the words make sense. "A gun?" she asked.

"In the woods just outside the breeding area. Just lying there. A . . . a Glock."

Cricket's skin grew cold, as if her body was preparing for an emergency, denying blood to the surface, sequestering it at the core. This couldn't be happening to her. She didn't run this far away for it to be happening to her here, in New Orleans with Pass. This dream was too young to die.

She stepped in front of him and grabbed his arm, shook it. "No," she said. "No."

"Cricket, I can't—"

"No. You knew this all along, and you didn't tell me. You knew why you were bringing him here and you didn't tell me."

"I didn't want to upset you. It's my problem, not yours."

She shook him again. "What else aren't you telling me? Did he kill Grace? Did he?"

Pass let his mouth open and shut again. His eyes flashed with anger, and he pulled away from her. "Of course not. He wouldn't. Jesus, Cricket. How could you think—"

"Did you ask him?" she interrupted. "Did you ask him what happened?"

"He wouldn't talk. He . . . he started to cry."

"The gun," Cricket demanded. "What did you do with it?"

"I took it into town, and I left it on the steps at the police department."

"The news didn't say anything about that."

"Of course not. It's probably not the same gun. Or else they're keeping it quiet."

"But . . . you didn't tell them where you found it. They should know."

"And where would that get them?"

"I don't know. You don't know either. You can't decide that. You can't live like that."

"Like what?"

"Like . . . like the rest of the world doesn't exist. Like there's nothing but you and your brother. You can't just decide what's true. You found a gun. Your brother was at the mall. You have to go to the police and tell them."

"What for?" he asked. "So they'll torture him with questions for nothing?"

"For nothing? People have to know. They have to know what happened to their children. How it happened."

"Well, how the hell did it happen?" Pass asked. "Who did it? The guy that sells the gun? The TV shows that solve all the problems with guns? The stupid world that tells people this is how you fix things? The way we don't know anybody anymore, and don't care? You tell me how the hell it happened."

"Somebody walked into the mall and started shooting. That's how. Somebody shot Grace. My *daughter*, Pass. With a gun. A Glock."

"Not him," Pass said, tossing a nod at Law, who sat on the curb rocking, listening to his music, not paying attention. "He didn't."

He was in denial, Cricket thought. Obviously in denial because he had no way of knowing if Law did it or not. It could as easily be him as anyone, and in fact more likely him. He wasn't evil, but he was broken. Broken people did broken things.

"You don't know what he did. You let him go to the mall alone, and you don't know what he did. You don't know the truth."

"I *know*, Cricket."

"How? He can't tell you. He didn't tell you."

"I don't need words. I know he didn't kill anyone. If you think he did, you've got a fantasy going that's—"

"Fantasy?" she cut in. "You . . . you live with birds and . . . and you think beauty is all that matters and you say I'm making up a fantasy? *I'm* facing the truth, Pass."

"You think something is more true just because it hurts? Used to be everything was beautiful, now it's all shit? It's still a fantasy.

Jesus, what is this? Is it too much for you, having someone really love you? Being who you are, and happy about it?"

"Stop it," she said. "Just stop it. Don't . . . don't pretend this is about me. It's about him." She jabbed her finger in Law's direction. They both looked at him, then turned back to each other. "You know what he did. You knew all along."

"I didn't lie. I didn't say anything."

"Lying isn't just what you say," she said. "It's what you don't say, and what you do. How you live. You lived a lie, treating me like I'm one of your birds you can fix. You had a story in your head and you just lived it, as if it were the truth. People do it all the time."

"I don't," he said pointedly. "I don't do that. You do. Except that now your lie is about pain. It's just another story you tell yourself. It's not *real*, Cricket."

She suddenly hated him. She wanted to slap his face and scratch at his eyes. How dare he? How dare he say any of this to her. He was trying to trick her into hope, and she wouldn't be tricked. He'd tricked her into feeling pleasure, wanting his body, his laughter, his talk about beauty and love, and she hated him because she didn't want to give all that up. She wanted to believe him. She wanted to be happy, and she hated him, hated herself for it.

She took a step back, then another.

"What're you doing?" Pass asked.

"I have to leave," she whispered hoarsely. "I have to leave." Pass was dangerous. What he believed in, hoped for, it was dangerous. She had to leave. Not to go back to Jim. Just to leave. Leave them all.

His face went tight and pained. He closed his eyes and opened them again. "Don't, Cricket. What we have, what we're doing, it's important. Don't run away from it."

She took another step away. He stepped toward her. "Law didn't kill your daughter," he said. "And you and me, we're not a

fantasy. We're real. Remember? Remember? Can't you tell the difference?"

She felt a cry rise from the bottom of her belly to her throat
and escape. She pulled her arm away from his grasp, put her hand
to her mouth, then walked quickly back to the car, got in, and
drove away.

The last thing she saw of him was his shocked face in her
rearview mirror, standing next to Law, who sat on the curb and
rocked.

DREAM #8

killer dreams

Cricket drove up and across. Up and across to Arkansas, to Oklahoma. She drove for five hours without a break, then stopped to go to the bathroom. She didn't look at herself in the mirror. She supposed she looked pretty awful. She'd stopped at the hotel to pick up her bags and leave some money because she didn't want Pass to pay the whole bill. She'd brought a large chunk of her savings account for the trip, and had enough to pay her own way. That and two credit cards would get her where she needed to go next.

She got back in the car and kept going until she was afraid she'd drive off the road. Then she pulled into a rest station, locked her doors, and slept fitfully, dreaming what the killer had dreamt all of his life. Not just one dream, but all the dreams he'd ever had.

Some nights he had nightmares, about his own death, the death of his mother or father, the death of his world. Sometimes he dreamt of aliens who were out to get him and destroy the world. Sometimes he had pleasant dreams of pretty colors, soft sounds. And when he woke, he sometimes couldn't tell where the dream left off, and the day began.

When he was a child, he dreamt that he had a miniature zoo in his room, where small elephants and giraffes grazed on tiny trees, and little kangaroos hopped across nearby arid lands. In his dream, he could pick up the animals, and they would walk across his hand, his arm, up his shoulder. He could still remember the feel of it, how pleasurable it was to have a dream that felt true. Then he would be despondent when he woke and looked for the animals, and couldn't find them.

After a while, he grew angry at the dream, and when he had it, he picked up the elephants and crushed them in his hand, their insides oozing out between his fingers. He took pleasure in watching the giraffes try to flee his hand, the kangaroos try to bounce out of his reach. He would catch them all, one at a time, and crush them, snap their necks, slam them against the wall. They were not real. None of them were real.

What was real was his waking life, which included a certainty of doom, and a persistent burning anger in his chest. He wanted his dreams to be real or go away. They would do neither. They stayed and burned him from the inside out. Even when he was awake, they called to him, talked to him in soft voices that were sometimes lies, and sometimes true, until he couldn't tell the difference anymore.

He told nobody about this, because he was afraid if anyone knew, they'd laugh at him, or punish him. Sometimes he'd offer hints, but nobody picked up on them. Nobody offered any advice. Most people seemed too busy or preoccupied to care at all. He began to suspect that everyone had their own voices to deal with. He learned to deal with his own, by himself.

Then, one day, while he was walking in the woods, he found an injured bird. He picked it up, and remembered the sweet feel of his childhood dream, of those small animals that were his to care for, to enjoy, to view with pleasure. He remembered that they weren't real, and he snapped the bird's neck.

The burning in his chest stopped. No voices spoke for a long time. From then on, he understood how to help himself, and he did it whenever he could.

Cricket dreamt this dream, and woke from it in terror. She sat up and bumped her head on the steering wheel. She looked around, not sure where she was or where she was supposed to be.

Then she remembered.

She was on her own. In Oklahoma still? Or Kansas? She didn't care. She was somewhere. Anywhere. On her own.

She got in the front seat and drove through a gray and foggy dawn, on gray cement, through gray air. The color gray was relentless, except for odd things she spotted along the side of the road. There was a sunflower growing on the edge of the highway. She did not know how it got there, or how, getting there, it survived. She saw an odd shoe and wondered what circumstance had brought a pink high heel to rest on the highway. She saw couch cushions. Strips of black rubber tires. Broken chairs. The sun set and the gray deepened to black. She found a rest stop, pulled over, locked the doors and dozed.

That night, the killer dreamt a new dream. In this dream, he was a shadow that moved through the world, untouchable, untouched. He could absorb no pain, because he had no substance. He could not be caught, because he was only the absence of light. When he reached out and stroked someone's skin with his fingers, they felt nothing. If someone tried to put hands on him, he did not feel their touch.

Cricket felt the relief of that, of not being touched or attached. It gave away all her pain, but it also made her feel as if she were spinning out of control, as if she were a balloon released from a hand.

She woke flailing her arms as if she were falling. It was broad daylight, with no fog, and in spite of the dream, she felt almost rested.

She stretched, got out of the car and saw by the map outside the rest room that she had somehow gotten to Texas. She went to the bathroom, finding the door that said women/mujeres. When she came back out, she realized it was hot, and the land was flat and the sky was very big. She stared into it and listened to the traffic whizzing by.

"I'm alone," she said to herself, amazed. "Alone."

She had never in her life been completely alone, her actions and thoughts unmediated by anyone except herself. She was terrified. She didn't know what you did with your thoughts if there was nobody else around for them to center on.

She brought her hands up to where she could see them, and flexed them. They were her hands. She patted her belly. It was her belly. She ran her hands up her belly to her breasts. They were hers. And her slim neck was hers, and her face and her hair. She went back into the bathroom and looked in the mirror. Her eyes were wild, her hair matted and greasy, the skin of her face mottled with sleep. But it was her face. It attached her to nobody but herself. It looked dirty and tired, but also relieved.

"I'm relieved," she thought, and realized she was. I am a woman with events in her life, she thought. I have lived events. But they aren't attached to me anymore, because I'm not attached to anybody. I am alone.

She went back to her car and got in. She didn't have to be grief-stricken when she was alone. Here she had no daughters, no lovers, no sisters, and so she had nothing to hurt her. If you're nobody, you can't be found, can't be touched. She would be nobody. She would be unfound. Untouched. Hadn't she always been, anyway? Wasn't that the modern condition? To be nobody, untouched and unfound. Her daughter was killed because she was nobody to a man with a gun. She lived in a world that saw its children as nobody and ate them. Pass still believed in beauty, but that was dangerous. Beauty touched you. Stalked you. Caught and stabbed you. She would be what the world asked her to be. Nobody. Unfound and untouched.

The thought elated her, elevated her. She told herself to be calm, but she couldn't, even though she remembered her mother saying that after laughter, came tears. That's what she'd say when Cricket and Peggy got the giggles. "Now, girls, calm down before you get upset. After laughter, come tears."

Cricket laughed, thinking of that. What did that matter, if she was alone, and driving. She turned the radio on, and scanned her way through preachers and more preachers. She realized it must be Sunday morning.

As she made her way across the Panhandle into New Mexico, she began to feel depressed, and wondered if her mother was right. Too much happiness depleted the system, and caused depression. That's why humans needed pain now and then.

"No," she said to herself, "I don't think so. I think I'm just hungry."

Hungry and tired, and not a clue where she was going. Maybe, she thought, she'd stay in Texas, get a room and a part-time job and just stay here until she felt like going somewhere else. She was just outside of Amarillo. That might be a nice place to stay.

She pulled the car over to the side of the road and got out. There wasn't much in the way of traffic, and you could see it coming from a long ways away. The sky was huge, and she asked it if she wanted to stop here. But when she stretched, a billboard caught her eye.

It was a giant crucifix, with Jesus hanging on it, almost dead. Underneath it said, in large, bold letters, "NOW IT'S YOUR TURN."

She got back in the car and drove.

She stopped in Tucumcari, New Mexico, just over the border, and found a place to get hamburgers and fries, which tasted better than any food she'd ever eaten, though from the looks of the kitchen, she was fooling herself about that. The heat of the day penetrated her in a different way than it did in New Orleans. There it sat on your skin with the humidity, making you feel enclosed. Here, you were permeable to it, and it entered you like water into stone, making you feel full of an energy you weren't sure your body was meant to contain. She glowed and buzzed and pulsed with the heat.

When darkness came around, she found a little hotel and a map. Her room was old and shoddy, and next door she could hear a couple having sex. "Call me 'big boy,' " he said. "Say, 'I want to fuck you, big boy.' "

They went at it for a long time, and at first Cricket was irritated, and felt her privacy was being violated. Then she realized they didn't even know she existed, much less want any of her privacy. She listened to them until he moaned and then, shortly thereafter, began to snore. After that, she heard water running in the bathroom, the door opening and closing, and she ceased attending to them.

Restless, she got out of bed and went to look at her map to decide where to go in the morning. Of course, ultimately where she went didn't matter, just as she didn't matter in a wild and random universe.

She closed her eyes and let her finger drop onto the map.

It landed on Farmington, New Mexico. That's where she would go.

She got back into bed and closed her eyes. The room was quiet. She was alone. That night she slept well, and dreamt nothing at all.

fifteen

Pass and Law stood for some time in the street in New Orleans, Law singing to himself and rocking on the curb, Pass staring at the emptiness that confronted him.

Then, he tapped Law on the shoulder and said, "C'mon, buddy. We better go."

He had the long habit of deferring his feelings to the necessity of caring for Law. Sometimes it seemed a lot easier that way. When his wife left him, he didn't end up at bars drinking his sorrows and himself to death the way some men did. When his mother died, he had no time to linger in his grief. He was needed.

They walked back to the hotel, the few miles not much to either of them. They often did a lot more in a day, and for Pass right now the activity was a good substitute for what he really wanted to do, which was scream or run until he found Cricket, or smash something or cry. His feet pounded pavement, and it provided some relief.

When they got to the hotel, Pass saw that Cricket had come back for her bags and left money. He crumpled up the wad of bills in his hand, humiliated by them. He was more used to caring for people than being cared for.

He turned to Law. "Here," he said, holding out the wad. "You should have some money in your pockets."

Law took it and straightened it carefully, and tucked it away.

Pass made arrangements at the front desk for a rental car to be dropped off, but when it came and he got in it, he realized he didn't know where he would go. The intern would be at the sanctuary for another week, so he didn't have to go back directly. But he didn't want to continue with the journey he'd planned with Cricket. His heart felt like a burden to him, and Cricket's absence a weight inside his belly.

He and Law sat in the car, Law listening to his tape and smiling out the window, Pass running his hands around the steering wheel, feeling the weight of his life. He'd have to accept this, he thought. This would be the way things were now, this heaviness, this emptiness, all living inside him. He'd have to get used to it, and go on.

He started the car and pointed it back the way they'd came, toward Mississippi. Toward his hometown. Though he hadn't wanted to see it with Cricket, who was about his present and his future, suddenly, he thought it would be a good time to visit.

He frequently dreamt about it, and more often than not his mother would be in those dreams. He came to think of them as visits from her, and always wondered if there was something in particular she wanted him to know when she appeared. Sometimes, a week or so after the dream, he would be able to piece it together with events in his waking life and understand the connection she'd been trying to help him make. While he didn't believe in analyzing dreams, he did believe in connections between dreaming and waking.

In the dreams of his hometown, he would sometimes be standing with his mother by a pond, listening to the early peepers singing. Hush, she would say to him. Listen. They're calling your name. Then, she would let go of his hand and walk away, backward, waving to him as she walked.

"Where're you going, Mama?" he'd ask. But she wouldn't answer. She would just keep walking backward, until he became aware of a great hole in the earth opening up behind her. He would see that she was going to step into it, and then he would see that it was a grave. But he was powerless to do anything about it. All he could do was stand and watch. There wasn't any way he could reach her before she fell.

Then, he would be an adult in the dream, standing by his mother's grave with a flower in his hand, Law standing next to him, smiling, not understanding.

Sometimes in the dream, Law would jump in after her, casually, as if it was an unimportant decision, and Pass would be left standing there alone.

When he got to the sign for the turnoff to Pass Christian, he found he could not take it. He just couldn't make the car go that way. He drove right past.

He kept driving for a while, wondering what to do next, and then realized there was only one place he could go, and that was home. Back to his birds. Back to taking care of Law, and watching children's faces when they first saw an eagle spread its wings. Back to doing what he did.

People thought he cared for birds because he was either very crazy or very good. But none of that was the truth. The truth was, the birds healed him. And not just him, but other people, other things, too.

Every time he released an eagle or a hawk or a crow, he would see something healed. He would see his mother flying out from her grave, soaring free not only of her death, but also of her life. He would feel in his bones that some child had escaped the stepfather who raped her, or know that some daughter had risen up from her coma and lived. He would have a sudden, sure sense that someone had put down their gun and decided not to kill. He would have a certainty that somewhere a father had stopped beating his son senseless.

And every time he made a home for a bird that would never fly again, he would know a homeless man was finding shelter, or an old woman was being fed, or a child finding a family, and none of them would ever know what the birds did for them when they weren't looking.

He didn't talk about it, but that's what he knew to be true. That every bird he cared for made a place in the world for something good to happen, beyond his hands. This knowledge was so clear in him that sometimes he felt guilty, as if he was using the birds, and they were caring for him, instead of the other way around.

He would go back to it. It might heal him again, and it might not, but he would go back to it anyway. It was where he belonged.

He stopped for a day at Virginia Beach, but the waves, the sun on his skin, the water, reminded him of Cricket and they didn't stay for a second day. He stopped again just over the Pennsylvania–New York border, when he saw a sign for an inn, with a restaurant attached. He would take Law out to dinner, sit and look at him over the dinner table and try not to be angry at him for being who he was, what he was.

He ordered steak for Law, fish for himself.

"Law," he said, whispering, "where did that gun come from?"

Law grinned at him, and cut another piece off his steak.

"Law, what happened at the mall?"

Law stopped grinning, stopped cutting. He put his knife down and stared at Pass.

"What?" he asked slowly.

"What did you do?" Pass asked harshly.

Law frowned. His eyes filled with water and the water spilled onto the steak.

The waitress came by and said jauntily, "Can I get you anything else?"

Then she took in the scene and whispered to Pass, "Is everything okay, sir?"

Pass ran a hand over his tired face. "Some more water might be
good," he said. "And . . . a Scotch for me." He was not a drinking
man, but he wanted to drink tonight. He did not know where his
soul was, or where it belonged. Not that he always believed he had
a soul. But he wasn't sure he didn't, either. And he knew some
essential part of him was missing.

Cricket was gone, and though he could live alone, what they
had together was the song his soul wanted to sing.

He wanted to try and deny this, because God only knew that
would be easier than feeling it. He wanted to tell himself that she
was just another woman, and there were plenty. Or that he was
better off on his own. Or that he'd get over it and move on. But
that wasn't true, and he wasn't the kind to tell himself lies. They
always caught up with you. Hadn't he just learned that all over
again?

Sitting and drinking his Scotch, he grew angry at himself. He
withheld the truth from her, telling himself there was no reason for
her to know, it didn't affect her, had nothing to do with her. He
knew better.

His work with the birds had taught him about the intricate
connections between one living thing and another. An event that
coursed through his life would ripple out to everyone else he
touched, and from there to everyone they touched, and on and on
and on. To forget that was to live a lie. It was the heart of trouble
and evil and pain, the sickness of the century.

But here he'd acted as if he was separate in some essential way.
Or that he was the healer, and she needed healing, which gave him
dispensation to withhold the truth. But his motives were com-
posed primarily of fear. Fear that she'd leave. Fear that she'd think
Law was a killer. Maybe fear that she was right, because if she was,
how could he face that?

No. She wasn't. She wasn't right about Law.

Maybe he should have gone to the police, but he knew what would've happened. It would have been a witch hunt, and Law was such an easy target. He was different. People were frightened of him. But he didn't do it. He couldn't have. He was innocent. It was his innocence that tortured him now, made him cry when he saw blood or heard shouting.

Whatever happened that day and night he was missing, it had hurt him horribly. Pass was sure that meant he was a witness and not a criminal. And it would be easy enough for him to pick up the gun if the killer dropped it. He would do that, unthinking, and walk away. But he wouldn't kill. Not Law.

Yes, sometimes he hunted with Pass, but that was bow and arrow, and though he was slow in thinking, his senses and his body worked better than most. Yes, he could butcher chickens easily and well. Yes, his mind was misshapen, mismade. But he wasn't a killer. He just wasn't.

The waitress returned with more water. When she put it down, she touched Pass on the shoulder. He looked up at her and saw that she was young, pretty, with soft breasts and softer eyes that looked at him as if to say, I'd like to help you feel better.

"Will you be staying at the inn tonight?" she asked.

"Yes," he said. "We will."

"Is there anything special you need for . . . for him?"

"No," he said. "Nothing."

"Well, I'll be here all night. I'm in the kitchen until eleven, and then I usually go to the bar for a little, so let me know if you do. Need anything. I'm Kara, by the way."

He nodded at her. "Pass. Pass Christian."

She wrinkled her face, not sure what he was saying. "That's my name," Pass told her, smiling at her confusion.

"Oh," she said. "How odd."

"Yes," he said. "Very odd. Suits me, I suppose."

She smiled at his joke, patted his shoulder. "Well, Pass Christian, if you're odd, you've come to the right place. Look me up later and we can talk about it." She left, her invitation remaining in the room, in his thoughts.

Pass pushed the water toward Law. "Here," he said. "Drink this. I won't ask any more questions."

Law picked up the water, and drank. In a short while, he was smiling again.

After dinner, Pass brought Law to the room and when he was watching TV, settled in, told him, "I'm going down to the bar for a while. I'll be back soon."

Law nodded, then giggled at a beer commercial. Pass left the room and went down the hall. He thought of how nice it would be to hold a woman tonight. He didn't need Cricket for that simple comfort. He'd found it in plenty of places before her, and would find it again.

When he got to the door that led to the bar, he saw her standing behind it, holding a bottle high to pour clear liquid into a glass. She was smiling at a customer, listening to him, nodding as he spoke. She was pretty, and welcoming.

And he knew better.

He watched her finish making the drink, then turned around and went back to his room.

"Hi," Law said, and pointed at the TV, where Animal Planet showed a man holding a snake.

"Hi," Pass said. He got undressed and climbed under the covers. He felt heavy. As heavy as a stone sinking into deep ocean.

He put his head down on the pillow, and fell asleep fast, tumbling into a deep and terrifying dream of his brother standing high on the edge of a cliff, teetering, unable to hold his footing. He held out an arm that was broken and bleeding profusely. Pass stood a few yards away, afraid to move forward because it might tip him over the edge, but afraid to stay where he was because then Law might fall.

He had to touch him. Somehow, touching him would fix his arm, and then he would be able to fly away. A voice in the dream, perhaps his mother's voice, said clearly, "Salvation requires touch." He had to touch him.

Pass ran to his brother and grasped him by the broken arm, seeing too late that in his hand, he held a gun. Law, smiling, fired the gun and Pass felt the bullet enter him, go through him, ripping him inside where he would never heal. He fell forward onto Law, who stepped off the cliff, walking backward into nowhere, bringing Pass with him.

No, Pass thought. This is horrible. I can't die. I can't die. I want to see Cricket. I want to kiss her, touch her.

But he knew he would die here, with his brother. He felt himself falling, falling with Law from a high place, into darkness.

sixteen

She was glad to stop in Farmington. She was tired of going.

She went to a diner that was filled with cowboys who stared at her, but she had a newspaper to look at for apartments, for jobs. The waitress who brought her coffee gave her a pen to circle places, then asked, "How long you looking to stay?"

"I'm not sure," Cricket said. "Awhile."

"I know a place. It's a sublet, and the owner'll be back in three months, but it's nice, and it's all furnished and pretty cheap. Guy who owns it is out of the country, and I'm watching it for him. Be easier for me to know someone's living in it. Must be nice to say that, huh? Out of the country? You interested?"

"Yes," Cricket said, responding to the last question. "I am."

"Great," the woman said. "Listen, can you hang around? If you can, I'll take you to see it when my shift's over. My name's Susan, by the way."

She stuck her hand out. It was rough, and she had long red nails that curved off the tip of her fingers. Cricket took it, and tried to think of something to say. It had been many days since she talked with anyone, and though she didn't find the inside of her mind much quieter, she did find that already it was easier not to talk.

"You got a name?" Susan asked.

"I'm Cricket," she said.

"Cricket? That's a pretty name," Susan said. "Is it real?"

Cricket frowned, not sure what she was being asked.

"I mean, is it a nickname?"

"Oh. Yes. My father gave it to me. But it's the name on my license and checkbook and everything."

"That's nice. Listen, I gotta get back to it, but wait here, okay? I've only got another"—she checked her wristwatch—"forty-six minutes and a few seconds. Then I'm off."

Cricket waited at the diner until Susan was off her shift, and then went with her to look at the apartment.

It was a small place on the edge of town, with curved adobe walls and slanting ceilings. The walls felt thick, but the windows let in the strange new light of this place. The furniture looked used, but not dirty, as if she'd find fleas or rodents living in it, which she was afraid of. And it didn't look so expensive she'd be terrified of hurting it. She saw a stereo and CDs, so she'd have music. Small kitchen with a gas stove and older refrigerator. Good enough, she thought.

"TV's over there," Susan said, pointing to it. "No cable, though. Used to have satellite, but he gave it up when he left. Reception's pretty lousy. Probably you'll want to rent a lot of videos, and I know a good store."

"It's fine," Cricket said. "Just fine."

"I'll call the owner, if you want it," Susan said. "He's an archaeologist and he's off doing a dig or something. Do you want it? Do you know anything about archaeology?"

Cricket wasn't sure which question to answer first. She was out of practice in following conversation. She smiled. "No, I don't," she said, and Susan's eyebrows went up again. "Know anything about archaeology," she said quickly. "I'm from New York," she added, as if that was an explanation.

"Oh," Susan said. "I'd be scared to live in the city."

"I don't," Cricket said. "Didn't. I live . . . away from the city."

Susan nodded, then put a finger to her lips and tapped at it with her long, curved nail. "You running?"

Cricket was startled at the directness of the question. It seemed intrusive, but she didn't know the boundaries or the rules where she was, so she had to assume it was okay.

"Not that it's any of my business," Susan added quickly. "I don't judge people. We all got troubles."

"I'm . . . taking some time for myself," Cricket said hesitantly, not sure if she wanted to go into it. When she ran the story through her mind, it sounded fantastic. Surreal. She didn't want Susan to think she was crazy. She could say she'd decided to live for a year as if she only had a year, and then she'd decide if she wanted to live at all, but that would probably sound even worse.

"Family trouble?" Susan asked.

Cricket nodded.

"Mm. I know how that goes. Probably some crummy man in it, right? Need a job?"

"I could use work," she said.

"We're looking for a waitress at the diner. Part-time, and it don't pay much, but it's something. Just to get you started, like."

"Okay," Cricket said. "Sure."

It sounded ideal. Part-time work doing something she didn't have to worry about failing.

"Huh," she said out loud.

"What?" Susan asked.

"I just realized, I never looked for a job I really wanted. That way I didn't ever have to worry about failing at it," Cricket said, then laughed lightly, trying to make it sound like a joke. Susan didn't take it that way, though. Her face was serious as she nodded and tapped her nail on the tip of her nose.

"I know just what you mean," she said. "I'm like that with men. I pick 'em to fail, so there's no surprises. You wanna come by the diner tomorrow, maybe around noon, and we'll set you up? You ever do any waitressing?"

"Sure," Cricket said, and left it to Susan to figure out which question she was answering this time.

The next day, Susan introduced her to the owner, who was also the cook. He looked at her morosely and said, "Probably have to lay you off soon's summer's done."

Susan slapped him on the back, which he didn't seem to like. "Larry, you ole optimist, you." She laughed. "You're probably right."

Right now, though, business seemed pretty good to Cricket. There were enough people who seemed to be regulars, since they knew what they wanted without looking at the menu. And there were the men dressed like cowboys who flooded them at lunch, wanting red meat of various kinds, or anything with hot peppers. "Who are all these guys?" Cricket hissed to Susan when she was juggling bowls of chili and plates of steaks.

"They're the rodeo show. Mostly from the East, guys who wear suits and sit in offices all winter. Summer comes, they show up here and wanna be cowboys, y'know?"

Cricket tried to ignore their blatant glances at her private parts, and went home alone when her shift was over, though on her first day, she got three offers to do otherwise.

Even Susan asked her to go shopping or to a bar after work, but Cricket declined. She wanted to go back to her apartment and sleep. Without dreams, sleep seemed safe, and sometimes she wouldn't even undress. She'd just lie down on her bed or the couch, and wake up there twelve hours later, when it was time to go back to work.

Susan didn't press her. She just looked at her and nodded and tapped her nails on her lips, considering her as if she were an oil painting that needed one or two more colors in it. Cricket ignored the looks. She didn't want to be seen.

"Y'know what you should do," Susan said. "You should go to Bisti Badlands, or Chaco Canyon. Probably Chaco. Nobody'd bother you there, and it's not too far. It's a good place to think."

"Maybe," Cricket said, not sure Susan had a clue about what she should or shouldn't do. But Susan gave her a brochure about it. Chaco Canyon looked spare and full of sky. There wasn't anything to see there except ruins. They wouldn't ask much of her. They would let her be alone, untouched, a state she craved even though sometimes it still terrified her.

It was disorienting to walk into an empty apartment and yell "I'm home," to nobody. The absence of people hollowed her out so that she could hear the wind blowing mournfully in the space they once occupied. Nobody knocked on her door, and her phone never rang.

She'd called Jim when she first arrived and left her phone number and address, in case she had to be contacted. She called during work hours when she knew he wouldn't be there and left the message on the machine. "Hi," she said. "It's me, Cricket. Here's my number, in case you need it." Nobody ever called back. She was untouched. Unfound.

But as the first week became the second, and the second became the third, she discovered many small pleasures in living alone. She liked staying up late if she felt like it. Not washing dishes. Eating TV dinners or cottage cheese and bread, depending on nobody's mood but her own. Nobody cared if she put on five or ten pounds. She could eat whatever she wanted. She could leave her underwear on the floor and nobody would step on it and say, "Ew, gross." Nobody picked it up for her, but nobody made her pick it up either.

She realized that for the first time, she possessed her own body fully. She would stand in front of a mirror naked, just to make sure it was still there in the absence of connection to another body.

She tried to imagine herself old, her body bent and her skin crepey and loose. She couldn't do it. She was thirty-seven and in good shape, her body firm and flexible. She described it that way to herself, and then realized it made her sound like Gumby. Maybe she thought of herself that way, though. It had been so long since she asked herself what pleased her body, in the absence of pleasing someone else.

And being alone, if she felt something, she could just say it however she wanted to, without worrying about hurting anyone's feelings. One night, she woke up from a dream about Peggy and Jim and realized she was pissed after all. She sat up and yelled, "Goddammit, what the hell were you thinking of? He was my husband, you shit. You shitty sister. You fucked my husband."

She realized she was yelling pretty loud, and clapped her hand over her mouth, but nobody came to knock on her door and tell her to shut up, so she yelled a little more. It felt good in the same way that throwing up bad food feels good. Painful, but a relief. She decided she didn't have to be angry at Peggy if she didn't want to, but if she wanted to, that was fine, too. It was entirely up to her.

Alone, she decided, was not as bad as she'd feared. Sometimes after dealing with hungry psuedo-cowboys at the diner all day, she'd crave even more of it than her apartment could provide. Then, she'd walk away from the streets to the place where the city ended and there was nothing but sky and earth. The land here was arid, full of browns and golds and soft tans. Brief hard rains would cover the land like hair brushed over the surface of skin, then dissipate into rainbows.

There was a deeper quiet here than there was in the Northeast, where cities sprawled into strip malls that stretched into suburbs that only gradually became country, punctuated by farms. Here, the city was a pocket of humanity that had sharply delineated boundaries. There was city. There was no city. There were people and sounds, and then there was just quiet, and a strip of highway that went untraveled for long periods of time. There were places where silence was its own conversation, where everything talked and nothing needed words.

The sage became sentient when the sun beat down on it after a short, sweet rain. The land under her feet had a heart that beat to the rhythm of dreaming, and she felt it course up through her when she stood in the quiet of the night, thinking she was alone.

Then, an eagle would call out its piercing cry, and the beauty of it would send her hurrying back to her apartment, to where the sound of it could not find her.

It made her think of Pass, and she did not want to. She had dreamt of safety and love, and in its absence manufactured a substitute so as not to disappoint herself. She had lived inside her own dreams, as if the world couldn't touch her there. Now she would live in the world, and remain untouched by dreams.

Or was that just another illusion she used to soothe herself? She could no longer tell if the fault was in the world, or herself, or if it mattered at all. Perhaps to be unconnected was to be able to kill. Perhaps it was to be able to live. Perhaps it was both.

Surety eluded her, and she lived balanced on the thin line of converging opposites, where she thought maybe she'd always lived, only she wouldn't admit it until now.

At night, she would stand in her darkened living room and listen to her heart beat out truths she didn't want to know, until somehow the room was her, and she walked in an ever-decreasing spiral, curling her way toward the center, each step bringing her closer to sorrow, fear, and peace.

seventeen

Cricket placed a cup of coffee in front of the man at the table, and as he picked it up, his hand shook so badly, he spilled much of it on the table.

"Damn," he said. "I hate that."

Cricket wiped at it with the dishcloth she kept tucked in her belt. "That's okay. We've got plenty more."

"No," he said, "I'll just spill it again. There's enough left, anyway."

He smiled at her, his craggy old face a study in weathering and strong bones that didn't seem to match his tremulous voice. Cricket wondered if he drank.

She took the rest of his order and went back to the kitchen to give it to the cook. She didn't have to rush, because it was quiet today. The owner said they were between rodeos, and they might as well enjoy it. Susan was in the back smoking a cigarette, which technically wasn't allowed, though nobody ever did anything about it. She stopped Cricket before she went out again.

"Hey, you got Old Man Sanders out there?"

Cricket frowned. "Who?"

Susan held up a hand and made it tremble. "Sanders."

She nodded. "Is he . . . drunk?"

"Nah. Parkinson's. Nice guy, though. Reason I ask is that if you talk to him a little, he'll give you a good tip. He's like that. Thought you should know."

Susan winked at her, and Cricket realized she was giving him to her as a sort of gift. Cricket chewed thoughtfully on her lip. She didn't know if it was very nice to talk to people for money. It seemed like prostitution, somehow. But she didn't mind being nice to him, whether he tipped her or not, so maybe it was okay.

She heard Susan chuckle lightly. "Look at you," she said.

"Me?" Cricket asked.

"Yeah. You're thinking a mile a minute about something. You're always thinking a mile a minute. It's not good for you, you know that? You gotta get out and have some *fun.* C'mon, woman. Let's go dance and pick up stupid cowboys. Tonight."

She'd been after her for some time to go out to a bar where they had a band. Cricket had said no enough times that she thought Susan would just stop asking, but she didn't.

"Susan," she said now, "what do I want with a stupid cowboy?"

"Sister, if I gotta explain, it's a lot worse than I thought. Come out tonight. Just tonight. Then I'll leave you alone about it? Just try it once?"

"Okay," Cricket said at last. It wouldn't hurt, she supposed. And it might satisfy Susan. "I'll go. Just this once."

"Great. First, we gotta get you something to wear, though. I know the cutest little shop. You take care of Mr. Sanders, and I'll take care of what you do with his tip."

Mr. Sanders's order came up, and Cricket brought it out to him. He chatted with her while she placed his plate on the table, bringing some extra napkins for him and hoping he wouldn't take it as an insult. He didn't.

"Now, that's nice," he said. "You thinking of me, bringing these.

That's real nice. But you look like a nice young woman. And you're new here, aren't you?"

"I've been here a month," she said.

"Guess I haven't been around for a while. I used to come in every day, the same time, for lunch. Now, some days, I can't." He shrugged wryly, but even in the shrug, she saw the tremor. "Parkinson's," he said. "Keeps me down."

"I'm sorry," she said.

He waved it away, with a shaking hand. "Everybody's got trouble," he noted. "I bet even a pretty woman like you has trouble."

She smiled, shrugged, but didn't offer any elaboration. She wondered if that was wrong, and would lose her a tip, but he kept talking. Maybe what Susan meant was not talking to him, but listening.

"There's this story I heard once. My wife told me, when she was sick. Cancer, y'know? She said once there was a woman whose family was killed, and the woman was so sad and alone, she thought she should just kill herself. But before she did, she went to the Buddha to ask his advice. She was an Indian woman. Not like Indians here. A real Indian."

Cricket nodded, to show she was listening.

"Anyway, she goes to the Buddha, and he tells her that before she kills herself, she has to take a year and go around the world, and find someone who's never known pain and learn from them. So, she sets out. And she goes all over, talking to people, asking their stories, and guess what?"

He paused, and she responded. "I can't guess."

He nodded and smiled. "She hears more sad stories, about people who lost their homes, their jobs, their legs even, or their children, which is the worst, I think. But she can't find any one person who hasn't known pain. Not one."

Cricket nodded. He cleared his throat and took a shaky sip of coffee. She wondered if that was the end of the story, and if so, what was the point. But then he spoke again.

"So she went back to the Buddha and she tells him she's not going to kill herself. She said she'd learned that everyone had sorrow, and so she was never alone." He nodded at Cricket solemnly. "Never alone. That's what my wife told me," he said.

Cricket wasn't sure she understood, but she smiled anyway. "That's lovely. Your wife must be a lovely woman."

"She was. She died about a year ago. But she was lovely." He smiled at her. "Never alone. That's what she told me."

Cricket brought him a piece of pie for dessert, on the house. When she cleaned his table after he left, she saw that the bill he left on it for her was not a one, as she supposed it would be, but a ten.

After work, Susan walked her down the street to a store Cricket had passed many times in her walk, but never gone into because it was used clothes, and she didn't buy used clothes. Susan dragged her inside, though. "It's vintage," she said. "You'll like it."

Susan beelined for a rack of black velvet, and Cricket gazed around at the racks of dresses, shirts, coats, pants, and skirts. She moved to a rack of dresses and ran her hand across it, stopping at something silky and red. It was a color that her eyes wanted right now, as if they were hungry for it. She pulled it away from the other dresses and saw that it was a red silk dress with delicate gold embroidery at the neckline and sleeves, and in parts of the body.

She ran her hand up and down the silk, pressed it between her finger and her thumb and slid her hand along the edge of the embroidery.

"Care to try it on?" a voice said, and she turned to see a woman smiling at her. She was an older woman, maybe in her sixties, her face deeply lined with wrinkles, her midriff bulging, and her hair black, but graying at the roots. Her skin was dark, and Cricket wondered if she was Hispanic, or Native American, or some combination.

"I don't know," Cricket said.

"You seem to like it," the woman replied. "Looks about your size. It's pretty small."

"I'm a three," Cricket said. "Everything's too big on me."

"No. It's the right size. My size, when I was your age."

The woman spoke cheerfully, as if she didn't mind being old and lumpy. Cricket smoothed the material of the dress with her hand. It was lovely, cut fitted at the waist and breast and hips, in a material that was soft with motion, moving as she did. And the red was saturated, as if it went down to the primal source of red. The gold embroidery at the square neckline and the hem, and up the side of the long sleeves, was a complex series of spirals arranged in three thin lines. She'd never seen anything like it.

"I don't have anywhere to wear it," Cricket said.

"You could wear it anywhere," the woman said. "I wore it to sing in."

Cricket stared at the woman. Susan appeared at her side with an armful of clothes.

"I bagged some quarry. You?"

"Not yet. You go ahead."

When Susan left, the woman grinned at Cricket. "You heard me right. I used to sing in it."

"You were a singer?" Cricket asked tentatively.

"For a while." As she spoke, she held the dress in one hand, smoothing it against her body. "Wouldn't believe this ever fit me, huh? It was my favorite, I have to say."

"Where did you sing?" Cricket asked.

"Oh, here and there. Clubs, hotels, lounges. I'm not someone you would've heard of. Just a lounge singer. I toured with a band. Long time ago. I'm Linda, by the way." She stuck her hand out and Cricket took it.

"Cricket," she said.

"Huh. You know what that means in Italian?" she asked.

"Yes," Cricket said. "But that's not why it's my name. My father said I was a dreamer, like Jiminy Cricket."

"Yeah," the woman said. "You look it. You wanna try it on?"

Cricket nodded. She felt obligated now. Probably it wouldn't fit, or would look horrible on her, but she did want to feel that silk against her, see that color on her skin.

"Back there," the woman said. "Let me see how it looks, okay?"

Cricket took it to the back, got herself out of her clothes and slipped it on. It poured over her like water, the silk against her skin a pleasure that made her not care how it looked. She kept her eyes closed while she smoothed it down over her body. Then, she opened her eyes and looked at herself in the mirror.

She gasped.

Outside, she thought she heard the woman chuckle. "Everything okay?" she asked.

"Yes, fine," Cricket answered.

"Gonna come out?"

"In a minute. I just have to . . ." She didn't finish the sentence because any finish would sound silly. *I just have to make sure it's me in the mirror.*

Cricket touched the face of the woman in the mirror, then touched her own face.

It was her. Really her. And she looked stunning.

She came out of the dressing room just as Susan was coming out of hers, wearing her own clothes.

"Nothing works," Susan said, then gaped at Cricket. "Holy shit," she said.

The store owner nodded. "Holy shit," she agreed.

"Yeah," Cricket sighed. "Holy shit."

She stood looking at herself in the three-way mirror. She had no idea she could look this way. She saw herself as someone who was in pretty good shape and not unattractive, but neither was she a head turner. And she didn't mind that. Being a head turner, she thought, was overrated. It would mean needing to be on your guard, it would mean fearing losing the power of your good looks. It would mean responsibility and vulnerability. But in this dress, she would turn heads.

"I don't have any use for it," she muttered.

"You got every use for it," Susan said. "You can't leave it here."

Cricket laughed. "What would I do with it? Frame it?"

Susan rolled her eyes. "Wear it to the bar. Dance in it. Make cowboys nervous. Yee-ha."

Cricket turned to the store owner. "How much is it?"

She reached over and caressed the cloth. "It was the first dress I bought when I went on the road," she said. "It's got a lot of living in it."

Cricket wondered how much that would raise the price. "It's old," she said, to put things in perspective.

The woman laughed. "It's got a story, too."

"Well," Susan said. "Tell it."

"I was twenty-nine years old in 1960. I had two little girls—three and five years old. I was going to be a singer, but I met my husband and got married instead, and we had a house and he was doing well at work. But something happened."

She paused a moment, then continued. "The doctor found a lump in my breast."

Susan and Cricket were silent.

"They did a biopsy and it was malignant, so they took my breast off without ever waking me up. That's how they did things then."

She smoothed the dress over Cricket's left shoulder, brushed off a piece of lint. "They put me through radiation therapy. They said there was a good chance it would come back, and I would die. I was terrified, but all I could think of was singing. That I never had the chance to do that, and that I'd die without ever getting it. So I found a band that was touring and needed a singer. I didn't tell my husband. They were just a two-bit little band, but I didn't care. I auditioned with them, and they said they'd take me."

"What about your family?" Cricket asked.

"I told my husband I was going," she said. "I didn't ask. I just told him, and then I figured I'd let him decide what he wanted to do. He said, Linda, you go. We can manage here."

Cricket tried to imagine Jim saying that to her. No. Never in a million.

"So I went. I had a great time, and after a while, I wanted to go home. The cancer never came back."

"That," Susan said, "is a great story. I been in here how many times and you never told me that story."

"You didn't need to hear it," the woman said. She turned eyes that were studious of pain toward Cricket. "You did."

Cricket felt visible in a way that only Pass could make her feel. Someone was seeing her. Really seeing her. She was being found. Touched. She had to do something to stop it.

"If you were going to live as if you only had a year to live now," Cricket asked, "what would you do?"

The woman grinned. "Just what I'm doing," she said.

"I'll take the dress," Cricket said.

"Yeah," the woman said. "I knew it was your dress now, anyway."

They met at a bar called El Diablo, which had a neon sign out front and a dim, smoky interior. Susan got there ahead of her, and was waiting at the bar, in conversation with the bartender. She waved enthusiastically to Cricket. "Hey. Here. You made it," she called, as if Cricket had breached the summit of Everest. "Ooh. Hot-dress woman."

Susan had talked her into wearing it, telling her it wasn't too dressy at all. People wore all kinds of things to dance in. She walked to the bar, careful of herself because she was wearing high heels, which she hadn't done in a long time.

"What're you drinking?" Susan asked.

Cricket wrinkled her nose. She hadn't had a drink in a long time, either. She had no idea what she was drinking. Susan leaned over and patted her hand. "Lemme make a suggestion, okay?"

"Okay."

Susan smiled at the bartender. "Give my friend sex on the beach, Charlie."

He chuckled. "Anything for my sweetie," he said, and turned to his work.

"Sweetie?" Cricket asked. "Is he . . . I mean, are you . . ."

"With old Charlie? No way. I'm my own best sweetie these days, and I think I like it that way. Last sweetie I had, he hit me. Only once, mind you. One before that I had to tell him when it was time to take the garbage out."

"What's wrong with that?" Cricket asked. She remembered she always had to tell Jim.

"And when to get a job, and when to get it up, and when to pee. Least, it seemed that way. You know, I'm from Texas, and I think in Texas they raise men wrong."

Cricket smiled. "How about in New Mexico?"

"I'm going slow, sister. Real slow." She closed her eyes and raised her hands and made groping motions. "Feeling my way in the dark."

Cricket laughed. The bartender brought her drink, which Susan insisted on paying for. It was very pink, and the first sip made Cricket less nervous about her skirt. The second sip made her much less nervous.

"You?" Susan asked.

"Me?"

"Yeah. You. What's it with you and men anyway? Got one? Lost one? Want one?"

Cricket felt a sinking feeling in her chest. She had almost forgotten she had a past. She didn't want to think about it now. She took another sip of her drink. "No, no, and no," she said.

Susan leaned in close. "Are you—you know. I mean, maybe you like women better? Not that I mind that, even if I don't feel that way. I'm just trying to figure out how to best get you some amusement for the evening, if you know what I mean."

Cricket didn't understand at first, then realization dawned. "Not women," she said. "I guess right now I just don't want anybody."

Susan nodded wisely. "They don't grow men right where you come from either, huh?"

Before she remembered that she didn't want to remember, Cricket spoke. "I'm from Dansville. Dansville, New York."

Susan stopped smiling and pulled back slightly. "Oh," she said. "Oh, wow. I'm sorry. Wow. I saw that on the news."

Cricket drank more, and realized her drink was disappearing very fast. Susan watched her, then shook her head.

"You had someone killed, huh?"

Cricket nodded. The animal in her chest, asleep for so long, woke with a start and demanded attention. She finished her drink to make it sleep.

"Husband?" Susan asked, then her mouth opened in horror. "Oh, God. A kid? Not a kid. Oh, God. Husbands are so replaceable, but kids. . . . Oh, shit. I'm sorry."

"Could we not talk about it," Cricket said. "I don't even know why I said anything. I thought that here I could . . . I mean, everything is new here. That's how I like it."

Susan reached over and patted her hand. "Don't say another word," she said. She raised her glass. "Here's to new. I like that, too." Then she giggled. "Hey, I made a poem. Hell, you need another drink."

They were three drinks in when the bar began to fill up with people and the band started setting up. Susan was beginning to slur her speech and, to Cricket's eye, blur around the edges, but she didn't mind much. She was a little concerned about what would happen when she got off her stool, but she didn't really have to face that yet. Right now, she was busy looking at a map Susan was drawing on a napkin. It was the way to get to church, she said. She thought Cricket might like to go to church.

"Not that I'm, like, really holy or anything. It's just a nice place, and the priest is real friendly. Some nice people go there and they have potlucks and dances and things. I thought maybe you'd like to meet them. And maybe it'd help, right? I mean, in times of trouble, where else can you go?"

Cricket winced. She didn't want Susan to think of her as troubled. And she didn't want to go to church or meet people. But, for now, she'd let Susan go on about it. It would keep her from asking questions. Susan said she'd take her, but then started drawing the map anyway, and explaining the route in detail. As she shoved it into Cricket's purse, the band began to play "Mustang Sally."

"I love this song," Susan shouted. "We gotta dance, girl. We gotta." She grabbed Cricket by the hand and led her out to the floor, but just on the edge, Cricket found her feet had stopped. She looked at them, then at Susan.

"I can't," she said.

A man in boots and a denim shirt, with a very ornate silver and turquoise belt buckle, put a hand on Susan's shoulder and whispered something in her ear. Her eyes lit up. "Sure," she said. She looked at Cricket. "C'mon," Susan said. "Dance with us. It's fine."

Cricket looked at her feet. She shook her head. She really couldn't.

"C'mon. You can." Susan reached for her hand, grabbed it, but Cricket felt a panic rising in her, and pulled away roughly. The song kept playing, and she couldn't make herself stop remembering, stop thinking, stop feeling.

"No," she said. "I have to . . . I have to go."

Susan's face expressed shock, but the man pulled her toward the dance floor and she went, giving one last glance at Cricket, who waved and mouthed good night, grabbed her purse and left.

Once she was outside the bar, she breathed in and out deeply. The sounds of conversation and music drifted toward her, muffled and confused. A car pulled into the lot near her, and a man got out. He was laughing, and moving toward the other side, then opening the door to let out a woman who was in the passenger's seat. She was pretty, and she smiled as she lifted a hand to him. Lovers, Cricket thought. Happy people.

As he took her hand and she rose and got out, Cricket saw that she leaned heavily on a metal crutch. Her skirt was not long enough to hide the fact that one of her legs was false.

"I love this song," she said as they ascended the steps to the door. "Will you dance with me?"

"Sure," the man said. "Anytime."

Cricket got in her car and drove back to the apartment, where she lay on her bed for a long time in the dark, waiting for sleep to find her.

D R E A M # 9

dancing

Cricket called Susan in the morning to make sure she hadn't been killed or gotten married or anything equally dangerous.

"My head," Susan moaned. "I don't know what hit it worse. Those drinks, or the back of that man's truck."

"What?"

"You ever try doing it in the back of a pickup truck?"

Cricket laughed.

"Not so loud," Susan said. "Listen, why'd you take off like that? I was worried."

"I'm not used to being out," Cricket said. "I have to go slow, I guess."

"Oh, sure, honey. I understand." Susan's voice oozed sympathy, which Cricket knew was real, though she suspected Susan was also dying of curiosity to hear the whole story. "I tell you what, though," she continued. "I can't go to church today. You got the directions I gave you. You go. Say a prayer for me. Make it a double."

Cricket didn't want to go to church, but she didn't want to stay home. She was restless, though she didn't know why. The motion of change, she thought, and shivered. It frightened her. Just when she grew comfortable, something would shift and she'd have to negotiate the new landscape forming inside her. She didn't want to stay home and think about it, or spend energy trying not to think about it.

She wanted to leave. She would drive.

When she got her car keys out of her purse, the directions and map written on the napkin came out with it. Okay, she thought. I'll go by. See what it's like. Might as well. It was just a meaning-less way to distract herself.

The directions took her outside of Farmington, and told her to turn left at a Texaco station. But there just was no gas station. So she took the next nearest left turn she could, and drove down another dirt road. Ahead of her, she saw a small brown building that might be it. It was an adobe building, and there were cars and trucks parked next to it in a haphazard way. When she drove up to the building and stopped the car, she noticed the small statue of a Madonna in an arch over the doorway, and thought this must be the church. But that didn't explain the pavilion next to it, or the music she heard.

She sat in her car, listening to the music, which sounded like a fiddle band. Folk music, or country. She couldn't really tell which. She got out of her car and walked toward the adobe building, almost running into a woman who was coming out. "Sorry," the woman said. "Hadda pee real bad, y'know?"

Cricket smiled, and stood there, deciding what to do next. Except for the Madonna, the building didn't look like a church, but she didn't know what churches might look like in New Mexico. She peered inside and saw a hall, dimly lit. She stepped in and saw a door labeled rest room, and another door, open, leading to a room where folding chairs were arranged in a semicircle. At the far wall was a picture, painted right onto the wall.

It was another Madonna, or at least a woman dressed in blue, but she wasn't carrying a baby, and she didn't look sad the way Madonnas usually did. Her long dress had spiral designs down the side, and she was surrounded on all sides by stalks of corn. Her hands were held out, as if to offer them to anyone who came by. She looked happy.

Cricket thought it was a church after all, but services seemed to be over. She walked around the building, and in back saw the pavilion. A band was playing inside it, and people were dancing. She walked over to it and watched.

Women of all ages in swirling dresses were being turned by men who wore purple pants and T-shirts, or green T-shirts and jeans. Even the older women had long silver braids and wore red dresses that moved around them like sunset-splashed clouds.

It was a garden of people, all in motion, which she followed just as she used to watch the emus run in spirals.

When she was a little girl, if her flying dreams became dreams of falling, she would sometimes call on a flock of colorful birds to save her. They always appeared immediately when she needed them, their fluttering wings soft against her skin, lifting her up. They were saturated with colors—clear reds and deep greens, rich and silky blues, shiny gold and pure white. Their beauty filled her with joy and she felt perfectly safe as they danced in flight around her. She knew they would never let her fall.

These were dreams she woke from with both joy and sorrow, because she knew she could only see the birds when she dreamt of falling. That was the only time they were there.

The song ended and everybody clapped and some people whooped joyfully.

"Thank you very much," a man holding a fiddle said into the microphone. "Now we're gonna do something to cool you down just a little bit. We don't want nobody overheating on such a hot day."

He turned back to the band and started a waltz. She leaned on one of the pavilion posts and listened, swaying in time, watching the people.

Two young women danced together in a corner next to the bandstand. She saw a man in a chiffon skirt, twirling a woman in jeans. A woman in a tight flowered dress and spiky black heels dancing with a man whose cowboy hat was the tallest she'd ever seen. There were people dressed in colors like flowers or birds. Girls with circlets of flowers worn like crowns on their heads. Purples and deep reds and orange, crimson flecked with yellow. Blue dotted with white. Wide dresses with Van Gogh colors, Picasso patterns. Women with Degas faces. Women with Frida Kahlo faces. A very tall, reedlike woman with long, dark hair. A woman with white hair and an emerald-green skirt and top. A man in a purple cotton tank top.

They were flightless birds and moving flowers, and they turned around each other effortlessly. She lost herself in the complexity of motion, and motion became all, like breathing.

This was better than church. Better than the bar. Here she didn't have to think. She only had to feel the pulse of music and motion. She only hoped nobody would ask her to dance, or try to talk to her, because she wanted neither. She wanted only to watch the swirling motion of the dance, untouched and unseen.

She stayed the rest of the afternoon, until the band stopped playing, and as if she'd cloaked herself in invisibility, nobody said a word to her, or even seemed to notice she existed. Nobody even looked her way.

The dancers breathed happiness out, and she breathed it in, and was content.

eighteen

Susan stopped Cricket at work on Monday. "Hey," she said. "You look good. You find that church?"

"Yes," Cricket said. "I like the dancing afterward."

"What dancing?" Susan asked.

Cricket opened her mouth, then shut it again. "Just kidding. I couldn't find it, your directions are so lousy."

"Oh, man," she said. "I give those directions to everybody. Nobody else ever gets lost."

Cricket shrugged and grinned. Maybe, she thought, they did. Maybe they all ended up at the dances, which was not where she meant to send them. Or maybe this was her church, and she didn't stay long enough after Mass to know about the dancing. Or maybe Cricket was the only one who could see them. Maybe they weren't even real, but just the solace of a madwoman. Cricket was tempted to tell her about it, but then she'd want to go, and she didn't want Susan there, encouraging her to pick up cowboys.

The door to the diner opened, and Mr. Sanders came in, smiling at her before he took his usual table. She went over with her pad and pencil and pulled out his chair for him.

"Well," he said. "If you weren't a lady, I'd say you were a real gentleman."

It took him a while to sit down, and she waited patiently before she asked, "What can I get for you?"

He looked up at her, and she noticed that today the tremors were affecting his neck and head as well as his arm. "Some of what you got," he noted. "You look happy."

She blinked, and said, sounding surprised, "I am."

"You have a good weekend? Meet a gentleman?"

"No," she said. "I mean, yes. I had a nice weekend. But I didn't meet a gentleman."

"Miss," he said, "if I was thirty years younger, you wouldn't be saying that. Of course, if I was thirty years younger, my wife would have had something to say about it."

Cricket laughed lightly. She didn't care if he gave good tips, or no tips. She liked him. He was a nice man. "Coffee?" she asked him.

"Of course. Then whatever the special is."

"Meat loaf," she said. "With mashed potatoes, carrots, and peas."

"That's fine."

She put his order in, and brought him his coffee. He managed it better this time, which was good since he'd brought a newspaper with him and had it spread out on the table in front of him.

"Look at this," he said, pointing down. "A terrible thing, isn't it?"

She read the headline he indicated: THREE DIE IN FIRE.

"Terrible," she said.

"Yes, and listen to this—one of them was a little girl. Four years old. She was in her room sleeping, and the baby-sitter who was watching her couldn't get to her. So the fire trucks get there, and the mother comes home, finds her house on fire and sees her little girl standing in the window, with all the firemen telling her to jump."

The old man looked up at her. "But she won't. She won't jump. And the mother's standing there, watching the whole thing. That poor mother, standing and watching that."

Cricket felt the blood leave her face. Her ears started to ring, and she was suddenly afraid she would faint. She pressed a hand into the back of the old man's chair.

"Whoa," he said. "Careful." He pushed at the empty chair across from him with his foot and told her, "Here. Sit. Sit."

She did so, and rested her head in her hands until she felt better. "I'm sorry," she mumbled at him. "I'm very sorry."

"Nothing to apologize for. Too much dancing? Or too much story? I hope it didn't bring sorrow home to you. I didn't mean to upset you."

He spoke so quietly, so kindly, she felt herself tearing up. But she didn't want to feel bad. She wanted to go back to the dances, be where the colors and motion were. She shook her head.

"Do you want to talk about it?" he asked. "Sometimes that helps."

"No," she whispered. "It doesn't help. What you say and do, no matter how much you love someone, it doesn't make a difference at all."

"Yes, it does," he said, his voice quaking with tremors or emotion, she couldn't tell. "It makes all the difference. Just . . . not in the way you want it to. The thing is, you don't get to write the whole script. You just get to pick your lines." He reached over and patted her hand. His palm felt very dry, like the skin of a lizard. "I don't know if it helps any, but remember that story I told you? Think about that. If you didn't have troubles, then you *would* be alone."

"Maybe," she said, more to herself than to him. "That's what I want. To be alone."

She heard him sigh. She didn't dare look at him. She could feel how keenly he regarded her, in spite of the tremors that shook his vision. And if she looked, she'd see what he saw of her. She would be touched. Seen. Found.

She sniffed, patted at his hand, and stood up. "I'll get your order," she said.

That day, when she cleaned his table, she saw that the tip he left was a twenty-dollar bill.

Cricket went back to the dances every week. Every week there was a different band. One week they were calling contra dances and fiddling, one week it was swing, and another it was something that sounded Latin. Sometimes she thought she dreamt the whole thing. The only way she knew she was really there was that every week, she'd put five dollars in the can marked "Donations" before she left.

That was fine with her. Cricket didn't want to know what this place was, who ran it, where all the strange and delightful children came from. The weight of knowledge would ruin it. No. She preferred to just go and get her breath of energy from the dancers, sitting in their breeze, taking in their joy. Then she could go home, feeling as if she'd taken a lovely cool shower and needed to think of nothing except what lotion to put on her skin.

She liked to watch one couple who danced together as if they'd been doing so since they were born. She was dark-haired, dark-eyed, and her face finely sculpted, her bearing proud. He was light-haired and light-eyed, and his arms were as strong as his carved features. They looked as if they'd grown out of the rocks of this place, and would go back to them someday. He held her so confidently in his arms, led her so well, and then he would twirl her away from him and she would dance, spin, all on her own, finding her way back to him as the music shifted. They had perfect timing.

Watching them, Cricket longed to be led, to be flung away so she could spin solo, and then be gathered in again. It must feel wonderful, she thought. But she didn't let herself linger in the notion for too long. That would be dangerous. Too close to wanting touch.

The week after the Latin group played, a fiddle band started their set with a song that was about autumn. When she heard them pull this sweet and mournful tune out of their strings, she realized it was that time of year when you know summer has to end. The days were getting shorter. The slant of the sun was changing. There were more thunderheads hanging in the distant sky, the lightning dancing its way across the land to them. It was August.

Janis would go back to school soon. She would be a senior. She had a birthday coming up that would make her eighteen. All Cricket's instincts told her she should be home, getting school clothes with her, but then she remembered there was no home left. No husband or family. Just an old reflex to buy clothes for a daughter who was frightened of her, and probably terribly angry at her for going away.

"Jeez," Susan said, looking out the window at work the next day. "The rains'll be here any day. Then, before you know it, the snows. Time goes so damn fast, don't it? Y'know that guy comes back in September, so I guess you'll have to find a new place soon, huh?"

"Yes," Cricket said, answering all of Susan's questions at once.

When Mr. Sanders came in, his tremors seemed worse. She had to mop up two cups of coffee for him, and talking seemed to take a lot of energy. "You should see me in winter," he said, sounding as if he talked while riding in a bumpy cart. "The cold. It's terrible."

She did not linger to talk with him too much. She was afraid of what he might say. In spite of that, his tips remained large.

Cricket slept a lot when she wasn't working. She didn't want to listen to what her brain was thinking. She didn't want to make decisions about what to do next. She didn't want to feel the motion of change.

The following week, a South American group played at the pavilion. They had drums and instruments that looked almost like guitars, and flutes and something they called pan pipes. These were rows of tubes strung together, and the player would blow through each tube to make a different sound. They came in different sizes, and the small ones were high and light, but the biggest ones, which were almost as big as the players, sounded like the breath of the earth, coming up out of the earth, deep and thrilling.

Cricket took her place by the post and watched the dancers. Lightning seared the sky, and a crack of thunder opened it up to let down the rain, which poured off the roof, driving the people all underneath.

"Ho," the guitarist said. "That's a good rain. We're gonna play a song for it now."

They started with the rhythm of a slow rain, then built it faster and louder, adding layers of drums and speeding the pan pipes. The people under the pavilion laughed and clapped and danced in a great circle with the youngest swirling about in the center.

Cricket smiled and clapped, and then felt a hand pulling at her. She gasped. Someone saw her. Someone touched her. She pulled back.

"C'mon," an older woman said. "Dance."

"I can't," she protested. "I can't dance."

"Dance with us," the old woman said, and pulled her into the circle as the music got louder and faster, and people began to kick and twirl. The music grew frantic with the pounding rain, and the people laughed and danced, not in couples or in sets of four, but as a whole, all dancing with the rain.

She was afraid. She'd been drawn in, unable to keep herself out of the dance. She was afraid.

She looked around, and saw that everyone was smiling. Were they friendly, good people who didn't kill each other? Were they the kind of people who would help her if she needed help? She saw a little girl laughing and kicking her legs out, and thought that she would help that little girl, if she needed it. She saw the girl's mother laughing with her, and thought maybe the mother would help her, if she needed it. And even if something happened, at least they were dancing. At least they had this moment to dance in.

Her fear begin to melt, replaced by something light and full of motion. She put her head back and laughed. She moved her feet, the rhythms of the rain and the music and the people all around her. She danced.

Then, the music began to slow, like rain going away. And as if commanded, the rain slowed with it.

The musicians puffed slowly into their pan pipes, beat softly on their drums. The rain beat slowly on the roof. With one more long breath, the pan pipe ran out of air.

The music stopped. The rain stopped. As if a faucet had been turned off, the rain stopped just as the music ended.

Somebody said "Aahh." They stood very still, until one of the younger people in the center of the circle leapt up and howled joyously. Then everyone was howling and clapping, and turning to each other and smiling and saying things as the circle became a mass of people in motion. She saw them all, so beautiful and so particular, a twisting spiral of connected parts like the double helix of DNA or the spiraling arms of the galaxy they all belonged to.

And in that moment, Cricket knew that it was only a knowledge of connection that kept humans from evil, and only being unconnected made it possible to kill without thought, without emotion, without limit. She knew that no matter what she did, she was touched, and that being touched, she could remain herself, found and seen.

Cricket wanted to say something, to smile at someone, anyone near her. A hand touched her shoulder and she turned around toward it.

She stood looking dumbly into a face she seemed to remember, but from long ago.

"Mom?" the face said.

It was Janis.

Her hands stopped midclap, and she held them that way, as if she was praying.

"Janis," she whispered. "Janis."

"Mom?" Janis said again. "Mom? He's dead. He killed himself. I came to tell you. He's dead."

It had been so long since Cricket had seen her, she'd forgotten how much Janis looked like her father. How much she sounded like him, her voice saying he's dead. Jim's voice saying Grace is dead. Both voices, talking to her, telling her things she didn't want to know, not caring about what it felt like to hear the words, only caring to say them.

"No," Cricket said. "No. He's not dead."

Janis opened her mouth to say something else, and Cricket turned and ran.

She kept running to her car, then got in and drove away, letting the dance and Janis and all the pretty people disappear behind her.

D R E A M #10

janis

Janis hadn't gone to camp that summer. At the last minute, she decided she didn't want to. There would be too many stories to tell, and she didn't want to tell them. For a while, after her mother left, all she wanted to do was stay in her room, but even that was no good because her aunt Peggy would insist on coming to talk to her, and her father was always mooning around the house looking for someone to complain to, usually about her mother.

Besides, lying in bed was painful. She couldn't sleep. Something seemed to dance under her skin with energy, some of it angry and some of it afraid and none of it pleasant. It wouldn't let her sleep. So she'd go into Grace's room and stare at her things, which were all just as she'd left them.

"Fuck you," she'd say to them and, by extension, to Grace. "Fuck you. Look what you did. You ruined everything."

Then, something in the pit of her stomach turned over, and she pushed her face into Grace's pillow, smelling her lavender smell, and she cried, saying she was sorry, over and over again.

She didn't like doing any of this, or feeling any of this, and she was sick of her father and her aunt Peggy and her mother and their warped lives. It occurred to her that all adults were screwed up, so they raised screwed-up kids who became screwed-up adults just like them, to raise more screwed-up kids. She didn't want anything to do with it.

To keep herself out of the house, she got a job at a day camp, and then a second job at a McDonald's. With the kids, she could run and yell hard, which felt good and seemed like a better response than her father's complaints, or her mother's cracking up and running away. She didn't want to be like them. She wanted to be strong. She should have been strong sooner, she thought. She should have been at the mall. Grace didn't know how to duck, but Janis would've gotten her out of harm's way. She knew she would have. But she wasn't there.

She wasn't there.

After the day camp, she worked as many hours as she could at the McDonald's, and came home exhausted, went directly to sleep. At first, Aunt Peggy would still come over at night, but after a few weeks she stopped doing that, and Daddy was even more pathetic than before. Now he started drinking when he came home from work—often whiskey instead of beer—and it made him look and smell raunchy. It also made him go from complaining to whining, which she couldn't stand.

One night, she came home and found him on the sofa in the living room, an empty bottle of whiskey on the rug next to him. He woke up and opened one bleary eye to look at her.

"You're disgusting," she said.

He pointed a finger at her. "Don't you get sassy with me, little girl."

She held her finger in the shape of an L on her own forehead, but he'd already closed his eye, and gone back to sleep. She moved the tip of her foot next to the bottle. Nudged it a little more. Then a little more. Then, she lifted it and sent it sailing across the room, smashing it into the wall, where it shattered.

Her father didn't wake up. It was funny that she always thought he was stronger than her mother. Now here he was just working and drinking, and falling apart. For the first time, it seemed like maybe a better thing to have the guts to just get up and leave.

"Y'know," she said to him, "I think when Mom left, it was the smartest thing she ever did."

In reply, he began to snore.

That night, she dreamt about her mother.

In the dream, her mother was wearing a red dress, and planting flowers at a grave. It was Grace's grave, but Grace was standing next to her, directing the planting. She wanted the little Lemon Gem marigolds that her mother always put in front of the house. She wanted poppies. She wanted a rosebush. Her mother was planting furiously, but she looked exhausted, as if she would die and fall into the grave marked for her daughter.

"Leave her alone," Janis snapped. "Can't you see she's had enough?"

Grace looked at Janis and rolled her eyes the way she used to when Janis would say something disparaging about the animal shows Grace liked to watch. "She wants to do it," Grace said. "You know that."

"Yeah, well, she's not strong enough," Janis shot back. "You'll kill her."

"Oh, no," Grace said, with a particular brand of condescension that always got them into a fight. "You aren't watching her. She's stronger than anything. She's stronger than death."

Janis pointed at her mother. "Just look at her," she said.

"You look," Grace replied, and Janis did.

She saw that her mother was made of vines and leaves, and of the petals of the flowers she planted, and a few feathers. She saw that her mother was ephemeral as thought, fragile as flowers.

"She's not made of anything," Janis said.

"She's made of everything," Grace said. "Look at her."

Janis looked again. She saw that as leaves fell from Cricket, they grew back. As one blossom scattered its petals on the ground, another one opened. And as her mother withered into nothing, her roots went down and drank in the darkness, waiting for the sun.

"Oh," Janis said. "Oh, wow."

"I told you," Grace said. "Didn't I?"

In the dream, Janis understood that her mother was strong, durable, and her durability somehow came from her faith in what was ephemeral. Janis didn't quite understand how that worked, because her mother was different than she was, but she knew it was good. Even the differences between them were good. Janis smiled at her, and she smiled back.

When she woke up the next morning, Janis wanted to see her mother again.

She wasn't sure how to do that, though. She didn't even have her mother's address or phone number. Her father tried to give it to her, but she refused to take it, and now she didn't want to ask him again. She was sitting at the kitchen table, eating toast and looking at the morning paper, thinking about it, when she saw the article.

It was on the front page, with pictures. It was about Pass Christian, whom Janis had decided at one point that she hated, and at another that she just didn't care about him at all.

The article's headline said, LOCAL MAN PLUMMETS TO HIS DEATH. It told how Pass Christian, who ran the well-known bird sanctuary that had bred a golden eagle, had hiked a mountain near New Paltz with his disabled brother, Law. There was a picture of Law standing in front of a tree, his face open and smiling, absorbing sunlight and the pleasure of warmth on his skin. Janis thought of the two of them walking up a mountain, passing through patches of shadow and light, silent and content.

The article said that at the top of the mountain, they stopped to eat a picnic lunch. Law was sitting a little distance away on a rock. Janis imagined them doing this. Law would be looking away into the sky. He would swing his legs if they didn't touch the ground.

The newspaper said that a family—mother, father, and two children—were eating lunch nearby. The children were playing a game, chasing each other with water guns. Janis imagined that Pass and Law watched them without speaking.

The mother said that Law seemed upset. He stood up, making noises and pointing at the children as he walked backward toward the edge of the mountain. Pass moved toward him, talking to him, but he never even got close. Law smiled at his brother, looked over the edge of the mountain, took one more step back and went over the edge. He fell three hundred feet down, and broke most of his bones on the rocks where he hit.

The family who witnessed the tragedy confirmed that it happened exactly the way Pass reported it. Nobody was being charged. The death was ruled accidental.

That was on Wednesday. On Saturday, when she didn't have to work, she took the car and went to the bird sanctuary. There was a sign in front that said it was closed due to a death in the family. She went and knocked on the door. Pass opened it, and stood staring at her.

"I'm sorry about your brother," Janis said.

Pass nodded. "You came here to tell me that?" he asked.

"Sort of," Janis replied honestly.

"What else?"

"I want you to tell me about my mother," she said.

He stepped to one side and she went in the house, where he sat her at the table and gave her coffee.

"What would you like to know?" he asked, his voice slow and gentle and inviting.

"You were her lover, right?" she asked, the word feeling strange in her mouth. She felt very adult, sitting here and calmly discussing these kinds of things.

Pass stirred at his coffee and watched it swirl in the cup. "Yes," he said, and waited for more.

"Why?" Janis asked, not sure if that question would get the

information she wanted, which was who her mother was when she wasn't being her mother. When she was just being herself.

"I fell in love with her," he said. "Didn't you ever fall in love?"

"Maybe." Janis shrugged.

"Then you know how it is. You see someone special, and you fall in love. She's a very special woman, your mother."

"Special?" Janis asked.

"Brave. Determined. When she believes in something, she lives it. She doesn't just talk about it the way some people do. You saw how she was with your sister. And you know she'd do the same for you."

Janis chewed on this thought. Her mother tended Grace out of strength and conviction, not out of delusion. Janis remembered her saying that if she had to pick one daughter to live and not the other, she'd shoot herself. For the first time, Janis believed this.

But she wasn't off the hook yet.

"She shouldn't have slept with you. She was married. And you shouldn't have slept with a married woman," Janis pointed out.

"Probably not," Pass admitted. "But I'm not sorry I did."

Janis stared at him hard. He meant it. He was speaking the truth. And she had to admire him for that. It was easy to say you weren't sorry you acted a certain way when everything turned out all right in the end, but this hadn't. He was alone, and her mother was gone. She eyed him up and down. She thought her mother had picked a nice man for a lover. Maybe that meant she was smart, or at least had good taste.

"Why aren't you with her anymore?"

Pass shrugged. "I can't tell you what she'll say. I'd say she just had to go away, be on her own for a while. She was hurt bad when your sister died. Hurt and scared. People run when they're hurt and scared. But probably you should ask her what she thinks about it."

He was right. That's what she'd have to do. She stood up, looked around the neat, spare kitchen. "I meant it that I'm sorry about your brother," she said.

"Me, too," Pass said. Then, "If you see your mother, tell her about it, would you? Tell her I'm thinking of her. Tell her not to feel so bad."

She got Aunt Peggy to give her Cricket's address and phone numbers—one for an apartment in Farmington, New Mexico, and one for work—but she didn't write or call. She just looked at them, not sure what held her back. But she figured she'd know when it was time to do something.

Three days later, she picked up the morning paper and read about another death, this time by suicide.

"Holy shit," she whispered to herself. "He killed himself."

Now, she thought, it was time. She'd have to tell her mother, and she should do it in person. She took the money she'd been earning, and bought a train ticket to New Mexico.

Her father told her she couldn't go, but Janis said, "You can't really stop me, can you?"

And he couldn't. Besides, since Aunt Peggy stopped hanging around so much, he had this other woman he was seeing, and he probably didn't mind having the house to himself.

Her train would take her to Santa Fe. From there, she'd take a bus to Farmington.

She wasn't afraid.

At least, not very afraid. Doing things like calling to find out train times, getting the ticket—they all made her feel young, and a little stupid, because she'd never done them before. But once she had that all settled, she began to feel as if the world was something she could take on after all. Her mother had, hadn't she?

The train was good, too. She liked the motion of it, rocking her to sleep in the two nights she had to spend on it. She liked hearing the conductor walk up and down the aisles, checking on people, announcing stops. She felt watched over, protected, and rocked in the arms of a moving animal that carried her to a new place. It was exciting. It was safe. It was everything good.

As she rode, she'd have little conversations that she'd include Grace in.

"I'm going to see Mom," she'd say. "She's all messed up since you died. I know you didn't mean to. It's not like it's your fault. But she's still all messed up. So I'm going to get her. It's really pretty out here, Grace. You'd like it a lot."

She watched the land change from green to gold, from hills to rolling plains, and she let Grace see it all with her eyes. She was almost eighteen, and she was having an adventure, and she wanted to share it with someone. Grace, she realized, was the one person who would always be there, from here on in.

When she slept, she dreamt of a white horse she was riding furiously to get to some unknown destiny. The feel of it was electrifying, full of wonder. She was flying over walls, over land, over streams. Speed was crucial. There was something she had to do, and she had to do it now, before it was too late.

The horse stopped in a cemetery, and she suddenly knew what her task was. In the middle of the cemetery, surrounded by the reaching, clutching hands of many dead people, she found a butterfly.

She was disappointed. All that way, such a hard, fast ride done so heroically, to save something that would probably only live a week.

But this was her job, and she'd do it the best she could. She got off her horse, picked up the butterfly, and rode away. When the horse had leapt over the cemetery wall, she lifted her hand and let the butterfly go.

There were many things Janis wasn't sure of. What she'd say to her mother. What her mother would say to her. What would happen next. But when she woke up from this dream, she knew she was doing the right thing by going.

She knew she'd find her, and whatever came after that, she'd deal with.

She was her mother's daughter, after all.

nineteen

On the drive home, and when she got into her apartment, Cricket kept asking herself why she ran. Why did she run away? How could she run away from her own daughter? What was Janis doing here, and what would she do now that her own mother ran away from her?

Her face. Cricket hadn't seen her face in so long. Her wild hair and eyes. She was so tall, so lean, like a wild tree. She was so beautiful. Her face wasn't a child's face anymore. It was the face of a young woman, so beautiful. So beautiful.

She said, "He's dead. I came to tell you." She sounded like her father, saying, Grace is dead. Somebody else was dead.

Who was dead? Not Pass. No, not Pass, he wouldn't kill himself. He wouldn't. If he had, that meant he had a reason to, and she didn't want to know what it was. No. She wouldn't think it. He didn't. Besides, why would Janis come to New Mexico to tell her Pass was dead? She didn't really know him, except as a man her mother slept with while she was married to someone else. She probably hated him. She wouldn't care if he was dead.

Jim, then. It must be Jim.

But that would mean Janis was an orphan. No. She wasn't thinking. Janis wasn't an orphan unless both her parents were dead. Cricket couldn't think. She couldn't.

Every time she touched something, it turned real. Every time it turned real, it shattered and died. It terrified her. What would happen if she touched Janis? Janis would die, too, because her mother was incapable of bringing any real thing to life that didn't end in disaster. Her daughter, her marriage, her home, Pass, all dreams broken like glass around her. She was wrong to think connection prevented killing. That only worked if you were a good person, which she obviously was not.

No. Let Janis have her life, she begged. Let her live. Please let her live, and let Pass be alive because it felt as if the death of either would rob the world of more than it could stand to lose. It would be loss beyond bearing. But everybody dies, she told herself, and nothing remains. We get old and we die, and that's it, and she knew that was true, but she didn't care. She didn't want Pass dead now. She wanted Janis to be alive.

Let him be alive. Let Janis live. She would not touch anything. Not ever again.

She got her small piece of luggage out of the closet, along with her tent and camping gear, grabbed cans of tuna, boxes of crackers, and whatever else might travel well and put them in a shopping bag. She looked around her apartment for a map, not sure how far she'd go or if she'd ever come back. Sitting on top of her road atlas was the brochure for Chaco Canyon. That would be perfect, she thought. She left the map and brought the brochure, went out to her car, got in it, and drove.

The road going into the canyon was rough and winding, with deep ruts from water runoff and hairpin turns going down. She was the only car all the way in, driving slowly, trying to avoid edges and potholes. She hadn't called anyone about Janis, but Janis would be okay without her. She'd gotten here, and she'd get back home. Janis didn't need her.

The land already had changed and become sparse, just splashes of gold and sand color mingled with the silver green of sage and topped by a turquoise sky.

At the bottom of the canyon, she went to the visitors' center and spoke to a man with a beard who told her it was eight dollars a night to camp, and gave her a booklet of the rules, which included staying out of restricted sites, not camping on the mesas, not littering.

"Okay," she said over and over again as he described wildlife and hiking trails and how to get firewood. "Okay. Okay. That's fine."

Then, he let her go.

It was late afternoon, and the sky was turning vermilion in the west. She saw flashes of lightning hanging in purple clouds just outside the rim of the mesas surrounding them. She set up her tent, opened a can of tuna and spread some on crackers. She was hungry, as if she'd run a marathon. When she was done eating, she lay down and was almost immediately in a deep sleep.

When she woke the next morning and stuck her head outside the tent, a hummingbird buzzed in her face. She was so startled she almost shooed it away, as if it were a horsefly. But she stopped her hand, and let it hover in front of her face as if it were asking what kind of flower she might be. Then, it shot off to the left, toward a cluster of red flowers on a little hillock that was set inside the curve of the mesa where she was camped. Other hummingbirds were feeding there, too.

The pain in her chest clawed at her. Hummingbirds, like the ones on Grace's T-shirt. Her chest filled with the feel of something shredding.

She didn't want to feel this. She wouldn't. She put herself on hold, as she had for so long in the hospital. She dressed, then looked over her trail guide brochure. She wanted to walk, and keep walking until she got to a place where she could see. She didn't know what she wanted to see, but if she saw it, she'd know.

She chose a mesa trail, packed some food and water and took it outside.

Hummingbirds raced past her, their wings a sound like no other. She breathed slowly, deeply, adjusting to the pain they caused, and the pain of beauty all around her, grabbing at her. She kept walking.

She passed a few other groups of campers, but none was going her way. As she walked across the sandy earth, the scent of sagebrush filling her, she had no human company. On her way, she stopped at a kiva ruin, read about it, then pressed her hand on the wall of it. In the mud that held the bricks together, she saw a fingerprint.

It was very small, like a child's. Children had built this place, over a thousand years ago. They were all dead, except for their fingerprints and these ruins, which archaeologists tried to preserve. Visitors should not climb into them, or touch them too much or take any stones. She didn't know if that was a good idea. She was sure the people who made it meant it to crumble someday, to go back to the earth it was made of. She didn't know if people believed in permanence until things like books and Styrofoam were invented. The people who built this place might want their lives to remain only in the whisperings of the wind that seemed to still catch and carry their laughter, their stories, their songs. The place had a feel to it of many gentle spirits watching her from the stones and behind the windows.

No, she told herself. There is nothing. You are nobody. You are unfound. Because if anything saw her, watched her, she would have to exist, and every time she did, something horrible happened. She wanted to be untouched. Hadn't she almost done that? Until the rainstorm and the dances, she had it all figured out. She would figure it out again.

She followed an easy trail up the mesa, watching how the earth changed as she climbed higher, starting with a black soil at the bottom, punctuated by pieces of a thin, micalike substance. Then the ground became smooth deep gold sandstone littered with small stones that were rounded and shaped by the wind. Some were pocked with what looked like many eye sockets, all empty. Others had intricate curving surfaces like the bodies of humans or animals. Each one seemed to be a miniature of the larger mesa, as if it reproduced itself in small stones, like the plant she had called mother-of-millions, which dropped tiny versions of itself everywhere.

She came to a plateau and sat down, drank some water. There was something very motherly about the place, she thought. It had stones that the wind had carved into enclosures, like couches or lounges in an arbor made all of stone. She found one and got into it, finding it was contoured exactly to her body. She opened her backpack, and sat eating her crackers and cheese.

After she ate, she continued walking up, following the trail markers. The color of the stones lightened as she ascended, becoming sandy gold, and then a soft white, as if the sun had bleached all color from them. She wasn't sure if she was on a trail anymore. She didn't know why she was going up. She didn't know what good it would do to be at the top. She was just going. Just going, to keep from being still.

As she rounded the last curve of wall and peered over it at the flat top of the mesa, a mule deer, a stag with a heavy head of antlers, looked at her from where he stood in the center of the flat, white table of earth, then kicked up its feet and ran straight toward where she was scrambling up the edge. She stayed very still, and it leaped over her, continuing down the mesa. Her heart beat hard in her chest, and she waited for it to settle down before she pulled herself up over the final climb to stand at the center of the mesa, where it had been.

The surface was flat and bare except for small ornaments of

stone, carved out by the wind into the shapes of miniature caves and little bowls. There was a piñon tree at one end, and a sagebrush that had managed to fight its way through the hard earth. She stood in the center, and looked out over the top of the canyon, over the tops of other mesas, beyond them to a land that rolled smoothly toward a very distant horizon.

The wind held the voices of the dead, circling her in whispers. They had let go of the same burdens she was trying to release. And then, above her, an eagle cried out, and she felt the sound as if it moved inside her heart. She pressed a hand against it and closed her eyes.

"Pass," she whispered. "Pass, please don't. Don't. Don't."

As if to mock her plea, she heard the sound of a crowd of people laughing. Or were they weeping? Or both?

I'm going mad, she thought, and she opened her eyes, expecting visions, but saw only the mesa.

The sound was still there, though. Was it ghosts, then? The children at the mall, screaming for their mothers, fathers, anyone to help them? Did the ghosts trail her here?

"Grace," she whispered, and listened hard, trying to discern her voice among the many. But the sound was fading now. Only one lone cry left, and it no longer sounded human.

Then she remembered. The man in the visitors' center told her there were coyotes. It was coyotes. Coyotes, singing their song. Coyotes, talking about it.

She found she was breathing fast, her heart beating hard. I will go mad, she thought, if I'm not already. I will go mad.

She lifted her eyes to look at the horizon. The deep gold sun rested in a sky that was purple and pink, the clouds full of long skeletal dancers of lightning who leapt down to earth, touched it, then were drawn back into the clouds. She looked down over the edge of the mesa, her hand clutching a pillar of stone to her right for support, in case she got dizzy. It was a long way down. She wondered what it would feel like to hit those rocks. She took her hand off the stone.

Her father had fallen farther than this. He had tried to unglue himself from the earth, but it dragged him back. Was he afraid, or elated as he saw the earth rise up to meet him? She'd read an article about a kamikaze pilot in World War II, who had written a letter the night before he was to fly his suicide mission. He said he wasn't afraid. "I do not exist anymore," he wrote, "except as a manifestation of the people's prayers."

Had her father become a prayer for someone? Is that why he didn't open his parachute? The police who investigated his death said sometimes the altitude made people forget what to do, but maybe he knew exactly what he was doing, and wanted to do it. Maybe he thought he was a prayer.

And if she should step over this edge and fall to the earth, would she become a prayer? If so, for whom? Her daughters, dead and alive? Pass, dead or alive? Or some other children, perhaps, who were in need of her.

She stood looking out over the edge, thinking about the difference between flying and falling, and wondering if she should make her own flight.

When Grace was shot, she'd learned that everyone is absolutely dependent on the goodwill of everyone else. She knew that the man in back of her at the grocery store could kill her if he wanted to. She knew she could kill him, if she had a weapon. There was no place you could be safe or ensure the safety of what you loved. The only thing you could escape was your own pain, and that only in ways that were bound to cause the pain of others.

She took a step closer to the edge.

Then, behind her, she heard the crunch of feet on sandy earth, and the thump of someone falling hard. "Oh, shit," a woman's voice cried out.

Instinctively, Cricket turned around.

She saw an old woman, facedown on the ground, her head over the edge of the mesa.

Cricket walked to her quickly, grabbed her ankles and pulled.

"Hey," the woman said. "Hey." She rolled over on her back, wiggled away from the edge, then pushed herself up on one elbow. She rubbed her head and looked at Cricket.

"Wow," she said. "It's a long way down."

Cricket let go of her ankles and stood with her hands on her hips, tapping her foot. The old woman was dark-skinned. Maybe Navajo, maybe not. Certainly not all white. She wore jeans and a T-shirt, and a hat Cricket recognized as an L. L. Bean porkpie hat, because her father had had one. Her face was etched into lines and curves like the stone, which shifted when she opened her mouth in a broad smile. Cricket saw the gap in front where a tooth should be.

"Goddammit," Cricket said angrily, "what'd you do that for?"

"I dropped my compact," the old woman said. "Right over the edge. Help me up, would you?"

Cricket did so, but without patience or compassion. The woman had interrupted her moment and now it was gone, irretrievable. The old woman stood and carefully brushed the dirt off herself, chuckling as she did so.

"Glad my granddaughter didn't see that. She'd be furious with me." She once again showed Cricket her smile. "You saved my life, didn't you?"

"No," Cricket said. She didn't think so, anyway. And even if she had saved her, she didn't want to. Why should she save the life of someone who had so many more yesterdays than tomorrows? Nobody could save Grace's tomorrows, all squandered for nothing.

"Maybe not," the old woman admitted, then grinned at her mischievously. "Maybe I saved yours, huh? You were pretty close to the edge yourself."

Cricket shook her head hard. She wasn't that close, and she knew what she was doing. Cricket wouldn't let her think she'd done any favors.

"Anyway," the old woman said, "you helped me. Thank you."

They heard the sound of light jingling, which preceded the

appearance of a teenage girl who climbed up over the top, stopped and caught her breath, then looked toward them.

"Jeez, Grandma," she said. "You didn't have to run ahead. You scared me."

"That smoking you do should scare you more," the old lady noted. "I ran up, and I'm not out of breath. You couldn't even walk."

The young woman rolled her eyes and walked toward them, jingling. She wore copper bells in her ears and a necklace of feathers. Her skirt was bright red and yellow and orange, fringed at the bottom. She wore a red tank top with a belt around her waist made of silver and turquoise. She was not much older than Grace. She put her arm around her grandmother's waist. Her grandmother patted her, kissed the top of her head.

The gesture pierced Cricket. Beauty stalked her, merciless and inevitable. Pass said it was all that mattered, but he didn't know how it stalked her, waiting to revive her pain. She gulped at a sob in her throat, but felt water running out of her eyes so fast she couldn't press it back. Beauty had pierced her. She was bleeding. She would never stop.

The old woman craned her neck and looked over at Cricket, considering her tears. Cricket wiped at her eyes, unable to choke out an apology or an explanation. The woman didn't seem to need one, though.

"It's good to cry sometimes, isn't it?" she said softly. "Reminds you you're alive." Before Cricket could answer, the old woman turned away. Cricket saw her back, and the back of her granddaughter through a misty veil of tears. They were an unstoppable river, silent and relentless. She heard the old woman humming very low, thought maybe she and her granddaughter were swaying to the rhythm of what she sang. Then the humming stopped, and there was silence, followed by a deep sigh.

"Look at that, will you?" the old woman said, as she faced the endless land and sky. "You can see forever out here."

She lifted a gnarled hand and swept it in front of her, as if tearing down a curtain.

"Look. There it is now."

Through watery eyes, Cricket saw it, spreading out beyond the land, into the sky.

There it was. Forever.

It didn't exist in words of explanation or description. It was the sensation of a moment, filling her, speaking in scattered images and sounds. It sounded like the laughter and weeping of coyotes. It was rich with lightning dancers, and sun. It held volumes of hummingbirds, and butterflies, and the song of eagles and silence. It was the beauty Pass said they made together. It was Janis.

It was the bottom of Grace's eyes.

The old woman turned around to face Cricket, her deeply lined face serious and calm. From here, you can see forever, it seemed to say. And forever is more friendly than you know, bigger than your pain can imagine. In time, the rocks speak to you. In time, you hear them. And, in time, you stand still and become stone. Whispering stone, telling stories to other women who need to hear them.

Cricket closed her eyes and pressed the heel of her hands against them. Sorrow and tears flowed through her, licking her clean.

"Time to go back," she heard someone say. The girl? The grandmother? They seemed to have the same voice. They had forever voices.

"Yes," one of them said. "Time to go."

Go? Go where? Home? She had none. She was her only home, and that a sad and lonely one. Nobody lived there, except in her hands pressed against her watery eyes, where she felt the cells of her children still move.

Grace was in her hands. Janis, too. Cricket had tried to run away from both her girls, and from Pass because she was imperfect and couldn't protect herself, or her children or her dreams, from harm, but they were in her hands. Now, she thought about them apart from her pain for the first time in a long time.

Janis would bow in front of audiences, on many different stages and never learn how to speak an untruth to save her skin. Janis would be beautiful and wild and alive in her own flesh, her own dreams, and she needed a mother to witness that, even if imperfectly. And Grace lived only in her hands, and the dreams Cricket would have of her if she chose to dream again. Grace needed a mother who would dream the dreams she couldn't, and live.

Cricket lowered her hands from her eyes and reached out blindly, wanting to touch something, someone. Her hand felt something smooth and cool, and she opened her eyes.

She was alone.

No old woman stood there. No young woman stood there. She stood on the mesa with her hand resting on smooth stone.

She looked out at forever and watched it watching her. She listened for any sound, human or animal or bird or wind, but heard none.

In the silence, she decided to go home.

twenty

When Cricket unlocked her apartment door and stepped inside, she let out a gasp.

"Mom?" Janis asked. She was crouched by the stereo system, looking over the CDs.

Cricket dropped her gear and walked toward her slowly. She had no words available to use yet.

Janis looked up at her and scowled. "Don't you have any good music?" she complained. Then, she grinned.

"Oh, God," Cricket said, and dropped to her knees, put her arms around Janis. "You're here. You're here. God, I'm so glad. I'm so glad to see you."

Janis raised her arms slowly, then put them around her mother's neck and squeezed. "Me, too," she said. "Me, too."

They had no food in the apartment, so they went to the diner where Cricket worked and ate chili and burritos. Susan waited on them.

"This is my daughter," Cricket said proudly. "Isn't she beautiful?"

"Mother," Janis groaned, but Cricket laughed.

"She's a looker all right," Susan agreed. "I saw that the other day when she found me and asked where you were. Then, off she goes to catch you at church. My directions were great, huh?"

"Yeah," Janis said. "Great."

"Like I told your mother. She tell you how she got here yet?"

"She was just about to," Cricket said.

"So go ahead and listen, and let me know if you want dessert." Susan left them alone, and Janis talked.

She told Cricket about not going to camp, about the jobs she got and about how mad her father made her. She told her how she read the paper one day and found out Law was dead.

"Law," Cricket said. "That's who you meant? He killed himself?"

Janis shook her head. "No. He . . . sort of fell off a mountain. Here. You can read it."

Janis reached into her backpack and pulled out a worn and folded newspaper article. She handed it to Cricket, and Cricket read it. As she read, she could see the scene unfolding as if she were there to witness it, or had seen it in a dream. She could see Law smiling. She could see him upset at the children. She could taste the despair in Pass's face.

"Oh, sweet Jesus," she whispered. "Poor man."

She found tears splashing down on the article, and thought that now she'd unleashed them, they would be difficult to restrain. Janis reached over and clumsily patted her hand. She wiped at her eyes, and patted back.

"It was sad," Janis said. "I thought it was sad. I went to see him, and— Well, he said to let you know, and to tell you he was thinking about you, and not to feel so bad. Then, the other thing happened."

Janis stopped talking. Cricket felt her heart thumping hard. This was it. This was what Janis meant when she said he was dead. Cricket folded her hands on the table and tried to relax, let the blow come.

"What other thing?" she asked.

"The guy who did the shooting. He killed himself."

The sentence sat in the air for a long moment. Cricket waited while it settled in to her, then she cleared her throat.

"The man . . . the one who killed Grace?"

"Yeah," Janis said. "Him."

Cricket breathed in, and breathed out. "Not Pass?"

"No. Why would he kill himself? Oh. I get it. Because of his brother. No. He's okay, I guess. Just sad."

Cricket sat very still, feeling her heartbeat regulate itself. Susan came by to see if they needed anything else. Janis ordered a chocolate malted. Cricket asked for more coffee.

"What happened?" she asked Janis when Susan was gone, though she didn't care half as much as she once thought she would. Whatever story Janis told her couldn't compete with knowing that Pass was alive.

Janis talked about it with anger and heat. "The bastard was a judge. The cops questioned him, but he had an alibi. His mother lied for him. Do you believe that?" Janis said, disgusted.

"Why?" Cricket asked. "Why did he?"

"He was crazy. I mean, he had this ex-wife who worked at the mall, and he thought she was taking his alimony and paying it to spacepeople who were gonna take over the world. He thought all the people at the mall were part of it. He thought he was saving the world. He wrote it all in a letter."

"God," Cricket said. "Not . . . spacepeople?"

"Spacepeople. That's what he wrote. I mean, you'd think somebody would've noticed he was nuts, right? Done something about it? Not let him have a gun, maybe. Y'know, I think you should write to a senator or something."

"You, too," Cricket said.

"Me?"

"You. You're almost eighteen, right? You can vote this year."

"Oh," she said, surprised at the notion. "I can. That's right. I will. But get this—it was Law who took the gun away from him."

"Law?"

"Yeah. That's what the guy wrote. He said he didn't know Law's name at the time, but he recognized him from his picture in the paper. He said he figured out Law was an angel, come to protect them, and now that he was dead, there wasn't any hope."

"He thought Law was an angel."

"The Angel of Light, he called him. The Angel of Light took his gun away, and never brought it back. He said he planned to buy a new gun and go back to the mall to kill more people, then he read about Law and realized it was all over, so he killed himself. Isn't that weird? I mean, if Law didn't die, this guy would've killed more people, and Law didn't even know. He saved a bunch of people, and nobody'll ever say thank you."

No, Cricket thought. They won't. He was too strange. Even she thought he was a killer. She felt a deep shame at the memory of her last conversation with Pass. There was nothing she could do to unmake that error.

"Anyway," Janis concluded. "The paper printed his letter. I forgot to bring it, but I can show you when we get back. I mean, are you coming back?" Janis asked and, for the first time, looked afraid.

"I'm coming back," Cricket said, and Janis relaxed.

"I . . . shouldn't have run away," Cricket continued, hesitantly. She wanted to explain, without offering excuses for her behavior. That wasn't easy. "I didn't know what to think, and I . . . everything I touched seemed to fall apart. But that's no excuse. I shouldn't have."

"Mom," Janis said, "you almost always do what you should. Maybe you needed to do it wrong this time. I mean, I can teach you all about that."

Janis was grinning at her, and Cricket thought she would swell up and explode with pride. When had this young person grown up, and how? What vital ingredient besides time had made her into a young woman of some wisdom? Cricket had a lot to catch up on, apparently.

"How'd you find me?" she asked.

"I got your phone number and address from Aunt Peggy," Janis said. "Then I took my money and got a train ticket. When I got to your apartment, you weren't home, so I called here and then came over. Susan told me where you'd be. I had to hitch a ride—don't yell at me. I hitchhiked, but it was okay. Just some old cowboy named Roy. He seemed nice."

"I don't think I want to know," Cricket said.

"Anyway, Pass told me you might run away from me and I shouldn't take it personally. He said he didn't know if you'd ever stop running. But if you did, it'd probably be for me. That's what he said."

Janis tried and failed to hide her pride in this. That she could be the one to change the course of someone's life.

"He was right," Cricket said. "Is that why you didn't just leave? I would have."

Janis shook her head. "I don't know if you noticed, Mom, but I'm kind of stubborn," she said, as if telling a secret she'd just discovered.

Cricket smiled. "Thank you," she said. "Thank you for . . . for being Janis."

Janis shrugged, blushed, and looked away. "When will we go back?"

"A few days. I can take you sightseeing first, if you want."

"That'd be cool."

"You know," she said, "when I go back, I won't be living with Dad."

Janis ducked her head over her plate. "I figured," she mumbled.

"You need to talk about it?"

"Not to you."

Cricket raised her eyebrows.

"I mean, I can find a counselor if I need to," Janis said. "Or I can talk with my friends. A lot of them have divorced parents. It's kind of common. And I guess . . . I mean, I can live with either one of you, right? Or go back and forth. Lots of kids do it. It's not like you're . . . you're dead or anything. And it's only for a year. Then I'll be in college."

"You will, won't you?" Cricket said, finding this thought made her as glad as it did sad. She would miss her child. And she would be glad to have her own life, too.

Janis lifted her face to Cricket, and it was softer than Cricket had seen it before. For once, her eyes looked inward instead of piercing everything they saw in the room.

"Mom," she said. "It wasn't my fault, was it? Grace, I mean."

"No," Cricket said. "Not at all. If you'd been there . . ." Cricket shuddered, and left the sentence unfinished. "It wasn't your fault. You believe me?"

"Yeah. But I still miss Grace. A lot."

Cricket felt the pain in her chest, but it was familiar now. It didn't frighten her, and she didn't need to run from it. Death didn't change her love for her daughter. The pain wouldn't go away. Neither would she.

"So do I," she said. "I think we always will."

When they got back to the apartment, Cricket set Janis to work cleaning and packing, while she called Peggy.

"Oh. Hi," Peggy said, when she heard Cricket's voice. "Where are you?"

"I'm coming back," Cricket said without preamble.

"Oh. You are? When?"

"I'll leave in a few days. Janis is here and I want to take her to some places first."

"She found you okay, then."

"She found me."

"I figured she would."

A long pause. They'd gotten through the pleasantries, and

there was nothing left to say except what remained unpleasant between them. Either they'd deal with it, or they'd have to be people who exchanged nothing more than pleasantries. Cricket waited.

"Cricket," Peggy said tentatively, then stopped. "I'm not . . . you know that Jim isn't . . ."

"You're not sleeping with my husband anymore?" Cricket said into the gap her unfinished sentence left.

Peggy sighed. "I was really stupid."

"That's one word for it," Cricket agreed. "How come?"

"I don't know. Part of me said why not, since you didn't want him anymore—I mean, you didn't, Cricket. I could tell that—and part of me said I was doing you a favor, because otherwise he'd be out looking for a woman who'd want to keep him. Part of me said I was doing *me* a favor, because he wasn't someone who could break up me and Pete. Then, sometimes, I think maybe it was just old jealousy?"

"Jealousy?" Cricket was shocked at the notion.

"Since we were kids, you had your way of seeing the world, and you stuck with it. You didn't need anyone else to believe in it. It always seemed like you were getting away with something I couldn't."

"Peggy, I had a bunch of well-oiled fantasies that kept me from seeing the truth," Cricket said.

"You believed in possibilities. Me, I just hated what was happening. With Peter and me. What happened to Grace. It made me want to— I don't know. Break something. Just break something."

"Maybe," Cricket said, "there were some things that needed breaking."

They were both silent, acknowledging this truth, knowing that some breakage precedes life, and some destroys it. Cricket thought of the judge, mad and desperate to destroy what was real to suit his illusion, and nobody paid enough attention to notice, or stop him, or help. He killed and died nobody, unfound.

"Hey, you know Jim's seeing Fran Tuttle now. You know. The woman who owns Catalina's Bar."

"God," Cricket said. "Not Fran."

"Yeah. Me and Pete are seeing a counselor."

"He agreed to that?"

"I'm pretty amazed. We're actually talking about stuff, the way we used to."

Cricket was glad to hear all this. All of it was good news, except for Fran Tuttle.

"Janis told you about the judge and everything?"

"Janis told me."

"Do you believe it? I mean, everyone always said he was nuts, but they didn't kick him off the bench for it or anything. His mother said he had troubles, but she didn't think it was anybody else's business. He was a family court judge, you knew that? Still hearing cases up until the day he killed himself. You can imagine what everyone's saying."

She could. They were saying he seemed like such a nice man. Not the kind of man to do such a thing. And he was a real Christian, too. Went to church every Sunday.

"I guess he actually told some people about it, but they didn't take it seriously. He had a lot of backing, politically, you know?"

"I know. Small town politics."

There was a longish silence, and then Peggy asked, "So when you come home, you'll come over and have dinner?"

"No," Cricket said.

"Oh. Oh, well."

"You'll take me out to dinner. Something really expensive. Your treat."

"You think so?" Peggy said. "Well, you could be right. Listen, call me when you get in, okay? You can stay with me until you find a place."

"I will. Okay."

She hung up. Janis came into the room, with two bags hanging from her arms. "Don't you have more stuff than this?" she asked.

Cricket shook her head. "I was traveling light."

"Still are," Janis commented. She dropped the bags near Cricket's feet.

Cricket took a last walk around the apartment, took a last look out the window onto a New Mexico vista. She would come back here, she thought. The stones and sun and sage had been a womb to rock her back to life. She would visit that particular mother again.

And she would leave a note for Susan, and one for her to give to Linda in the dress store, and one for Mr. Sanders, to tell him she'd learned she wasn't alone.

Janis waited by the door, for once not tapping her foot or making noises of impatience.

"Time to go," Cricket said, and they did.

DREAM #11

home

Since she was a little girl, Cricket had dreams of a particular house that she knew was her home. It wasn't the house she grew up in, or the one she shared with Jim, or any house she'd ever seen in waking. It was adobe, U-shaped with a fantastic garden and fountains inside the U. The upper level had slanted windows that showed the whole sky. The light had the same quality as the light of New Mexico and the walls had the colors of the stones there. The attic had a bed covered in red silk. The kitchen was large and had a fireplace that kept it very warm. And she always recognized it as her home.

She used to think the dream was predictive, and someday she'd build this house. Not that she didn't like the house they had together. She loved it. But it was a house that belonged to everyone else, while this house, the house of her dreams, was hers.

On her first night home from New Mexico, she got a room at a Red Roof Inn outside of town. The room was clean, anonymous, generic. It smelled like a motel. She lay in the king-sized bed alone and thought about what she'd do next. She wanted to sell the house she owned with Jim and use her part of the money to go back to school. But first she'd need a place to live. A place to call home. It would be the first time she picked a place just for herself. She wondered what it would be like.

That night, she dreamt she saw a little girl with golden hair sitting in a meadow, intent on some task. Cricket walked over to her, and saw that she was building an elaborate, miniature U-shaped house of moss and sticks and leaves.

Cricket laughed, because she remembered that when she was a little girl, she used to build little houses of moss and sticks and leaves, images of her dream house, for the fairies. She wished and wished for the fairies to come live in them, and would leave tiny sandwiches and thimbles full of juice to coax them in. She would drop rose petals on the leafy roofs, and make little pools of honey outside. And she was always terribly disappointed when the only thing she got was ants.

"I used to do that," she told the girl, "I wished for the fairies, but they never came."

The girl looked up at her with eyes that were very old and very solemn. "Of course they did," she said.

"I never saw them," Cricket said.

"How could you?" the girl replied. "You didn't have a mirror."

Cricket tried to understand. You need a mirror to see fairies? She didn't know that.

The girl rolled her eyes impatiently. She swept a hand in front of her, and Cricket's dream house appeared, a large version of the fairy house the girl was building, with a fairy at the window.

"It's *you*," the girl said impatiently. "The fairies you wished for are you."

With the nocturnal capacity for absorbing mystery, Cricket felt a profound sense of resolution.

She awoke to the sound of the maid knocking on the door. She understood that her dream house was something she'd already built. Now she just had to occupy it.

It took her less than a week to find an apartment near the community college, where she planned to take some courses in botany. It was a nice old Victorian building set up on a hill so that she could search for forever. Her apartment had a window seat in the living room and a claw-foot tub in the bathroom. It was on the third floor, and there was an oak tree right outside her bedroom window, which faced east. When she woke up on her first morning there, green-gold light trickled through the leaves into her room.

She stayed with Peggy before she moved in, and then Peggy helped her move and unpack.

"The boxes," she said. "You survived the boxes. God, you're a better woman than I am."

"No," Cricket said. "If you wanted to leave, you'd leave."

"Yeah," Peggy said. "You're right." Peggy pulled a statue of a bird out of a box and held it up. "You gonna go see him?" she asked.

"Who?" Cricket asked.

Peggy waved the statue back and forth. "Him. The bird man."

Cricket stopped what she was doing. She didn't know what to say.

"I talked to him at his brother's funeral. Did I tell you that?"

Cricket was surprised. "You went?"

"Yeah. I felt bad for Pass. Y'know, after Grace died, when we brought you back to the house, I said some nasty things to him, but he wouldn't leave. He kept looking at me with those funny eyes of his, not saying a word, and just staying. He's like that, isn't he?"

"Yes," she said. "He's like that." She turned the statue of the bird over and over in her hands. "I don't know if he'd want to see me, though. The way we left things was pretty bad. I thought . . . I thought his brother shot Grace."

"Jesus," Peggy said. "That is bad."

"I know," Cricket agreed.

"But it's not more messed up than I was," Peggy noted, "and here you are."

305

"We're sisters," Cricket said. "It's different."

"Okay, lemme ask you, then. Are you afraid he'll hate you, or afraid he won't?"

Cricket closed her eyes and rocked back on her heels. What if he hated her? What then? And what if he loved her? What if she loved him?

She thought of beauty, and how terrifying it was to love. She was afraid that she believed him. She was afraid he was telling her a truth she'd always believed. She was afraid she didn't know how to live within it.

Two days later, when she was unpacking boxes of books, she looked out her window and saw two cardinals at the feeder she'd put up. She watched how the male picked at seed, offering it to the female, and how he followed wherever she went in the yard. "Okay," she said to them. "Okay. I'll go."

She could at least apologize to him. She owed him that. Maybe then they could be friends.

When she pulled into his driveway and got out of the car, she stood for a moment inhaling the particular smell of the place—birds, loamy earth, things rotting and growing, manure and lavender. She heard the sound of feet on gravel behind her.

"Hi," Pass said.

She stayed still a moment, then turned. He was holding a bag of leaves in one hand, a rake in the other. His eyes focused on her as if nothing else existed in the world.

"Hi," she said. "How are you?"

"I'm okay. Doing the fall mulching. Getting ready for winter. You know. How're you?"

"Better," she said. "Much better."

She stood on one foot, then on the other, then put both feet firmly on the ground, uncomfortable as Pass scanned her. He put the rake and the bag down next to his feet, brushed his hands off against his jeans.

"You're different," he said.

"Yes," she agreed.

He studied the difference for a moment, then nodded. "Janis found you?"

"She did. She told me about Law. It must've been awful for you," she said.

"I couldn't stop him," he said, as if he'd gone over the event repeatedly, and was still trying to see if there was anything he could have done to change the outcome. "I started to walk to him, but I couldn't get there."

"I know," Cricket said. She wanted to touch him, but was afraid to.

He looked out toward the trees, away from her, and shook his head. "When the judge killed himself, all kinds of people showed up here with food. I've got enough baked ziti in the freezer to last the rest of my life. None of them came to Law's funeral, though."

"No," she said. "They didn't understand. Neither did I. Pass, I'm so sorry. The things I said in New Orleans, what I thought— I was so wrong."

"Wasn't all your fault," he said, shaking his head. "I should've told you a long time ago about Law and the gun. About what I was doing with him. I thought I could just take care of it myself. I thought— I guess I was afraid to tell you."

"We were both afraid," Cricket said. "Both of us."

Pass rubbed at the back of his neck, keeping his eyes on her. A fly found her arm, and she swatted it away. This was good, she thought, talking this way. They could tell each other the truth. They could forgive each other and be friends. That was good.

"Where are you living?" he asked.

"I found an apartment near the college," she said. "I'm taking classes in botany."

"Come here," Pass said.

A moment passed.

"What?" she asked.

"Come here and live with me," he repeated. "I want you to."

She frowned. That was not what she expected him to say. Just like that, come here. Live with me. It wasn't something she knew how to answer. How could she answer it? She wasn't ready for the question, much less the answer.

"I love you, Cricket," he said. "That hasn't changed for me. You know I love you."

He loved her. Yes. She was glad. Very glad. It was good to be loved. But she couldn't just say yes, she'd come here and live. People would talk, and she had already signed a lease. And there was Janis to consider. How would she feel about it? They had to talk about it more. Think about it more. They didn't even know each other, really.

She opened her mouth to speak, but was outvolumed by the eruption of conversation among the geese in the pond nearby. She looked toward them and waited for their discussion to subside.

While she waited, she saw that the zinnias she'd planted were still blooming, red and orange, with tiny Lemon Gem marigolds sheltered beneath them. The herbs outside the butterfly house, fennel and parsley and dill, were flourishing in shades of green. Her hands ached to feel the dirt around them, brush the soft tips of the marigolds and the dill across her palm, to touch and smell the material realization of her dreams.

The geese grew quiet. She turned back to Pass.

"Okay," she said. "Okay."

"You will?"

"Yes. When school lets out," she added. "There's Janis, and I've already got my own place for the winter."

"In the spring," he agreed. "Time enough then."

He took a step closer to her, lifted his hand and stroked her face. She admired the miracle of his fingers, reaching for her. She felt the cells of her children swimming inside her.

In the yard, the sand hill cranes stretched their long necks and clacked, and the eagles called out their piercing song.